Daddy Dead

a novel by
Julia Van Middlesworth

Serving
House
Books

Daddy Dead

Copyright © Julia Van Middllesworth

ISBN: 978-1-947175-11-2

Cover art by Cassandra Keenan: sharpietaboo@gmail.com

Serving House Books logo by Barry Lereng Wilmont

Published by Serving House Books
Copenhagen, Denmark and Florham Park, NJ
www.servinghousebooks.com

Member of The Independent Book Publishers Association

First Serving House Books Edition 2019

"You're in for a major brilliant read with Julia van Middelsworth's *Daddy Dead*—right from the first paragraph. With strikingly original characters—Aunt Oink, Mother Blind, Knife, King Car, Brother Willy, Toro of the red bow-tie, the first-person narrator spins an entire world of language and imaginative wonder that is breath-taking. The linguistic vitality and imagination compels you to keep reading in dazzlement and makes you regret coming to the end lest you leave that world behind: Encore, Ms. Van Middelsworth! Encore!"

—Thomas E. Kennedy, author of the four novels of *The Copenhagen Quartet*

"*Daddy Dead* is the astonishing first-person account of Zoe King, an eight-year-old girl with a vivid imagination whose family is coming apart. Julia Van Middlesworth brings us Zoe's secret world--full of vision, hijinks, and dark humor. This is an unusually beautiful and unforgettable novel."

—Rene Steinke, author of *The Fires, Holy Skirts, Friendswood*

"You might think the precocious, luminous little girl making rough poetry out of a rotten life is all too familiar—but meet Zoe King, narrator of Julia Van Middlesworth's *Daddy Dead*, and think again. She wears Knife, her punk Barbie and closest confidante, in a holster. She knows damn well what her Aunt Oink is up to. And in re her feckless father's injunction, "Children should not be seen or heard," has she got a story to tell. Steeped in the s southern tradition of poignant hilarity and clear-eyed bewilderment, Daddy Dead has a voice all its own. It's inspired and earnest. It's brash and insistent. And it's madly, heartbreakingly good."

—Ellen Akins, author of *Life Like a Knife, Little Woman, Hometown Brew, Hometown Movie, Public Life*

"Julia's writing style is punchy and original. Like Flannery O'Connor, she takes reality and makes it both strange and ominous. Like David Lynch's films, the images have the power to attract and disturb at the same time. As the narrator gets closer to her escape, the prose brings images of running pigs feet, feathers and a flying car."
> —Jennifer Matthews, Poet, Munster Literature Centre, Cork, Ireland

"The winning story, 'Daddy Dead', captured me from the first nine words: 'You can buy baby pigs feet in a jar.' That's an opening to stop you in your tracks. This is a sparky, witty story with dark depths; in it a young girl observes the non-too-savory activities of the adults in her life with great humor and sadness. The story folds back over on itself, with clever and restrained use of several motifs: pigs, feather, Paris, clouds and pillows. Here is a writer in control of the material: nothing is overdone and everything fits. I read and re-read it and found more to enjoy each times."
> —Nuala Ni' Chonchuir-O'Connor, Judge Sean O'Faolain Short Story Award, Munster Literature Centre, Cork, Ireland. Author of *Miss Emily, The Closet of Savage Mementos, Nude, Becoming Belle, Joyride to Jupiter*

"Julia Van Middlesworth's skillful, fast paced stories are always surprising. Again and again, clumsy human disaster is redeemed by quixotic human creativity."
> —Penelope Schott, author of *A is for Anne, T, The Pest Maiden, Baiting the Void, Crow Mercies,* Serpent Love,*House of the Cardamom Seed, Bailing the River, How I Became an Historian, Lovesong for Dufur*

"Reading Julia Van Middlesworth's stories is like sliding into a sequined shift and heading out for a night on the town. It's a heady feeling. I laugh more, shimmer a bit, delight in quirks."
> —Darla Bruno, Editor

For Larry

Part One

Pig Feet

MY AUNT BUYS PICKLED PIG KNUCKLES in a jar and chases me with them. She is probably the only girl in Lockwood High who eats pig feet. She's seventeen. We call her Aunt Oink but that is our secret. I feel bad for the pigs. They didn't ask to be born. I shake the jar and watch them skip away through the yellow grease. There is probably a farm full of piglets without feet somewhere in Nebraska.
She shoves the jar in my face.

"Hungry?" she says.

On the label there are silver, gold and red letters that say:

Victoria
Pig's Feet
Cooked Bone In

Her black hair is in a twist today and she is wearing her red short-shorts, a white halter-top and leopard print slippers and there is a pig foot pinched between her two red-nailed fingers. Knife is in my holster punching the air and my dog Toro is on his hind legs snapping. He jumps high and nips a toe and Aunt Oink jerks it away then bends over me and Knife aims her pistol dead center.

"You've been spying on me, haven't you, little rat," she says, and digs her red nails into my arm then jams the pig foot in my face. The vinegar smell burns my nose and I gag. I know things about her, things she does in the living room. She will be sorry. Today we found the key.

Knife is my doll. She thinks something bad is going to come down on our house, maybe the pressure cooker will blow up, maybe a mattress will catch fire, maybe Aunt Oink will choke on a pig foot, but that wouldn't be bad. Knife says a juju is on Aunt Oink and everything she touches.

"But she touched me a lot of times," I say.

We stare at each other.

I got Knife for Christmas when I was seven but she wasn't called Knife, she was called a Revlon and wore a pink satin dress and a long blonde ponytail, boobs and high heels. She doesn't look like that now. My mother said it was a bad idea to chop her hair because she cost a lot and they quit making her this year, 1956, so now she is ruined as a fashion queen. I named her Knife because she dresses sharp and can stare anything down with the blade in her eyes, even the sun.

Let's go, she says.

We're making a getaway out of North Branch, New Jersey, where you can walk for miles through blue fields under trees with green hair. We're moving to Florida to get away from the juju in our house but first we're getting married Holy. I'm already eight so I'm old enough. We make our own rules and fish the garbage for empty Budweiser cans, the ones my father didn't smash flat. We're getting married Holy and tying the cans to King Car's fender. I punch a hole in the bottom of the can with a screwdriver then pull a string through the hole, in and out, can to can. By the time we finish we have 38 beer cans tied to the fender, a long dinosaur tail. We shake them and they crash together and here comes my brother Willy running in all directions, his white table cloth tied at the neck blows up over his face but he keeps on racing toward us anyway.

"*Wey* back *dere.*" he says, and points to the woods where he thinks there is a buffalo. There are some wires tangled in Willy's brain but I understand him. I heard Grandma say he might have to go to the genius school. Sometimes, he gets so mad he turns blue and Grandma and Grandpa have to hold him down on the floor so he doesn't hurt himself. A few times he was so mad he passed out and then Grandma had to throw cold water on his face.

It might be that his favorite jeans are in the washer and he has to wear another pair and this makes him very upset because no other pair will do. But he was born knowing how to fix televisions, toasters, hair dryers and cars. He also does things like start fires and jump from the top-pest part of our swing because he thinks he can fly. He makes up words a lot too like qua-qua and dasher, but I always know what he means.

I used to talk funny too because by the time I got to kindergarten I'd copied my father's southern accent so no one could figure out anything I said. Daddy says: *tawk* instead of *talk* and *dee-vorce* instead of *divorce*. Sometimes I still say words wrong like *faar* instead of "fire," or *be-fo-wah* instead of before, or *git* instead of get.

"*Wey* back *dere*," Willy says again, this time it's more important to him then the first.

"I can't go now," I tell him. "I'm busy getting married." I watch as he disappears into the blue corn.

I am making Knife a wedding dress made of toilet paper. I wind it around her body so it is tight because she doesn't like puffy. She says it's so-so, but what about a veil? So, I take a napkin and pin it to the back of her short hair and it hangs down her back but Knife thinks it's blah. So, I get the scissors and snip until there are white streamers that fly out in the wind. Knife says it's better but to do something sharper. There's black paint in the garage so I dip the ends of the veil in the can. Then I paint one black stripe across the gown from the shoulder to the waist.

Bullseye, Knife says.

We get married under the cherry tree and all the blossoms wave over our heads and a pink fog colors the air. Our only guest is Toro in his red bowtie that I found in the closet. I'm the minister then the groom back and forth, back and forth again till we say, "I do" and we sign the marriage license we made out of a grocery bag.

After we kiss married and holy we hop into King Car and see Willy has snuck back from the cornfield and is jumping on the back seat. We drive in a straight line over all the beaches that lead to Florida. Everything there is green: orange trees, parrots and coconuts that roll down the streets toward the blue of the ocean. Toro races in the sand. We have a seashell and fire party on the beach and the ocean waves ice our toes and foam sprays our faces. I dig a hole and light sticks on fire. We are never getting a dee-vorce. I have the key in my cowboy boot. When we get back from honeymoon we'll hunt down the jewelry box and when Aunt Oink works on her tan in the sun she'll catch on fire. The only thing left will be a pile of ash that smells of stink cheese.

Burn, Knife says.

On the way back to New Jersey, Willy stands on the fender with his cape pinned around his shoulders, a red fox on his head and a pistol in his hand. He likes it when I let Knife drive and she guns the gas and we fly down the sandy beach road, Willy on the back bumper with his arms out, his silver eyes staring up at the black clouds that race us all the way to the end of Cherokee Road where the sun has landed.

We get home from Florida and we're sitting in King Car when my father's truck blows smoke up the driveway. His arm hangs out the red door of his truck that is so shiny it looks like red water. His shirtsleeves are rolled up and there's a lit cigarette pinched in his fingers.

We grab our ski masks from the back seat and sneak to the garage.

Willy flashes past and says: *dasher* and runs into the house then down the hallway the way he always does, skidding in his socks, holding half of his army to his chest.

My father wears his baseball cap and his black hair flops over one eyebrow and his blue eyes flash. I bet he had his head out the window all the way up the interstate singing his Hank William's and honking the horn at women with big boobs. Knife and me slink tight against the cement wall and pretend we are black cats. The truck door cracks open and he crushes his cigarette into the dirt, then rubs a dust spot off the hood with a rag. I ask Knife why can't he be like Before? Before, when he took me, only me, to wait in his new truck while he chucked beers and gabbed to Marlene Travers who works at the Elbow Room. Knife says it can't never be Before ever again. Before is over. I can smell his aftershave, his whiskey, his Hostess butterscotch cupcakes. He'd be burn-up mad if he knew we've been spying on him.

We sneak back around the house and climb in the open bedroom window and fall onto the bottom bunk. It's cool out and clouds slide over the trees the color of ashes after a fire. I hear a crow call.

My father slams the front door and we slide down the hallway to our corner so we can peek through the crack in the closet door but he catches us on his way to the icebox where Aunt Oink is popping ice cubes into her jar.

"What you lookin' at girlie? You know what I told you. Children should not be seen or heard. Now get in the bathroom, wash those dirty hands and get in bed before I spank your bare behind."

"But it's not late," I say. "I didn't get to watch the detective show yet. Mommy's not even home."

I see my face in his shoe and Knife tucked in my belt with her arms up. He was in the Army.

"I'll tell you about it tomorrow," he says. His teeth are very white. "Now do as I say. Hop to it. And bring that mutt with you," he says.

"He is not a mutt," I say. "He's a Chihuahua."

"He's a rat," he says.

"It takes one to know one," I say.

"Wha'd you say?"

"He ain't hurtin' no one," I say.

"I need a light Hollis."

Aunt Oink holds her cigarette between red-nailed fingers that match her lipstick and red bathing suit. All day long she bakes brown in the sun, white lines on her bare shoulders, the red straps hanging down.

He turns away, digs in his pocket for the lighter.

"I can't find the key to my jewelry box, Hollis," she says.

"You were wearing it around your neck."

"Damn. Can't find it."

She catches me staring at her.

"What about you Zoe? You see my gold key? You're always spooking around."

"No," I say.

"Well if you do you, hand it over, you hear? I got some head cheese in the icebox I've been wanting you to try."

We pretend to go to bed but when it gets quiet, we sneak back down the hallway and peek through the crack in the living room door. My father and Aunt Oink are smack against the pine wall and he has his hand on her boob. Then she slides to the floor, fall-down-drunk on her knees like saying a prayer. We escape out the window to King Car and sit in the dark staring up at the moon.

The cracked windshield is smeared with our fingerprints, butter from sugar sandwiches, grease from Willy's thumbs. King Car is our favorite place, especially when Aunt Oink babysits. We have meetings and make up names for our family. Secret names we write on pieces of brown paper that we burn when we get mad. The names curl black then we bury them in the dirt and make new name tags that we keep

13

stored in a coffee can in the trunk until the next time we need to burn.

It started when my mother asked Aunt Oink to babysit a few times a week so she could go to town and shop. This is what Aunt Oink does: sits on her butt on the living room sofa wearing her tight red sweater, blows smoke from her red lips, sips a Tom Collins and waits for my father and that is called babysitting. I don't need a babysitter. Aunt Oink thinks she is boss of everything. My brother Willy is almost six and he is with me.

"We don't need a sitter," I tell Knife. "Do you ever wish you were never born?" I ask her.

I was born? she says.

"Under the pillow, remember?"

We go back inside, Willy on the floor snapping the heads off his soldiers. He has something called a speech pediment like I said and sometimes he stutters too and I have to say the word for him and then he gets mad and whacks off another soldier head.

He's wearing the cape and his crown made from Grandma's fox stole. Willy thinks he can fly. On our rooftop, where the peak is, there is a flat ledge about eight inches across. He shimmies up the drainpipe, lands on the roof, holds his arms out at his sides and when the wind lifts his cape in the air he thinks he is flying and zips along the shingles to the end where the roof drops off. The white cape flaps over his head. He can do this for a very long time in his own Willy dream. Sometimes he runs across the roof and I get scared because he has lots of crashes. My mother said some people just have a lot of smash ups because they were born upside down like Willy was—feet first.

"Accident prone," she says.

"What's prone?" I say.

"Likely," she says.

"You can't really fly you know, Willy," I tell him.

I sit in the corner with Knife on my knee and we make a telescope with our hands and watch Aunt Oink through the crack in the door.

Aunt Oink's real name is Margaret Alice but people call her Allie for short. I call her Allie when I have to say her name out loud but I never say Aunt. She used to be fun in the Before. At Grandma's she read me stories about rooms with walls that crush and a heart beating under a floorboard and one with a table that has a sword swinging over it. She likes that sort of stuff. It's called *Poe.*

"A near death experience always makes my day," she tells me, and Cheyenne, her big red cat sits on the shoulder of her chair sharpening his claws.

Paris

WE HIDE IN THE BACKSEAT of Aunt Oink's car and follow her into the bookstore where she goes to read about her future. We can always tell where she is in the store because of her perfume. It's called Evening in Paris and it comes in a dark blue bottle with a silver label and shiny screw top. The tower on the label is very tall. We draw it on the wall of our closet but it don't look the same exactly:

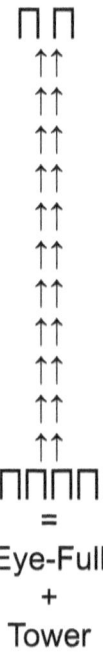

But Evening in Paris perfume doesn't smell Paris at all and when I look at the label again the tower is gone and that is when I know I dreamed it up. I'm a day and a night dreamer. It was never on the label in the first place. I know Paris doesn't smell like that. It has lights and jugglers and loaves of bread long as arms. People wear berets and black and white sweaters with stripes—smart people who think and see French and know how to drag one another across the dance floor.

We see the photographs of the dancers in a shiny travel book at the back of the store.

Knife is wearing the black beret I made her out of Willy's Lone Ranger puppet and we sit on the floor and stare at the pictures of Paris. Aunt Oink is in the next aisle hunting down her horror scope magazines. Paris has a river named Seine but we don't know how to say it. We ask Mr. Collins the owner and he says the letters out loud: S-A-N-E.

Paris has a lot of lights at night. It makes me think of the stars on Mr. Zagoria's class trip to New York one time. We sat in a movie theatre, but the screen was on the ceiling. You are in a big bowl filled with stars. It made me feel like a feather skipping the shiny stones in the sky and not caring where I land. I think Paris is like that. Knife and me flip through countries and plan our vacation to islands with caves. I like to read. We have a trailer library that comes to our school every month but there aren't that many books. I am in the A group of the reading class in school. Reading is like taking a vacation. Right now I am reading *The Adventures of Huckleberry Finn*. He has a drunken bum father too. Before that I read *The Adventures of Tom Sawyer* who goes to his own funeral. I'm thinking of trying that one myself.

I hear Aunt Oink snort from the next aisle.

She pays for her fortune books and we slink behind her when she wiggles out the door and hope Mr. Collins don't see the picture book under my shirt but he's not looking at us anyway, he's watching Aunt Oink's boobs and saying good-bye.

We walk behind Aunt Oink, Knife riding my back tucked into my shirt and she whispers into my ear: Rabbit jelly and chicken livers for supper. Snort, snort.

Besides pig feet Aunt Oink eats cow tongue and head cheese and most times when she laughs a snort comes out. Once I called her Aunt Snort to her face and she chased me with her sharp fingernails that left red half-moons on my arm. I squeeze the half-moons to bleed out her poison. My mother says I have bad blood from my father. I don't need any more because Knife and me are going to be something someday. Maybe a skating pair on television and dance across a frozen pond in silver pants.

When we get home Aunt Oink piles her books on the kitchen table:

The Temple of Fortune
Reading Tea Leaves
Making One's Own Crystal Ball

The books have shiny gold and nickel colored covers with drawings: signs, goats bulls, crabs and a girl holding weeds and that is my sign. Maybe Aunt Oink should have started reading the fortuneteller books a long time ago. Grandma says she should take a correspondence course and learn to waltz, or type or take shorthand and that way she don't have to finish high school and she can get her own bungalow.

Tribes

WE LIVE ON CHEROKEE ROAD, a dead end where the dirt is cocoa powder and when a car makes a U turn at the dead part it blows chocolate clouds from the tires. The beginning of Cherokee Road is where the toilet tribe live and the faucet tribe on the dead part by our house. They came from the drawings we made, stick people on the unpainted walls in the hallway and bathroom. They were trapped in the walls till they escaped and multiplied so that now we are surrounded by them hiding in trees and even burying themselves in the dirt where you can't see them lying flat. Once Willy mixed the dirt with water and drank it down in one gulp. He says it makes him run faster because of the dasher zoom left behind by the car tires and the Indian power in the red dust where the Cherokees did their war dances.

Another thing that's buried is a creepy house. It's hidden with vines that tangle around the chimney and bushes grown so tall all you can see is one dark window and only if you look hard. We sit by the road and stare wondering who lived there and why they left and if there are monsters or ghosts inside.

One day, Willy brings Grandpa's big choppers.

"I chop-chop," he says.

"I'm scared," I say. "What if someone's in there?"

"Chop-chop," Willy says, and opens the giant blades then closes them and they click and snap in the air.

Willy doesn't wait for me. He charges ahead until I follow because I don't want him to have an adventure without me even if there are monsters inside.

Armed and dangerous, Knife says.

We saw that on a sign with a photo of a crazy man that time we went to the post office with Grandma.

Willy hacks and slashes the twisted vines and splits wild branches, the long creepers catching in his hair until we see the broken front door and the peeling strips of red paint.

"Willy," I say. "Wait."

But of course he can't hear me from his cloud and kicks open the creaky front door holding the chopper blades out and ready to slash. My heart is in my ears but I follow him anyway, Knife in by pocket holding her arms out like a zombie.

With every step the floor cries and it's hard to see anything except a door where a slice of sun has shot through the glass on the other side.

Willy puts his hand on the door knob of what might be a closet of skeletons.

"No, Willy," I say. "Let's go back," but of course he won't.

He turns the knob but the door is swollen with rot and the knobs comes off in his hand then he wedges the blades in the crack and pries the door open and there is something long and white like a sheet inside and Willy pokes it with the chopper and it moves.

"It's a mummy," I holler, and we trip over the boards and things on the floor that feel spongy like mushrooms and we pound up the lane so fast dirt flies in our eyes and we collapse at our front door, Willy still holding the chopper blades.

Something died, Knife says.

We ask Grandma about the house and she says it was a murder, someone's head chopped off years ago in a fight over land.

"Don't ever go near there," she says. "A spirit can get caught in your windpipe and strangle you."

We don't go back but Willy eyes it every time we pass in our wagon. When we race our wagon down the road the dirt blows in our eyes. Wind roughs up the dust and it races up and down the road in funnel tops. Willy's right leg out, left leg in, my left leg out, right leg in, Toro in the middle. We roll to the end of the road then back to the dead part. Willy's leg is shorter so he has to lean and sometimes he falls out and I run him over. It's downhill on the way back and we wind through twisters of dust. In the dark we set our flashlights side by side so the tribes will think we are an Army tank and run away.

The faucet and toilet tribes are at war over who owns the road and they try to kill each other with poison tipped arrows. It's a war about property and we get caught in the crossfire and sometimes they hit us and we fall in the dirt and die with arrows through our heads.

Our house is at the dead part of the road and dirt ends in clumps of crabgrass. Our hallway is made of something like cardboard that you can poke holes in. It has white stripes. Knife says it's a runway and we race Willy's iron airplanes down the stripe, lift off for Paris, Florida or an island with white sand and blue houses on rocky hills.

It's also a battleground like all the walls in our house.

Yesterday Willy crayoned a monster fish, blue and green and yellow. It swims around the tub and it eats all the tribes. Willy pokes holes in the wall with a screwdriver to make two fish eyes. There are wires back there and the fish eyes look scary when he pulls the wires out. He calls the fish Foamy. Knife says one day Foamy is going to eat the entire house. I hope we're in Florida by then.

Sometimes, the toilet tribe people climb up from the cesspool into the toilet and it gets choked. The cesspool started as a puddle and turned into a black lake in the backyard. Willy calls it qua-qua.

The qua-qua makes Mother Blind smoke a lot of cigarettes. She used to think when you were in love with a guy, my father for instance, and the guy is in love with you, it don't matter if you have a nice car or house.

"I could live in a cardboard box as long as I'm with Hollis," she told Grandma. But that was before she knew about cesspools and houses that never get finished and little sisters that trespass on your property and try to break up your tribe.

The trees on our road are giants. Wild things live in the trees, buffalo and creatures with jelly eyes and long beaks that can pick you up and fly you away to their cave. They have furry babies and dig secret places to keep them. Secret faucet and toilet babies are even hidden under our house. Everything has to get born and die except for Willy, me, Knife and Toro. We won't ever be old because we don't know how and don't plan on learning.

Ugly Things

MY MOTHER DOESN'T LIKE UGLY THINGS. They make her nervous so she studies Shakespeare and that makes her calm because the stuff that happens in Shakespeare makes her feel better about how her life turned out so far.

She is in the kitchen frying chicken parts and chopping cabbage for slaw and baking lemon pie with white peaks and biscuits cut out from a glass pickle jar—my father's favorites from Virginia back when he lived on a farm in Highland Springs with a pig and a milk cow and his mother in the kitchen skinning rabbits. I don't like her. I killed her pet duck. I thought you were supposed to pick it up by its neck. Daddy Dead is cranky about his supper if it isn't cooked the way his Mama cooked it. But Mother Blind is good at it and practices every day, rolls the dough, dusts the wings, browns the biscuits and whips the peaks.

Knife and I sit under the kitchen table and look through the glass oven door. There is a gap between the panes of glass where the rubber melted and a black French fry is stuck in there. We watch the white peaks of the lemon pie toast and then Mother Blind has to take the pie out of the oven fast before it burns under the broiler. We like to watch biscuits get brown and white elbows bubble in Velveeta cheese. My mother said Velveeta is a miracle food like Bisquick.

Phooey, Knife says.

The floor is shiny from all the wax and Knife ice skates circles all around the green tiles under the table square. She spins and floats with one leg up one leg down then she leaps up in the air and lands on one foot.

My mother hates dirt and that is why she calls Willy and me pigs. She scrubs and polishes until you can see yourself in the floor like looking in a lagoon. Everything is so clean Jesus could visit. Willy and me are always dirty because we have fun outside in the mud, grass, rain puddles, the mushy swamp ground that we pretend is quicksand. Sometimes there is dirt in my ears and under my toes and fingernails and I don't even mind.

22

"Cleanliness is next to holiness," Mother Blind, says.

Plop, plop. Knife says.

Knife does a figure 8 on the floor then swirls around so fast she disappears. I watch Mother Blind's legs and her blue high heels as she clicks from the stove to the sink. When she turns to the window Knife skates out from the table behind Mother Blind's heels, then does a flip and lands on her hands with her feet in the air.

"When will you learn to be a lady?" Mother Blind says. "Get out from there and get cleaned-up for dinner."

Knife sticks her arms out and does a little dance and her leather trousers fall down.

"You need a bath," my mother says. "You're disgusting."

I wiggle my foot inside my sock and feel the edges of the key.

My mother rolls the chicken parts in flour with one hand and holds a cigarette in the other. Flour puffs are in the air all around her. Flour fog.

Maybe it gets in her eyes, Knife says.

That is how we gave her a secret name, Mother Blind.

We watch the yellow breasts turn white with flour dust then she drops them in the black frying pan and they sizzle and crack. Knife wants to know where all the feathers go. Maybe they stuff the clouds with them? Then Mother Blind drops in the little wings. They lay sideways in the hot fat and are folded like little baby arms. Knife wants to know if chickens and pigs have a way to cry.

The fire under the black pan is blue then orange then blue, high then low then dead when the pilot light goes out and Mother Blind has to light it with a matchstick. Sometimes she cries into the biscuit and dumpling batter. Once a teardrop fell dead center in my mashed potatoes and when I ate that part I felt sad.

I used to cry but I learned a way not to because cowboys don't cry and neither do soldiers like Knife. When I wish I was dead Knife tells me to stop because if I die what will happen to her? What will happen to Willy? I don't cry anymore even if I get the pillow trick or the belt on my bare butt because my father always says: Don't slobber and makes me stand in front of him till I stop. I make the tears go inside not out and the first time I did it, it felt like winning at checkers. Knife taught me how because she doesn't cry outside either. She says she has to empty her leg out in the toilet once a week so she don't drown. There might be tadpoles in my legs. Knife said so and I think I can feel them tickle my knees swimming circles looking for a way out.

At night I look out my bedroom window into the dark woods and think about wolves with yellow moons in their eyes.

Mother Blind sits on our bed and reads Willy The Three Little Pigs from the storybook. When the wolf tries to blow our house down Willy yells:

Stay.

Toro lifts his head from the pillow, his ears perked and stares at Willy then squints his black eyes and goes back to sleep.

Willy used to be a wolf before he became a fox. It's because he found Grandma's stole, a real fox that used to sniff through the forests with all the other foxes and wolves till someone decided he should be in a fashion show.

I dream about the wolf who is sometimes a red fox but on other nights he is still a wolf and does a jig up our driveway on two feet like a person but holding his tail in his paw. He leans down over my bed and howls in my ear:

Bloooooooooooow-dooooooooooooooooooooooown-yoooour-hooooooooooouse

The words stretch like chewing gum across my bed. I'm not afraid of him. He knows secrets and paths in the woods because he has to escape the trappers. I want to follow him and in my dreams I do. We blow down the house all night, first the chimney then the window glass and the cinder blocks fall one by one onto Aunt Oink until she is flat. Then we fold her up into a tiny square and put her in the ground and a big crow sits in the grass pecking for worms.

The Key

WE FOUND THE KEY in Aunt Oink's Bible. I flip the pages and smell her perfume. We hold our noses. I read the words: "thou shalt not" and Knife's forehead gets a dent over her eyebrow.

There is a creak from the hallway and we look up into the mirror and see ourselves and almost scream. My brown hair twisted in knots, Knife's spiked and she is wearing the leather pantsuit I made her.

The key is on page 564 where it says:

"If anyone reviles his father and mother …"

We slam the Bible shut and I drop the key in my sock.

"What's revile mean?" I say.

She is not our father or mother anyway. Knife says. Besides it says: *his*.

Aunt Oink's big bra hangs on a nail inside the closet door. It's hard to get away from her boobs. They are everywhere like the universe so we name them Pluto and Mars and hope they'll spin her into the galaxy.

Camera

DADDY HAS A CAMERA with a flash bulb and a room with a red light. One night, Knife and me hear the camera click three times then a sizzle sound. We peek through the crack in the living room door, purple and black spots exploding in our eyes like tinfoil and we are blind but then not, Aunt Oink's naked boobs flashing off and on.
Are you crying? Knife says.

That was the night we made it our mission to track down the photographs.

Knife thinks the jewelry box is buried in Aunt Oink's closet. She doesn't actually live in our house, Aunt Oink, but she hardly ever leaves anymore and after a while everything we thought was ours is hers like the closet where she throws her dirty bras, fortune books the blue scorpion crawling out of the pages. If we find the jewelry box we'll find the photographs and have our proof. We already checked the darkroom for the negatives but it's not easy with only a few minutes to do our bandit work.

On Sunday night, I stick Knife in my holster and we slink down the hallway, slip into the closet and dig in Aunt Oink's smelly wash and poke harder till we reach the edges of the jewelry box. Once we have our evidence she'll be gone, folded up in a tiny square that the crow will eat.

Listen, Knife says.

Toro's ears perk and he sniffs under the door.

Heels tap up the hall so we leap out the window and find Willy crouched in the lemongrass. He runs alongside us and we fly to King Car, Toro in the back seat digging at the stuffing.

King Car

KING CAR IS A TUNA FISH CAN. A big one. An old rusty one with jelly jar windows and wheels flat as pennies. It's a little rotted and smells of dirty socks and gasoline and there are some holes in the floor. Willy thinks if we put our legs in the holes and run we can make it to the comic book store on the interstate. King Car is hidden in a bunch of bushes with berries and silver leaves. We don't know where King Car came from but Knife says it might have come from a king or princess because there is a duchess that lives on a state not far away. She is a tobacco queen and wears a crown of crinkled brown leaves. Knife said maybe King Car drove the queen to get her diamonds and bubble flavored water. We ram the gas pedal and go to important places like New York and Paris. Places without pig farms.

Jewelry Box

IT'S FRIDAY THE THIRTEENTH and today we found the jewelry box hidden under the wee-gee board and opened it with the key.
Liver paste, eyeballs and giblets, snort, snort, Knife says in my ear.

We find a small book that reads: *Positions for Christian Intercourse.* Inside are drawings of acrobats not wearing clothes. Ladies with beards on their private parts and men with swelled up henrys. The left side of Knife's forehead dents.

A correspondence course? On the interstate? she says.

"Like on the billboards?" I say.

Or a book of matches, Knife says.

We dig deeper through silver and gold chains until I feel the square edges of the photographs wrapped in slingshot underwear. I shove the photos down my jeans and a door slams down the hall.

Go, Knife says, and we slide out into the hall to our fort in the bedroom closet.

"Jane you seen my gold key?" Aunt Oink hollers.

On the closet floor we string out the loot and examine the evidence: photos showing Aunt Oink's naked boobs taken from different positions: above, below, sideways upside down, close up and not.

Gurp, Knife says.

Willy knocks, then turns the knob 3 times to the left than once to the right. It's our code. We let him in. He stares at the photographs and touches the boobs with his pinky right on the bull's eye—the nipple part.

"Beep, beep," he says.

At night we like to watch Million Dollar Movie. Tonight it's *The Hunchback of Notre Dame,* Willy's favorite. Mother Blind is in the kitchen showing off her Shakespeare.

"By the picking of my thumbs, something wicked this way comes," she reads out loud. "That's from *Macbeth.*"

"Anybody can memorize," Aunt Oink says, and bites on a pig toe.

Mother Blind knots her yellow and orange scarf under her chin. She's going shopping and the jeep is running outside the door because if you shut it off it might not start again. She is wearing her brown monkey coat.

Hear no evil. Speak no evil. See no evil, Knife says.

"'A little more than kin, and less than kind.'"

"Hamlet," she says, and walks out the door.

"Hoity toity," Aunt Oink snorts.

"Tennessee Williams," Mother Blind hollers. *Streetcar Named Desire.*

"Hmph," Aunt Oink says.

We watch Mother Blind step down the muddy driveway in her black heels. Her yellow scarf flies out in the wind from the open window and she sees us watching from the stoop and yells out: "Don't let me find a filthy pig pen when I get back."

We hear Daddy Dead's truck grind up the driveway and we slink along the wall to the mop closet wearing our black leotards, ski masks, and leather gloves. My father stomps in in his work boots.

"Where's the little uglies?" he says, and Aunt Oink gets up from the kitchen chair and they kiss and Cheyenne slinks out of the room, his orange tail high in the air. I open the door a little so I can see all of them and not just a slice but I kick over the mop pail by accident and it makes a loud crash and I hear his shoes march up the hall.

"I told you two to go outside." she hollers.

"Liar." I say, and then I make a snort sound on purpose.

We watch my father's shadow move along the wall getting bigger and then he opens the door and finds us there in the dark. His eyes are blue fire. If he spanks me he'll find the photos and then I will be dead.

"Show some respect," he says. "You don't talk back to your elders that way."

"Maybe she needs is a treat," Aunt Oink says, opens the icebox and the light turns her face green and when she opens the freezer door white ice breath fogs her face and we run to our room and shut the door.

We wear our black outfits and boots under the bed covers and dream about Paris. There are clouds hanging over the roof. They can smother you like the Daddy Dead pillow trick where Knife was born.

I put a jar of peanut butter, crackers, a banana and a book called, *Guide to the Milky Way* in a pillowcase along with the map of Paris I robbed from the bookstore. We wait till everyone is asleep and all we hear are snores and whistle sounds and the hoot owl then we tiptoe down the hall toward the kitchen where it is black except for a roll of tin foil in the moonlight from the window.

I feel for the third drawer on the left of the stove and roll out the flashlight then spotlight the stove.

"You're a military genius," I tell Knife.

We line up the photos on the counter.

Let's blow evil wolf breath on these, Knife says.

We huff and puff and the photos bounce across the counter.

We pry open the rubber strip around the double glass window and the burnt French fry pops out. We pry the rubber with a spoon till it is loose enough to slip in the three photos. Mother Blind can't miss them even with flour in her eyes and Aunt Oink and Daddy will burn in the oven and turn to ash along with the bits of corn muffin. Knife says the stove will fire up on its own now and by morning it will be 1000 degrees.

We wait all night for the day. Willy is sleeping on the top bunk. I think about the pigs in cabbage blankets that Mother Blind rolls in cabbage leaves. We count cabbages instead of sheep and wait for the sky to color pink. When it finally does, I hear Mother Blind's slippers swish against the hall tiles. A hiss from the faucet, the coffee pot dinging with water A click from the knob on the stove, the blue flame rising. Her cup and saucer clang and coffee clouds drift over us. Then a lid lands on the floor and I hear it spin forever. Then quiet till a cry sound. Mother Blind's. First soft, then loud and long.

We hop the windowsill and crash down into the weeds and hear Mother Blind yell: *filthy pigs*. Aunt Oink scream: *Jesus*. My father: *What the fuck?*

We fly to King Car, crack the door and Toro leaps into his seat. I grab the steering wheel and we rock side to side, back and forth until the engine zooms. In the broken rearview mirror, I see my mother, my aunt, my father in the ruined window.

"Don't look back." Knife says.

I jam the gas pedal with my toes and the kitchen window floats away.

"Faster," Knife says.

King Car lifts up, higher till the stars rocket past the jelly windows and light a path.

Cold Slaw

WE FLY ALL NIGHT through the clouds until we finally spot the Eiffel Tower.

"Look. Paris." I say.

Knife is so excited her leg falls off.

Finding Paris is easy but now that we are here King Car stalls.

"May day, May day," I call into the radio. "Stalled over Paris, France."

"Roger doesn't answer," I tell Knife and this makes her eyes cross.

We've been flying all day, twenty thousand miles. Fog leaks into the broken windows and Knife and me hold hands and the smog starts to clear. It's been a rough day. We lost King Car's bumper over Kansas and the tires over Jupiter. Florida, that is.

Now all we have to do is land. I should know how. All the times with my father landing his Piper Cub. But I always pass out when he does his belly flop rolls so I can't think which way to pull the throttle or how to make the wheels go down. Then I remember we don't have wheels, Knife's leg is on the floor and the gas arrow is on Empty. King Car coughs and wind hisses through the cracked glass and down we go, close our eyes, lock our fingers.

Knife's forehead dents then the roof caves in with a loud *crunch*.

Go, Knife says, and snaps her leg back into the socket.

I kick my boot against the door, jump out and see it's my brother spread eagle on the roof of King Car with his arms pointed straight ahead like Superman.

"Hey Willy, get off. You're wrecking King Car."

But he can't see us. He is flying over foxholes and rivers, blue islands with white caves. I grab his cape at the corner, put my finger through a hole and pull. He makes a fist and yells: *dasher* and that means: go away, run. The fox legs fly out around his ears and the safety pins that hold it all together flash in the light from the kitchen window.

"Get down Willy."

"Me no Willy." he says.

We give up and run to the swing. The kitchen window is lit and I see Aunt Oink at the sink drinking a beer. Knife rolls her eyes.

This is a problem, Knife says.

"If she didn't leave after this morning she never will," I say.

The sun melts red into the hills, the moon full and golden over the pines. Clouds ride over our house and the silver antenna pokes through, a tin man with wires spiking out of his head, the Eiffel Tower.

We sit on the top of the swing and hang our legs down.

"Now what? Mother Blind is *never* going to kick her out if she hasn't by now. Our military plan didn't work. We're in trouble."

Sleepwalkers, Knife says,

I know what she means. They'll pretend not to remember the fight, the oven door, the photos. When your sister is eleven years younger than you she gets away with a lot. It's the Eleven-Year-Rule that says when your eleven years older than your sister you are almost her mother.

Willy leaps from the roof of King Car and shimmies to the top of the swing. He tight walks the pipe with his arms out at his sides. He wants to fly like Daddy only he wants to be the plane not the pilot. He dives from the top of our bunk bed at night, runs down the hall straight out the front door and down the dirt lane and Toro leaps behind till Willy is the size of G.I. Joe and Toro is a black bean and I wonder if Willy is diving off the end of the earth.

Aunt Oink spots us from the kitchen window and points a finger.

Remember, we don't know *nothing*, Knife says.

"Let's go. We can't stay out here forever. I'm hungry."

We shimmy down the pole.

"We didn't put any nude photos in the stove," I say.

What photos? Knife says. We weren't even in the country.

We hold our breath, our heads high like we are innocent. The kitchen smells of burnt toast and there's a pile of ashes and broken glass in the garbage can.

Aunt Oink leans against the counter; bags under her red eyes but she can still do her witch-eye, no problem. All she ever has to do is cry and Mother Blind forgives her anything.

"I think I smell a rat in here, she says, to Mother Blind. "I'll have to sic Cheyenne on it. His claws are killers."

33

"I don't know about smelling a rat," Mother Blind says. "But I do know a rat can cause a lot of trouble."

"Well, this is a peculiar kind of rat," Aunt Oink says, and gives me the finger.

Mother Blind chops cabbage heads with a butcher knife. She makes the best cold slaw in the world because she uses a sharp blade and slices the cabbage heads thin as confetti. Her eyes are puffy like Aunt Oink's and her hair is still twisted in pin curls and she always takes them out in the mornings but now it is night.

Knife gives me the told you so signal: she holds a finger to her eye then points at me then points at her eye again and that means: told you they'd pretend to forget.

"What's for dinner?" I ask, like I'm in a show playing a part. "Mother? Are we having the Vanderbilts for dinner? It would be lovely to take out the good china."

I memorized it from a Cary Grant movie. No matter, my mother ignores me.

Steam rolls out of the pressure cooker on the stove and makes clouds in Mother Blind's hair. It shoots up from the escape hatch next to the dial, the needle, the red and black numbers, the words: Maid of Honor. There is a round glass window that sits on the lid like an eyeball. It is a dial with black numbers all around: 0 IIIII 5 IIIII 10 IIIII 15 IIIII 20 IIIII. The needle in the glass dial bounces toward the word: Caution.

We check out the room to see if anything has changed. The photos are gone, the oven window busted, the glass punched out with a hole the size of my father's shoe and the clock on the wall is upside-down. Next to the washing machine is a plastic basket, a Jell-O lime color filled with dirty wash, Aunt Oink's giant black brassiere hogs the space, the straps inching the other dirty clothes, a black widow.

Knife notices me stare at the bra and gives me a signal: she moves her hand out in front of her in one smooth wave, a half circle and that means to coast.

Aunt Oink has moved to the table with her horrorscope books and her stink cheese, Mother Blind's face shrunk tight. Knife and me are under the table and she is doing her ice dance in the skates I made her. We shoot bullets at Aunt Oink's legs with our finger and thumb.

Knife works it into her skating routine. Then Aunt Oink starts to read out loud so the whole world has to listen.

"*An unexpected and surprising event will change the course of things,*" she reads, Cheyenne curled on her lap, his orange tail tick tocking.

"Well, that's a relief," Mother Blind says, in her snippy voice.

"*There is a thief in your life. A thief and a troublemaker but this individual will get what's coming to them,*" she reads, and looks at me.

"Is that a thief in your life or mine?" Mother Blind says.

Your love life will heat up to a boil after the new moon rises.

"Is that *my* horoscope?"

"It's mine. Scorpio," Aunt Oink says. "I didn't read Gemini yet."

Knife accidentally scrapes her skate against Aunt Oink's leg and the blade leaves a light mark across Aunt Oink's calf. Then Aunt Oink is all over us, hissing, scratching, pulling my hair, digging her red claws into my arm and Mother Blind says to "get up off the floor and sit at the table and act like a normal child."

Knife holds two curved fingers in the air and points them at Aunt Oink and that means a Knife curse is on her.

"Don't scrape your dirty shoes against the table," Mother Blind says to me. "It's not even paid for yet. Get out from under there and get that awful doll out of my sight. Look what you've done with it. It was very expensive. They don't make them anymore."

Knife narrows her eyes at Mother Blind.

"*Making one's own crystal ball,*" Aunt Oink, reads. "*To divine the past, present and future you must use beryl or a transparent stone such as rock crystal to create a cloudy effect and an irresistible current.*"

Then, my father walks into the room after his shower and in the living room the television freezes and Knife and me hold our breath. I can smell the soap and the aftershave and he has a mooneye, purple and blue and he's drinking tomato juice for his hangover. He's probably been sleeping all day. His shirt is stiff and white and his black pants have creases up the front. Mother Blind is an expert ironer and she uses lots of starch and sprinkle water then puts his shirts in the icebox so they iron smooth.

"Who left the front door open?" he says.

Willy pops out of the kitchen cabinet under the sink.

"Ziggy do it. He *fryin'*."

"Well Ziggy will have a red behind if he does it again."

"Ziggy ready have red bee-hive."

Aunt Oink snorts. She thinks everything Willy says is funny. Well, it usually is.

"You should put a steak on that shiner," Aunt Oink says.

Mother Blind sets the green leaf platter on the table and slices the pot roast but it falls in strings not slices.

"Jesus, Jane" my father says, and smacks Mother Blind on her butt. "*Lordy*. Looks like that heifer's been around the farm a few too many times."

"I'd like to say a prayer," Aunt Oink says, and my father gives her a look, laughs then pulls on a lock of her hair. She just wants an audience.

Mother Blind smacks the spoon against the pot and looks at Aunt Oink who is wearing her hair down in black waves and then she looks at my father.

"They'll be no prayers from you at this table," she says.

"Heathen," Aunt Oink says.

"Hollis," Mother Blind says and she gives him the look that he says could burn down the house. "Can we all act like adults at the dinner table, please? Allie, this is dinner not church. Not the boardwalk. Get your gypsy books off the table."

"Jeezy," Willy says.

Mother Blind sharpens the chopper on the flint wheel but the roast still don't cut right so she sets it down and sets a bowl of cold slaw and a basket of biscuits down, then gravy in a boat, the mashed potatoes, the corn. She scoops the food on our plates and everything smells of biscuit and vinegar and brown gravy.

Aunt Oink lights a cigarette.

"Allie, for the last time no smoking until we've finished dinner."

Aunt Oink sticks out her tongue when Mother Blind turns her back and then she blows a long pipe of smoke her way and it lands in my mother's hair.

"Put it out," Mother Blind says with her back turned.

Willy stuffs a mouthful of coleslaw in his cheeks and they puff out like a cartoon cloud then he lets all the cabbage strings hang out in a cabbage beard.

"Get your elbows off the table," Hollis says to me. "Mind your manners."

"Willy's are," I say.

"Hey. Speak when you're spoken to."

"I just did."

"You need to show some respect young lady," he says.

"You need to show some respect young lady," I say.

"Stop that or I'll get the belt and you'll go to bed hungry," he says, and the cat jumps down from Aunt Oink's lap and pounces on a shadow.

"Stop that or I'll get the belt and you'll go to bed hungry," I say.

"Okay that does it." He starts to get up from his chair.

"No. I'm sorry Daddy. I won't do it again, I promise. I was just teasing like you do."

"One more chance, young lady," he says.

"Lady?" Aunt Oink snorts. "More like a rat. Look at her dirty claws."

Willy's chair slips backwards and slams on the floor and when he grabs the tablecloth his plate goes down with him and Toro tries to get to the plate before my father grabs it. Willy hops back on his chair and blows the coleslaw back into the bowl before anyone can stop him.

"Pigs," Mother Blind hollers and a pin curl pops out like a jack in the box. She twists her apron and two more bobby pins ding off. "'Pearls before swine.' All of you," she hollers, but she is staring at Aunt Oink and Daddy Dead.

"Boy, you sit at this table till you eat every carrot and pee on your plate, you hear?" he says, and spoons the spit-out coldslaw into Willy's bowl.

He says that all the time. He thinks it is funny. He thinks a lot of things are funny like holding a pillow over my face for instance.

Aunt Oink smacks her fork on the table.

"Are you calling *me* swine?" she says.

"Yes I am," Mother Blind answers.

"This roast is overdone. I ain't eating no shoe-leather-meat. I'm going home."

Yay, Knife says.

"Hollis are you going to just sit there and let her speak to me like that?" Mother Blind says.

"Now just a minute. I'm not putting up with no catfight. Jesus. Turn 'em upside down and they're all the same," he tells Willy. "Lordy."

"You ought to know," my mother says.

Aunt Oink slides out of her chair and gets up from the table.

"You'd drive any man crazy," she says. "No wonder he never..."

"Who do you think you're talking to?" Mother Blind hollers.

"Bitch. You're not my mother for Christ sakes."

Mother Blind takes Aunt Oink by the shoulders and slams her into the hallway.

"Get your hands off of me. You think you're so smart with the Shakespeare..."

Mother Blind melts onto the floor and cries into her blue and yellow flowered skirt and I wonder if she will turn into a puddle of melted crayons.

"I'm cutting outta here," Hollis says.

"Allie get in the truck, I'll give you a ride home."

"How dare you." Mother Blind hollers.

"Jane. I drank too much the way I told you, okay?"

"Like hell." Aunt Oink says.

"Nothing happened. It was innocent."

"Innocent?" Mother Blind says.

"You know I love you," he says, and Mother Blind cries on the kitchen floor, her skirt spread on the polished tiles.

"Are you taking me home or not?" Oink says, one hand on her hip.

"*Dasher*," Willy says. Then Knife gives me the *go* signal with her thumb and we take off. drag our blankets, our pillows and books into the closet and slam the door tight. I read Willy The Three Little Pigs and Toro curls up on my pillow.

After the screaming ends it goes silent and we sneak down the hall on tip toes and peek into the kitchen mess. There are voices coming through the window screens. We peek out and see three cigarettes burn red from the trees by the barbeque pit and we hear beer cans ping the tin barrel where my father burns dead leaves and garbage.

"*Dey in dingey barrow*," Willy says.

"She never left," I say.

We sneak back into the kitchen, Willy in his cape and crown, empties the cabinet and rolls cans of tomato soup across the counter and they crash into the sink. I put Toro on the kitchen table so he can lick up the pot roast. Broken plates and cold slaw are on the floor and the chairs are sideways and upside down. Willy finds a box of Oreos and shoves a fist of them into his mouth then he flies down the hall and black cookie crumbs make a path. He hops onto the stove and holds his arms airplane at his side.

"I *fry*," he says.

"You can't fly," I say.

"I Ziggy," he says. He leaps back on the counter and walks the windowsill over the sink then points to the backyard.

"*Wey* back *dere*," he says.

Out the window I see the outline of King Car in a circle of weeds but then I see two yellow eyes.

"Let's go to bed," I tell Willy.

From the screen door we spot three red-hot cigarettes loop in the air like fireflies.

The Eleven-Year Rule

THIS IS THE Eleven-Year Rule:

Your name is Jane and you have a sister who is born when you are eleven. Her name is Margaret Alice but Grandma calls her *it* and this makes you mad. Grandma can't take care of baby *it* and this makes you sad.

"Could you feed *it* the bottle for me, Jane?" Grandma says.

Grandma won't get out of bed due to meloncola.

You feed the baby mashed peas then you roll her up and down the sidewalk in the baby carriage with the silver handle and the blue hood. You shake the pink rattle and change the yucky diaper and you still have to fry pork chops and make Grandpa's work sandwiches and run the wash through the wringer, go to school and feed the baby all at the same time. This is hard.

In school you study typewriting, hygiene and how to get stains out of pillowcases and bake a pretty meatloaf with a bacon strip on top. You have to learn how to sew a skirt. You study Shakespeare—fun. But now there's no time. When Grandma finally gets out of bed and takes a shot of whiskey you are already a sort of a mother though you are eleven and the baby is zero. When you are almost a mother to your sister who is minus eleven years, that means you aren't just a sister. You are a sis-mom-ster and that makes everything mixed up and hard to understand like multiplication tables and fractions and decimals. So if your baby sister does something bad to you, you can't beat her up like a regular sister or chop off her hair or cut up her clothes on the wash line. You can't hate her and even if you do you have to turn the other cheek and get smacked forever. And that is the *eleven years' rule.*

Sisters, sisters, sisters. Holy.

High Horse

IT'S THREE WEEKS SINCE WE STALLED OVER PARIS and quiet for now. Knife says people do normal things to forget the not normal: wash clothes, dishes, babies, roll pies, mash potatoes and go to a lot of movies. Grandma beats rugs, Grandpa mows grass till it's almost gone, Daddy Dead goes to the Elbow Room, Mother Blind burns shirts with the iron and reads Shakespeare. Aunt Oink eats pig feet and reads the Bible, Willy and Knife and me race our wagon down Cherokee as fast as we can go--ducking low so the tribes don't get us.

This morning, we watched the sun come up orange and red over the hill, then played bakery and made mud pies in empty pot-pie tins. We decorated the pies with leaves and wild berries. It's Daddy Dead's birthday and Mother Blind set up the table under the trees with the blue Christmas lights hung twig to branch. She's baked a double devil cake in the new oven and Grandma, who didn't want to come because, you know, makes hamburger patties and ate eats some meat raw with salt and pepper and I almost puke. Her pockets are stuffed with cough drops and chewing gum.

Nasty bum, rotten bum, no good bum, I hear her say to herself.

But she is here anyway because she doesn't drive and she's lonely.

Everyone is trying to get along because: "What else can you do?" Grandma says. "Life is short, and it gets shorter every day."

In the afternoon Willy and me blast each other with the hose then stand in front of the fan. Grandma says we will catch our death but she says that about eating apples too. Apple skin can get stuck in your windpipe and then you choke to death, die, like the cartoon where skeletons dance and sing: Dem bones dem bones those dry bones. It's funny but scary too. Willy always shakes his bones with them. They are lit up bright white with a black background singing: The ankle bone connected to the leg bone and on and on until they put together an entire skeleton. Every time we watch it we want to see it again.

"Can you really *catch* your death?" I ask Knife, and she gives me the coast sign and her eyes go dark.

No, she says. It catches you.

Knife makes me calm when I am about to have a fit or drown myself in the bathtub or get smothered by a pillow. Without Knife I'd be dead already.

Daddy Dead's party starts at nightfall. It's magic under the trees, the air honeysuckle, and a chocolate breeze from the kitchen window. We eat corn from the grill and let the butter melt down our arms and bare chests then rub it around and stick leaves to our skin. After the double devil cake Grandpa breaks out his trombone and Willy and me bang sticks on the tin barrel. I steal a half can of beer. Grandma says you have to require a taste for beer and she is right. It's not sweet like one of Aunt Oink's highballs.

We spit the beer out on the dirt and it makes a dark shape on the ground and Toro comes over to inspect it with his nose.

Cocktails over beer any day, Knife says.

Mother Blind and Aunt Oink sing a song about *misters* and *sisters* from the movie called *White Christmas* and Daddy Dead plays along on his guitar. After they do shots and beer chasers, they square dance, whip up dirt clouds with bare feet. But Knife and me know that before long there will be a catfight.

Twisters, Knife says.

Mother Blind is wearing the silver sparkle dress and Aunt Oink has on white short-shorts so she can show off her tan.

"I could have been in a traveling show," Mother Blind says, and combs her fingers through her hair on one side and swings it over her shoulder so it covers her right eye in a wave. She's is in her *whatever will be will be* mood. Happy. If you can't change the future because it is written in a horrorscope book, why worry?

"Kirby Hoagland said I had the kind of voice that deserves a full piece orchestra."

"Garbage," Aunt Oink says.

"When I was fourteen and Mom and Pop had a band. I sang the "Tennessee Waltz" and did cartwheels on stage."

"I'd like to see you do one a those right now," Daddy Dead says.

"You can't do those after having a baby," Aunt Oink snaps.

Mother Blind puts her shoulders back and lifts her chin.

"The troupe wanted to bring me on the road but Mom wouldn't hear of the stage. I told you this story many times, Allie."

"Hmp, well I forgot," she says, and squirts a big plop of white lotion in her palm and polishes her legs with it.

"Had my picture in the newspaper," Mother Blind says, and Aunt Oink cracks the cap back on the bottle and sets it down hard.

Willy and me, flat out on the ground, look up at the blue fairies strung together in the trees. We like to listen to grown up talk. The ground is a soft with powdery red dust and clumps of stiff grass like I imagine porcupine needles feel.

"I don't remember that either," Aunt Oink says, and kicks her bare foot up on the bench.

"Well of course you don't remember," Mother Blind says. "You were only three-years-old. Things were different then."

"Hunky-dory for you." Aunt Oink says, then takes out her compact and puts on more red lipstick.

Mother Blind says she was a trained tap dancer and when she was a girl she got everything she ever wanted because she was an only child.

"You two just won't quit," Daddy Dead, says, and asks himself a question about why did he ever leave Richmond.

Aunt Oink crosses her bare legs and swings one toward Daddy Dead and he grabs her foot and tickles it.

"Well after you moved out, *I* was the only child," Aunt Oink says, rolling her hair up in a high ponytail so tight I can see her scalp stretch.

"I guess you could say that, as spoiled as you are," Mother Blind, says. "You see I got attention, you were spoiled. There is a difference."

"Always riding a high horse," Aunt Oink snorts, and Cheyenne struts across the lawn with a dead mouse and drops it at Aunt Oink's feet.

"Get that thing out of here," Mother Blind says, and Willy picks it up by the tail, spins it around in the air then tosses it into the woods.

"Hollis says I've got class, right Hollis? He said no one has more except maybe Audrey Hepburn. But he never met her," Mother Blind says.

"Oh yeah? I don't tell you everything.," Daddy Dead says.

Willy and me play puppet with our toes and make them talk along with Mother Blind and Aunt Oink, squeezing them up and down like lips.

"That's the first honest thing you ever told me."

"Well, you always were a lady," Daddy Dead says. "Always good manners."

"Did you go to high horse school too?" Aunt Oink says. "Miss Manners."

Mother Blind sure didn't get her manners from Grandma because Grandma eats with her mouth open and burps out loud, even spits out the window whenever she says the name "Hollis."

Where *did* Mother Blind get her high horse? Knife asks.

Mother Blind knows her forks and knives. Also, she has a high walk and practiced with books on her head. Maybe she got it from Grandma's mother Emma who came on a ship from Switzerland and brought the high horse with her. The horses are high there because of the Alps, everybody in Switzerland has a high horse.

I mouth the words to Willy: *Look, the stars are out,* until Willy figures out what I said. It's a game we play along with read my mind and Indian burn. Finally, he looks up and stares at the sky and all its diamonds. We find the big dipper first, then the little dipper and after we stare for a long time we see the outline of Pegasus. Grandpa taught us about all the stars and tonight we can almost make out all of them and they are making everyone tipsy, Mother Blind doing her Shakespeare again.

"A hall, a hall, give room. And foot it, girls.

More light, you knaves, and turn the tables up;

And quench the fire, the room is grown too hot."

"Who knows what that is from?"

"Emily Post," Aunt Oink says, then sucks at her beer can and shoots cigarette smoke at Mother Blind and it wraps around her face like mummy gauze for a second.

Romeo and Juliet, Mother Blind says.

After a few more beers and whiskey shots they forget about the high horse and Mother Blind drags Aunt Oink by the arm and gets her to dance to Daddy Dead's guitar strings playing "Hey Good Lookin'."

Grandma and Grandpa leave and the fire goes dead. Willy and me go into the house to find a cowboy movie on television but there is only a movie where people give Hollywood kisses. Outside the window I see Aunt Oink's white shorts glowing in the dark like twin

44

ghosts. We run out into the night.

Willy races past and I catch his cape and he gives me a fist. I figure I'll really rev him up just for fun.

"Hey Willy I think you were really flying there for a minute. I saw you lift up a few inches. Let's play airplane."

"Up *dere*." he says, and points his finger to the sky. "I pie lot."

He shimmies the drainpipe to the roof and onto the shingles in his bare feet until he reaches the peak and the skinny flat ledge at the top. In the moonlight the flecks of grit on the roof are sprinkled with glitter.

Flashlight, Knife says.

"Wait Willy."

I run into the kitchen and snap up the flashlight. It has a dial on it and tiny buttons that flash it white, red or green.

"Hey Willy. I'm the tower, okay? When I flash red it means wait. When I flash green it means the runaway is clear and you check the controls and get ready for lift off."

He stands at the end of the roof with his arms held out at his sides and the white cape flaps at the moon.

"I think you should take your crown off," I say. The fur waves with the breeze.

"No," he says. "I Ziggy."

"Stop at the chimney and turn back around. Just keep doing that until I say you can land. You ready?"

He stares ahead and his eyes lit like foil.

"Start your engine," I say

He turns knobs made of air.

I flash the light red and it colors his cape.

"Check the indicator,"

He looks down at the panel.

"All signs are dasher," I say.

His arms are stiff at his sides, his face set and fixed ahead.

"Get ready for lift off."

I turn the red light on then off.

"Ready."

He dips his wings side to side.

"Set."

He makes an engine sound.

I flash on the light, green and steady.

"Departure aircraft 777. Have a nice flight. Roger. Go."

That really fires him up and he runs like a horse taking off at a race, the glittery peak shining under his feet all the way to the far end when I watch his crown slip over his eyes like blinders.

"Turn back." I holler. "Willy stop. *Stop.*"

His cape lifts and disappears over the edge then a loud thump and I scream his name.

I see the white threads from Willy's cape float past the chimney. I am numb. Mother Blind's scream stretches from the trees and echoes. Willy is out cold on the ground with his face flat against the dirt and Knife is in the lawn chair giving me the *space* sign, circling her finger over her head and this means to float around the moon.

Mother Blind flips Willy right side. There is blood from his head.

"Call an ambulance." she hollers.

"But we don't have a phone." Aunt Oink screams. "They shut it off."

"The neighbors."

"What neighbors?"

"Down the lane," Daddy Dead says. "That old house. The Perfumos."

"No, there's a mummy there," I say.

"Run," Mother Blind says.

"Wake up. Wake up. Willy, open your eyes." My father is on his knees holding Willy's head. "Willy Boy," my father says. "Wake up."

"Hollis," Mother Blind cries.

"He'll be okay, he's breathing."

But Mother Blind is crying hard and wipes her tears with her silver skirt and I think this time she might cry herself into a lake.

Willy opens his eyes and the earth stops falling.

"That a boy," my father says.

"Don't go back to sleep," Mother Blind says. "If he falls asleep he could slip into a coma, Hollis."

Her tears make holes in the dirt around her feet and my father rubs her hand and then the sky cracks and the rain comes down in cool sheets.

"Stay awake Willy boy," he says.

For once they don't fight.

I grab Knife and run into the house. It's my fault he fell. I'm supposed to protect him.

Knife tells me to stay in moon orbit for now.

I watch Mother Blind climb into the ambulance. It spins red light around the yard and flashes the walls of my room then the sirens fire down the lane racing away, the siren stretching down the interstate. After Knife fixes her head, we put the pillow over both our heads and hope death don't catch Willy, or us, in our sleep. But we can't sleep anyway.

I tuck Knife onto my shoulder and we shiver. Blood on the ground. White threads in the air. Moon cold and pale, a crystal ball, the future all cut up. It's midnight and the wind blows shadows across the yard.

We get up and go into the closet and I read a book called *Misty of Chincoteague* about a boy named Paul and his sister Maureen and a wild pony named Phantom and her colt. She is a shaggy horse and lives on an island off of Virginia. When Paul finds Phantom, he at first thinks her colt is part of the mist so when he finally sees the colt he calls her Misty. On the way from the island to the mainland the horses have to swim but Misty is too small and is drowning so Paul jumps in and holds her safe as he swims to the shore. In the end, they set Phantom free because that is how she is meant to be but they keep Misty.

At daybreak the sky spills onto the hills and turns flat as a blanket, a gray one and there is a cloud that holds a ghost moon. I float there in the haze a while longer till Willy comes home and Knife says it's okay to come out of orbit.

Frankenstein

WILLY COMES HOME THE NEXT DAY with fifty stitches across his forehead and he thinks he is Frankenstein--black thread sewn in his skin, a zigzag, the skin puckered tight at the edges like hems of Grandma's handmade curtains.

"Willy, I shouldn't have let you go up on the roof at night," I say.

"Why?" he says. "I *fry*."

"No Willy. You didn't fly. That is why you have fifty stitches in your head."

I stare at the dark lines across his forehead. I never saw Willy cry from hurting himself. Every fall or cut or bump on the head, he never bawled and I wonder how he does it and then I remember he probably learned it from me because I've had more practice than him.

He walks toward me with his arms straight out.

"I not Willy," he says. "Me Frankenstein."

"Why weren't you watching your brother?" Mother Blind says, standing in the hallway in her blue raincoat. But I don't have an answer. "He could have died," she says, and I look past Willy at the knives lined up on the wall in the kitchen. They have to be very sharp for her cold slaw.

"I knew you'd be trouble," she says. "Born on Friday the thirteenth."

As if I had anything to do with it.

Don't worry, Knife says. Look at me.

Outside it's windy and rain pounds the ground and I think about Misty almost drowning.

"Willy? Does it hurt?"

"No." he says. "Me no hurt. Me *drown-did*."

"What?" I say.

"Ziggy *dasher* in ocean. Dive," he says, and dips his hand through the air.

"But didn't it hurt when you hit?"

"No," he says. "*Qua-qua*," and runs down the hall.

"But you hit the ground, not the water." I tell him but he runs away.

From the window I see his cape and crown are heaped in the mud and rain so out I run and grab them and the fur smells like wet dog. I shake them out in the garage and hang them to dry from an extension cord that is looped from the workbench to the outlet on the wall.

"Why weren't you watching your brother?" Daddy Dead says. "Another of your big ideas?"

"No. He thought it up. He did it before. A lot of times."

"And you didn't tell him not to?" he says.

"I told him to take his crown off but it was too late."

"Listen, don't you understand? Your brother isn't afraid of anything. His brain is screwy."

I watch a black ant creep across the floor carrying a graham cracker crumb. Daddy Dead stomps it dead with his shoe and it makes me sad to think the ant didn't get to enjoy the crumb after so much work.

"Keep your eye on him, you hear? There is nothing he won't try."

Willy spends the rest of the day playing Frankenstein and I spend the day wearing one of Grandma's curtains over my hair and running from the monster made of many dead body parts who is about to kill me.

Red Light

THE DAY DADDY DEAD AND MOTHER BLIND bring Willy to get his fifty stitches out, I'm stuck home alone with Aunt Oink for the first time since we cooked her in the oven.

I hear her pop a cap off of a beer bottle. I can see her at the end of my room through an empty wrapping paper tube. She pours a glass of whiskey and lights her Salem.

"Get your telltale ass in here this minute." she says.

If I run through the garage I can make it out to King Car. Aunt Oink gives me snake eye, narrow and dark. I run to the garage door but she grabs my arm and twists it backwards till it kills then squeezes my wrist in an Indian burn that hurts so bad I stop kicking and she slams me into the corner.

She says never to lay my hands on her personal things *ever* again. Says I'm being sent to a school where you can't come home, a Betsy-Wetsy school for pee-pee children who don't belong in the normal world and by the way, where the hell is her key? I don't tell her it's still in my sock and I see Knife is under the kitchen table giving me the coast sign.

"You little bitch," she says, her black eyes blacker the madder she gets. "You caused a lot of trouble." She drags me down the hall and into the room with the red light. She is Poe all the way tonight.

"Nobody's allowed in the darkroom," I say. "Daddy said."

"Shut your mouth."

She unlocks the door and I wonder how she got the key but then I know how.

The darkroom smells of vinegar and hard boiled eggs. A string is looped from one wall to the other and photographs of airplanes and cars hang snipped in place with little wooden clothespins. The chemicals are lined up on the counter in silver trays and one tray has an upside-down photo floating on the water. A metal cabinet sits in the corner and she pulls out all the drawers one after the other and cars, trucks, airplanes, babies, boats slide on top of one another until she finds the drawer she is looking for and flips through a new stack of photos.

"Look here," she says, and holds the photo up close to the light bulb and I try a hex on her to catch fire but nothing happens.

It is a black and white photograph of two little girls sitting on an odd-a-man like the one in our living room, white with slices of black pie shapes all around in a circle. One girl has curly blonde hair and the other has straight brown hair with bangs. Their eyes are wide and round and frozen. They're naked. I stare into the eyes until I see that two of the eyes are mine and the others belong to my Kindergarten friend Wilma who wore a white pinafore with ruffles and I think I must be looking into a crystal ball to the past instead of the future.

"It's not me." I say.

"Of course it's you."

My face gets hot and I remember.

It is summer and I am the only one born. My friend Wilma and me are in the backyard playing on the tire swing. The sun is shining and we eat tomato sandwiches under the apple tree. Wilma's white dress has a bow in back and stiff ruffles at her shoulders but there it is brown around the hem from the dirt underneath the swing. Daddy pulls in the driveway and after a while my mother calls us in the house and she brings me into the bathroom but Wilma doesn't come.

Mother Blind shuts the bathroom door and tells me to take off my dress and my underwear and I say: *WHY?* Then *NO.* and she says *YES* and I say, *NO, NO, NO,* but Daddy says *do what you are told* and then my clothes are on the floor and I think of a cartoon where a girl disappears. Mother Blind drags me into the living room and there is Wilma naked same as me and sitting on the black and white oddaman. Daddy tells me to sit down next to Wilma with her bare body parts showing and skin like a ghost. We stare up and into the eye of the camera and he clicks and flashes, our bare shoulders touch and our legs lock together, our butts stuck to the plastic, red and purple exploding in our eyes. When he is done flashing I have to walk naked across the living room to get my clothes and Wilma does the same but we only look down at the floor and not at each other. After that we were too shy to be friends anymore.

"Your daddy is a photographer," Oink says.

I hear stones spit up the driveway and Aunt Oink flicks out the light and locks the door. Daddy Dead won't like the mess she made. A place for everything and everything in its place, only he keeps getting the places mixed up.

Down the hall the door pounds open and shuts and I hear footsteps and wait for my mother and Willy but I hear Daddy Dead say he dropped them off at Grandma's for dinner.

He is in the corner talking to Aunt Oink and I quick slip into the kitchen and grab Knife from the ice skating rink and she asks what took me so long and her head is loose again. I say I'll tell her all about it in bed and we make a getaway, skating in our socks on the waxed floor to our room.

"Get back here young lady," Daddy Dead, says.

He tells me to stay out of people's personal things and that children have no business in the affairs of adults and how there are a lot of things children don't know about and don't need to know about for a long time.

In our room we crawl under the bed and make plans for another trip to Florida where we can build sandcastles in the sun and practice skimming waves on a paddle board.

"I'm never taking my clothes off for anyone," I tell Knife. "There's a photo of Wilma and me naked. You never met Wilma but she was my best friend in Kindergarten. I forgot about it till now but Aunt Oink made me look at it and called it *art*. She said the photographs of her are *art* too."

Knife throws up her hands and spins her head around.

What if you have to go to the doctor's? she says.

"They can't *make* you take your clothes off right?" I say.

Not if you have a pistol, she says.

We hear Daddy Dead say, "not tonight," and slam the door on Aunt Oink.

Yay. Fisheyes and ground hog livers, Knife says.

The sky is black and the moon drips gold across the cornfield. Knife says: let's have a dream now and I say okay and we close our eyes and go to sleep till the dream comes but it's not a good one.

My mother is in the woods polishing the trees with Windex and Butcher's Wax.

What is she doing? Knife says.

Knife is in pieces on the ground, all her parts popped off but her head is in the grass but she can talk. Above us are rolls of clouds, bed pillows with feathers raining and Wilma drowning in her white dress.

"I just waxed her dress," Mother Blind says and I notice a pressure cooker dial attached to the top of her head, the numbers rising.

I pick up a can of lighter fluid, make the letter Z in the dirt and light a match.

Our House

THERE'S THREE BEDROOMS IN OUR HOUSE, two small and one not and that is the one where Daddy Dead and Mother Blind sleep, all the red leaves waving in the wallpaper. I see Aunt Oink go in the red tree room and Daddy is in there and THAT IS NOT ALLOWED. No Trespass. A trespasser breaks property law like if you step on your neighbor's grass.

Daddy Dead said our house can't burn down. He built it from cement blocks. Good idea because there's a lot of fires at our house. In the living room there is a big window—a picture and that means when you look out of it everything has a frame. Maybe if Daddy finishes our house we can hang some drapers. Grandma says she can sew some for us with her threads and needles but the truth is she don't sew so good. Grandma's afraid of sewing machines. Grandma is afraid of just about everything.

In our living room and kitchen, the walls are made of wood, not fake wood but the kind with black eyes staring out like bats. I kick the planks with my cowboy boots when I get mad and I get mad a lot because I see Aunt Oink and Daddy Dead kiss by the oven with all the fish sticks burning black.

There is a stone fireplace in the living room and wall paper with giant birds frozen over the wooden panels. Mother Blind picked out the wallpaper, birds with long tails of brown, gold, white and orange but the kitchen and living room and one bedroom are the only rooms finished.

I told Mother Blind about how Aunt Oink trespassed in her room with Daddy Dead but Aunt Oink said she was just studying a book about how to fly a small plane and he was showing her the way to operate the control panel.

Hollis King

MY FATHER'S REAL NAME is Hollis King. He used to be Daddy and bounce me around inside a sheet or let me ride on his shoulders or do pony boy but that was Before. Now he holds a pillow over my face just for fun while Aunt Oink tickles me. He is a *tease,* my mother says. He's just *horsing around.* He is Poe when he does this. Funny—NOT. I can't breathe or scream under the pillow, so Knife was born there in the space with no air. Knife says: Daddy Dead over and over. That is how he got his secret name. The pillow smells of chicken feathers and Knife takes me to a sleepy place on the ceiling and we look down.

Supernatural, Knife says.

When he lifts the pillow off my face, he laughs and Aunt Oink giggles and I run to my room and rocket out the window and breathe all the air in the sky.

That's when I snipped off her hair, sliced off and buried her breasts, tore off the pink silk dress and made her a black outfit out of Daddy Dead's leather glove.

Let's go start a fire, Knife says. Her forehead is dented and she stares at the sun and doesn't blink.

On television we watch a story about a wife who kills her husband with a frozen leg of lamb then she roasts the lamb and feeds it to the detective and that way: *no evidence.* My mother might do that now that she found out about Daddy Dead's lie, one of them anyway. They fight all afternoon about married.

"She won't give me no dee-vorce. She's cat-lick," he says.

He says I have a half brother and sister. I don't like halves or sharing either. I don't want any new relatives.

Mother Blind says she was married by a Judge Travers at the courthouse but she didn't wear a bride dress but a gray suit with a lily in the pocket and a hat with a crisscross veil. Knife says lilies ae for funerals. Daddy Dead forgot he is already married by Virginia. Maybe you can have different wives in different states and be married to one in New Jersey when in New Jersey and one in Virginia when in Virginia.

"Well I'm just going to keep having babies until you do right by me." Mother Blind says.

"You know I love you," he says.

"Don't you ever mention that woman's name to me again."

"But that was before I met you."

"Shut up."

She says she's gonna lock all the windows and doors so he can't get back in the house, then she lights a cigarette.

My mother is twenty-six but today she looks about thirty.

The Ghost Pond

WHEN MOTHER BIND AND AUNT OINK start to fight and Grandma screams opera and Grandpa gets his rifle and starts talking rotten apples and skunk, Willy and me make a getaway into the woods.

A breeze waves the tall ferns along the path, green combs that brush my bare legs. Each time we go further than the time before. Sometimes I am afraid we are lost but it's more fun than knowing where you are all the time.

We look for footprints, Indian arrows and shrunken heads, gold and silver, two-headed snakes, toads, turtles and rabbit kittens. We heard on the kitchen radio a rabbit kitten was found at Sheepfield Park and it is very important to call the station if you see it. I write the number on my foot with a marker pen.

We walk over hills and through the thick trunks of trees and tangled weeds and then over a dirt bank and when we look down we discover a pond and for a minute we just stare at the reflections on the water: trees waving, clouds swimming, shadows crawling.

"I didn't know this was here," I say, and I notice a blackbird stare at us from high in the tree as if we don't belong here. As if it is his pond.

"Whoa," Willy says, and we run down the bank to the still water.

We draw maps of our adventures on ripped up grocery bags and now we can add the pond. I grab the brown paper from by back pocket and the crayon and draw.

"Let's give it a name," I say. "How about Ghost Pond."

"Huh?" Willy says.

"Because it was invisible and hiding from us like a ghost," I tell him. He stares at me with sun in his eyes that have changed them from gray to blue.

"Ghost *qua qua*," he says.

Yeah, Knife says.

The pond is muddy at the edges but clear further out and we study the tadpoles slipping through weeds that wave over pebbles and rocks smooth and white as bone.

By noon the sun eats the clouds and the sky is hot white and the water is clearer and we can't believe what we see drowned in the watery grass: a blue bicycle stuck in the mud.

Maybe a kid was riding on the path speeding down the hill so fast she didn't see the pond?

Willy says he'll swim down and get the bike.

"Grog," he says, and points his finger toward the bicycle.

Grog means swim and water at the same time. Grandma says maybe there is a way to fix Willy's brain with Vaseline if he eats a teaspoon a day to grease the twisted wires.

Willy stares at me, eyes round as quarters. He wears his Ziggy costume and I can tell by the faraway look in his eyes he is cooking up a scheme.

"*Dey dash* bike on *grog*," he says. "Ziggy get it."

"You can't swim wearing your Ziggy cape," I say. "We have to get back, remember? Grandpa is getting us a blow-up swimming pool."

That gets his attention.

"*Hunky*," he says.

"Come on let's go."

We gallop like horses, Knife stuck in my back pocket says: Whoa.

Skunk

GRANDMA BEATS A RUG ON THE WASH LINE with her big wooden spoon and Grandpa cleans his rifle on the front lawn with his pipes and his rags and polish cans. Grandma's black hair is piled on her head and tucked into a donut ring and she has jelly dots and sour balls squirreled in her pockets. She honks her nose into a red bandanna then pulls a jar of Vicks Vapor Rub from her pocket, sticks in her pinky and shoves it up her nose. The kitchen window is open and the air smells applesauce. Grandma can peel a green apple in one curl.

"Good Lord, Oscar," she says. "All the rotten apples in the world and we get the one most rotted. The devil is in on this."

"Whelp," Grandpa says. "What can you do but pray?" He shoves his shine rag into the barrel of the gun.

"Are you gonna put up our swimming pool, Grandpa?" I say.

"Maybe," he says, and goes back to his polish rags. "After I get the skunk."

Mother Blind is in bed today nursing her heart. Grandma says Mother Blind has a broken heart and that's called meloncola. Things didn't work out so hot with Daddy and now nobody knows what's going to happen next. Grandma says we're going to have to live like gypsies in a covered wagon because Grandpa is losing his job.

She thinks she can sell her pies on the side of the highway to make some money. Daddy Dead has a good job firing iron and silver and copper pots but he can't weld the hearts he broke, I heard Grandma say. She says he makes good money but spends it all on his airplane and a new Buick every year and a motor boat. Everything for him and the law won't help us with the matrimoney because, you know.

Snort, snort, Knife says.

"He ought to go hang himself,"Grandma says in her opera voice, and I follow her wooden spoon into the kitchen.

Mother Blind shuffles in from her heartbreak bed, crying.

"What's wrong Mommy?" I say, as if I didn't know.

"Everything," she says.

I hug her around her skirt and Willy squeezes her from the other side and for this moment I'm not mad at her but at Daddy Dead and Aunt Oink. I remember her reading me Little Black Sambo in bed, the tigers churning into butter. How she let me make doll shapes out of the pie crust and wear her pearl necklace and try on her silver dress. It's warm here by the oven.

But Grandpa is still talking about the skunk. He is dressed in his tan trousers and shirt that says: Mack Truck on the pocket. But Mack is moving to Ohio and Grandma says no way is she leaving her daughters. When Grandpa argues she tells him to go to the devil. I heard her say he is lucky she's not in the sane asylum like his sister Aunt Elsie who is never getting out.

"Grandpa's not putting up the pool today," I tell Willy.

Rats, Knife says, and Willy has a fit on the kitchen floor and kicks his boots against the tile, his fists slam the green squares. He screams made up words like: dammmfruckzoo and his face goes bluer every second till Grandma throws cold water on him and Grandpa holds him down till he stops and that doesn't happen until all Grandpa's veins are popping out.

By morning, Mother Blind turns her other cheek, it's Grandpa's birthday, and she pretends she didn't have a fight with Daddy Dead the night before but Grandpa is still polishing his gun.

"Let's get out of here," I tell Willy.

We drag our wooden play chairs and table through the weeds to the pond and set the table under a tree, sit Knife on the chair. I put acorns in the blue teapot and cover them with pond water. When the water is clear, we stare at the bicycle. Willy finds a branch and ties a rope with a loop trying to fish the bike.

"Me get it," Willy says.

"No I'm scared," I tell him. "What if you get caught down there?

Willy dives in and tadpoles down to the bike, tugs the wheels and spokes but they jam in the gunk. He frogs to the surface, grabs the wash line we stole along with a meat hook, a soup scooper and a potato smasher. He jumps back in but the bike only shakes and sends clouds of mud in his face, his cheeks puffed, his eyes narrow. Grandma said if you stay underwater too long the water will go into your ears and you will die from water on the brain.

"Willy hurry," I say. "It's getting dark. It's Grandpa's birthday party, remember? Birthday cake.

Back home, coal glows hot from the barbecue grill and Mother Blind hangs blue lights thst loop treee to tree.

"Let's get some dry clothes, I tell Willy and in the hallway he stops to draw the bike on the wallboard, a stick person on the seat, spaces between all the body parts.

Aunt Oink is wearing her red bathing suit and drinking a Schlitz beer from the brown bottle. Knife gives her the juju claw. Grandma made blue cake with M&Ms stuck into the frosting.

"*Hunky.*" Willy says.

There is chicken and biscuits, gravy and corn on the cob, melted butter and watermelon all set out on the wood picnic table under the birch trees. Daddy Dead lights paper lanterns and hangs them from the tree branches and the blue lights glow like stars. Grandma says everything will be okay now. We will all get along because she prayed for it, very hard, and the lord gave her a sign when the oven heated itself up to 400 degrees without her even firing the pilot light or turning the knob.

Bicycle

WE SPEND EVERY DAY AT THE POND trying to fish out the bicycle till finally one day we pull it out of the mud with a rope. We dive into the belly with closed eyes, pinched noses, weed slimes tickling our bare skin. The sky is melting red to purple when finally we drag the bike up to the bank, stare at it, dripping puddles from our hair and underwear. The chain is twisted, the seat chewed and shot up with rusted holes. Willy spins the tires and cranks the gears. The tires are flat as Grandpa's sardines and there's a wire basket growing hair.

"I fix it," Willy says.

The pond seems empty without the bike, like its heart is missing. I stare into the water and see tadpoles wiggle up from the bottom, millions, exploding, fizzing from their tails.

From the corner of my eye I catch something by the trees. A wooden sign:

No Trespassers.

I never saw that before.

That's when I hear a hiss.

"Willy do you hear that?"

He's perched on the busted seat not paying me any mind. Deep in the trees a sound like firecrackers gets closer, branches snap and I grab my jeans. That's when I see the yellow hair.

I watch it weasel around the trees.

"*Wey* back *dere*." Willy says.

Shush.

A black cloud rolls and the moon goes bright and I can see it's not a wolf or a bear, it's a boy ducking from the black trunks of trees. His white shirt glows.

I reach for my jeans, hop into them but my sweater with the sparkles on the front is out of reach. We're good as dead and there's glitter on the ground.

The boy carries a stick, clicks his tongue, whistles through his teeth and walks a circle around the pond, taps his stick then stomps our way in his black boots. He picks up a branch with dried leaves and rattles it over our heads.

"This pond belongs to me," he says, and kicks the tree with his boot. "You're trespassing on the Stovekin Estate. I can fix your arrest."

He pops a cigarette, fires a match and holds it over our faces and I think he will set us on fire.

Willy's fox crown is on the ground and the kid picks it up with his stick and stares at the beady eyes.

"Are you the ones who killed it?"

"No, no." I say. "It's my grandmother's."

"Cause I'll kill the mother fucker who did."

He chucks the fox at a tree and I hear the little legs clack.

"Do you know you can be fined for trespassing?"

"We didn't know."

"Can you read?"

"Nope," Willy says.

"We didn't see the sign till just now," I say. "It was covered with leaves."

The moon rips a black cloud and shines the pond and the kid blows smoke in my face. He's tall. A teenager.

"What kind of dog is that you got there? Looks like a mole to me." Toro eyes him steady as the boy walks a circle around us.

"He's a Chihuahua," I tell him.

"Where's the bike?"

Willy and me stand frozen.

"I said where's the bike?" He scopes around, spots it, walks toward the tree, stoops over the bike, spins the wheels and gives us bad eye. He grabs the handlebar, combs his fingers through the muddy hair but it's not hair at all. In the moonlight I see it's plastic streamers caked with mud. The kid kicks at the pedal, spins it around.

"You've destroyed the grave," he says. "This is my dead sister's bike."

When he says the word *dead* it's like a body fell from a tree.

"She was eight. Came here to fish. How old are you?" he says.

I feel hollow inside. I never knew a kid my age that died.

"I'm almost nine," I say. "Next month."

"She *drown-did?*" Willy says, and the boy sits next to the bike and crosses his long legs Indian style.

63

"No," he says.

The moon shines on Willy's forehead and I see the track of fifty stitches.

"Ever hear of Fun Day?" he says.

I did but don't say.

"Well, my sister went to Fun Day on her bike and never came home. Gone just like that," he says, and snaps his fingers.

Willy's eyes are wide and shine silver.

"She left Fun Day, probably bored, I know I would be. She was on her way here to fish. I taught her how to cast the line. He draws the number 8 in the dirt.

"Big *foamy kilt* her?" Willy says.

"He means a big fish," I say.

"No, a little fish. She stopped at the bridge by the road and caught a catfish. It's slippery. She drops it. There's a big car. Little car. Big car passes. She bends down to grab the fish. Little car throws her in the air, over the hood. Smack on her head. Water on the brain. Dead."

I picture a girl, a girl like the boy, tall and bony, flying over the roof of a small car.

"The bike made my mother cry. She asked me to dump it here because it was my sister's favorite place."

He kneels down, picks up some white stones and skims them across the pond.

"You had no right to mess with it," he says: "It's a federal case. I should call the sheriff." He draws a stick through the dirt and makes a circle around us.

"Who *kilt* her?" Willy says.

"Best friend's mother. Had to move. Avoid Hemlock Road. You can't go nowhere unless you go Hemlock. We called her Flipper but her real name was Francine. Came here to ice skate too."

He tells us about children who die young and stay mad forever, mad because they won't learn to drive a car or steer a boat and girl ghosts who won't get to have babies, just rubber ones.

"Aren't you the kids who live on the dead end of Cherokee?"

He breaks a branch in half and swings it into the pond and it makes a loud splash.

"My father's gonna notify the Board of Health about that

cesspool."

"I don't want any babies," I say, out loud and almost look over my shoulder to find out who said it.

"Well, then I guess if you die young you won't be mad," he says, lights another cigarette. "Girls are supposed to be mothers. What do you think you will be then? That is, if you get to grow up."

"A pilot," I say. I never thought about it till now, like there's another kid inside me that I just met and now we're going to have to arm wrestle.

He shakes his head and laughs and the moon lands in the crook of a tree.

"You? You can't be a pilot," he says. "You can't afford a plumber."

"My father has a Piper Cub," I say. "He'll teach me. I've been flying with him since I was a baby."

"Well if he can afford a plane and that spanking new Buick I saw parked at your house he can clean up his god damned cesspool."

My face burns hot and my heart too.

He looks around at our fort and kicks at a pile of ashes, puts his hands in his pockets and points his stick at me.

"You're going to do as I say. "You know what this is?" he says, and pulls the thing from his back pocket.

"A walkie-talkie," I say.

"You know who has the other one?"

"*Kilt* sis?" Willy says.

"Yeah, right. The sheriff."

He pulls up the antenna and it wiggles it over his head.

"You're not leaving my property till you bury the bike back where you found it. Hear me aviator girl?"

He slides the antenna down.

"Looks like you guys been setting up camp here," he says, then he kicks over the wood we piled to build a wall. I think maybe he's a murderer.

The water is black and the moon is behind a cloud. The kid says we can start a bonfire next to the pond for more light. He wants the bike back where we found it, dead center. Now.

Willy and me find sticks and branches and build a stack next to the water and the kid sits by the bike and stares at us as we break thin branches from bushes, then more to keep the fire burning. I find some

65

rotted boards over by the well and stack them.

"Don't you know how to build a proper fire?" the boy says. "You have to crisscross the stack so there's air in between."

We take the stack down and start another, this time crossing the sticks and branches—X on X on X—each X in a different direction than the one beneath it.

"We'll go through these in no time," he says.

It's dark under the trees but we go farther in, almost to the creek. I hear the water splash over the rocks and we find branches and tow them in—a pine tree, tall as the kid, downed from the storm. I look over the tall trees, black against a waxed paper moon, low to the ground and ready to roll.

"Okay, it's time," he says. "Time for burial."

He strikes a match and lights the pile of wood, stands up, drags the bike out by the handlebar, rolls it into a spot where the firelight is brightest, holds the bike steady and squeezes the shifters and the brakes.

"Dearly beloved," he says, and gives us a sideways squint to make sure we're paying attention.

"Flipper Stovekin died on Fun Day."

Then he is quiet and I'm thinking he doesn't know what to say next.

He puts one foot on the pedal and his silver buckle shines.

"She had cocoa for breakfast," he says. "And then I never saw her alive again," He scratches a big R.I.P. in the red dirt, wheels the bike to us and we each take one side of the handlebar.

We roll the bike down the bank and the streamers blow out against my arm, the rusted fender scrapes my leg and here we go into the black water: slugs and snakes, pee-pee children pulling us down. Scary. So, I pretend I'm a pilot and the pond a black sky and the bike is a plane and I steer steady and straight. Flames wave on the water and we tow the bike out into the center of the fire, the water up to my neck. Willy steers the bike from beneath, swimming under, guiding it, with the other hand he holds his nose and kicks his feet.

"To the right," the kid hollers. "Okay, stop. Stop right there. Let it go."

I dive under and yank on Willy's hand then point to the bottom and we let the bike sink into the center of the flame until it disappears in the deep mud. I hold Willy's hand and we swim toward the shore. On the bank I wipe my eyes and shake gunk from my hair, check my skin for sluggers. When I can see again, the kid's face and hair are red from the flames and he is flipping stones in the air.

"You know this wood you used to build your camp? This wood is my property and you destroyed part of the estate. What did you think you were doing?"

"We were just playing house," I say.

"Play house like this?" he says, and his fingers make a circle, then pokes a finger in and out. "You mean play this kind a house?"

"We drink tea and draw maps and stuff," I say. I bring my doll.

"You mean that scary thing over there?"

I'm thinking Knife just might stab him. Her fingers are pointed in his direction.

"The fire's too high." I say. "What are you doing?"

"It's my property," he says.

I scoop up Knife then Toro and tuck him under my arm. I feel his heart beat hard against my chest.

The boy has flames in his eyes when he kicks my play table and chairs, the ones we dragged there and pitches them into the blaze. I watch the legs burn and there is a loud whoosh over my head and a tree branch catches the flame and Willy runs for his bucket of water.

"Willy. No. Run."

He looks at me and then at the boy. He snaps up his cape and crown and we rocket out, our bare feet pounding the dirt path. I turn to see if the boy chases us and there is a big heap of wood like antlers burning, the flames higher and higher and no sign of the boy.

The meadow glows red and we hear the fire gaining behind us as sirens cut the air and the giant wheels mow the cornfield. The engines flash by, mirrors of us caught there for a second in the shine of the doors, the tires rolling the cornstalks flat.

When we get to our house there are strangers standing on the lawn watching the fire burn and I hear someone say

"That's state property. No one's lived there since the Stovekins moved to Maine."

North

THE SCHOOL BUS STOP IS AT THE CORNER where the Elbow Room Bar sits, its chimney blowing smoke signals to Daddy Dead that say the beer is cold and the shots are hot. Marlene Travers works the bar and she is what he calls "built."

I kick the stones in the ditch with the leather toe of my boot. Everyone at our house is fighting over north and south, married and not married and: *she, she, she, her, her, her, you, you, you,* until the moon goes pale and thin and you can see right through it to the milky way.

"You have to throw the rotten apple away. The whole bushel will go bad," Grandpa says.

It's gray today, clouds so low they might land before the school bus comes and I can hop on one and go somewhere but then I see the yellow bus climb the hill through the fog. I sit next to Shari Collins with her pink cheeks and blonde ponytail. She is twelve and lives in a house that looks like someone colored it with rainbow crayons. Maybe we'll live in a house like that when we move to Richmond, Virginia.

"He doesn't like it here because we're North," I tell Knife. "South people are his friends and his relatives."

Let's never go there, Knife says, and curves two fingers in the air.

But now we *have* to go South. Mother Blind says we're packing up in two days and driving straight through Washington, DC and on to Richmond were the Civil War happened. Daddy Dead said it is better in Virginia. Besides, his middle name is Lee after a general with a sword and a white beard. There is another reason we have to move but I'm not sure what it is yet. I heard Grandma say: "What will the neighbors think?" We don't even have any neighbors. Everything is hurry up and secret. I'm not supposed to tell anyone what goes on in our house. I can't even tell anyone we are moving away.

I tell Shari and she says they hang people in trees down south. I tell Mrs. Ponyberg and she announces it to the whole class and to the principal Mr. Graves that we are moving in two days. David Cease makes me a card out of a paper plate that reads:

Good Buy Luck

Suzy Striker hands me a cap gun and a Bazooka. Everyone says goodbye for all of two days but three days later I'm still in New Jersey. I feel stupid so I tell everyone our car broke but we are leaving tomorrow when it gets a new duster.

That was six months ago and we're still in New Jersey.

Tadpole

IT'S ON ACCOUNT OF A TADPOLE AND A RABBIT that Grandpa lined up the apples on the fence and shot them to bits. I watch the apple seeds explode and stick to my shoe. He is practicing so he can get the skunk with one bullet.

In the kitchen Grandma skins a bushel of apples for her pie sale and the peels curl in long strips and slip into the tin bucket on the floor. She can do an entire apple in one twirl. She says when she goes home to the caretaker house she'll take me and play "When You Walk Through a Storm" on her piano. Sometimes when she sings I get scared because it don't sound like her voice. No way. It gets deep and loud like there's a man inside her.

"I sang on the radio," she tells me. "I was the first one to ever sing on the radio."

Maybe no one had a radio back then except for the one she sang on.

Mother Blind is practicing her typing in the bedroom: *tap, tap, tap, tap, tap, tap, brrring, slide, click, ring.* She's going to get an office job, buy a car, apply her high school diploma, a business major, straight A's and a head full of Shakespeare.

The sky is dark blue and ready to crack. Grandma says we're getting a hard rain. But flood rain can drown you and float your house down the river but not our house. Our house would sink. Knife says it might be tadpole rain, all the guppies coming down on our heads and jumping in puddles trying not to die.

Aunt Oink is reading about the future again. She plops on the sofa in front of the picture window, her toenails painted red, her cigarette ashes on the rug but she don't care. She says the world is coming to an end next Friday.

Great. Next Friday the 13. I turn ten but I guess only for one day.

"Good," she says, and takes a drag. "I'm tired of living."

"But your just eighteen," I say.

I heard Grandma say the high school is going to "let Aunt Oink graduate *anyway*." I ask what's *anyway*? But she won't say. Only that it's because of the rabbit.

"Zoe?" Aunt Oink says.

I'm on the floor gluing sticks together in the shapes of people and deer and even a rabbit kitten and a fox. I hunt the yard for just the right ones. Knife says maybe we can sell the stick figures on the side of the interstate and save enough money to live on our own.

Zoe? She holds up her empty glass and waves it at me. Her face is red and puffy because she's always crying about the rabbit.

"Please," she says, Cheyenne is stretched out on her lap licking his orange fur.

I only do it so she'll get drunk and leave me alone. Besides, I like to play bartender. I'm thinking I can be a pilot *and* a bartender. Knife says she can be copilot and steer the plane while I shake the cocktails.

I put in two ice cubes from the silver tray, whiskey it up to the top, one sugar cube, a lemon squirt and a lemon slice fixed on the side of the glass, a half moon. Tasty.

"You forgot my cherry," Aunt Oink says.

I tell her she ate the whole jar and she calls me a liar and her eyes go skinny and her claws come out but she changes her mind and downs her highball instead.

She puts a cigarette in her mouth and I light it for her the way a good bartender does. I throw a lemon in the air and catch it in my mouth.

This is good," she says. "But make the next one a little stronger."

"Come here and sit by me for a bit," she says.

I tell her she's taking up the sofa by herself and anyway, I'm busy with my sticks and glue.

I was eleven when you were born," she says.

"I thought you were the most beautiful baby in the world and you were so teeny. I put you in the wash pan and gave you a hot bubble bath."

Her black eyes are spiked with eye pencil. Everybody says she's a good looker, everybody but me.

"I don't want to go to graduation anyway," she says, out loud.

"If you don't go to graduation then how will you graduate?"

She starts bawling, all the black eyeliner going spider down her face and I feel bad but Knife kicks her boot in the air: Don't go soft on Aunt Oink. She was there when Daddy Dead was holding the pillow. Laughing.

"I don't know what to do. What should I do?"

"Why don't you move to Florida," I tell her. "That way you can stay tan all year the way you like."

I glue an acorn on a stick woman. Her arms are pointed toward the sky. It's a hold up.

Snow

IT'S THREE DAYS BEFORE CHRISTMAS EVE and snowing, but not just any snow—it's blizzard snow frozen and sparked by moon and blue stars and wind blows flurries, waves of white so soft the flakes make beds across the lawn.

"It's a white Christmas like in the movie," I yell to Willy. But, still no Christmas tree.

Toro jumps and makes a path in the snow with his nose. All I can see are his black ears.

Snow blows sideways over the weeds, brown, now white, then it swoops over the woods, the pines like tall ghosts and I imagine the pond multiply crystals. A web of ice. Even the dirt road is sugar. I see stars on a path to King Car lost in a polar bear drift, the headlight eyes, the tire paws, the grill dripping snowflakes.

"Whoa." Willy says.

Over the cesspool, a lumpy white sheet floats and hides the black water—all the flies frozen-dead and shining.

Willy and me slide down the hill, run up the hill, down again in our orange snowsuits and the trees bend over our heads and shake snow onto our wool hats. We lay on the ground and open our mouths, fill Grandma's silver bowl with snow and stir in sugar and blue food color and eat it with spoons on a snowbank, our rubber boots touching, the bowl set between us.

I roll a snowball and sit Knife on it. She is wearing her purple velvet cape with a hood that I cut out of Aunt Oink's prom dress and the snow sticks to the velvet so the entire cape sparkles and Knife likes that.

Off to the prom, she says.

Snow falls where it falls. If it wanted to it could fill our house from the chimney and bury us. It doesn't care if it's our property. Weather doesn't care about anything.

We fill a silver pail with stones and aim them at the drainpipes and gutters and knock the snow off. We play Civil War and draw a line. I am in Richmond and Willy is in New Jersey. He tapes a Kotex bandage around his forehead and squirts ketchup blood on it. He dives into a drift and screams up the drainpipe: *Loch Moigh* and that means WAR.

We refuse to move from our house. And just in case they capture us we'll destroy everything. We make a snow baby from three small snowballs then poke it with sticks. By dark, our fingers and faces are bright orange but feel blue and so numb it seems they are missing.

Inside we pull off our boots and the snow melts on the floor and Mother Blind shakes a broom at us. On the television, a movie about the man who wants to jump off a bridge and Grandma twists knots of pie dough and sprinkles them with cinnamon and sugar. Mother Blind wraps cardboard angels with tinfoil to hang on the fireplace. Daddy Dead and Aunt Oink are at the Elbow Room because Aunt Oink *had* to have a ham sandwich.

Livers and cow hearts and polliwogs. Knife says. Oink, oink.

Yesterday in school, Suzy said tadpoles are made of jelly the same as jellyfish, same as Jello and green jam. She says we were all tadpoles at one time and swam in faucets and toilet pipes.

"Like tribes?" I say.

"Well, there are a lot and two teams."

Emily said that's not true. She says a boy goes pee inside a girl's triangle and that makes a baby. I think of the boy in the woods and how he said girls only want babies and I remember the other girl inside me who wants to be a pilot and ride the sky. I tell that girl to *stay* and not disappear.

Runway is clear, Knife says.

"But it's not."

Well pretend, she tells me.

We sit in front of the TV, our fingers still cold and red and eat knots of warm pie crust and the man in the movie can't get out of town and has an old house where everything keeps breaking like our house. The film plays all day and night so we watch it again from the beginning, memorize the words when, George Bailey says:

"What is it you want Mary? You want the moon? Hey that's a pretty good idea."

Mary says she'll take it. He's going to lasso it and I forget about the missing Christmas tree and moving to town.

George tells Mary she can swallow the moon and it will dissolve like candy and how the moonbeams will shoot out of her fingers and light the ends of her hair, and Willy and me both say: *Wow* at the same time.

Mother Blind is still gabbing about moving. It's like the Million Dollar Movie. Yesterday we're moving to an apartment in a town. The day before Grandma is staying with us. We're staying with Grandma. Daddy Dead and Aunt Oink hopscotching to Richmond with the polliwog. But not really. Now they're going to live in a trailer in our backyard. Aunt Oink and the jelly baby.

"We can't stay in this house," Mother Blind says.

I tell her it's our house and she says: "History is unkind."

If you're married you divide the house into two parts and each gets one side. So where's our side? What about the married rule? What about the holy?

Mother Blind wears a tight red dress and black heels and black stockings and a snowman pin with red rhinestone eyes. When I ask where she is going she says: *Out.* She goes out a lot lately but she never says where.

It's nighttime and the car might break down, I tell her, but she stares out the window without a word. Then: "Don't give your grandmother a hard time while I'm gone," she says, and clicks her heels out the door. I stick my face against the window. I see a car. No ordinary car. It's a police car.

"Mommy got arrested, look." I tell Willy.

Sharp, Knife says.

On Christmas Eve the kitchen smells of Grandma's cookies, chocolate chips melting, and she is singing "Silent Night" in her opera-man-voice. Scary.

It's still snowing and our rubber boots make stamps and when we get to the porch we look across the yard and in the moonlight the boot prints look like alphabet letters, Willy's lowercase, mine upper. We stare back and try to read our fortunes.

Daddy Dead's truck chugs up the driveway, still no Christmas tree but a blue submarine hooked to the fender. They get out, link arms and disappear into the white trees toward the liquor store on the highway and I hope they never come back. But they do, Daddy Dead dragging the pine tree he sawed off of somebody's lawn.

We put blue lights on and it smells like the woods. I hang the red Santa from my first Christmas, the green bell from my second, a silver snowflake from the third, blue angel from my forth and that's the one I remember best. Daddy Dead gave me a *special* present wrapped in silver paper. When I open it, it's a brown baby with big eyes staring back looking as scared as I feel. Daddy is laughing.

"You can't play with that new white doll no more," he says. He says it is my *nigger baby*. I'm not scared of the doll so much but scared of him. I hang the blue angel on the highest branch then the glass bird, the candy cane, the elf, the reindeer and the gold star.

I hear Mother Blind in the kitchen with Aunt Oink, saying everyone has to *act normal* because, "You know, the kids."

"We don't want to ruin their Christmas."

"They don't remember nothing." Aunt Oink says.

I hide around the corner. I like to listen to them talk. In the toaster I see their faces melt together.

One day, I ask my mother why she still talks to Aunt Oink when she got a Daddy tadpole?

"She's my sister. I brought him into the family. What am I going to do?"

Everybody asks me the same question.

"I hate them," I tell her.

She lifts her hands from the blue bowl of cornmeal and yellow dust floats over the sink. I spot Daddy Dead outside the window, in the backyard, in the snow, with the blue submarine.

"What's that blue thing for?" I say.

"Just temporary," she says, and pours the batter into a muffin pan. "A trailer." She looks at me and grabs my chin with her hand.

"Stop trying to make sense of things. 'There is nothing either good or bad but thinking makes it so.' *Hamlet*," she says.

On Christmas morning I get a baby doll, a holster, a Mickey Mouse watch and a View Master, my favorite because you can go to a pretty world for a while. Knife says to play with the baby doll for five minutes

76

and we can dump her later. I don't get the aviator goggles and the leather jacket I asked for. Willy gets a silver airplane, a fire truck, a toy rifle and a new set of Army men.

From the kitchen I hear Grandma sing her turkey song. She holds a raw turkey by the wings, dancing it in a sink full of water. Then she rubs it with butter and stuffs in apples. Aunt Oink fixes Bloody Mary's with celery sticks. By the time the turkey is roasted, the potatoes mashed, the string beans cooked, she and Daddy Dead are Bloody Mary drunk and Mother Blind is mad and tells us to pick up our toys and Willy broke the lever on my View Master so I break the trigger on his rifle and we wrestle on the floor rolling until we knock into the Christmas tree and the lights blow.

Daddy Dead lives in the blue submarine. Knife says we can nail the door shut so they can never get out. If we push hard enough we can slam it into the cesspool.

Mission. Knife says.

When Aunt Oink's baby gets born in six months we might have to move to a row house but it's not on a river. Mother Blind has to get a typewriter job.

"What about child support and the alimoney?" I holler.

"Maybe you should study the law," she says, and I stomp out the door.

It's the day after Christmas and there is a baked dome of something that Aunt Oink made on the table for dinner but I don't eat it. When Mother Blind goes shopping Daddy Dead and Aunt Oink get drunk and decide I need a haircut.

"No," I say. I like it *long*.

"Look at it," Aunt Oink says. "You've got trees growing in that nest."

"Shut up," I say. "I don't want a haircut."

"You've got to cut the knots out. No way you can comb them."

"Get the bowl," Daddy Dead says.

I run into my room and jump out the window into the night but Daddy Dead stomps out and catches me by my hair.

"Get back here," he says, and pulls me back into the kitchen and shoves me into the chair.

"Sit," he says, and Aunt Oink puts the yellow mixing bowl over my head and the scissors cut around the edge up to my ears. I try not to cry but then I can't stop.

A curse on them, Knife says.

Meloncola

EVER SINCE CHRISTMAS IT'S ONE THING after the other like Willy's broken train set, the box cars filled with the soldier heads he's snapped off, the tracks busted. Nowhere to go. Now Mother Blind has to see the doctor for her meloncola. She makes me go with her to sit next to Willy while Dr. Spencer gives her some pills. I'm never going to the doctor's. He made my mother walk around naked in her high heels so he could see what was wrong with her back that time. I'm never taking my clothes off for anybody.

When Mother Blind comes out of the office she is white as flour. We walk out to the Jeep. Grandpa rigged it to run but the doors still don't open and the windows don't close so we have to pop in one at a time. It's cold with frozen snow everywhere shaped like blocks even though it's almost spring and I'm going to be ten.

Mother Blind turns the key and the engine smokes and the heat comes on but she don't step on the gas yet. She stares out the window at the road ahead and says:

"I have to tell you something."

I can tell by her face the something isn't good.

"I'm going to have a baby," she says, and stares ahead. "You can't tell anyone because your father and I are getting a divorce. We have to move. I'll have to—I don't know. What will I do?"

"Move to Florida?" I say.

She steps on the gas and Willy and me stand up and bounce in the back seat hitting our heads on the roof when we go over all the bumps in the road.

Goodbye

GRANDMA STIRS THE BLACK FRY PAN with a wooden spoon and there's onion clouds around her face and she jumps with a scream when we slam the front door.

"You scared me," she says, and a long strand of black hair slips down from her bun and she pushes it behind her ear with the red clip-on earring. "I told you not to slam the door. I have an enlarged heart."

"*Chunky*." Willy says, then Mother Blind walks in.

Well?" Grandma says. "How did it go?"

Mother Blind leans over and whispers into Grandma's ear then Grandma sets the fry pan on simmer and the two disappear into the bedroom.

We put our ears up to the door and hear Grandma say: Lord help us.

But we already know about the new polliwog. Grandma shuffles back into the kitchen in her slippers and holds the collar of her dress even when she stirs the brown onion rings and I know she is afraid and I draw a wolf on the new map of the woods with the Ghost Pond dead center of the grocery bag. I color the trees and the flowers and a stick boy with blond hair.

"Be careful," Grandma says.

"Of what?" I say, but she doesn't answer.

Mother Blind wears the bathrobe Grandma made with the upside down horses. Her eyes are red and her pockets stuffed with Kleenex.

"I've heard there are doctors," Grandma says, in her secret voice and this makes Mother Blind cry harder.

Where? She cries into her Kleenex, but Grandma doesn't answer.

Willy flips his spoon across the room at Grandma.

"Willy. Stop." Mother Blind says. "My nerves."

"Go to bed now Jane," Grandma says. "I'll fix you a hot-whiskey-sugar-water."

"Can I have one? With lemon?" I say.

"After your pray-dens," Grandma says.

80

It's what her mother said, Emma who came from Switzerland on a ship at seventeen and left a baby in the Alps. I tell her I won't forget but most times I do. But this night I do pray and ask Jesus to let us stay in our house and to please get rid of Aunt Oink.

Later, when the house goes quiet, I wake up Willy.

"I can't sleep."

"*Whelp*," he says, rubs his eyes with the sheet.

Outside the wind howls down the chimney and a tree scratches our windows with hairy branches and Willy's eyes grow big.

"What's going to happen?" I say. "I don't want to move to town. "

Ask the G-board, Knife says.

We tiptoe down the hallway. In the living room the Ouija board sits next to a stack of horrorscope magazines. One has a picture of a scorpion and that is Aunt Oink's sign. Poison.

On the lid of the box it shows two sets of hands, one with rings and a bracelet. Both sets of hands are over the glass eye, not touching. Above the hands it says: Mystifying Oracle.

Whatever that means, you probably can't see it. The board has an alphabet and numbers. At the top is a smiling sun face that says: YES. On the other side there is a moon face, not so happy, and that says: NO. At the bottom it says: GOODBYE underneath the numbers. On each side of GOODBYE there are two scary faces. One is the head of a man that floats in space and the other head is a voodoo woman who looks like Aunt Oink with her black hair blowing back and her hands flying in the air.

"Willy, you can't move it with your fingers. You can't touch it."

"*Chink*." he says.

I hold my hands in the air over the oracle and shut my eyes. You have to practice concentration. I tell Knife to think about the same question:

"Will we stay in our house?"

Wind rattles the windows and the storm door.

"Will we have to move to the row house?"

Nothing.

I repeat: "Will we have to live in a row house?"

"Knife are you thinking hard?" I say, but she is. So hard, her forehead is shrunk.

"Okay, let's think of a new question," I say.

"Will Zoe King from New Jersey be a pilot?"

I say it over and over in my head and out loud and then the oracle slides a bit at first, side to side, faster, then it starts to fly around the board like crazy. I want it to go to the happy sun not the sad moon. Faster, then the glass eye stops. I open my eyes and see the oracle over the word: *GOODBYE*

We run back to our room and hide under the blankets.

"Goodbye?"

Knife's forehead is still shrunk and I tell her it's okay to stop thinking.

"Where are we going?"

Are we going to die? Knife says.

"*Wonk-wonk.*" Willy says.

"It didn't answer any of our questions. It only said: *GOODBYE*".

Knife says maybe we are going on a trip. She says the *GOODBYE* meant I *am* going to be a pilot and say *GOODBYE* to the earth.

I tell Knife we have to study flying like saying prayers every night before we go to sleep through the signals in our brains and her hair goes sideways. I send her the message that we are going to practice flying on our own now. She sends me a message back that says: *Let's exchange heads.*

Okay, I say and we take off our heads and I put on her and she mine so now I have a tiny head on a big body and she has a big head on a little body this way she can read my mind even better than before.

"Zoe to mission control. Ready? Over".

Knife to mission control: Mission go. Over.

"Rodger. Over."

Rodger. Over.

I close my eyes and practice the inside of Daddy Dead's Piper Cub but I am seeing it through Knife's eyes so everything looks very big. The cockpit, the flashing lights, the radio, the wings out the window, the propeller, all of it magnified.

Sharp, Knife says.

"Always empty your pockets," I tell her.

Why?

"For when Daddy flies upside down."

He's not flying, we are, she says.

"But I might try a few tricks for fun."

I take out a rock and pencil, a quarter and dime then Knife checks the wings and looks for loose screws in the rudders and locks the doors and we taxi.   Knife talks to the man in the radio. She checks the indicator. Ready for takeoff. Roger. We taxi along and she jams the throttle. The tail lifts, then the wheels and she rams the handle toward the nose then yanks it back to the throttle to balance the wings straight. We climb the steps of clouds. Knife does a daredevil trick, turns the throttle off and we glide through the sky until the nose points toward the earth and there is blood in my head.

We're going to crash, I holler.

No we're not, Knife says. Watch this.

She turns on the throttle and angles the nose back toward the dark sky.

"The rules of the sky are like the sea," she says. "There is only one captain."

"And that is you," I say.

No, it's *you*, she says.

We lift in a stream of air and fly steady over the black ocean. Up here everything says GOODBYE.

Fox

AT TWILIGHT WE RACE TO THE POND and tie our horses to the willow tree. The sky flashes white lightening and I see a lump moving on the ground tiny as a kitten. Maybe the rabbit kitten. It's red with a bushy tail and I see it's not a kitten but a fox curled around a pile of leaves. Alongside the fox is something bigger and redder, furry and flat and a cold wind blows the red fur back.

"Willy look."

His eyes open wide and I know what he's thinking. He's thinking his fox crown came to life after he lost it here last summer.

Willy walks over and squats down by the baby fox.

Another fox, a big one, is flat on the dirt, the baby balled up next to it. The tail is flat and greasy and fixed to the ground and that's when I see its leg is torn up from a set of silver teeth. There is a chain hooked to an iron circle and the fox eyes stare up at the dark sky, the pupils yellow and blind.

Toro sniffs the fur. I put my hands under its belly and pick the baby fox up. It shivers under my vest, I think I know him, his heart, the smell of his fur, the chill of his black nose against mine. Silver spreads across the sky, the pond clear and full of stars. I hold him to my chest and his heart beats inside mine then the moon cuts out from a cloud. I know him. I've been waiting for him. I can't explain.

Willy kneels on the ground and stares at the dead fox for a long time.

"*Clapper* bad," he says, his cowboy hat flipped back on his head.

There's a rustle through the trees then a hum and crack and I see a tall shadow, a red cigarette tip. It's the blonde boy.

"Hey." he yells.

I jump and so does Willy but I don't drop the baby fox.

The kid moves closer.

"What are you bums doing back here?" he says. He tosses a stone into the pond with a loud splash.

We stand frozen.

"We're not doing nothing," I say.

"You're standing there aren't you?" He points a flashlight in my eyes.

"If there's one thing makes me mad it trespassers." His cigarette gets brighter in the dark. I want to tell him New Jersey owns the land but I don't. He walks toward a clump of trees, shines the flashlight, snaps the heels of his black boots, spots the dead fox and flashes the light in its eyes.

"What the fuck?" he says, and kneels. "God I'm fixin' to kill somebody," he says and crouches next to the mother fox, yanks the chain, clicks a lever and the teeth snap open and pop.

"No trapping allowed." he hollers. This is Stovekin property. This is a capital offense do you know what that means?"

"*Git shot done dead,*" Willy says.

He squats on the ground and lays out the trap and yanks a lever and the teeth snap shut.

"This is the last time this fur trap bites," he says.

"We kill them," Willy says. "*Done dead. Kilt.*"

"I can get Grandpa's shotgun," I say.

I feel the baby fox squirm in my jacket right under my arm. Warm.

The kid drags the mother fox by the tail.

"I'll give this fox a proper burial," he says, and that's when the baby's tail falls out along the hem of my vest.

"What's that you have there?" he says.

"Nothing," I say.

"Looks like something to me."

He yanks open my jacket.

"Well, well, look see. Get a load of that. That kits about a month old. If there's one there's at least five others in a den. Somewhere. They come out to play. I bet the mother was looking for the kit when that trap snapped. She tried to chew her leg off."

A low mist rolls over the pond and the kid's words blow through me.

"The kit is my property. Part of the estate and you're breaking the law by trying to steal him. Hand him over," he says.

I hold him close.

"It's just a baby," I say.

"It's called a dog, the male, not a baby but it's a kit for now. He belongs to the woods. Hand him over."

I nudge his black nose with mine and smell the woods in his fur.

"But he belongs with me," I say. "I'm sure of it." I remember a photograph. A baby photo of me with a fox.

"He belongs in the wild," he says. "Hand him over."

When I do, my heart goes with him.

He puts the fox under his coat.

"Can we visit?" I say.

"No," he says. "No more trespassing *pilot*. And stay away from my sister's bike, stay away from the pond, hear? Next time I'll fix the sheriff on you like I said."

"We were just riding our horses," I say. "I mean pretend horses."

"Well now Lone Ranger, you get back on those horses and ride yourselves off my property."

He walks off into the trees dragging the mother fox by the tail with its nose on the ground and one blind eye looking at me.

The sky is dark then a hard rain comes and we fly over blue mountains, the beat of the fox's heart wild in us.

We find the key to the darkroom in a empty beer can under the sink. That night I unlock it and search for clues, for the photograph I remembered. In the third drawer a stack of photos falls out and fans across the floor. Baby photos of me in a carriage outside Daddy Dead's airplane, then I see the one I'm looking for. It reads: Zoe 6 months old with Waco

I'm on a rug playing with a little dog but when I look closer I see it's not a dog but a baby fox just like the one in the woods. I rub my eyes and hold it up underneath the light bulb and see that it really is a fox. I find another, me and the fox in my crib, his ears are up and his tail is fluffy, his front paws are in the air as if he's doing a little jig.

Knife reminds me of the scary pictures of Wilma and me not wearing clothes and sitting on the leather oddaman. I flip through photos: airplanes, cars, motorcycles. There is one of Mother Blind wearing a silver sparkle dress and smiling into the camera's eye.

Then I find them: the photographs of Wilma and me naked. I tear the photos up and flush the pieces down the toilet. I make for the kitchen. Mother Blind is there ironing, all the fog around her, steering the iron like a steamboat around the collar.

"Why did you let Daddy take naked photos of Wilma and me?" I say.

She shrugs her shoulders. "Oh, he thought it would be cute," she says, and steam lifts through the air in watery clouds.

"Well, it wasn't."

"He's a photographer. They like to compose things."

"Did he ask Wilma's mother for permission?"

"I suppose. I don't remember. It was a long time ago."

"I told you I didn't want to. You made me."

"How do you even remember?" she says, and presses down on the iron to make a sharp crease in a pant leg.

"It wasn't right."

"Well, at the time I was madly in love and wanted to please him. It was only a photograph."

In the corner of the kitchen the iron radiator knocks from inside the pipes where Willy and me think the radiator people live banging the iron with little hammers, everybody trying to get out of the boiling water.

"How come you never told me about the fox?" I say.

She sets the iron up, stares hard at the photos.

"It's Waco," she says. "Your father found him. He played with you like a puppy.

"What happened to him?"

"Oh, it was sad but your father said we had to let him go because he was wild. 'One touch of nature makes the whole world kin.'" She smooths out the sleeve then steams out all the wrinkles.

I remember now, staring through the screen door: "Where's Waco?"

"He's out there," she said, and pointed to the trees, and that is probably the first time I was sad because I still remember.

"You should of let me keep him," I tell her.

"I know," she says. "But we were scared."

Inside I feel an ache and I wonder what happened to Waco and if the fox in the woods could be Waco come back to life or maybe a relative. I wish the kid let me keep the fox. Now I always have to miss him.

"You loved him," she says, and irons through a wrinkle. I stomp out of the kitchen and slam the door to my room.

That night I have a dream that I'm in reading class, naked, hiding under my desk.

I'm so scared I fly to the moon.

There is a nurse with a wing cap on her head. When she comes close I see she is a girl pretending to be a nurse.

"Here take this," she says, and puts a spoon in my mouth. "Swallow and everything goes away."

Across the room I see Knife on a stretcher, naked.

"Knife," I say.

They are doing surgery, putting all her pieces back together. In the corner by the wax wall someone is crying. The nurse hands me bubble-flavored water in a clear jelly jar. I stare at a boy holding needles and then at the nurse. They look alike.

"I'm fixing to have papers served on you for being naked in the woods," he says.

I laugh because the syrup doesn't let you cry.

"You took my bike," the nurse says, and unscrews a glass jar filled with white moths.

"He said a girl can't be a pilot," I say.

"If I said any different would you want to be one?" he says, and sticks a needle in my arm.

That's when I wake up crying and one white feather floats over my bed and lands on my shoulder and I see there are sparkles on it from the woods.

Pray

GRANDPA IS ON THE PHONE with Daddy Dead and Grandma peels peaches so fast the skins pile up on her blue slippers. Grandpa picks peaches by the bushel from the orchard at the caretaker house where Willy and me are spending the weekend.

"Rotten," Grandpa says, and hangs up the phone. *Bang.*

Grandma spits into the sink, her lumpy fingers zip the peeler blade over the peach around and around until the rind makes a curlicue at her feet and she quick picks up another peach.

"The phone rings again and Grandpa answers. "Staying with us," he says. "I shot more than one skunk in my life."

"No good," Grandma says, a long pink skin hanging from her thumb. She shakes it off and begins another

"Tell him to go back where he came from," she says. "Back to hell."

Grandpa slams the phone down and lights a cigar, his hand shakes the flame to the tip of the cigar. It catches fire and he blows out a big O.

"He's not coming here, is he?" Grandma says.

Grandpa doesn't answer. His boots, muddy from the apple and peach and orchard, leave brown boot stamps on the floor. We're crammed under the kitchen table catching the peels. The garage door creaks open and slams. Willy looks at me. Grandpa keeps his rifle out there where all the skunk and raccoon tails wave from the ceiling. Spooky. We always run away. We don't like Grandpa for this but he's Grandpa.

Willy has a peach skin wrapped over his shoulders and he twists it around his neck and grabs it hangman then rolls his eyes back and sticks out his tongue.

Grandpa's boots walk past us and we spot the barrel of his rifle drag by. Willy ties the peel over his eyes

"One rotten crab apple," he says.

"One spoiled peach will do the same," Grandma says, and her hands shine with orange peach meat. She spots the rifle and throws the peeler on the wood table, wipes her hands on her dress.

"Oscar *no.* Don't. No more trouble."

Grandpa opens the cupboard where he keeps his whiskey and bullets and we listen to him unscrew the top. fill the shot glass and load the bullets.

"Get the kids outta here," he says. "He ain't getting his hands on them. Hide em' in the closet."

"Lord help us." Grandma cries, drops a pit and it spins across the floor and hides under the stove before she can nab it.

"Zoe? Willy?" she hollers.

We pop up from under the table and Grandma screams.

"Giving me a heart attack." she says and holds her hand to her heart.

The doctor says her heart is too big and might explode. She tells us to get upstairs in the walking closet. Willy and me skip up the staircase, rounding out the curve, two steps at a time, Knife tucked into my shirt, riding my shoulder.

Are you crying? she says.

I feel my face and it's wet.

She gives me the orbit code.

Grandma huddles in the closet with us. It's big enough for ten people. Willy and me sit on the floor. Grandma hangs onto the doorknob, her ear smack up to the door. We wait for Daddy Dead's red truck to growl up the long curvy driveway, the rev and hum, the down click of the engine when he ticks off the ignition and cracks open the door. It seems like a long time and Willy grabs my wrist and starts to arm wrestle then we hear the growl, tires over stones. Willy lets go of my arm, shuts his eyes, covers his ears.

The carnival is coming, Knife says.

"Pray," Grandma says.

I close my eyes and say: "Please God," but I don't know what to say after that.

Outside we hear shouts, voices that get louder then a shot, another and Grandma cries into the daisies on her dress. Willy throws himself face down, his arms over his head on the closet floor.

A door slams and a motor starts and we are scared someone is dead and hope it's not Grandpa.

We wait for a long time, mice hiding in the woodwork. Willy sits up and holds his head in his hands and Grandma is bunching her collar. Then a shuffle across the floor moving up the staircase, then:

"Anna." Grandpa hollers. "You can come out now."

I shake Willy, tell him it's okay and nobody is dead because I heard the truck tires down the driveway and a dead man can't drive.

"Lord have Mercy. What happened?" she says, and opens the door.

"Shot him in the foot," he says. "One at the moon for good measure. He won't be back. You kids get to bed now."

Grandpa drinks a shot and a beer and goes to bed and Grandma boils a big pot of saltwater.

"Thank the lord." she says. "What don't kill you..."

It's 11:30 pm and *Million Dollar Movie* is on.

"Let's eat," she says, and walks to the pantry. "Here. Husk this corn for me," and we dive into the bushel basket and juggle the ears.

We sit at the table and skin the papery husks, the long brown hairs. Willy sticks them on his chin like a beard. It's a corn party.

We watch Frankenstein and eat buttered corn on the floor, play typewriter with our teeth. Grandma gives us warm peach pie with vanilla ice cream and whipped cream and Frankenstein lets the little girl go and walks away sad.

Daddy Dead didn't press no charges or serve papers on Grandpa. He told the doctor it was a hunting accident and the doctor put a bandage on where the bullet went through his heel. Now we can stay at Grandma's when we want and she mixes us whiskey sugar water before bed and we sleep in the room with pink roses on the wall, a white fireplace and a hoot owl in the giant oak outside the window. I wish we could live here.

Late in the night I heard the phone ring and then Grandma tells Grandpa Aunt Oink's water broke.

"What's that supposed to mean? Water can't break."

Knife don't answer but her eyes spin bright in the dark.

The Chili Poe House

Aunt Oink had a baby girl named Zuzu after her water broke but we still don't understand about the water or how it can break. Knife said maybe it wasn't wet water. Wet is what we call water but the water isn't wet, she tells me. This gives me a headache but that was nine months ago after Grandpa shot Daddy Dead in the foot.

I wish I had a gun. I'm so mad, I smash a blue willow plate against the wall. I tell Mother Blind it was an accident and then I have to sweep up the blue houses and trees, the blue birds all because Mother Blind is making me spend the weekend with Daddy Dead and Aunt Oink and the water baby at the Chili Poe House.

Puke. Rat tails, bird feet and toad eyes. Snort. Snort. Knife says.

"I'll hang or drown myself, stick my head in the oven," I say.

Aunt Oink said Mildred Franken, a girl in high school stuck her head in the oven and died from baking.

Let's go to Florida instead, Knife says.

Aunt Oink and Daddy Dead live above the Chili Shack now but just till they find something else. It might be fun to stay at the Chili Shack only it closed a year ago. Daddy Dead knows the owner and for a plane ride to North Carolina he is letting them stay there for a month, rent free.

"Why do I *have* to go?"

"You just do," Mother Blind says, as she dumps the crumbs and soot from the dust pan into the garbage. "It's only a weekend."

I heard her tell Aunt Oink kids were only cute up to age six or seven. That's why she is making me go.

"I'm NOT going." I say.

"You're going." She says.

Knife says I need to soldier on, keep my guns loaded and my blades sharp. So we sit in the back of Daddy Dead's car and pray curses.

"What do you think of the velvet sofa?" Aunt Oink says, after we climb the stairs.

I shrug my shoulders and walk away to the kitchen

I slide open the window to air out the Evening in Paris smell and the screen makes a loud screech that scares the turkey vultures out of the tree. So many the tree looks like a poesy of black roses. That's what Mother Blind calls a bouquet.

Knife is wearing an aluminum foil outfit today so she looks like Flash Gordon.

I hear Aunt Oink clink around in the bathroom and I snitch a cigarette from her pack of Salem. She says I'm gonna smoke anyway so I might as well start now so I can develop my lungs. Zuzu is out in the yard under her mangy blanket in the wood playpen. I like Zuzu now. It's not her fault half Aunt Oink and half Daddy Dead=Zuzu. Mother Blind never had her baby because it dropped out on account of being too fat, the baby that is. But Mother Blind didn't cry. She wasn't sad about it. Not really.

We learned in school about pregnant and period and how after it comes, you can grow a baby. I hope I never get a punctuation mark. Knife says I might be able to spook it away with nail polish remover and a lit match.

Now Aunt Oink's name is Margaret Alice King and it's the holy law. I found the marriage paper with a stamp on the bottom, official and signed on all the lines. Mother Blind says her and Daddy Dead got a divorce. Lie. Grandma told me. I'm a bastard. Sometimes though, I don't believe her all the way. She wasn't there with the judge and Mother Blind in a gray suit with a lily.

Aunt Oink shuffles in wearing her black silk slip and I pull the window screen up.

"You'll let the flies in," she says. "And I don't want Cheyenne outside."

"You left Zuzu outside." I say, and she blows her nose into a napkin and says something only the napkin can hear. I skip down the stairs two steps at a time toward the burnt grass in the backyard.

On the ground next to Zuzu is a pile of gray and white stones. Crackers are stuck to Zuzu's face and a plastic see-through bowl jellies over her head. I give her some stones and sticks to play with. Better than the spatula and eggbeater.

I cut flat doll shapes, snip, clip, glue, press hands together in chains long enough to hang from trees. Poke a hole through the first, stick a paper clip through it, bend it to hang in from a twig then rainbow colors drag on the grass until the wind picks up and they coast above us, paper sounds like tiny wings in the air.

Aunt Oink hangs her head out and cracks a beer can.

Zuzu looks up and giggles, her tee shirt half-off, half on and raggy around the edges, her hair dandelion dust.

Aunt Oink opens her fat Bible and leans over the windowsill but she changes her mind about the Bible and I spot the gold binding of her Poe book.

Chop-chop. Knife says, and clicks her elbows together. That means to ignore Aunt Oink.

Aunt Oink reads out loud *The Tell Tale Heart* from the window but she doesn't start at the beginning of the story like when I was in Kindergarten. This time, she wants to get to the good parts right away.

If still you think me mad, you will think so no longer when
I describe the wise precautions.
"We're not listening to you."
... I took for the concealment of the body.
"N-O-T-L-I-S-T-E-N-I-N-G."
"Not." Zuzu says
The night waned, and I worked hastily, but in silence.
First of all, I dismembered the corpse.
"S-t-o-p," I say.

Zuzu giggles so hard she falls down. I tickle her stomach and under her arms so she laughs harder.

Oink always has to have an audience, Knife says.
...I cut off the head and the arms and the legs.

Finally, she stops and chucks a bag of garbage out the window and it knocks over the trash can, all the deviled ham cans rolling down the hill toward route 22. She thinks it makes more sense to throw trash out the window otherwise you have to carry it down the steps.

Daddy Dead pulls up the rocky driveway with the radio blasting "Your Cheatin' Heart." I know that song because he plays it on his guitar. He cracks open the blue door and walks toward us lighting his

94

cigarette, wearing his mirror sunglasses.

"What you up too miss smarty pants," he says, and a row to paper dolls blows and smacks him in the face. "What's this supposed to be?" But he doesn't wait for me to answer, He bends down and picks up Zuzu who starts to cry.

"You little devil baby," He says.

His work boots climb the steps: *stomp, stomp, stomp,* up to the end of the world. Before long, I hear his voice slide out from the kitchen sink telling me to get my *bee-hind* upstairs to the supper table.

"Head cheese stew, pig's ears and cow tails for dinner. *snort, snort,*" Knife whispers.

Dinner is served: Spam in tomato sauce with chunky pineapple. Gag. I figure I can stuff the Spam in the pockets of my jacket and jeans when he's not looking but first I'm going to ask him the question.

Daddy Dead points to the platter and says, "What's this?"

"It's Hawaiian," she says, and chucks the Poe book on the floor.

Zuzu is in the highchair playing with the tatters on her tee shirt and smearing them around in mashed carrots.

"I thought you were making fried chicken."

"I forgot," she says, and looks over at the counter, the bleeding grocery bag she forgot to unload, Cheyenne on the counter licking up the evidence but Daddy Dead don't notice because he's looking at her slip and her boobs falling out.

"Daddy?" I say.

She gives me her narrow black eye, afraid I'm gonna tell him about the spoilt chicken. Mother Blind would never leave a dead chicken bleeding on the counter. She'd be frying it till it was brown and crispy and tender next to her fluffy mashed potatoes and biscuits with gravy.

Knife gives me the *go-ahead* eye.

"When you gonna fly your plane again, Daddy?" I say, and try to sound nice. I slop the spam around my plate with the fork.

I tell him I want to be a pilot and Aunt Oink snorts.

"Will you teach me how to fly? Can I go next time?"

Aunt Oink slams down her can of beer.

"I'm older now, eleven, (in case he forgot) so I won't pass out anymore when you do your airplane tricks."

95

"You can't bring her," Aunt Oink says. "There's not enough room for both of us."

"I'll see about that," Daddy Dead says. "You're not gonna be a fraidy cat?"

"You can't fly no plane," Aunt Oink says. "Besides, I own half that plane now. We're married."

Razor, Knife says.

After the Hawaiian dinner, Aunt Oink puts on her "Love Me Tender" record, a new one since Daddy Dead cracked the last one in two and stabbed her in the thigh with it. He hates Elvis.

I sit on the damp ground under the witch tree, three trunks grown together and spy on them in the window: She pours a highball, he lights his cigarette and downs a beer. After a few more beers and highballs their voices get loud and he grabs her by the wrist then she smacks his cheek, and I wonder if they notice me. She tosses stuff from the window: sheets, blankets, pillows then quiet.

In bed Knife and me are alone with the stars. We hear Aunt Oink and Daddy Dead's voices in the wall, they jiggle ice cubes in the silver shaker, we hear words in the plaster we can't make out then the buzz stops and there are loud knocks from the wall next door.

I roll under the bed with my blanket and pillow and a pencil slides out of a ball of dust.

"Let's draw," Knife says.

On the wall with the most space I pencil in armies and faucet tribes and toilet tribes the way Willy and me used to do. I draw a big stick woman with a beard.

Knife says to draw a plane, a Piper Cub, the one I'll fly when I'm a pilot, official, all the papers signed and stamped.

I draw the body big, then wings, the propeller, windows. doors, the wheels and tail. I notice the moon in the window, a super moon, so big it doesn't seem real and I can see all the moon countries. A blue night fog blows in from the window and the plane I drew is flying in the shadows and I see something I didn't draw. Knife holds my hand. A girl is in the pilot's seat staring at me. I feel dreamy and grab onto the bedpost. The plane flies a loop around the yard, glides through the wall without a sound. Knife's leg hits the floor, the airplane is near my bed by the window, under a star.

"Hey Kiddo. Are you ready?"

"Who are you?"

"I'm the girl in brown who walks alone," she says.

I notice she is wearing a brown leather skullcap and jacket, brown boots with gold buckles, the goggles on her forehead are caked with mud and wax.

I think she must be made of stars.

"Jump in. That is if you're ready."

I don't have to open the door, I just pass through and wonder if I'm dead. She says we are flying over the Atlantic to Paris. The nose dips to one side and she says she needs to give it more rudder. We pick up speed, she angles the wings and dips in and out of clouds.

"You can't fly north and south at the same time," she says, and I think that makes sense.

Far out, Knife says.

I notice the pilot's fingers are blue. We fly light as paper over the backyard. Zulu's playpen sits in a spot of light; the wooden spokes a shadow that gets smaller as we climb. My paper chains in the wind on the twig ends of branches. The stars are straight ahead.

The Perfumo Boys

THE PERFUMO BROTHERS moved into he mummy house. They wait at the end of the lane where I also wait for the yellow school bus to chug up the hill. Even though they go to a different school a mile from mine they still have to share the bus with kids like me.

They talk to me because they are from a city. A surprise since I am younger and they are tall and wear their dark hair long and smoke cigarettes down to the stubs so that the ends of their fingertips are stained brown. I want to ask them about the mummy but don't. Instead they ask me about my cowboy boots and compare theirs to mine and say mine are sharper and ask where I bought them.

"Texas," I say. "Where I grew up."

That ought to shut them up, Knife says.

"Oh," they say in unison but I hear the tallest one scoff like he knows I am lying.

They tell me they lived in Newark till Mr. Perfumo lost his job.

"Where in Texas?" the tall one, Gabe says.

"Houston," I say, since I know about it from a tv show. He squints his eyes at me and kicks up dirt with the tip of his boot.

After school the bus lets us off at the end of the lane where it picked us up. Willy comes home on a different bus a bit later. The Perfumo boys let me walk with them but mostly talk amongst themselves about football and wrestling matches and girls.

One day, Gabe, he oldest one, says: "Want to show us around the woods? We're not used to having trees as neighbors. We're used to streets and sidewalks."

"Sure," I say, proud I know something they don't.

"Tomorrow then," he says. "After school."

I tell Willy and he says he wants to come but I tell him no, they just want me and he gets mad and has a fit on the floor and destroys my stick collection.

The next day after school we leave our books and lunch boxes at the beginning of the Perfumo driveway and head off toward the trees, me leading, pretending I am a real cowboy, in Texas, with my posse. They grow more quiet the deeper we get. I am leading them to the ghost pond through an open field, my thumbs tucked in my back pockets when I notice them spreading out, making a circle. Around me.

"What are you doing?" I say. "The pond is this way follow me."

But they spread their legs and stand silent with crossed arms, staring. At me.

"Take off your clothes," Gabe says.

I think I am hearing wrong and wind blows my hair across my face.

"What?"

"I said to take off your clothes," he says, and takes off his belt.

You know what to do, Knife says.

If you touch me I'll kill you with my bare hands,"I say, but it seems as though someone else said it. Maybe someone from a movie but it doesn't matter because the circle opens as I walk straight toward the tallest one and I can feel inside that I meant what I said even if it was impossible and they believed it too. I walked right past them toward the lane.

"There's a mummy in your house," I holler, but they stand frozen.

You put a spell on them, Knife says.

Blue Pontiac

Tomorrow Grandpa and Grandma are taking us to Lake Hopatcong but today Grandma browns her pork chops and boils sauerkraut and potatoes on the burners and the kitchen smells like bad eggs but I don't tell them about the Perfumo boys. Grandma's heart might get bigger and Grandpa will polish his gun.

Grandma is talking to herself again, saying Aunt Oink is "Drinking up a devil" and she isn't "Fit to be a mother." Then Mother Blind swings in from the yard lugging a basket of wash and wearing her blue dress.

I sit at the table by the window, put my palm against the fog on the glass. I pull my hand away and it leaves a handprint like a ghost was there trying to get out.

"My hands are full," my mother says, and I hold the door open for her.

She spots Zuzu sitting on the floor in the center of the room with her plastic bowls and spoons.

"Zuzu again? I can't take care of her kid, I have enough on my hands."

"No good," Grandma says, and shakes her head at the potatoes boiling in the pot taking off their jackets for her.

They talk about Aunt Oink and how she doesn't take care of Zuzu who is always dirty, her hand-me-down clothes ripped. Willy calls her *Raggy*, because her baby-tees are shredded around the hem from her unraveling the threads.

"I don't know what to do or who to call," Grandma says, and holds the collar of her dress tight. "What about a pastor?" Grandma says. Then she bites into a purple deviled egg. "At least we have a roof over our heads, thank the Lord."

I look up at the ceiling and see a hole where a rat ate through.

Grandma sits in her chair and turns on Search for Tomorrow only the television is on the fritz and won't stop rolling so she hollers for Willy to come fix it.

On the way to the lake, Grandpa drives with the windows rolled open and his lit cigar pinched in his lips and we see our faces in the rearview mirror. Grandma has a pint of Lord Calvert whiskey, a jar of water, one empty jar in case we have to pee, hard boiled eggs and jelly beans stuffed into her pocketbook in case the car breaks down. We stick our heads out and watch the clouds race Grandpa's blue Pontiac. Grandma throws a soda can out the window and I watch it flip down Route 22 till it gets squashed flat by a red tractor-trailer. I wave when the truck zips past and the driver looks down at me and honks the horn.

Grandma asks Grandpa the name of that fish restaurant by the lake, the one down the beach with the saggy porch and the blue spotted pony—the place they took Aunt Oink when she was Margaret Alice and in kindergarten and looked so pretty in her yellow sundress and braids. Back when they were happy with no troubles except making ends meet. Grandma wants to go back to that place but Grandpa's not listening.

"When we gonna get there?" I say.

"Not sure we'll get there at all," Grandpa says, and Grandma sips some whiskey as Grandpa downshifts and we stop on the hill at the red light. When the light turns green we roll backwards down the hill but then we jump forward and Grandma says: *thank the lord* and peels a hardboiled egg, throws the eggshells out and they fly away like moths.

At the lake there is a long gray walk made of boards, planks like on a pirate ship a gang plank only with little bright houses made of fabric where stuffed snakes, bears and monkeys spin in the air and wheels turn numbers and ducks sit in a row ready to shoot. There is a glass both with a fake gypsy who, when you give her a quarter, she gives you a fortune.

Grandma takes a zebra on the merry go round, I win a kewpie doll with pink hair and Knife says it's an alien. Willy wins a wind-up King Kong.

"Are you going on the rollycoaster?" Grandma says.

"It's a roller coaster not a *rollycoaster*, Grandma."

"Are you going to ride the rollycoaster?" she says.

Ugh.

"Yes," we say, at the same time then hop down the boardwalk away from Grandma, past the cones of cotton candy, the fun house mirror.

The roller coaster is built of rickety wood. When the carts go down the hill they roar over our heads and the wood rattles and blows my hair in my face. I watch a girl coast down on a strand of hair then the girl throws up her hands and screams: *mistah stop this thing.*

A boy in a baseball cap straps us into a little red cart and I look at Willy with candy apple smeared all over his cheeks and he's not scared. Knife tells me not to be afraid because in the history of rollercoasters only a few kids have died.

We climb a hill and when we get to the top everything looks like a toy. I look down and scream as we zoom toward the Ferris wheel so fast everything is smeared together: trees in the lake, Grandma and Grandpa standing on their heads, the lake in the sky. The air smells of popcorn and peppermint and stinky lake water and we fly down another loop until we come back to the boy in the cap and our car comes to a stop, Grandma waiting there by the gate.

"I was so scared." Grandma says, right in front of the boy with the cap. We run down the ramp toward the funhouse.

When we get home, Willy and me decide to build a rollercoaster by the cherry trees in the woods. Willy is a genius. He makes broke things work and draws formulas on grocery bags, symbols and numbers that look like this:

$$\leftarrow \rightarrow \uparrow \downarrow \rightarrow = 36 \text{ PEOPLE}$$

It means the speed of the roller coaster will be as fast as the weight of 36 people in a box with wheels going down a hill. He turned whiz on me last summer when he started taking stuff apart, old radios, a hair dryer attached to a chair, a broken toaster and a record player. He guts all the screws, nuts, wheels, wires and figures out how to put them back together. Sometimes he gets them to work like when the hair drier went on and scared Grandma out of her soap opera chair. Grandpa showed him how to take a car apart and put it back together, but truth is, he already knew how.

He draws rollercoaster plans on the wall.

$$\cap\cap\cap\cap \rightarrow \rightarrow \rightarrow x = \text{speed} + 64 \text{ lbs.}$$

Or, four cars double the speed to equal 64 pounds of speed times 4 people. Don't ask me to explain.

Sometimes, he scribbles formulas on his hands and legs with a marker pen. He even writes things on his knees but Mother Blind makes him scrub them off with a *Brillo* pad.

In bed, me and Willy talk about how when we finish our rollercoaster we can put up a billboard on the highway so people will come and we can charge them for rides and sell popcorn and lemonade, enough money to take a train to Florida where the sun always shines and there's room for everyone to be happy.

Musical Houses

THESE ARE DADDY DEAD'S IDEAS IN FOUR PARTS BUT ONLY ONE CAN WORK:

1. Sell King Car House/ We Move to Town/They Move to Virginia

2. Daddy Dead and Aunt Oink Move into King Car House/ We Move to Town.

3. Daddy Dead and Aunt Oink Move to a House in Marsville. We Stay in King Car House.

4. We Move to Their One Bedroom in Lockwood and Use Daddy Dead's Two-Year Leash/They Move to King Car House

The only one Willy and me will agree to is number 3. but that doesn't matter.

Mother Blind said okay to number 4. because "cheap rent" and she can work in an office.

Number 4 wins.

Pretend to be someone else, Knife says. She says to remember they are adults and you know how that is.

Knife was right. Aunt Oink and Daddy Dead never did move in, or sell King Car house, they moved to the apartment in Marsville. We got kicked out of the garden apartment with, one- bedroom after two-weeks because for one, there were too many of us, and two, no animals allowed. While we were there we had to go to a new school and hide Toro from the landlord. Mother Blind said I could buy two new dresses but I don't even like dresses.

We went to a store in town called Cuties (Knife calls it Cooties) with a fake pony outside that you can ride but not go anywhere for twenty-five cents. Mother Blind picked out a green dress with a painter's palette pocket and a real paint brush sewn on.

Oh god. Knife said. But I was too sad to care.

In class there is another girl wearing the twin to my dress only she is a colored girl. We look at each other for half a second, like the time with the black baby doll, both of us scared, and after that we steer clear the rest of class.

Back at the Ranch

ON THE FIRST DAY BACK from the one-bedroom apartment we discover the termites nibbling our house, all the wood parts, the knotty pine cabinets and walls. Mother Blind sprays bug killer from a red can with a yellow pump that says Shelltox in red letters but the buggers multiply anyway, black, buzzing, tiny critters with little cellophane wings. We cover our ears and run outside into the rain.

It's April and that means lots of showers. Our yard is flooded, King Car floating in the brown swamp of grass. Grandma says it might as well rain nails the way things are going

Willy and me are so happy to be back home with the ghost pond and the woods we don't care about the rain or the termites. We think of ways to fix things. Willy has a plan to start King Car once the rain dries out. That's one thing we can fix.

"We get *tryers*," he yells, from the porch.

We might have to steal the tires. We search every barn and torn up garages.

I run behind Willy and try not to lose my cowboy hat. He points down a path where he hunted for tires and found a dump in the middle of Neely's Field. There's stuff there, wheels, an angel without a head and a dummy.

I follow down a footpath of tire tracks that weave in and out of the mud and trees where the sun never breaks the shade. There are witch hazel weeds that pop from the sloppy ground—little bunches of yellow under a sky floating thin white clouds.

At the junkyard Willy shows me the dummy, a doll with a cracked head and a mouth that when you put your hand in you can make it say things.

He's dressed in a little suit with an orange bow tie. Willy says we can use him to test out our roller coaster.

We find an old tricycle and a wagon with three wheels.

"No *tryers*," Willy says.

There are rusted cans of paint, glass doorknobs, cinder blocks, oven doors, wooden planks from a fence and Willy says he can use them for the roller coaster track. Under a rusted oven we find an iron lamp in the shape of a crown.

Let's crown King Car and have a car-a-nation, Knife says.

Car-A-Nation

IT RAINED ALL DAY YESTERDAY. Today the sun is everywhere and from the open window I can smell the grass cook.

It's been seven days and Aunt Oink is still a missing person.

"Where did she go?" Grandma says, again.

"Kingdom Come," Grandpa says, from his grumpy chair.

I teach Zuzu how to play peek-a-boo with the pillowcase, the one with black cats jumping over the moon and I slip it over her head and pull it down then up again and she laughs. When I yank it off she tugs the other end so I let her keep it in the playpen and she crawls inside. Sometimes I pick it up with Zuzu inside and I swing her around and she laughs herself silly.

Mother Blind is nagging Grandma again.

"You left a pile of dirty diapers. The whole house stinks. They've got to be soaked in a bleach bucket for god sakes."

Grandma pretends not to hear and Mother Blind sinks down into the sofa next to Grandpa in his chair and lights a Salem.

"I didn't get to it yet," Grandma says, talking into her handkerchief.

Willy and me head back to the junk hole. Chipper, from across the highway, says you can catch a bad spell there from the gypsy wagon. It's buried at the dump from the days when gypsies roamed the earth.

At the bottom of the junk hole we find a big dolly lamp shade made of burlap with a straw hoop skirt and a painted face, red lips and the word: Fortuneteller across the skirt.

I hang it in a tree and the fringe blows spooky in the wind and I think maybe I can sell it to Aunt Oink and she can tell her fortunes on the side of the highway.

We find more paint. Some not even open. We decide to paint King Car yellow and red so it looks like a race car. I paint the roof red and Willy paints the hood yellow then we do a checkerboard on the doors, paint the crown lamp the same colors and we sit in the sun eating warm cherries waiting for the paint to dry. The iron crown is heavy. Willy climbs onto the roof and pulls and I push and we set the crown down easy on the roof. Then Willy makes the final touch to the trunk with the paintbrush and writes:

"King of the Thrown," in big black letters.

I don't tell him he spelled it wrong. He'd get too upset. Not his favorite subject but in the special class they don't care so much. He has better things to do like fire up King Car's engine. I'm a great speller when I write the words down on paper but when I think of certain words they are spelled differently in my head. Mother Blind said it's called phonetic. But only certain words like: odd-a-man get scrabbled in my mind's eye.

"But when we get King Car to start the crown is going to fall off," I say.

Willy scratches his head.

"Cone wires," he says, and looks up at the telephone line that runs from our house to the pole to Chipper's house across the highway.

I follow Willy, through the pines to the telephone pole. Willy climbs with his monkey legs and pruner shears.

"Willy be careful," I say.

He clips the line and a long snake of it whips down with a swoosh. I wonder if our phone still works and hope Chipper's doesn't.

Willy cuts the phone line into four pieces and ties them to the iron crown. Next he screws a hook inside the roof

We stand back and stare.

"Boss." Knife says.

We light candles all around the car, birthday candles we found in the kitchen drawer. We stick them into the mud.

Willy gives me a list of things to look for in the garage:

"Find," he says, and hands me a brown paper bag with scribbled words:

> oyl
> wyer
> gasolean
> rages
> bataree

rench
raideator cape

He cranks the hood and unscrews things, parts like the pieces of a puzzle, everything fits together. He takes out the battery, black with white stuff growing on it and uses a Brillo pad to scrub it off. He says the cap is missing then fills it with water. If I don't find a cap in the garage he can steal one from another car. Steal a battery too. There's a diner on the interstate called House of Toast and we know a short-cut to get there. We can lug the battery in our wagon.

Grandpa's lawn mower is in the garage and I find a jug of gasoline he keeps there and Willy pours it in the gas tank, his face is black with grease, his hands, legs and arms but he just keeps going, fiddling with the pedals, the starter, the stoppers, the duster, he fixes the tires with the patches from the blow up swimming pool Grandpa bought.

Grandpa taught Willy all about cars. He took his Pontiac apart piece by piece and explained how each part worked with the other. How all the parts have to work together like a team. Willy loved when Grandpa did that and he can remember every step like playing back a movie in his head. It's part of what makes him different. He didn't tell Grandpa that he already knew how to take a car apart and put it back together.

Only thing is, we can't find the key to King Car.

Willy says he can trip some wires

His eyes light silver. "Tomorrow. We get *tryers*," he says.

Tryers

IN THE MORNING WE CUT THROUGH the woods to the highway, Knife in my holster, and walk along the shoulder, kick stones, chuck black rocks across the road to see who can throw the furthest until we get to the red star on the other side of the highway, the metal pole hits the sky, a white circle that reads: TEXACO in black letters, a green-T-in the center, a giant lollipop. We cut across and pretend we just crossed the border into Texas.

"We get *tryers*," Willy says, and a tractor-trailer zooms past so loud we jump into the weeds and watch as it mows around the bend and disappears into the orange sky.

"That truck could of hit us," I holler and a chill creeps up my neck.

"We in *Texit* now," Willy says.

I imagine both of us rolled out flat on the highway, sunk right into the white stripes. But Knife says:

Scared = Grandma. Just stop.

In this part of Texas there is: The Circle Inn Bar & Grill, the Blue Jay Dance About, the Elbow Room Bar on the corner, the Greyhound bus stop, yellow school bus stop, the House of Toast Diner and Joe's Texaco.

The Diner is made of shiny metal rounded at the corners of the roof so that it looks like a gigantic toaster, which is why we call the diner House of Toast.

We cross the highway and cut to the back of Joe's Texaco where Willy spots a stack of tires. A man stands outside and leans against the chipped paint, red hair, wearing a blue bandana.

Willy turns my way, moving his mouth but no words come out he is so excited. He turns red from his neck to his face.

"You," he says, and points to the Texaco sign.

He doesn't stutter all the time now like when he was younger, just when he's about to break the law, not scared, he's excited.

I already know he wants me to get Joe's attention so he can work on the tires. I need to ask him a question. Knife says to check out the signs on the garage.

Auto Parts, Auto Repair, Oil Change
Motorcycle and Bicycle Repairs

Willy heads into the field. I walk toward the star, my boots snap, my hands in my jean pockets finger the screws Willy told me to hold. He said he can spin the tires two at a time into the field, then roll them up Cherokee Road before Joe misses them. But what's the question?

Broken bike, Knife says.

My heart is wild.

Scared = Grandma, Knife says.

"Hey mister." I say, and he turns.

"I'm looking for some bicycle parts, pedals and a seat. You got any?"

He blows out cigar smoke and squints at me.

"I might," he says.

"Could you show me? My bike got run over."

He throws his cigar to the ground and smashes it, not like Grandpa who saves what's left.

"Where'd your partner go?" he says.

"Huh?"

"That boy was with you a flash ago."

"Oh, him. Just some kid got off at the bus stop. Don't know him."

He has a red beard and grease on his hands.

"I need my bike back on the road. I gotta deliver papers."

I look down at the dirt and kick it with my boot.

"Where?" he says.

"Up Burnt Mills Road and back."

His eyes are dark blue and he stares dead into mine.

"That's a ten-mile haul."

"Yeah. I need my bike."

Okay, let's take a look," he says.

There is an oily bin inside the garage. The man picks through the sprockets, chains, hubs and rusted spokes and I see Willy out the window punching a tire.

"I think I see a seat down there at the bottom," I say, but there is a thump from outside when Willy knocks the top tire off and the man looks up and my heart pops. He's staring at Willy just as Willy jumps back up on the tires to whack off the next one.

"Son of a gun." the man hollers.

I run like hell out the door.

"Willy scat," I scream.

Willy jumps down and dives into the weed and I'm running so fast my heart's on fire and I can hear the man pounding behind me with his big paw out.

"I see you around my station again I'll run you over." he hollers.

I look over my shoulder and see his blue bandana blow away, his red hair on end. I fly down the hill and dive straight into the burning sky. Willy is mad, kicking trees along the way and yelling *Fruck*.

But Willy doesn't give up. At midnight we drop out the window and race up the lane toward Texas

"We get four *tryers*. Two you, two me," Willy says.

"But what if the lights are on?"

"Not," he says.

At the Texaco there's a spotlight lit but no people around and hardly any cars on the highway but no tires stacked by the side of the garage.

"*Fruck*." Willy says.

He motions me to follow and I think this is way scary but then Knife gives me the Grandma sign, two fingers running away.

Willy drops to the ground and I follow and we crawl like lizards in the grass till we get to the back of the Texaco. Willy cracks a wide window with the screwdriver he scoops from his jeans. The sill sticks to the paint on the frame but he pries the hammer prongs till a small space opens then he runs the flat end of the driver around the wood to pop it. I wait for the glass to blow but then the window just opens.

I scope the highway for cop cars and trucks, blue bandanas. It's quiet and all I see is the blue neon light across the road blink: The B J-A_Y, the "L" and "U" and "E" knocked out, an orange moon sliced over the chimney.

Willy leaps into the black space. He finds his way in the dark, a shadow looking for a spot of moonlight and the tires are stacked like pancakes in the corner. He rolls one then two until four tires spin toward the window   They hardly make it through but with Willy makes it happen. We yank and squeeze, push and pull, the first, the second, the third, the fourth. The tires are heavy and smell like our swimming pool. Willy races past me ramming tires with both hands, driving them down the dirt lane like toys. If he can do it so can I. It's not as hard as I think and even though I fall down a few times and get knocked over, I catch a rhythm and push on downhill Willy up ahead with the moon lighting his hair.

We crash the tires into the bushes by King Car. Willy takes the can of red paint and writes his name in big fat letters around all four tires just in case anyone tries to say we stole them.

"Put the *tryers* on *morrow*," he tells me.

In bed we both smell like rubber and oil but don't care.

Willy is up with the first light and wakes me with the: *crank, crank, crank* of him jacking up King Car and we work all day and before we know it it's suppertime, the sky turning rose and we are starving.

"We get *batter wee* at dark," he says, and I know tonight will be another Texas adventure but first we run after Grandpa because he is carrying a big box of pizza into the house. Grandma hands us paper plates and when we finish the plates are stained with grease in cloud shapes.

We hop out the bedroom window and roll the wagon to the shortcut that leads to the House of Toast.

The parking lot is packed. We creep between cars hoping for a Henry J. but any battery might work. Willy spots a Henry on the corner of the lot, a white one with a black top. It's far from the lit windows where people eat their stacks of toast,

I see a man with black hair and a baseball cap and white shirt sitting at a booth next to the window and I freeze—it might be Daddy Dead back from China or Kingdom Come or wherever. There is a woman across the booth with blonde hair, not black, but she has big boobs sticking over the table and I wonder if Aunt Oink went off and bleached her hair so no one can identify her as a missing person.

The hood is rusted and hard to open so Willy gives it a whack and it snaps and makes a loud rumble.

"Hey there," a voice from the parking lot hollers.

113

We duck down, crouch behind a black Pontiac, close to the ground but our wagon is still there right next to the Henry J and Willy has a hard time leaving it. Being the hip shooter he is I'm afraid he might just jump up and grab it and blow our plan.

"I'm talking to you." the man yells.

"Willy let's run," I whisper but I can tell Willy's not going nowhere without the wagon and the battery.

"Why I be damned. How you been boy?"

Whew.

We watch the men smack each other on the back and light their cigarettes and hope neither one of them owns the car with the popped hood or the Pontiac we're hiding behind.

After a few more high fives the men walk into the diner and we quick skit over to the Henry J.

Willy works fast and hunches under the hood, lifts the clamp and pops the battery. It's a new one. I can tell because nothing is growing on it and the black part smacks a shine. Willy spins off the radiator cap and pops the clamp. I can almost hear him buzz electric as he works.

We make our escape down the shortcut. The battery hammers the side of the wagon. All the stars are out and Cherokee Road is lit a yellowy color from the moon, the brick road in the movie. Gargoyles in the sky. We wait for sirens and the red-headed man until morning when Willy clicks in the battery, screws on the tires, sticks a wire into the ignition and the headlights blink on.

"Yay, "we holler.

The motor growls then dead so Willy pumps the clutch and twists the wires until it starts up again. By dark we are covered in grease but King Car starts. This time it don't die.

"Get in," Willy says.

Toro leaps in the backseat.

"You sure you know how to drive?" I say.

Willy looks at me with eyes like new nickels and I know he can drive the car. He was born driving a car.

I jump in next to him and King Car jerks forward then it grinds across the yard, rolls the weeds flat and irons deep tire tracks in the mud. Willy steers around toward the road but then there is a loud bang on the windshield. It's Grandma in her nightgown and curlers, her face shining, her pocketbook on her elbow.

"Hey," she hollers.

Faster, Knife says.

Toro makes his vampire face.

"Where are you going?" she screams.

"Florida." I holler out the window.

"She has pie money." I tell Willy.

Willy steps on the gas but not before Grandma opens the back door.

"Well? Let me in," she says.

Crash Test

WELL, OUR TRIP TO FLORIDA didn't go so great.

When Willy steers King Car toward the road, he guns the gas all the way to mow over a bump of gravel but the wheels stick, spin in place then swerve in the opposite direction smack into the picture window, all the glass window panes crashing.

Grandma screams.

We sit and stare for what seems like forever and try to wind back to the Before—turn King Car around, zip down the interstate headed for Florida instead of into the living room window.

Dang. Willy punches the steering wheel.

"God help me." Grandma says. "I have a heart attack."

Smashing. Knife says.

Toro hops on Grandma's lap in the back seat he's so excited.

"Get off a me," she screams and opens the door crying: "Lord have mercy. I thought you could drive."

The side view mirror is bent and broken and hangs from a loose screw and it falls to the ground with a *clunk* that sounds like the end of something.

Willy rubs his head over where he got the stitches.

"*Fruck.*"

The porch light flickers on and Mother Blind steps out, frozen under the light, her face as white as her nightgown, thin trails of smoke rising from the lantern behind her.

"Dear God. What the hell? Willy, are you alright?

"Not *kilt*," he says.

"Tell me I'm dreaming," Mother Blind says.

"You dreamy," he says.

"Zoe. Why didn't you stop him?"

A pickle, Knife says.

"Grandpa just fixed the window from that time with the stone," I tell Willy.

Mother Blind blinks her eyes at Grandma fixed there in her curler helmet clutching the collar of her nightgown.

"What on earth are *you* doing out here?"

"They said they were going to Florida."

"And you *believed* them?" Mother Blind says.

"If the good Lord willed it."

Mother Blind is inside a cloud of brown dust from the tires spinning the soft dirt.

Grandma shakes her head and clicks her tongue. Curlers coming loose.

Mother Blind's eyes are on Willy as if blinded by the headlights, or she's seen a ghost or been turned to stone, or all three.

I'm going away now, Knife says.

We decide we'll have to get out sooner or later so we kick the doors open.

Willy points to the roof where King Car's crown has not moved an inch after all that commotion.

"How did you get that jalopy to start?" Mother Blind asks in her high voice, as if Willy is either a mystic oracle or just plain crazy. "You could have been hurt. You can't drive."

Willy just hunches his shoulders.

"Yes I can," he says without even a stutter.

Mother Blind says the entire window will have to be replaced and that costs money. She says she thought her life couldn't get much worse but it just did.

"It could be worser," Grandma says, then opens *Vicks Vapor Rub* and jams a dollop up her nostril. "Look on the bright side. I could of got killed."

"What's your father going to say?"

"I don't care," I tell her, and that's when I know I don't.

Willy sets to work, hunches down and works on getting King Car started again. He jiggles the wires and revs the engine, backs up and around to King Car's spot in the weeds. The grill is bent and so is the hood, caved in where it hit the cement blocks but Willy says we're not giving up on Florida. He's set on fixing King Car come hell or high whiskey as Grandpa always says.

In the morning, after Grandma scrambles eggs and burns our toast, we get down to business, bang out the dents and touch up the paint where it scratched. Grandpa works on patching the broken windows and while he grumps and growls at us for causing him more work and a trip to the credit union to borrow money, I think he is downright impressed that Willy conned King Car into starting.

"I'll be damned," he says.

I'm glad there is finally something to make his eyes bright. He's been steaming mad all week— still no word from Aunt Oink and nobody knows if her and Daddy Dead are dead or alive.

"They flew the coop," Grandma cries into her tissue over her plate of runny side eggs. Zuzu is on her lap sticking her fingers into the eggs, smearing them around the table like finger paints. "I thought we'd be in Florida by now," she says and gives Willy the eye.

"Literally flew the coop," Mother Blind says and sets down a blue bowl of green apples Grandpa picked from the caretaker orchard.

"Where could they be so long?" Grandma dips her jellied toast into her coffee.

"Probably on a beach somewhere in Florida," I say. "So she can keep her tan going."

"Please don't speak with your mouth open," Mother Blind tells Grandma.

"How you supposed to do that?" Grandma says.

"I meant eat not speak," Mother Blind says. "That plane won't go far without refueling. They'd never make it over the Atlantic so we can assume they are still in the country," she says, and snaps the dish towel against the sink. "Too bad about that."

"What don't kill you..." Grandma says and runs her fingers over the bowl of apples feeling for bad spots. "I hope he burns in hell," she says, and a chunk of ceiling falls and hits the floor.

Zuzu hangs onto Grandma's knees and manages to pull herself up with bubbles fizzing out of her mouth. "Blah-blah," she says, looks at me and giggles.

"Willy that telly is rolling again," Grandma hollers. "Can you fiddle with it. I can't miss my soap."

And Willy does fix it so Grandma can watch Search for Tomorrow and find out if Shelly will walk again after her car accident, and if John will recover from amnesia, or if anyone will find the kidnapped girl and Grandma won't have to think about Aunt Oink for a half an hour but that doesn't work out.

Here comes Oink crashing through the front door out of the blue, as Grandma says, wearing her red rose lipstick, black capris, a tight black sweater, her hair waved over one eye.

"Where's Cheyenne?" she says.

Grandma's eyes go big and her mouth open. I can see her gums because her false teeth are out and her face caved in. She jumps from her chair, Zuzu on her hip, Grandma looking as if the Loch Ness monster just stomped through the front door.

"Where have you *been?*"

I smell stink cheese, Knife says.

Grandpa grumbles then lights a cigar, pays Aunt Oink no mind as if she's still a missing person but I can tell he is glad at the same time he is mad by the way he stares at the floor and blows out cigar smoke in a long tail.

"Oye," Zuzu says, and blows a bubble down her chin.

"Mom was worried sick," Mother Blind hollers, and pitches Zuzu's string of lids across the room to the sofa where they slide onto the floor.

"Well, I'm sorry about that," Aunt Oink says, and brushes her hair back from her eyes. "Hollis had trouble with the plane in Virginia. It stinks in here."

"From you," I say, but she doesn't hear.

"Virginia?" Mother Blind says.

I'm steamed up she got to fly in Daddy Dead's plane.

Toro sniffs Aunt Oink's ankles and she tells him to scat.

"Mommy's home, Zuzu," Grandma says, and Zuzu blows more bubbles, holds out her arms. "My lord. I was sick with worry. I prayed and prayed you were alright. Why didn't you call?"

"Have you checked the phone lately?" she says, and walks toward the liquor cabinet.

Willy jumps up and lifts the receiver on the phone.

"*Done dead,*" he says.

"Oh Christ." Mother Blind says. "They turned it off again?"

Willy gives me a look and I know he's thinking about the cut wire.

"You dumped the baby on us?" Mother Blind says. "What the hell is wrong with you?"

"Me?" Aunt Oink says and reaches to pick up Zuzu. Zuzu clings to Grandma.

"No respect," Grandma says.

Aunt Oink pours whiskey in a jelly jar then adds some ginger ale and two ice cubes, takes a sip and says: "That's better. Where's my cat?"

Daddy Dead and her didn't fly *no coop* like Grandma thought. They were flying all right, but not the coop, the cub. When they got to Virginia the plane had a cough. Tried to call home. Phone is shut off. Grandma says she ain't getting no younger and she got room-a-tizz-hymn but Aunt Oink isn't listening, she mixes an another Four Roses highball and stabs a toothpick through a cherry.

"What the heck?" Grandma says. "You know how I worry."

Aunt Oink shrugs, looks away, grabs Zuzu with one arm, balances her drink with the other. Zuzu starts to cry but sees Aunt Oink's black cat earrings and pulls on them.

"Zoe, grab Cheyenne for me and put him in the truck."

"You've got to tweeze those whiskers from your chin," Aunt Oink says to Grandma and grandma gets up from her cornbread and runs to the tin mirror over the sink.

"I'll be back tomorrow," Aunt Oink says. Just like that, as if she hasn't been a missing person for two weeks. "Do you want me to pick up some hair dye?" she asks Grandma. "You've got a band of solid gray going on."

"Well, I haven't had the time. It's coming in fast." Grandma says.

"I'm sorry," Aunt Oink says and slams the storm door so hard everything not nailed down rattles.

Tango

ON FRIDAY, THE SUN IS ORANGE behind the trees and Aunt Oink is back with a black suitcase. She walks in and looks around deciding how she is going to arrange her trashy furniture, her shiny black lamp, the bull with gold horns, a green velvet sofa, a lumpy red chair.

"I brought the hair dye," she tells Grandma, and sets Zuzu in the playpen. "I can do it in the kitchen.""

"What are you doing with a suitcase?" Mother Blind says.

"Tango wants to be in here by next week," she says. "Figured I'd start bringing my stuff. He put the deposit on that apartment in Lockwood for you."

That's Daddy Dead's south nickname, *Tango*. Everybody in the south has a stupid nickname but nobody calls Daddy *Tango* in the north except Aunt Oink who after two weeks in Virginia fakes a southern accent.

"Tango wants to git this show on the road, y'all."

"I hate her," I say out loud.

Lamb livers, pig snouts and jelly fish, oink, oink. Knife says.

Elizabeth Taylor's photo is on the hair dye box. I hope Grandma don't think she's going to look like that. Aunt Oink mixes the chemicals at the sink and the smell stinks and burns my nose.

"Tell Tango we're not leaving," I say, from the corner of the kitchen where I am counting the pennies I've saved, dropping them into stiff rolls of red paper. Willy shimmies up the swing set out back. I see him from the kitchen window doing his tightrope routine across the top pipe, waiting for me. We're going to work on our roller coaster later.

"Tango will just have to wait," Mother Blind says, from the other side of the room. She is folding wash into neat squares.

"You need some help packing? *Tango* said Charlie has a truck you can use. Not that you have that much."

Mother Blind ignores her as she folds Willy's tee-shirts, doubling over, smoothing wrinkles, straightening pockets until the shirts are tight and small as handkerchiefs.

"You need a towel around your shoulders," Aunt Oink tells Grandma.

Grandma's hair is in four sections and Aunt Oink paints the goop on the gray band but then says it's better just to squeeze the whole bottle on and lather it up.

"It burns my scalp," Grandma says. "How long?"

"Forty-five minutes," Aunt Oink says, and molds Grandma's hair straight up with a curve on top like a question mark.

"You could go blind if it gets in your eyes," Grandma says.

Grandma looks in the hand mirror.

"Look, my forehead is dripping.".

"Here," Aunt Oink says and throws Grandma a wet dishrag. "How about a beer, Jane? You're folding that wash to death." she says, and pulls two out of the fridge.

"What about me?" Grandma says."

Aunt Oink turns on the radio and a song is playing about washing a man out of your hair.

"Someone should invent that shampoo," Grandma says.

Mother Blind don't drink much except when Aunt Oink is around. Once they start there's no telling. Aunt Oink hits the Four Roses and Mother Blind forgets the laundry and turns up the radio. They light cigarettes with the lamp light shining down, but not Grandma, with her head full of black hair dye, she sticks to beer.

"Stinking dope," Grandma says, and waves away the smoke. "Can kill you."

"Well, something's gonna kill ya anyway," Aunt Oink says.

"When my mother died," Grandma says, filling her glass, "Her white hair turned jet black."

Whoa, Knife says.

"How?" I say.

"The Lord works in mysterious ways," she says.

The answer for everything.

Supernatural, Knife says.

By the time Daddy Dead rolls up the driveway Mother Blind says Aunt Oink is "nine sheets to the wind."

"Why nine sheets?" I say.

"One sheet is one drink. By the time you get to nine sheets your

122

blind drunk," she says.

Aunt Oink tells Mother Blind she's sorry but it's *Tango's* house so there's nothing she can do.

"It's the law," she says.

The sky turns dark and rain clouds roll shadows but I hope it don't rain so we can work on our coasters.

"I'm so sorry," Aunt Oink says.

"Actually, you're not," Mother Blind says, and turns on the oven.

Willy and me watch Aunt Oink trip from the storm door into the wind.

Then the rain pours down so we can't work on our roller coaster till tomorrow.

Roller Coaster

NEXT MORNING, WE RUN TO THE WOODS and the sun lights the tops of trees. I watch as Willy hammers, jams a post in the ground then glues under and over, up and down and the planks of wood snap together. He twists pieces of metal and winds wire, measures with his fingers and feet, spins wheels till they spark, screws the handlebars on the coaster, greases the track with Crisco. He rubs grease into the planks until the wood turns shiny and dark in the sun. He jumps from the roof of the shed and back to the ground until the moon shines the glass doorknobs and all the stars come out. In the light from the full moon we put the dummy in the coaster, the wooden champagne box we found at Grandpa's, wheels from a carriage, for a crash test and his arms go up before he smashes to the ground and his head rolls down the path and we run back through the dark trees.

When we get home Grandma says she saw a magician on the telly and he took a hat and made it a parakeet and cut a lady in half but she didn't die.

"*Dang.*" Willy says.

He likes to watch magicians so he can figure the tricks out.

When the phone rings Grandma says not to answer, it's the bill people. Grandpa paid the phone but only money collectors call.

Grandma's band of gray hair is black now and she sticks her finger in a jar of Vaseline and scoops out a swirl of grease and lets Toro lick it off. She's says it will keep his coat silky and add some shine to his eyes.

The phone rings twice then and stops, then rings again, a signal it's not a bill collector, it's Oink which is almost the same. She tells Grandma she is on her way and Grandma's fingers leave Vaseline prints on the phone.

I'm drawing a picture of a pig, copying from a picture book and Aunt Oink shows up wearing a leopard spotted skirt and red pumps and a black leather coat she calls her bomber jacket and she sets Zuzu down on Grandma's lap.

"That's no bomber jacket," I tell her. "That's a fake from the department store. If it were real you'd have to be in the military to get one."

"You don't know nothing," she says. "By the way, *Tango* is teaching me to fly."

"Is *not*." I say, and I am so mad I think I might catch fire but Knife signals me to coast.

Aunt Oink gives me her cat eye. Her boobs don't fit inside the fake leather anyway and she broke the zipper trying. She tells Grandma when she moves in to King Car house, Grandma and Grandpa can move back to the caretaker house.

"That would be nice," Grandma says.

Aunt Oink looks at me with her cattail ticking, then she pops a can of Bud and kicks the icebox shut. "Tango's itchin' to get outta that apartment," she says, still staring at me.

"This is our house," I say.

"Not according to the law," she says. "I told y'all how *Tango's* going to fix the place up and finish the rest of the rooms. Cover up those scribbles you brats drew. Put some fresh paint up. Get rid of that damned cesspool out back."

Now I'm so mad my hair is on fire thinking about Daddy Dead making our house nice for HER not us.

"It's not your place to call them brats." Mother Blind says. "I'm the only one allowed to do that. Besides, what do you think you are? You're the biggest brat of all. I suppose I had something to do with that. Unfortunately."

Mother Blind mops down the kitchen counter with a rag, wiping it in tight circles across the length then back in the opposite direction and I wonder if she's trying to rub the counter away.

"You can have this dump I'm getting a job," she says, staring at the dishrag.

"Doing what?"

"Making money."

"Maybe you can work as a waitress," Aunt Oink says. "Or, the perfume counter at Woolworth's. Hold your nose in the air."

Grandma looks like she's about to cry, Zuzu standing on her knees, pulling at her bun.

"Stop, that hurts," Grandma says.

125

"I keep her in the play pen all day," Aunt Oink says. "You don't need to coddle her. I don't want her to be spoiled like the others." She pours a glass of Grandma's whiskey.

"You shouldn't be drinking during the day it can make you blind," Grandma says.

"Don't tell me what to do."

Mother Blind don't say a word she just keeps wiping circles.

"No good," Grandma says. "You should wait until Zuzu is asleep at night."

"I'm a much nicer mother after a drink," she says. "I'm gonna redo this kitchen."

"No." I say. "We are NOT leaving."

"Zoe," Mother Blind says. "We have to move. I found a job in town."

"No way, I'm not leaving again."

Aunt Oink grabs Zuzu from Grandma and this makes Grandma sad, her sad moves from her to me and back again. Even though she is old and tired, Zuzu makes Grandma laugh.

"I'm out of here," Aunt Oink says.

"You get attached," Grandma says. "You can leave her with me."

Aunt Oink slams the front door and revs up the truck and she drives off still holding onto her glass of whiskey and Zuzu sliding across the passenger seat.

Blinded

MOTHER BLIND FOUND A TYPEWRITER JOB in the newspaper and she can walk there from the new apartment.

Willy is on the floor taking a toaster apart. He says he is going to get King Car on the road again as soon as we test out the roller coaster. We won't have to move to Lockwood if we make it to Florida.

"Let's go," he says, and we run like horses through the trees.

Our roller coaster is just about ready to ride: handlebars screwed on, wheels waxed, track greased and ready to roll. We drag the wooden boxes by the wheels the top of the plank and I tell Willy he can go first. I hold the cart while he gets in, grabs the handlebar, crouches low, head down like a racecar driver.

"Tell me when you're ready, say Geronimo."

Toro sits with his paws neat.

"*Onnerrow*," Willy hollers, and I give him a shove and watch him race the track, the wheels roll smooth and the cart rocks side to side, Willy's head down between his knees and he rockets away on the grease until he gets to the bottom and smacks dead into a tree. I hear the coaster crack and Willy flat out cold on the moss.

If Willy dies who's gonna start the car?

His eyes are closed and he don't move and I holler:

"*Willy. Willy, wake up*," I yell, and shake his shoulders. Then I smack his face and tug at his arms to try and get him to sit up. Then he opens his eyes, blinks, rubs his eyelids and stares up at the sun.

"*Fruck*. I blinded."

"What do you mean you're blinded? Cut it out. It's not funny Willy."

This is not good, even Knife looks scared with her hair pointed up.

"Get up, Willy. Get up now. Quit joking."

"Blinded" he says, and stumbles, holding out his arms for balance.

"No." I tell him. "Cut it out."

He bumps into the tree and I get a sick feeling in my gut.

The sky is coloring red along the outline of the hill and soon it will be dark.

"Come on Willy."

He wobbles forward.

"Okay. Let's go home."

I'm so scared I'm shaking.

"Hold onto my shoulder and follow me."

Willy don't have a scratch on him and I can't believe this is happening.

It is, Knife says.

We make our way in and out of the trees and thorns, Willy hangs onto my arm, Toro sniffs along behind us and it's slow going and I'm spooked. By the time we get home it's almost dark and bats swoop over our heads. Willy freezes.

"Can you see now?" I say.

"See *Raggy* fallin'," he says.

"What?"

"See *Raggy* fallin'"

"Stop it." I say.

Mother Blind is watching her alien show, her feet up on the sofa, smoking her cigarette and drinking a cup of coffee. Willy trips behind me then the metal door slams and she looks up.

"We were playing in the woods on our coaster and Willy hit his head on a tree," I say.

"What?" She smashes her cigarette in the ashtray and jumps from the sofa.

"What is it? He looks fine," she says.

"He's blind," I say.

"Quit joking."

"Back *dere*," Willy says.

"You really can't see?"

Willy nods.

"My god! Poor baby."

She lifts his face in her hands, tells him to close his eyes, then rubs his eyelids with her thumbs. "Now open," she says. "You can see now, right?"

"No. Blinded."

"Follow me," she says and takes his hand.

128

Over the kitchen sink she dunks his head with cold water.

"Splash the water in your eyes," she says. "With your hands. Again."

She dabs his eyes dry with the yellow towel.

"Now?"

"No," he says.

"My God, Willy," she says, and guides him to the kitchen table.

I'm glad Grandma is at the grocery store. Grandpa dropped her off for an hour then he picks her up but he might be late because he has to drive Mother Blind and Willy to the hospital in the blue Pontiac.

Knife and me go to our closet and shut the door.

There is a chip of paint on the floor and I find the spot it fell from and peel off some more and the flakes scatter on the floor like shingles, chunks of blue until I have a half of a wall skinned down to the white plaster beneath but I can't stop there I have to keep going till the entire wall is bare and I have a pile of paint bark.

"What if he really is blind?" I say. "He won't be able to drive."

Knife doesn't answer at first.

Seeing eye, she says.

She says we should practice being blind ourselves for a while so we'll know how he feels. I tie a black sock around her eyes and the other sock around mine then we reach for the doorknob but we're turned around. I keep my hands on the walls feeling for doorways until we find the one to the kitchen and I trip over a chair and Knife pops out of my pocket.

"That's not funny!" Grandma hollers. "Blinded for life, maybe."

"I was just practicing," I say. "So, I can help him."

"Pray for your brother," she says, and cries into the towel.

We keep our blindfolds on and feel our way back to the closet and shut ourselves back in.

Let us pray, Knife says.

We pray in our heads that Willy won't be blind. Then we wait for the sound of Grandpa's Pontiac up the lane.

When they get back from the hospital Willy walks in by himself.

Knife and me stare at one another, wondering.

The doctor said Willy has a concussion. It was temporary blindness like when the television rolls.

Knife's leg drops off and we both say, *holy*, at the same time. Maybe our prayer worked? In bed we say another prayer for a new blue bicycle.

The next night, after everyone is asleep, Willy and me run out to King Car for a meeting. Knife sits in the open glove compartment and the moon looks down through the windshield. Willy points his ring and middle finger like a slingshot, one finger pointed at each of his eyeballs.

"I see *sumpin*," he says.

"Huh? What?"

"Went I blinded."

"What?"

The moon is full and seems so close to earth.

"*Raggy* fallin,'" Willy says, his eyes far away and the words hang in the air.

Control Panel

WHATEVER WILLY SAW WHEN HE WAS BLINDED he don't want to see anymore. When I ask him about it he covers his ears. It's eleven o'clock at night and Willy and me are having a pancake party. We cook pancakes in the black griddle and wait for each to bubble, flip, flop—a few drop on the floor but we don't care. It's quick with Bisquick, just add some eggs and milk. Or, use water if you don't have eggs or milk. No butter? Use Crisco. No syrup? Sprinkle sugar. Tonight, we have syrup and Willy slugs some from the bottle.

"Shiny *puddy*," Willy says, and wipes his sticky lips with the bottom of his tee shirt. "*Wey* back *dere.*"

There is thunder from the ghost pond, rain clouds over a chip of moon like a broken dish.

"Yay. A storm," I say.

"Boom." Willy says.

We load the pancakes on the white dish Mother Blind uses for birthday cakes and set out the matching plates, the blue willow ones with birds, trees, boats, little scalloped houses. I fold paper napkins into triangle shapes like Mother Blind does and set out the jelly jar glasses.

Why is everything the same? Knife says.

"Not true," I say. "The pancakes aren't all the same.

You're growing buds, she says and points at my chest.

I look down at my tee shirt and the two small lumps growing there.

"I don't know how to stop it," I tell her.

Now we won't be the same, she says. Tie a washboard on.

Lately, Knife's been moody.

Why do we fail? she says.

"Willy is going to get King Car back on the road."

I put her in the kitchen cabinet and shut the door

Willy pries the sack down on the Taylor pork roll.

"Careful with the blade," I say.

Willy tosses circles of pork roll into the fizzy grease until they get

131

so hot they bubble up about to explode.

"*Chingy,*" he says, and flips a piece.

Rain sheets the window and lightning strikes the trees spooky.

Willy has his platter of pork roll piled high and ready to go when the phone rings and Willy and me lock eyes. No one calls us late at night. Bill collectors again, I tell Willy. I don't want it to wake Mother Blind so I snap the phone up.

"We can't pay no bills now. We're flipping pancakes." I say, and slam the phone down on the wall hanger.

I drizzle more syrup when the phone rings again.

I answer and say, "Go hang yourself." then slam the receiver down.

Willy giggles and digs into his black pork roll and the phone dings again. This time he jumps up and grabs it.

Go fry you *sulf,* he says, and we laugh our heads silly.

Let me out of here, Knife hollers, so I take her out of the cupboard and sit her on the chair.

The phone rings again and this time Willy answers: "Bang, bang you kilt." But then his face turns white before he slams the phone and sits back down. He tears into his pancakes but he's not smiling.

Knife puts her arms over her head like in a hold up.

Juju, she says.

"Stop." I tell her. "I'm trying to eat."

Pancakes make you fat, she says.

"Shut up" I tell her.

When the phone rings again, I answer it and this time I hear a familiar voice: Grandpa.

"Hi Grandpa. We aren't doing nothing. We didn't know it was you."

"Get your Mother," Grandpa says, and in the background I hear Grandma screech opera. Grandpa is dead on serious. I run to the bedroom and shake Mother Blind awake.

"What is it?" she says, and rubs her eyes.

"Grandpa's on the phone."

"Grandma?"

"Grandpa."

"Grandma is crying."

She trips out of bed, wraps the sheet around her and drags it into the kitchen.

Willy has his head down and he gobbles his burnt pork roll.

"Pop?" Mother Blind says, "What is it?"

Silence. I watch as she goes pale as flour.

"What? No. No. Don't say that."

Willy scrapes his plate.

"How? I don't understand. How? God, no."

JUJU, Knife says, and this time I know, as usual, she is right on.

Mother Blind, rubs her forehead.

"Valium. The elephant teapot by the stove," she says, and pulls the sheet tight. "Give her two with whiskey. Better Allie spend a few nights. Are *you* okay?" she says, but Grandpa already hung up.

Mother Bind stares at the telephone, then the Gumby and Pokey salt and pepper shaker on the stove, Gumby with his eyebrows high and his eyeballs rolling back.

"What?" I say. "Grandma's heart?"

She looks at me but she's somewhere else and I notice my pancakes alone on the blue willow plate, the steam gone, cold, flat, the bubbles squished. I want to hide in the closet.

"This isn't going to be easy," she says, and plops down in the chair, covers her eyes with her hands. "Zoe get my cigarettes from the bedroom. My pocket book."

I'm scared and Knife looks as spooked as me, her eyes spin.

Mother Blind swallows a pill from the bottle in her bag and lights a cigarette then starts to cry.

"Bring me that bottle, please," she says, and points to the cabinet with the Four Roses whiskey. "And a shot glass."

"What is it?" I say, reach for the bottle, fill the shot glass and hand it to her.

She wipes her tears with the sheet. "It's too much," she says, and kneads her forehead, then downs the whiskey. I notice her hands shake and she puts one over the other to stop them.

"Dear god," she says.

Willy stands facing the wall, his hands over his ears and his eyes shut.

"It's Zuzu," she says.

133

"What?"

"Zuzu," she says, and wipes her tears with the sheet again.

I am stone, my feet stuck to the floor, my heart moved over in my chest.

"Zuzu is dead," she says.

Blood in my head, my heart beats in my ear.

"No she's not. How?"

"A broken neck. She didn't make it."

"No," I say.

Willy makes a sound like a buzz saw and plugs his ears with his thumbs.

Mother Blind eyes me pistol hard and I know that it's true. But it can't be real.

"How?" I say.

"The open window," she says. "A fight, a basket of laundry."

"No." I scream. "No." I feel like a helium balloon stuck in the corner of the ceiling. Supernatural.

"Not really," I hear my voice say. "Not for real."

"Don't make this harder on me."

I'm drifting in space, a balloon stuck in the corner of the ceiling. I see Knife's leg pop off and hit the floor and Willy knot a dish towel over his eyes. Knife makes a circle above her head with her finger. Go into moon orbit, she's telling me but I can't get there yet, I can't stop staring down at the kitchen: the pancakes stacked on the cake dish. I picture Zuzu limp in the dirt outside the kitchen window. I don't like this picture in my head. I shut my eyes, cover my ears, scream: NO.

Knife says: Orbit. NOW.

Mother Blind shakes me by my shoulders and smacks me in the face.

"Stop it."

"It's not real," I say, and white space fills my head.

"It's as real as it gets."

I trip out the kitchen door into the dark and puke pancakes under the cherry tree. It's my fault. The pillowcase trick. Everything is melted, the wash on the line, the mud pies on the bench, brown puddles growing, the moon leaking wax. Zuzu's face in my head. I

134

run back inside.

Mother Blind is on the phone. I can't find Willy but I scoop up Toro, tuck Knife, in my back pocket. We hide under the covers. Can't stop the shakes, ice in my blood but Knife says to go into orbit *immediately*. So, I try and think of the control panel in Daddy Dead's flight manual. I memorized the dials and instruments and drew the flight controls on my bedroom wall spelling out the name of each one:

Flight Indicator
Compass
Air Speed Indicator
Gyroscope
Radio
Autopilot

I pretend I'm flying my plane, Knife in the copilot seat and all the dials lit up.

Outside the wind howls and the clouds spread apart in a net made of fog.

But there is another plane. It's the girl in brown, her gold hair whips her face, the propeller spinning silver through the air, but the plane is stalled.

"Hey Kiddo. Hop in."

She wears a brown tie same as a guy and the air smells of honey.

I hop in.

"Ready?" she says, and I nod my head.

"I've hit a few bad storms," she says. "But I managed to stay my course."

I stare at her brown boots, the earflaps of her hat strapped down snug. But I can't say much with words stuck in my throat.

"Do you know my name?" she says.

"No," I say.

"I like that kiddo. Someone who doesn't know my name. Someone who thinks I'm alive."

Knife and me watch frozen to our seat as she jumps out of the plane and balances on the left wing holding her long arms out at her sides, laughing so hard I think she will fall into the black space but she

135

doesn't. Instead, she starts to tap dance, clicking the heels of her boots against the metal wing.

"Do you know this one?" she says.

And then she starts to sing in a low voice a song I know:

Dem bones, dem bones, dem dry bones,
Dem bones, dem bones, dem dry bones,
Dem bones, dem bones, dem dry bones,
Now hear the word of the lord.

"Stop," I holler.

She looks blue in the moonlight and I wake myself up screaming.

Jagged

THREE DAYS AND ZUZU IS STILL DEAD. Not real. Is real. In the sky. Not earth. Somewhere else. There is a string with silver baby jar lids hanging from a painted hook, it dangles from the eye in the knotty pine wall. Last week Zuzu jiggled the rattle and the lids rang in my ear. I loop the string over my finger and rock it back and forth and the lids click together like jewelry. Willy stares, hypnotized, his eyes tick as I rock the lids on my finger and they make a kind of music, Zuzu's buttery finger prints smudged in the tin. We shiver in cold stars.

"Raggy kilt," Willy says, three times, as if he's trying to believe it, and each time I feel a chill, tiny ice cubes down my back bone.

I think of Mrs. Freezer in first grade class with her sharp eyebrows and pointing sticks, gray cloud of hair and she is saying there is no Santa Claus, icing us over in our chairs with her steel eyes. And there *is* no Santa Claus and babies drop from open windows and die and we will die too.

Why? Knife says. Why are we born?"

Grandma is blue down to her bones, her face a like a shrunken head from all the crying. I'm glad Grandma doesn't know I'm thinking this. Grandpa's chin rests on his chest, Aunt Oink slip-sliding in cocktails, Tom Collins all the way, Daddy Dead in silver mirrored glasses. Willy covers his eyes. Mother Blind polishes forks and bakes mac and cheese, says we have to "Snap out of it," but we can't yet because it is a very bad dream, an icy nightmare we can't wake up from.

Jagged, Knife says.

"I taught Zuzu to crawl into the pillow case, "I whisper.

That's neither here nor there, Knife says. This is Poe.

We hide in the closet and plan our vacation. Knife says it is important to work out all the details.

Remember Paris, Knife says.

I try to think Paris but Zuzu is in my head. I see her smile, hear her giggle, touch her brown dandelion fuzz, look into the shine of her root beer colored eyes, clear and bright. Her tiny fingers touch the hairs on the back of my neck. I didn't know I would care.

What is a soul? Knife says.

"An invisible heart?"

Water and sand?

"Leaves and bark?"

Queer, Knife says.

"What's eternity?"

Evermore.

Shadows tag us in and out of rooms and knit spaces with shade. No sun. Grandma has her face in her hands and she can't yell opera because her voice is gone. Grandpa is sunk into his chair but gets up and pours whiskey then sinks back down and drinks his tears.

Mother blind rolls dough on the counter, slices circles with the top of a water glass. "We can't *all* go crazy," she says, and twists the glass rim into the dough, dusts it with flour then places it next to the last and side by side they look like ghost eyes.   Last night I saw her cry and it made me sad to see a tear land on her cigarette like rain. It scared me too.

"It's a curse," Grandma cries, her voice sandpaper low, her eyes bulging, her hair falling out in black clumps that leave white patches of scalp. "A terrible curse."

I cry too but Knife said to be careful or I will drown.

Coast the ceiling, Knife says. Like when Daddy Dead held the pillow.

I do go back there and so does Knife and for a few minutes we look down at Grandma with her shrunken head in her hands.

Grandma thinks Zuzu is in heaven but I can't believe there is a god because if there is then who made him? Also, how can all the people who ever died fit in heaven? Grandma said the streets in heaven are paved in gold.

Who cares? Knife says, if you can't wear it.

Aunt Oink believes in heaven too but it's not much good. She had to be put down for three days in the hospital and then the police asked her a lot of questions but she just cried the whole time. They asked Daddy Dead a lot of things too but he didn't have answers because there aren't any.

Willy thinks Zuzu is dead because of the weegee board or a gypsy spell from the dump, the fortune teller lamp with red lips and fringe skirt flapping from the tree. A hex. We are the only ones who know what Willy saw when he was blinded. He is the only one who knows I taught Zuzu to hide in the pillow case. We run to the pond and under a nick of moon we cut our arms with razors and mix our blood together in a promise, fix our wrists as one and bleed into each other, Knife's skinny arm in the middle.

"Forever," I say.

"*Fev-vor*," Willy says.

Evermore, Knife says.

I wonder if Zuzu is mad. I don't think so because she didn't know anything yet. I feel her heat follow me.

There is a crematorium. A barbeque house, Knife says. That's where Zuzu is going. I don't like to think of Zuzu on fire, her hair orange flame but Knife says the worms won't get her. We can't afford to bury her fancy in the ground under the apple tree with a stone angel to hold her down.

Today Zuzu is riding home in a white coffin. They emptied her blood and put antifreeze or something in her veins and fixed her up with wax and paintbrushes. I'm scared, I don't want to see Zuzu dead, her broken neck. Knife says we'll cut out, go somewhere else.

I wear my navy blue dress with the white collar, my cowboy boots, my hair combed and twisted in a ponytail, Knife in the shiny black outfit, tiny gold safety pins down the front holding it all together.

A man with a big butt sets Zuzu's coffin on the skinny table Grandpa brought from the caretaker house. The coffin is small and white and terrible. Zuzu dressed in a snowy gown with sparkles, a lace bonnet cupped around her face like a flower. I know she'd rather be in her tee shirt with the tatters to pull on. She looks the same as before but she's gone and I feel a pain from her to me and back around to Willy, something invisible like a blade of sad slicing us together.

Willy wraps a blue bandana over his eyes.

"Gone," he says.

"*I* didn't know," Aunt Oink cries from the living room. "I was fighting with *him*," she says, and points a finger at Daddy Dead hiding behind his aviators. "I was throwing *his* stuff out," she cries.

Daddy Dead tries to hug her.

"Don't you touch me." she says.

Toro jumps to nab a slice of bologna from the kitchen table then barks at a squirrel scatting up the dogwood tree. I wish I was him.

All three mornings since the pancake night, I wake up and forget Zuzu is dead. When I remember it feels worse than before I forgot.

We watch Zuzu in the coffin and wait for her eyes to open. I think I see her fingers move.

Willy won't take off his blindfold but I see him peek.

Aunt Oink bends over the coffin and cries. Grandma holds on to the collar of her black-eyed-Susan dress as if it's going to save her. Her tears dot stains on the yellow part.

Daddy Dead doesn't take off his aviators, he just stands at the coffin iced-over and still till he bows down and kisses Zuzu's forehead.

Aunt Oink, cries, stop, drink, cry, drink, cry, blow nose, drink, cry, blow nose, honk, honk, snort, drink, cry. Even Knife feels bad for her.

Sniff, she says.

Grandpa sips his whiskey, his gray eyes far away in clouds, the rain filling up. Grandpa tries to hide it but I saw the tears. I heard him cry but then I think he is laughing so I laugh with him but he wasn't laughing and my cheeks catch fire.

Willy and me don't go in the room with the coffin. I watch it from the kitchen, baby doll in a white box. Toro jumps. His ears tick above the casket. He is trying to wake Zuzu up. Willy says she is a ghost baby now, a white shadow spooking us in the dark, hunting for her pillowcase.

"Boo," Willy says and I jump, look out the window at King Car frosted over and remember what the boy said, the angry dead children at the bottom of the pond, Zuzu underwater tossing stones at the rusted bike. Swimming. A tadpole. Free.

Daddy Dead wears his black suit and tie and his shoes spit shined same as his hair. He leans in a corner and smokes his cigs one after the other like railroad cars. Grandpa just gives him his grumpy stone face but Grandma stops saying her prayer and screams across the room in sandpaper voice:

"Louse. You brought the devil on this family."

Grandpa says if you make room for the devil he'll move right in and start a fire.

Mother Blind lines up the food, lights a candle and sets out the blue bird plates.

This is what's on the kitchen table: a plate of rolled up bologna, cheese with toothpicks, Ritz crackers, a lemon meringue pie, green Jell-O in a fish shape, a jar of purple eggs and a lemon platter of white fish, the kind that is frozen in a box that says: Filet of Sole.

A minister knocks on the door, stinks of whiskey and says things happen for a reason.

What is it? Knife says.

Babies die, babies get born with half a brain or are joined at the head, children get hit by speeding police cars, but god has a reason, the minister explains.

What is it? Knife says.

The minister says you can't know the reason. Knife says the reason is that there is no reason and he is scratching to get more money for his breadbasket. We don't like him. Knife saw him sneak a peek down Aunt Oink's blouse at the same time he grabbed a plate and slapped on a stack of bologna and two purple hard boiled eggs.

"Excellent pickled eggs!" he says.

Grandma looks up from her crying. "I made them," she says, in her squeaky voice before she goes back to bawling.

I'm afraid Grandma will melt. Or, she might go crazy like the women I saw once in a movie—women wearing long nightgowns and rocking baby dolls in their arms, talking baby talk as if the rag dolls were real babies not sown from seed sack and rags of cotton. I wish Grandma's Vaseline could make her better. Maybe she should eat a little and see if it helps.

Knife says Grandma believes in Vaseline and if she thinks it works it just might and grease the valves of her heart and stop it from getting larger.

Willy rips off his blue bandana from his forehead and slaps his hands over his ears when the minister talks.

When the under men come, Aunt Oink drops to her knees, her black scarf a dark puddle on the floor. Mother Blind tells her to "Snap out

141

of it" and Grandpa's glass hums across room, his hand gone limp and everyone watches as it bangs into the woodwork.

"Grandpa?" I say.

The man in the grey suit snaps the lid of the coffin shut

They carry it out to a big black car.

"Why can't *we* ride with them?" I ask Mother Blind.

We follow in the Jeep and it chugs and smokes a tail behind the Cadillac, Aunt Oink's head poking up in the back seat.

"I never knew there was a crematorium so close to us," Mother Blind says.

Willy and me stare at one another, all eyes, ears, fingers, toes.

Inside, Grandma honks her nose from the front chairs where the preacher man prays about the "Shadow of death." Grandpa locks his crying back but it bubbles up and comes out of his mouth in a choke. Willy keeps his head down and his hands over his ears. I try to think something happy like when I get my pilot's license with all the boxes crossed and the "i's dotted and the papers stamped and signed. Then I can pick Zuzu up from her comet and take her for a spin.

"Lord," Grandma cries.

"Calm down, Anna," Grandpa says.

Blocks of sun from the windows light tissue lint that floats in the air.

Grandpa pulls out his whiskey flask and Grandma takes a sip and he takes a swig but it only stops her from crying for a few whiskey minutes.

Daddy Dead bows his head then rests his forehead in his palm but I can't see behind his sunglasses if there are tears.

"Let us pray," the preacher says.

The air smells of talcum powder and worn leather Bibles. We flip through the psalms, Bibles so old there's squashed flies stuck between the pages that are thin as onion skins.

Aunt Oink sits in the front row in her black dress and a fortune teller scarf tied around her hair. She bawls, sniffs, blows her nose so hard it sounds like wild geese. She even giggles once when the undertaker bends over and his pants slide down and show his ass crack. Grandma says laughing and crying are the same relief.

142

Mother Blind sits next to Aunt Oink in her dark suit. Her back is very straight and her shoulders stiff, her hair rolled in a twist, pearls pinched at her ears. She says there is "special provident in the fall of a sparrow" but we don't know what that means.

Knife says to look out the window at the chimney behind a row of tall pine trees. Smoke curls from the chimney. White snakes. Knife says they slide the bodies in on giant spatulas and bake ghosts in a big black oven.

A ghost factory, she says.

They set the hair on fire first. If there is no hair they put hay in and light that. Knife says Zuzu will be a comet now and when we look up at the night sky we will see her flame.

Grandma and Aunt Oink stumble to the door. Outside the air smells of fire and burnt sugar and we watch the smoke lift from the stack and pinch our noses with cold fingers.

"Vultures." Knife says, and I look up at three fat, black birds with red and wrinkled faces, their jagged claws dig into the grey shingles and they watch us walk to our car with black beads in their eyes.

The shadow of death, Knife says.

Daddy Dead's truck pulls in front of us and rolls its way to the Elbow Room. No one wants him around. It's like *he* dropped Zuzu out the window. I feel sad for him. I can't help it but Knife says not to go there. He is the sad in everything.

Back home, Grandma calms down for a few minutes and tells Aunt Oink she bought her some pig knuckles at the market and that she should eat something because she had a lot to drink.

"No," Aunt Oink says, her face swollen, her nose red and it seems as if she shrunk like my wool sweater that time Grandma put it in the washing machine.

Zuzu's ashes are in a jar. It sits on the mantel and I touch the glass with my pinky. Willy don't say nothing, he just keeps marking numbers and letters and signs on a brown paper bag trying to fix the ashes and bring Zuzu back.

$$\sim 20 + \partial \pm X \cong \ni \; \exists \; = Z$$

He says the fire makes a gas when the body burns and if you can get some of the gas from the ashes you can start a person over.

Aunt Oink flops in the chair in front of the television that won't stop rolling a woman chopping up a raw chicken.

"Zoe, come here. Please."

She tells me to get her a highball. Grandma said don't give her no more because she's on a roller coaster. All she does is drink and cry and drink and fight and drink and go crazy.

She likes Zuzu more since she died, Knife says.

I mix the sugar and lemon and add an extra shot of whiskey then stab a cherry with a stirrer and set it in the glass.

"Thanks," she whispers. "Sneak me some of those pills your Mother has. The yellow ones. In her pocket book."

"Maybe," I say.

Mother Blind took the pills away from Aunt Oink because she might kill herself. That's not such a bad idea if she has to cry the rest of her life.

The pill bottle is hidden in Mother Blind's sunglass case. I flip the lid and shake out two yellow pills. Aunt Oink gulps them down with the extra whiskey highball I made her.

I mix a highball for myself and pour in some cherry juice.

Let's get out of here, Knife says.

Willy follows. We crunch through the weeds to King Car, rock it till it nearly flips.

The sky turns black.

"I wish we could sleep out here," I say.

"Jumbo," Willy says, and we go inside to warm up.

Grandma is at the sink washing dishes. Aunt Oink spots me from her chair and shakes her ice cubes at me.

"Neat this time," she whispers.

I pour it into the Popeye glass, straight vodka and she swallows it down to Popeye's hat in one gulp.

"Listen," she says. "I'll give you some money so you can go to the Elbow Room and ask Kirby, the guy with the beard, to buy a bottle of whiskey and tell him it's for me. You can keep the change. Deal?"

I shrug my shoulders and she slips me a twenty.

"Don't let nobody see you with it, especially Grandma," she says.

I shove the twenty in my boot.

I almost hug her but don't then she hugs me and I let her hang on bawling her eyes out. She blows her nose in a rag and slumps back in the chair. Her black hair is greasy and sticks to her cheeks and her eyes look rubbed out.

When everyone is asleep, Willy and me make a beeline to the woods. We carry candles and matches and cans of beer and the wee gee board. Willy thinks if we can communicate with Zuzu he might be able to copy her ghost and bring her back with silver gelatin paper.

It's cold out and the moon is covered with fog. We light the candles and sit cross-legged under the willow tree and set the weegee board between us.

"Ask *kit*," Willy says.

Wings flap over our heads and the air smells clean and still as snow.

"Okay. Remember not to move your hands on purpose or press down on the oracle in any way," I say.

"*Yep*," Willy says, and stares down at the woman with the flying hair.

"First question: Can Zuzu see us?"

We wait but the oracle is still.

"Can Zuzu see us?"

The oracle slides to the right then the left then upwards to the sun:

Y E S

"Is she here now?"

Y E S

Toro perks his ears.

"Where?"

P O N D

My neck tingles and Willy and me stare at each other than at the black pond shining a moon face.

"Let's not ask anymore Zuzu questions," I say.

"Will we have to move?" I ask.

It slides to the bottom to the woman with flying hair and her hands in the air, the man's head floating over her shoulder, and it stops dead.

"What's that supposed to mean?" I say.

Willy stares down.

"Let's try another. I know. Will I be a pilot?"

The oracle zooms around the board, our fingers hardly touching, circling over the alphabet then it stops and begins to spell a word and Willy and me watch as it spells:

P   R   I   S   O   N

Divorce

AUNT OINK AND DADDY DEAD are getting a divorce and Daddy Dead is selling our King Car house and keeping the dough. Aunt Oink can't pay for a lawyer, besides, she says he's dead to her, even his money. He shot Cheyenne because he said she loves the cat more than him. I remember the time he broke "Love Me Tender" in half because of Elvis. I know I will never forgive him. Cheyenne was washing his fur in a circle of sun, purring in the warm grass. I don't want to look but Willy did and poked Cheyenne with a stick just to make sure. I won't go in the backyard or look out the window till Willy tells me: "Cat gone." Grandpa buried Cheyenne under the dogwood.

"You can get half the money when he sells the house. It's the law." Grandma says.

"What about us?" I say.

"I don't need money from the devil," Aunt Oink says.

Zuzu's blanket covers her knees, the blanket with the fringe and the flying elephants and it seems like she is here, in the room, in the kitchen with her silver jelly jar rattle.

Willy and me try every night to start King Car before it's too late. We ask Grandpa if we can bring King Car with us to the apartment house and he says, no, he don't have towing hooks and besides there's no place to park it there. Even Grandma and Grandpa are moving because they don't have the caretaker job at the movie star house now. The movie man died and his new wife got everything and his promise to leave Grandma and Grandpa his house don't mean a hill of jelly beans as Grandma says.

We're all gonna live in our own square apartment in Lockwood: Grandma and Grandpa in A 10, Willy, me, and Mother Blind in B 13 and Aunt Oink in A 16. I pretend I'm a lawyer and have to argue my case.

Argument 1: We're living here and he isn't and possession is 99% of the law. (I learned this on television.)

Argument 2: In the state of New Jersey you have equal property

147

rights when you are married. (Oh well, cross that argument out. I keep forgetting what Grandma said but maybe she was wrong?)

Argument 3: We don't want to move back to town where all there is to do is get in trouble.

Argument 4: It's not fair

I don't stop. I hammer my case every day and Mother Blind gets tired.

"Listen," she says. "I'll let you have your own bedroom and buy you new furniture for it."

"How you gonna pay for it?"

"Credit with Mr. Owen. It's his store. I already asked him. You're going to be a teenager soon. Don't you want your own space? You can fix it up nice."

"Where's Willy sleeping?"

"He can have the other bedroom," she says. "I'll take the sofa."

I never thought about having my own room like girls on television with flowers on the walls and ruffled curtains on the windows with the moon shining through. I think I like the idea.

That night we spin King Car's old tires down the path just for fun and in the dark we watch with the flashlight as they spin into the hole with all the other busted stuff. Since we were here last there is a black oven with silver knobs and a soft yellow chair that Willy says he can use in King Car because the driver's seat is broken and held up by a cement block. The chair is heavy so we drag it all the way back and the stuffing bleeds a path all the way back to King Car.

"King Car zoom," Willy says

"What if we get stopped by the police?" I say, and Willy says he has another route in mind and we're going to take that route tomorrow night.

In the morning we see that Daddy Dead hammered the "For Sale" sign on the front yard. Willy and me paint "NOT" in front of "For" and when Daddy Dead pulls up the drive in his red truck we act dumb and say we saw the Perfumo brothers running away. Every time he fixes the sign we paint "NOT" again.

If we can't live in our house nobody can. If we can't drive away in King Car or tow it to Lockwood or drive it to Florida, no one else will.

148

We have a plan. Knife says maybe we should cremate King Car and put the ashes in a jelly jar or a tuna fish can so we can bring it with us like Zuzu.

The doctor said Aunt Oink has double meloncola. She mopes around in her nightgown, doesn't shower, eat and won't go back to the apartment to get her stuff because Zuzu's playpen and crib and toys are there. I make her cocktails and ride my bike to the Elbow Room to buy her cigs and Kirby gets me the liquor. I steal yellow pills from Mother Blind. Knife says to give her what she wants. She's only nineteen and her life is already a junkyard so I ride my bike to the Elbow Room.

Kirby is so tall he has to bend down the take the twenty-dollar bill and his long beard brushes my arm.

"You sure this is for your aunt?" he says.

"Yes," I say. "Her baby died."

"Well, that's a good reason to drink," He says.

Kirby says to meet him around the corner where there a no windows and he hands me the bottle in a brown bag and I stuff the change in my pocket.

Midnight

WE SKIT OUT THE BEDROOM WINDOW and yellow berries tick off around our feet.

King Car shines under the orange moon. In the morning, the moving truck will come. Willy checks under the hood and the new spark plugs glow white and gold and green. He pours the can full of rainwater into the radiator and I smell tin and mint in the night air. When the moving truck comes, we'll be gone.

Toro is sleeping in his cardboard box. Mother Blind says they don't allow dogs at the apartments but she found him a home on a farm faraway. Sure. I know about the "farm" where they gas dogs and cats in an oven. I toss the dog food, water bowl and biscuits into an old potato sack. Toro's with us.

Willy is at the wheel in the yellow winged chair. He wiggles the wires and King Car's engine chugs and white smoke puffs from the duster. Willy and me stare at each other then he guns the gas pedal and steers King Car in a circle, the headlights round the trees then light the bumpy road ahead. But we're not on Cherokee Road.

"How come we're not on the road?"

"*Cutroad,*" Willy says.

He thinks we can motor down the hidden skidders in the woods, the back paths and lanes, the truck treads and secret dirt roads all the way to Florida. We follow the tracks the fire trucks stamped in the dirt.

"*Loch Moigh,*" Willy hollers out the window.

"You did it Willy."

"We are really driving."

Holy, Knife says.

I wonder how long we can go before we run out of gas but Willy will know a way to spot gas from another tank.

Faster. Knife says. Don't look back.

She's wearing the aluminum foil bathing suit I made her. She wants to learn to surf. I don't have a suit but I brought my cut-off jeans and tee shirt and towels.

Willy grins and points to the radio knob.

"What?"

He turns the knob and out comes a voice singing about poison ivy.

"How'd you get it to?" I say. But then I wonder why I asked. Willy is the Einstein of cars.

King Car climbs over the hill that dips toward the pond and there is a loud knock and the hood starts to smoke then the engine clunks and we roll to the edge of the water and Willy jerks the emergency brake and we stop hard. King Car coughs and clanks to a dead stop but the radio keeps going, singing about a moon.

Dang, Willy hollers and slams his fist on the dashboard and we stare at one another and wait for the pond to swallow us.

"Now what?" I say.

Willy holds his hands tight over his ears and squeezes his eyes shut.

"*Fruck,*" he hollers and his face goes red.

The headlights make yellow paths across the pond. The water is black and in the light beams I see mosquitoes circle the water and walkers move their long thin legs on the dark shine of the surface.

"We can't go back. Toro will go to the pound and that can NOT happen."

Willy drops his hands down from his ears and opens his eyes. He keeps the brake on but trips the wires in the ignition but it doesn't spark and his face gets redder.

He jumps out of King Car, pulls out the tire iron and beats till the hood is one big dent. Toro howls and I get the spooks.

"Hey Willy quit it. We're still in here."

We get out, sit on the ground and throw stones across the pond. Knife says to think about all the sour balls we can steal in town.

Willy pops back into King Car, unlocks the brake, jumps out. King Car rolls toward the pond. Willy pushes on the trunk and gives me the sign to help him. Together we push and King Car picks up a roll and slips down the bank, into the water, silent, until we see the roof disappear into the watery grave.

For a long time we just listen to the gurgle, the bubbles, the rings on the water. That's when the kid shows up carrying his stick and lit cigarette.

151

"I knew you'd be back," he says. "Like I said, once a trespasser always a trespasser. This time I'll call the sheriff," he says.

"Go ahead," I say. "Arrest us. I don't care. I'd rather go to jail then move to town."

"I see," he says. "Well, I'm sure the sheriff can put you up. He knows your family. I hear there was a kid killed. An accidental death with questionable and unusual circumstances."

I don't say nothing and neither does Willy.

"Sheriff says he didn't file any charges, though."

"Why would he?" I say, "I didn't do nothing."

"Well, I guess we're in the same club then," he says.

"Club?"

Willy sits on the ground hugging his knees.

"The dead sister club. That was your sister right? Has the same last name."

I don't answer.

"The club of the dearly beloved. I guess I'll give you another pass," he says," Since you two are members now."

He drags his stick across the dirt.

I hope King Car is at the very bottom sunk in the mud so the boy can't see. I look at the water and see a line of bubbles boil up from the bottom.

"Where is it you're moving to?"

"Lockwood," I say. "To an apartment house."

"Well now what is so bad about that? Soundberg Airport is there a few miles out. I bet you can walk there and watch the take offs and landings since you think you can be a pilot."

"But our dog isn't allowed. He'll go to the pound."

The boy kneels and Toro stares at him.

"Well, it just so happens I've been looking for a Chihuahua. Most people don't know it but they are fierce watchdogs. I bet if there's a trespasser three miles away I'll know about it."

Toro's ears go straight up and he stares at the boy.

Willy and me lock eyes and Knife's hair goes sideways.

"But we don't want to leave him," I say.

"Well, it don't seem to me you have a choice. You can't camp out here. They'll be searching for you."

152

He leans against a tree and lights another cigarette.

"Listen," he says. "I'm kind of used to you guys trespassing and I'm thinking maybe you can come back and see the dog if you want. Or, if your situation changes you can take him back. I'm a few miles east, you'll see the old place. Look for the sign that says: Stovekin Estate. I'm a gamekeeper," he says. "I know how to take care of animals. It's what I do."

"You promise we can have him back?" I say.

"I don't make promises," he says.

We pet Toro and rub his belly and he kicks his paws in the air. I lay down beside him and pull on his ears the way he likes and he licks my face. I try not to slobber.

Willy looks at my wet face.

"Don't look at me." I say.

On the way back home the tears keep coming but I stay quiet and the weeds rattle in the wind, the moon through the papery pods and for the first time I am sure the boy in the woods is real and not a dream.

The Circus is Coming

GRANDMA SAYS WE CAN WALK to the movie show and see *Some Like It Hot* and *Suddenly Last Summer* on a big screen.

"I already know that," I say. "You took me there."

"I know but we can walk now," she says, drawing on her pink lipstick.

There are lots of places we can walk to like Woolworth's, and the eyeglass store, Grandma tells me.

"Change is good" she says, like riding my bike on the sidewalks and streets, plus the hospital is practically in the backyard. "We can go to a restaurant and order ravioli," she says. She thinks maybe she can get a job at the movie show selling tickets or candy and that way she won't have to pay.

"What the hell you talking about getting a job?" Grandpa says. Then he picks up his coffee cup and lights his cigar looking like he just drank some vinegar.

"You need to forget about things for a while," Grandma says. "That's why they invented the picture show. So you can go somewhere."

When the movers come, I run through the trees to the pond, a razor in one pocket, Knife in the other and clouds trail me till the wind bites the clouds into shreds and they rip over the pond like oily rags.

I call out for Toro and watch for his ears between the stalks of grass, his black body speeding toward me. But he doesn't come and all my pieces' slip into a black shadow, a hole in the ground.

I pull myself up and lean over the pond and the girl staring back at me is different than before, my hair longer, my eyes hard, scary like a crazy girl I saw in a movie. A girl called a *bad seed* who could kill anyone with a smile. I pull out the razor and hold it up to my arm. I'm going to cut the four letters there, T O R O but I don't. I shave off my eyebrows instead. I don't know why. Knife thinks it looks spooky-good. She sits under the tree in her silver bathing suit with her toes in the water.

I *want* to scare people in Lockwood, I say.

Are you crying? she says.

I look away toward the field so she doesn't see me leaking all over the ground.

The circus is coming, she says.

I hear Grandpa yell my name through the trees and reach for Knife but she is gone.

"Where are you?" I say.

Grandpa's boots trample over twigs.

"Knife?"

I search through the tall grass and think maybe she decided to take a dip in the pond since she was wearing her bathing suit. I don't see her but I can hear her snap herself together and I listen to her words inside my head.

Here, she says.

"Where?"

Where things end, she says.

"What do you mean?"

They begin.

I have to go to a new school. Willy thinks it's going to be too bright there. Too many cars. Strange people. He'll have to keep his eyes shut and cover his ears and you won't be there.

Everlasting to everlasting, she says, and I feel her click inside me like a skeleton.

"You mean it?"

Today. Tomorrow. Next Day. Day After That, she says.

I see Grandpa march through the tall grass and there is a crack of sun and the clouds draw shadows on the ground. I fish the pieces of me out of the shadow and fall into place but not the same place.

Grandpa looks down at me, his rough hands on his hips, his knit cap pulled down on his forehead.

"I'll drive you back sometime," he says, pulling me up off the ground by my elbow. "Things don't happen the way we want," he says, and looks at me queer. "Where's your eyebrows?"

But I don't answer and I couldn't explain anyway. He takes his cap off and puts it on my head slipping it down to cover my missing brows then he drags me to the car, Willy in the backseat with his hands over his ears, the car rumbling, Mother Blind in the driver's seat, waiting.

We look out the back window and watch our house and the trees get small then disappear till there is nothing but trucks and the interstate. I think of Toro there in the trees, trotting alongside the tall boy like a tiny Misty, Toro's nose to the ground sniffing for me. I reach for Knife and then I remember.

Mother Blind follows Two Men & A Truck wearing her soldier-self and the soldier-self does what has to be done.

"Okay," she says. "Where's the dog? I know you have him hidden. He can't come. We'll be thrown out. I know a farm…"

"He's not going to any farm," I say. "He's staying on the Stovekin Estate with the Stovekin boy until me and Willy get our own place."

"What Stovekin Estate? What boy?"

"Behind the house. By the pond."

"That land belongs to the state," she says. "Only estate was ten years ago and that's long gone.

Willy's eyes go big and wild and we stare at each other.

"No, he lives there," I say.

"Well anybody who lives there is trespassing," she says.

Willy looks at me.

"Squatters," Grandpa says. "Sheriff finds out they're gone."

"No Grandpa, he's friends with the sheriff. He's related I think."

"Where's the dog?" Mother Blind says, in her snippy voice.

"I just told you he's with the boy. I'm not lying."

"Well if I catch wind of that little stinker he's going to the farm," she says.

"You're so mean." I say.

"'Cruel to be kind,'"she says.

"I hate you."

"How sharper than a serpent's tooth it is to have a thankless child," she says, and the Jeep blows smoke out the tailpipe till Mother Blind can't see and we ride a cloud all the way to Lockwood.

Part Two

Clothesline

GRANDMA SAYS YOU SHOULD always look *presentable*. "You can't go around looking like a sock-doll," she tells me. "Town people are nosey."

I remember the times Grandma listened in on other people's conversations on the three-way phone back at the caretaker house, Grandma's ear at one end where the sound comes out and her hand at the other end covering up the holes where the sound goes down.

"Looking for dirty laundry, town people," she says. "Can't run out to bring in the wash from the clothesline in my nightgown and hair curlers anymore. Spy on your wash too to see how big your underwear is, and how white," she says and looks at me. "Comb your hair once in a blue moon, Zoe. Townspeople notice if you're dressed willy-nilly."

"Not properly groomed, is what she means," Mother Blind says.

I think of my shaved eyebrows, pull Grandpa's hat down lower.

We park at the curb and stare out the window for a while-- garden apartments without a garden, more like the prison I saw in a gangster movie with Grandma, brick buildings like alphabet blocks. Across the street a football field, bleachers, a steel fence I figure Willy and me can cat jump.

Even though we lived here that time for a few weeks in the Before—me and the colored girl staring at one another wearing the same stupid dress with the pallet pocket and the paint brush sewed on—everything looks different now. Maybe this is what the weegee board meant by PRISON.

In my head, Knife says not to forget about the candy man with the missing finger, the ice-cold orange-cream pop in my back pocket. She says there's ice cream on every corner in town and at least fifty different flavors, not like the country where there is only vanilla, chocolate, strawberry and napoleon.

The sky in town is different too even though they say it's the same sky. It's white and empty today and the trees along the streets look tired and not so tall, just stumps compared to the trees back home, even though back home isn't that far away, trees have more room to grow there in the wild.

Willy and me lug our suitcases, the color of oatmeal with the leather punched and torn, that belonged to Grandma's mother from another century and some other country across the ocean, a place Grandma calls the snowy Alps where her mother rode a high horse. We set our jaws and pretend to be soldiers off to war and bust through the door so hard the knob leaves a hole in the plaster and here we are, looking from one wall where the apartment begins to the wall where it ends without moving.

"I thought our house was small," I say.

"It's a roof," Mother Blind says, and sets down a box filled with half broke dishes. "It'll do for now." But when she sees the teeny stove, her shoulders slump. At least we had a big oven in the other stove. "I don't see how you could fit a turkey in there," she says.

I think of the glass window in our oven where we fit Aunt Oink's photos, where Grandma's apple and peach pies bubbled, the naked turkey roasting brown. I think of the wallpaper in the living room with the pheasants staring out all day and in the backyard the dogwood tree with the papery white petals.

"You can fit a couple chickens," I say. "I told you we should have stayed in our house," but she doesn't answer I guess because there is no answer.

Willy whispers in my ear we should head back to our house and the woods.

"How?" I say.

He holds up his thumb.

Knife says to wait. Check out the candy and department stores first.

This is how the apartment goes: first, you walk into a living room with a picture window but not so big like the one at home and only thing you see is another brick building and a lady on the stoop sweeping out the pockets of a man's trousers with a whisk broom, then a skinny kitchen with a radiator, a small bedroom, bigger bedroom and tiny bath with pink tiles and a cracked toilet bowl. I get the big bedroom with the blonde furniture from Owen's and Willy has a fit because my room is bigger. "She promised me," I tell Willy. "It's not my fault I'm selfish."

I move the new furniture around the room in different arrangements: bed by window, bed in front of window, bed up against the side wall, bed in middle of room, bed catty corner. Knife says to leave it there because that way we have a view of the garbage house which is a garage where everyone throws their broken stuff. Knife says it might be full of treasures and that night we case it out and find: a dirty bride gown with a torn veil, a wooden box shaped like Popeye, a yellow pair of smelly rubber boots, a cracked doll's head, a ratty bra and an old toaster that Willy snaps up.

"I fix this," Willy says, then looks at himself in the chrome Sunbeam.

"Your face is melting," I tell him and he chases me down the zig zag path with the toaster tucked under his arm, the black cord beating his leg until we make it back to our place, all the apartment windows lit in yellow squares and Mother Blind picking out paint colors at the kitchen table. She looks up at us and spots the toaster.

"What do you want with that old thing?"

"Space station," Willy says.

"Forget I asked," she says, and goes back to her squares of paint but then she looks up again.

"Zoe where are your eyebrows?"

I reach up for my hat but it's missing.

"Why? You look ridiculous."

"I just wanted to see how the razor worked," I say.

"I'm going back to picking paint colors," she says, and for the next few days, she paints the living room Robin's Egg Blue, the kitchen Cornbread Yellow, the bathroom Tea Rose, Willy's room Sandstorm and my room Brigadoon Green. She presses curtains on the ironing board and the steam chugs out around her face so she gets a facial at the same time and that's a good thing because she has to start her new job in a few days. The curtains are white and see through with ruffles all around like ghost brides. She's polished the windows and wood floors and when she hangs the curtains she crisscrosses them just so.

"Don't smudge," she says and she stares at me. "Your sticky fingers," then she slips the last curtain through the rod. I look at my fingers, blue and sugary from an ice pop.

161

There is a clothesline made of twisted silver ropes in a spider web shape at the garden apartments. Knife thinks maybe they used to hang children there in the olden days.

"For what?" I say.

Red hair, she says. Freckles. Green eyes.

I imagine the steel ropes hung with red-haired girls, their necks limp, strings of hair twisting out in the breeze, freckles on their noses.

We never saw a steel wash line in the country. Willy and me go out to see if it spins and it does but not with us hanging on it. We lay on the grass and look up at the underwear, sheets, the pillowcases blowing out like ghosts and at the same time we both say, "Zuzu," and stare up at the sky turning dark. Then we have what Mother Blind calls *another bright idea* and run back inside for the scissors. We slash and cut the wash up in long strips. We take turns slicing up the long men's underwear. We don't touch the pillowcases though. Afterwards, we run across the street to the field and shimmy the fence, fall in the grass and can't stop laughing for so long we get scared. We don't know the people the wash belongs to but every apartment house has a spider wash line. So, by morning we hit every single one.

Then a day later there's a rolled-up newspaper on the porch stoop that Grandma picks up and brings inside where Mother Blind cooks breakfast, scrambled eggs the same color as the walls, Willy and me with our box of Frosted Flakes, Grandma soaking her jelly bread in her coffee. Grandma unrolls the newspaper, stares at the headline then reads out loud:

Lockwood Clotheslines Vandalized:
Cutters on the Loose

When Mrs. Simmons went to collect her wash
the morning of June 15 at the Garden
Apartments in Lockwood...

"That's us," Grandma says. 'Isn't that the woman across the way? The one always with the whisk broom?"

"I believe it is," Mother Blind says.

Willy and me sit frozen to our chairs, staring at one another, our spoonfuls of Frosted Flakes frozen midair, halfway to our mouths, then Grandma reads on:

> ...what she found instead were rags. All of her
> clothes had been snipped to shreds.

Grandma shakes her head and clicks her tongue, her soggy jelly bread half floating in her coffee, she reads on:

> "I've lived here from the beginning" Simmons said.
> And I've never known any trouble here except for
> the peeping Toms. But there's been a lot of new peo-
> ple moving in."

"Who would do such a crazy thing?" Mother Blind says, and Willy coughs up his corn flakes.

"Don't eat so fast," Grandma says. "You could choke to death," then she goes back to the newspaper.

Willy covers his ears.

> Simmons was not the only victim. Several clothes-
> lines were vandalized.

"I'm never setting foot," Mother Blind says, "I'll use the dryers."

"There's rapist down there," Grandma says, then goes back to the paper and reads:

> Lockwood Police are searching the area for the prank-
> sters. If you see any suspicious individuals call: 908-
> 877-Help.

"Must be lunatics," Grandma says, and spoons the jelly bread out of her coffee.

Willy and me quick dump our half-eaten cereal in the garbage without Mother Blind catching us and make for the door, run to the garbage house where you hardly ever see anyone during the day.

"Man, we're in trouble," I say.

"Fruck," Willy says.

Knife says to destroy the evidence. We could be the next to hang.

That night we discover a park in the center of town. We put the scissors in a sock filled with stones and drop it in the creek that loops around the apartment block and Grandma's kitchen window but she'd never see us from here, in the dark.

Grandma lives in the next apartment building to ours facing Orchard Street and Aunt Oink lives in the one after that on Brown Street, so we can hop from one to the other when we get bored, everyone with their own apartment divided up like a nesting house for birds. The one at the caretaker house was white with red perches and holes where finches knit bits of straw snatched from the barn and threads pecked from Grandma's sheets on the clothesline. Willy and me never thought of slashing those up. But that was country.

Town

WILLY SAYS HE'S GOING TO RUN AWAY. He thinks he can hop a flying saucer to outer space because Mother Blind said he'll have to move with Daddy to Virginia because of, you know, his problems. We've been here for months, I forget how many, and he still isn't interested in English or history, only the future. Outer space. He is building a radio that he says aliens can speak through.

"But how will you understand them? It will be a different language," I say. But then I remember he already speaks a different language. "You have to try harder in school, Willy. "You don't want to live in Virginia, do you?"

Gong to a new school is tough but for Willy it's a witch. They put him in a special class but he says the lights are too *sunny*, the long tubes on the ceiling sting his head with their green flash so he covers his eyes with his hands. Then there's Mrs. Cramer's voice that he says is too *boom* so he has to cover his ears. But in auto shop he is all in. Even though he is only just ten, they put him in a freshman auto shop class after he got Mrs. Cramer's Chevy to start when it conked out in the parking lot. He made the Freshman look like space heads after he put a Chevy Turbo-Fire V8 engine back together in a record thirty minutes. I know this because they sent home a report from the auto shop teacher, Mr. Gremlin, saying that with permission he could take the advanced class. I bet he could teach the class without ever saying a word. But he is still doing crazy things like digging his fingernails into his arms till they bleed, shaving patches of hair from his head and setting fires.

"I make fire," he says, and I look out the window and see a pile of twigs burning behind our apartment.

"Willy, you can't do that," I say, and I run outside, Willy pounding behind me, and we stomp the fire out. "Don't ever do that again," I say. But he just stares at me, says: *cracky*, and grins.

"*Cracky*, can kill people. You'll have to live with Daddy or worse, go to prison," then he points at me.

"Zu-zu," he says, and I remember the weegee board by the ghost

165

pond and get a chill up the hairs on my arm. The word PRISON.

Hocus-pocus, Knife says.

We walk to Grandma's apartment house because she has butterscotch ice cream.

Grandma is hanging pots and pans in her bedroom window. She's afraid there might be burglars hiding in the lilac bushes, stories of thieves in the night and people being murdered in their own apartments, a woman in building 66 hacked to death at 11 o'clock in the morning and then there was the headless skeleton found under the bridge, the man who was hit by a train scaring people up and down Main Street with his one eye in the middle of his forehead, a puff of white hair hanging over and only two holes for a nose, the full size girl with munchkin parents and the man who is six foot ten and the color of ink who collects life size statues of jackals that he keeps on his front porch like guard dogs. Mother Blind says they are rumors because people talk too much in town. You have to see someone every time you walk out the door: Hello, Hi, goodbye, see ya, how ya doing? Nasty weather. Nice weather. Where are you from? Did you hear? When? Watch out.

Grandma's pots hang from a curtain rod and play music when the wind blows through the window screen. Grandma isn't taking chances. She keeps her iron skillet next to her bed.

"You never know," she says. "And the coloreds next door."

"But you watch Amos and Andy," I say.

"Well. They're on television."

"How about Paul Robeson? You love him. Grandpa worked with him that time at the brickyard. Grandpa said he sang the whole day."

"Well, he's a great singer," she says, and closes the curtains.

There are no colored people at the garden apartments. Not one. They live alongside the apartments on Davenport Street.

There is a man who has a garage on Davenport. His name is Jones and he fixes cars and plays a saxophone. Outside is a rusted Chevy with a twisted hood that Willy has plans for. Jones sits on an upside down tin pail greasing engines, setting things right. Sometimes Grandpa walks over and talks to Jones about cars and Mack Trucks and Grandpa hands him a cigar. One day, Grandma walks over and they talk about Grandpa's trumpet, her apple pies, her piano, her opera lessons. But Grandpa and Grandma have a fight a week later because Grandpa says Grandma hung her brassieres on the wash line so Jones can see how big they are.

That's the thing about town. But there are lots of places to work: Burke's Fine Clothing, McGowan's Stationary, Woolworth's and Joey's Pizzeria and in the next town over, Manville, there is a building named IBM and that is where Mother Blind got a new job. She was working in the upstairs office at Burke's Fine Clothing where there was a small fire then a Fire Sale and the owner, Mr. Burke, marked all the clothes up not down. Mother Blind catches invoices through the air in tiny carts across the wired ceiling, wires that run from the cash register below. Mother Blind says it's so the sales girls can't mess with the receipts but it's really because Mr. Burke has a college degree.

But, the better job came up.

Tomorrow is her first day. She hangs her new green dress on the closet door and sets out her yellow heels, pocketbook and slip. She bought them on installment at Burke's. She doesn't know anyone at IBM like at Burke's where she dated the window dresser, a tall man with curly reddish-blonde hair like Danny Kaye. He is a painter but the only thing he paints are clown faces. Once they went to the beach and he said: "I am going to go change into my *macaroonios*." After that she didn't see him much.

Now she has to meet strange people and learn how to punch holes all day. She is going to be thirty-one next week and she's getting wrinkles around her eyes.

"Use Pond's Cold Cream," Grandma tells her.

There is a little kitchen in the apartment big enough for two people but Mother Blind sets the table for us and we squeeze in. On the stove is a big pot of tomato sauce she made and water boils in another silver pot and when the spaghetti is done we dig in. Sometimes it doesn't seem so bad living here in the apartment. There are always people to watch when you get bored, Victoria Spain dressed in black tights and ballet slippers pushing her baby. Grandma says she plays loud music, drinks wine, speaks French and has men over all times of the day and night.

Cool, Knife says.

Next to Victoria Spain is Ivy Shapiro who is Jewish and boils whole chickens in a pot, Mrs. Simmons on her porch stoop dusting out trousers, a girl with red hair who is my age and has a transistor radio and a leather jacket. Sometimes I see her walking at night, the red button lit on her radio, the antenna poking up silver in the light.

In Lockwood it's hard to see the moon and stars because of all the rooftops in the way so Willy and me cross the street and duck under the fence to the football field. We lay flat in the center where there is nowhere for the moon to hide. We think of King Car covered with water, fish swimming in and out of the windows and tadpoles rushing around the tires. We wonder if the race stripes are still on the hood. Every day we miss Toro's black face, even his peeing on our shoes. We think of Zuzu and wonder if she is in the ghost pond swimming in and out of King Car's broken windows wearing her white dress and bonnet wondering what happened.

Now that Aunt Oink left him, Daddy Dead won't leave her alone even though he can't come near her because she has papers on him so if he does the police will arrest him for trespassing on her. He tells her he is going to kill himself. She tells him to go ahead and do it, it'd be a service to mankind. We don't see Daddy Dead anymore and that's okay with me but sometimes he calls when I'm there.

The phone rings and Aunt Oink says. "Tell Fat Daddy I'm not here."

That's what she calls him since the divorce but he's not fat. It's a South thing like his nickname *Tango*.

I take the phone and he says: "You know I luv ya." I go along with it because I want to get off the phone but before I can, he asks me if Aunt Oink is dating anyone and how much he'll always love her and I say, "What about Mommy?" Then he says she wouldn't stop having babies and I hang up the phone.

When Mother Blind comes home with bags of groceries we go gorilla and eat everything, the cookies, cereal, cheese and the loaves of bread and then she gets mad and starts to cry. She says she don't want to go on the well fair but if we can't control ourselves she might have to and that's called charity.

"We're poor," she says.

"No we're not." I say. "Poor people are in Russia. We're not poor."

"We are, "she says.

"We are?"

"The school is donating money so I can buy you winter coats. We're in a pickle."

"I don't want any donated coat. Poor people don't have nothing."

I never thought we were poor before. In the country, with the trees and the ghost pond, the moon over the hill, the grasshopper weeds, you don't feel poor. Town is different. For one thing you have to buy everything. But not always. I robbed another popsicle from the man with the missing finger and there was another person in the store, a colored girl looking at sour balls with her back turned and I saw her put two in the pocket of her jeans.

The street next to the garden apartments is Davenport Street and it is called the *colored* section like I said. Grandpa and Grandma and Aunt Oink sometimes say *nigger* just like Daddy Dead. If I go up Davenport Street the colored girls cross to the other side of the sidewalk. I'm the only white girl who walks to school on Davenport but it's shorter and I like how the colored girls wear their hair in a beehive.

I hate eighth grade. For one thing, Diane McGowan has it out for me. She is blonde and has muscles in her arms and Jimmy says she carries the lid of a Campbell's soup can in her pocket, sharp enough to carve up Susan Stryker's cheek. I don't know these kids.

There is a tall girl with dark blue eyes and blondish hair who sits in the corner of Mrs. Lambert's eighth grade classroom. She taps her foot and writes things with a black pen in a notebook with a silver cover but when I look closer I see she is drawing rows of different shaped bottles, bored like me. She wears black capris, a tight white sweater and ironed hair down her back with the ends squared off. Someone blows their nose and another coughs, a pen rolls across the floor and she turns and our eyes meet then she looks away.

One day she stops me in the hall and says:

"Everyone in this class is an asshole."

She is wearing a tight black skirt and sweater and her arms are long and thin. "I'm just cluing you in. They'll chew you up if you let them."

"I'm Zoe," I say.

"Kat," she says. "Kathy Blue."

"Later," she says, and walks down the hall and out the door.

Wind howls down the alleyway and the sky colors dark gray and purple. I skip over puddles shining beneath my boots and the boys at my side are strung together in the water and shadow me puddle to puddle.

Baptism

BACK IN MRS. LAMBERT'S ASSHOLE CLASS, the boys move on to Sally Manford's short skirt and the way her ass rounds out beneath the clingy fabric and the girls chew on the rumors that Sally Manford had sex with the entire football team in an empty school bus.

But at lunch they ask me things: the reason we moved, Kicked out? Divorce? Why I wear cowboy boots, Live on a ranch? I say, "Yes." We did live on a ranch with seven black horses. Not a lie since it was a ranch house and we did have horses, pretend ones. I tell them we moved because my father was hired for a very important job. He builds stages for rock n' roll bands and flies all over the world in his own airplane. He even built a stage for Elvis. I didn't plan it, just fell out of my mouth like gum. Then, I told them if we have a party my father will build us a dance stage and bring the Everly Brothers to sing "Bird Dog." Except for Jimmy Kip, that is.

Ten lies in a row equal a tribe, Knife says.

"Why did I?"

An Itch, Knife says.

I sit in class rolling a pencil back and forth and count the pieces of chalk on the little shelf at the bottom of the blackboard. White chalk, *Plankton* Willy calls it, blue, green, yellow lines that disappear-- ghostwriting when Mrs. Lambert wipes it clean and writes:

The Civil War was a war between the North and the South.

I already know this stuff.

After class I walk past girls quiet and narrow-eyed.

"If I catch you outside," a girl with a black ponytail says, and flashes a soup lid in her fingers.

Knife says a juju is coming and I ask her how many jujus can one person have? But she doesn't answer.

On the walk home Kat catches up to me.

"This town is the pits," she says. "I'm headed to the city."

"You need a partner?" I say.

"Maybe next time," she says. "I'm with my brother tonight."

"How will you get there?"

"On the train of course."

When I find out it is the train that goes through Lockwood that brings you to New York, I like the town a lot better. But not school.

I nab the lunch Grandma hands me: an fried egg sandwich, a green apple and a bag of Planter's peanuts. The bag makes a crumple sound that smells egg. Grandma is at the stove stirring her soft eggs and I smell the boiling water in the air and it reminds me of King Car's radiator when Willy poured in the water and the engine was hot.

Grandma bangs the metal spoon against the pot where she's making noodle soup on the other burner. She says to have fun at school but I'm not going to school. I'm going to the park that runs miles of green through the center of town. I stomp out into the fog and it wraps around me like sleep.

At the park there are no swings or sliding boards only tall trees and a brook where water slips over rocks and weed. I skim stones and the tadpoles scatter. I step barefoot over moss and stone, the water is cool, the crows fix eyes on me. There is mist and the willows stir the grass with weeping leaves. I think I can live in the park. A bridge is bent over the brook and I hide there where the water runs fast over stones and there are islands of grass to hop on and off of. Pink flowers with fat faces stare from a garden and I find a white birdhouse made of wood and big enough for people. A place to get married in then dance down the stairs to the path of trees and the brook. Knife thinks we are safe from the bad thing here, but I feel her hair going sideways.

Clouds swim over, dark now and filled with rain and it comes down hard so I hold my sweater over my head and walk the hill toward town, past the moviehouse and the ravioli place with the red and white curtains blowing out in the rain. I shake off the water and slip into Woolworth's Department Store where the air is warm and smells of roasting hotdogs and burnt toast.

The cashiers wear pink uniforms and tick their time away punching clocks. They gab over tubes of lipstick and rhinestone earrings, not paying attention to customers. A lunch counter with red leather stools and a hotdog spit sits in front of a big window of mannequins in underwear. I smell burnt cheese from the grill where a lady stands wearing a yellow uniform, her hand on her hip as she flips hamburgers and eggs.

I duck behind the stationary aisle.

On the middle shelf there are diaries, black and brown, plastic and leather. I flip through blank pages. On the bottom row I find one made of smooth pink plastic and on the front there is a girl with a ponytail sitting on a comfy bed and she is writing. I open my jacket and pinch the diary under my armpit and glide toward the door.

On the way out, I see a woman float in the storefront glass, she wears a pea green hat and coat and spoons confetti ice cream. She stares at me. I'm scared she can tell I'm a thief so I wave to her and split out the door.

That night in bed, I tuck the diary under my bed covers and write: I hate everyone.

Not Toro.

Not Willy.

On the third day I skip school and fill my pockets with bracelet charms, silver and gold, a wolf, a fox, a bird with red rhinestone eyes and a blue collar, a silver airplane. The more I get the more I want like eating potato chips. Cashiers look past me and at themselves in mirrors, fixing their lips and hair. I steal a jar of Vicks Vapor Rub for Grandma.

At home I spill the treasures onto my bed and lock the door. It's hard to sleep. I keep thinking about the charm I didn't get but I'll get that one, the seahorse with the green rhinestone eye, tomorrow.

On Friday afternoon, I slip down the fishing pole aisle. I'm learning different techniques. For instance, you can pick out any lunch box you want and just walk out the door with it. I'm deciding between Roy Rogers and Lone Ranger when a tall man in a dark suit and tinted glasses taps me on the shoulder.

"Why aren't you in school?"

"I'm sick."

"Why aren't you home in bed?"

"Nothing you can catch. Asthma."

"Where do you live?"

I tell him I'm not from these parts and I'm staying with relatives but I forgot their address. He says if he catches me during school hours again he'll notify the police.

I fly home and the rain hits me sideways, my hair dripping in my eyes. Grandma is watching *Search for Tomorrow* from the kitchen at the stove where you can see the TV blinking in the living room.

"Home so early?" she says.

Joan is telling Vic she is pregnant with triplets.

I tell Grandma I had an asthma attack and went to the park to lie down.

"But you told me you were divorced," Joan says.

I figure I'm off the hook thanks to Joan and Vic but then the doorbell rings. I catch my breath. It's the school nurse and I've been out of Mrs. Lambert's class all week. Maybe the nurse knows about the stealing, what if the man in the store told her? Maybe I'm going to jail. I crouch on the sofa and wipe my sweaty palms on my knees as Grandma opens the door.

My grandmother tells her I suffer from asthma. I hold my breath.

"Oh, I'm sorry to hear that," the nurse says. "You're soaking wet," she says.

"I was in the shower," I say. "Breathing the steam."

"You'll be in Monday then?"

"Yes," I say.

"I'll check in on you then," she says, and takes fairy steps out the door, dots of sun lighting her patent leather heels.

It is a miracle. I am off the hook but my gig is up.

On Monday, I pretend I'm the other girl and go to class counting the days till summer.

On the last day of school, I feel happy—all the blank days of summer ahead.

Now that we live in Lockwood Mother Blind decided we have to get baptized and I say, *no way*. The minister comes to our apartment and I jump out my bedroom window and speed down the path, wait in the football field until I see him leave. Mother Blind is drinking the Jesus juice, getting hooked on "the shadow of death."

"This Sunday," she says. "Both of you are getting baptized."

She tells me not to give her a hard time and that I don't have to do

174

anything except stand up so the minister can throw water at me. I tell her no again and again.

"That's for babies," I tell her. I tell her it's against my religion. I don't believe in it. It's not going to change anything. I'll still be a bastard but she says if I don't do what she says I won't get to go to the diner afterwards and order French fries and coke.

At the church, I stare at the floor. I'm wearing a stupid yellow dress with buttons up the front and a white collar called Peter Pan. Willy wears the brown suit Grandpa bought him.

We have to stand up in front of the stupid minster so he can say our names and splash water on our heads and that is supposed to mean you go to heaven?

Afterwards, Mother Blind is happy all the sin is washed away and everything is squeaky clean and shiny like a floor.

I meet Kat on the corner that night.

"We can buy cough medicine to get high," Kat says.

"What?"

"You never did it?"

"Only when I was sick," I tell her. "And I hated it."

"Well, you have to get the right kind," she says, and lights a cigarette. "The good stuff is behind the counter. You just have to sign for it."

"Why?" I say.

"It's got the stuff that makes you high in it. Codeine."

"What is it?"

"I don't know," she says, and stomps on her cigarette. "I just know it makes you high and everybody is doing it. I'll go in this time and sign," she says. "You go next time."

I watch as she walks away in her black boots and in no time she is back with a brown bottle in a brown bag.

"Here it is," she says. "Happy water."

We sit in the parking lot behind the drug store in the dark and the gulp the cough syrup but it tastes really bad and we never do get high because we throw it up pools of red all the way down Bridge Street.

The Married Sisters

Last week I turned thirteen and Grandma gave me thirteen dollars and Mother Blind made a double chocolate cake that Willy ate in the middle of the night. Not one crumb left, Willy saying a devil was in it and it wasn't his fault and there is a ring of chocolate around his lips that makes him look like a monkey. I'm thirteen and one week old now and I can still see the chocolate around Willy's mouth.

The devil always leaves her tracks, Knife says.

Under the window the radiator hisses at Mother Blind's stockings and bra hung there pressed over the iron pipes, nylon legs under a bra as if a person disappeared into the steam. She is going on a date with a Navy guy from her office so she is wearing a white cotton dress and navy blue shoes.

Mother Blind has girlfriends now, women from IBM, Marlene, Betty and a tall woman Willy calls *Doorshock*. They play beauty parlor and color and curl one another's hair, paint nails and drink wine. Aunt Oink comes too sometimes and usually gets drunk and starts a fight but tonight she's home alone and calls, asks me to come over. She's not happy about Mother Blind's date with the Navy guy.

"Come over," she says. "I'll play some records. I just bought a new album, the *Grand Canyon Suite*."

Lately she's been into classical stuff that puts you to sleep.

"I'm going out tonight," I say, but she starts to cry.

When I get there she is on the sofa wrapped in a dark blue blanket. Paint and *Tigress* perfume are in the air along with the smell of greasy sausage and it gives me a sick stomach. No more Evening in Paris perfume though, that went out with Daddy Dead and the divorce. Next to her on the table is a bottle of red wine in a straw basket and it's almost empty and she scrapes at the red wax seal with her sharp nails and tells me her life is a horror show and nothing is worse than seeing your dead baby and how come the horoscope books didn't warn her about the laundry basket.

"I wish I was dead," she says. "Don't tell nobody I said that."

"I won't tell anyone," I say. "Do you need more of those pills?"

176

"Yeah," she says. "As many as you can get. The ones they gave me don't do nothing but make me fat.

And she is fatter than ever and reminds me of Grandma's dough when it rises up to the top of the bowl.

"I need the yellow ones. Better off dead," she says. "What does living get you?"

"But you'll get over it." I say. "You're not that old and you can still be something if you want. You can move to Florida and serve drinks on the beach and stay tan."

"You don't know nothing yet," she says. "You'll see when you get older. You need to drop out of school and find a good man and get married."

"I can drop out of school?" I say.

"Yeah but first you have to turn sixteen," she says, and slugs her beer.

"So why go to school now then if I'm gonna drop out anyway?"

I think about getting a job at the airport, waving planes in and out. You can see the football field dead on from Aunt Oink's apartment since it's right across the skinny street.. The band is marching to the far side toward route 22, the purple hills in the background solid against the night sky, the white mansions looking down at us with lighted windows.

"Find a man," she says. "With money."

"I don't want to get married," I tell her. "I'm gonna be a pilot."

"Sure," she says. "Good luck with that."

She tells me she's not surprised though, I was always itching for action, made my way to town from Grandma's house when I was three, kicked the spokes from my crib then the window screen and crawled out on the roof.

"Always causing trouble," she says.

"That's no reason I can't be a pilot," I say.

"You'd kill people," she says. "Besides, who's gonna pay for the lessons? It's a man's world and you better find you a rich one."

I feel hot inside my chest, the heat moving up to my neck so I have to open my mouth to cool off.

"Why did you mess with Daddy?" I say.

She scissors her legs and my words hang jagged in the air.

177

"He told me I was beautiful and asked me to sit on his lap. I was eleven. Nothing happened then but that's when it started. I don't know how. It just did."

Zuzu is dead and Aunt Oink is sad but I still want to kill her.

"Well, you didn't have to do it," I say.

She gets up from the sofa and goes into the red kitchen, everything red, even the ceiling and it's tinier than ours because it's a three room apartment and the kitchen is small enough for one person to bake in.

"You don't know nothing," she says. "I don't want to talk about him ever again."

But Aunt Oink and Mother Blind do talk about Daddy Dead. A week later, after the Navy guy found out about Willy and me and never called Mother Blind back, they sit in the kitchen making fun of him.. We call them the married sisters because nothing ever breaks them apart for more than an hour or a day. They've always been married and always will be. Holy.

They sit at the kitchen table and joke about Daddy Dead. With bottles of red nail polish and hair dye beneath a bare light bulb, they laugh and say Daddy Dead can't keep his pants on, running around with that Rose woman with the short hair like a man. Then there's one called Sadie with the black spit curls. But he still calls Aunt Oink and tells her he loves her. Mother Blind don't get mad and I don't understand because it makes me mad instead of her but Knife says to remember the reason we call her Mother Blind. Aunt Oink rolls curlers into Mother Blind's hair then Mother Blind does Aunt Oink's listening a Johnny Mathis album, a song called "The Twelfth of Never" spinning on the record player. Mother Blind gets up to stir a pot of chili and Aunt Oink pours another glass of wine then twists a hot towel from the radiator around her head so her curls will set. There is a egg yolk beauty mask drying on both their faces and cucumbers under their eyes.

They flip through magazines and talk about the peeping Toms who creep around apartment window sills hoping for a peep at a half dressed woman. They talk about Elizabeth Taylor and Grace Kelly and how beauty can buy you the world. Sometimes they put mayonnaise in their hair then wrap their heads in wet towels and smear Vaseline on their hands, then cover them with gloves, they gab and gab, smoke and drink, Johnny Mathis singing "Misty" and "Wonderful, Wonderful" until the words and the tunes get stuck in my head forever. And then they fight.

"I need a man," Aunt Oink says, and pushes her wine glass back and forth on the table. "Every woman needs a man to live."

"That's not true," I say, from the living room sofa.

She looks my way with her yellow face and waves her hand at me like swatting a fly.

"We were put on this earth to fall in love. That's the meaning of life. The reason God made us, to have babies. It's says so in the Bible and you can't argue with that. You'll end up just like the rest of us."

"Whoa!" Knife says.

"Hollis says there ain't no woman in the world can light a candle to me," Aunt Oink says, and presses the cucumbers tight against her eye bags and stares at Mother Blind over the half-moons. My mother, her face tight from the dried egg, her muumuu hiding her curves, stares at Aunt Oink like shooting arrows, Aunt Oink pinned against the wall, then she turns back to the stove and hits the pan with her wooden spoon and the chili boils steam straight up to the ceiling and when she smacks the spoon down on the counter, the egg cracks around her mouth.

"He tells every woman that," she says. "Fools' paradise."

Aunt Oink flicks her cigarette in the ashtray and gulps red wine.

"You know what he told me? He said I look like Ava Gardner."

"Ava Gardner has a full mouth," Mother Blind says, and scrubs at a spot on the counter. "Besides, she's tall and well proportioned. An hourglass," she says, and slaps the wet rag at the hook on the wall. "We're going to be eating soon. You can stay if you want but that's it for the wine." Mother Blind says, and swipes the bottle from the table. "You're not supposed to be drinking with those antidepressants. I have to work in the morning."

"Who are you to tell me what I can do? Miss *nose-in-the-air*," Aunt Oink says, then gets up from the table and kicks her chair then forgets the egg on her face and the cucumbers stuck under her eyes and she slams the door and walks down the path right past old Mr. Winger who does a double take but Aunt Oink don't pay him no mind and heads straight for her red kitchen.

179

"Beware the green-eyed monster," Mother Blind says to herself and the radiator people hammer from the center of the basement where the washers and dryers are, the peeping Toms spying on women and their dirty laundry.

It happens at least once a week, a man's face at the apartment windows too, till we have to keep the shades rolled down all the time. Once it looked like Mr. Winger then one night the screen from my bedroom window is gone and the light on the side of the building is unscrewed and dark. Willy and me are alone and call the police but they never come. It's a hot night but we lock all the windows and the door and wait with our butcher blades.

One night Kat and me hide in the laundry room drinking our zombies and I look up and see him there, a face and we scream and grab the mop and broom from the corner and run up the stairs swinging but he is gone. "This is a street thing," Kat says. "We've got to take care of these guys. The cops won't do a thing."

"So, what can we do?" I say, but Kat just stares at a hammer clawed onto a wooden peg and I wonder if someday Kat and me will be like the married sisters--friends for life. No man to break us. When we get to the top of the stairs there is no man there at all, it's Willy playing a trick on us. He laughs so hard he falls in the grass when he sees the look on our faces and Kat standing over him with the hammer ready to strike.

"Not funny Willy," I holler.

"I could have killed you," Kat says, but this only makes him laugh harder.

Kat and me stare at one another and shake our heads and it feels like we will always be friends.

Red

AUNT OINK'S STOPPED EATING and lost all her salt and sugar weight and the only thing in her tiny, lipstick-red kitchen is booze, pig's knuckles and a moldy loaf of bread. I heard Grandma say that's not a good sign that she painted everything red and maybe Aunt Oink needs to talk to a head doctor.

"Why you painting everything a devil color?" Grandma says.

"I don't want no boring color," she says. "I want red everywhere. I want to swim in red."

"No good," Grandma says, then clicks her tongue and stares at the floor.

For the last month, Aunt Oink is awake all the time instead of always sleeping like before. After she paints the kitchen red she decides to do the whole apartment. In the bedroom she takes black paint and runs lines over the red walls, dips her hands in the paint, finger painting, the red showing through the other side of black.

In town, she picks through garbage and hauls home boxes of left over carpet squares from the home decorating store, all the colors and patterns scrambled and mismatched.

"What are you doing?" I say.

She is pasting them onto the walls of the living room.

"It looks groovy don't you think?"

She's so thin now her eyes seem bigger and blacker than before, even her boobs are shrunk to half their normal watermelon size.

"It's different," I say.

She's playing Spanish music and there is a big china bull on the coffee table, black with gold eyes. Mother Blind says Aunt Oink is seeing some guy from Spain who only comes late at night and is married with eight children.

"Want some wine?"

"Sure," I say.

We sit on the sofa and stare at the carpet squares, a crazy checker board.

181

"I'm in love," she tells me. "For real this time. Not like before with your father."

All that trouble for nothing, Knife says.

Aunt Oink says she's going to be a veterinarian or maybe a brain surgeon since she always liked slicing up frogs in biology class.

"What?" I say. "You gotta go to college for that."

"You're just jealous," she tells me.

Her breath stinks and I can smell her underarms and I know she hasn't showered for a while or washed her greasy red hair with all the black roots showing. Then there's the crazy talk about god and sinners. She says she is pregnant with Zuzu by immaculate conception. Zuzu is coming back. Isn't it a miracle? She talks so fast I get a headache. When I leave, she is pasting the carpet squares on the ceiling.

Some nights I mix her highballs and light her cigarettes and after a while she falls asleep with the drink in her hand and the cigarette still smoking from her lips. The doctor says she might have to get her brain hooked up to electricity so all the circuits get their fuses replaced.

"Could you get me a pig's foot?" she says.

"No. I'm not touching those."

"Then just bring me the jar," she says.

There's not a lot in the refrigerator. She's on well-fair. If she gets better, they want her to go to nursing school and learn how to give people needles and take their blood.

I hand her the jar of pig's knuckles and the feet bounce up and down.

"Why aren't you in school?" she says.

"Today is Lincoln's birthday," I tell her.

"No it isn't," she says. "That was two months ago. I remember because I bought these at Royce's Market on sale that day."

The gold lid rattles and I smell the sour pickle juice across the room and gag.

"Today's a school day," Aunt Oink says. "I know your skipping. Maybe they'll let you quit before you're sixteen so you can get a job at the supermarket and quit wasting their time and money. You'll never use what they teach you anyway. Except maybe

182

in home economics."

Sun hits the lipstick wall and I hear the train whistle blow its way toward New York City puffing a ribbon of red smoke along the steel tracks.

Frogs & Liquor

IT'S NIGHTTIME AND WE'RE IN TOWN the day before my biology class and Kat's algebra exam and we want to get high so we wait outside the liquor store, lean against the rough brick storefront, Kat in her beehive and me in my tight jeans that were Willy's. We've squirreled up the babysitting money we made from Ivy Shapiro and Victoria Spain to score a bottle of Thunderbird for our basement washer and dryer party. It's not so scary down there when we blast Kat's radio and down a few shots.

"Watch this," Kat says, and pulls out a Salem. There is a guy walking our way wearing an Army jacket, brown boots and a cigarette pointing out of the back of his ear. He's pretty cute, older, about twenty-two with dark sunglasses.

"Got a light mister?" she says. She's wearing a short blue skirt that ends halfway up her thigh and she bends her leg, rests it against the brick and the skirt rides higher.

"Sure," he says. "For a cutie like you."

"Sorry," she says. "Cute is an insult."

"Well, well. E-x-c-u-s-e me," he says. "For a beauty like you then."

"Nice try," she says and knocks out a cigarette.

"Let me get that for you," he says.

She holds her Salem between her fingers and waits for the flame then pinches the filter with pink fingernails sharp enough to kill then throws back her head back, flicks her hair and inhales one long drag.

"Merci," she says. "Would you be hitting the liquor store by any chance? My friend here Zoe and me are headed to a party over on Mountain Avenue. Some kid's parents on a skiing fling. Party time."

"Well, it just so happens I am hitting Liquorland," he says, flashing his white teeth.

Kat pulls a five from her back pocket. Thunderbird, she says. "We'll wait around the corner," then she gives him a big smile.

"Be back in a flash," he says.

We walk away laughing at the lie Kat told and wait in the front of the Candy Kitchen, the after school hang out, cherry cokes, ice cream sodas, whipped cream and strawberries, goofballs and pills that wind you up or down Kat tells me. Heart medication.

The air smells of chocolate cake mixed with hamburger grease, curtains pulled back so you can see the line of chrome stools and matching green counter that takes up most of the space in the front and in the back are green vinyl booths, smooth and slippery where kids sometimes make out or trade stolen pills.

"I could use a downer before biology class tomorrow," I say, and rattle my airplane charm on the chain. Kat taught me about downers, hard to get until you're at least a junior.

A silver Corvette slows, the radio blasting "Monster Mash" and the driver yells out: "Hey Baby!"

"Get lost," Kat yells back.

Thunderbird struts around the corner, collar turned up, a cigarette hanging from his lips, the bottle in a brown paper bag tucked in his armpit.

"Here you go," he says.

"Nice," Kat says.

"Hop in," he says, and points to a green Malibu. "I'll drive you to the party."

"Oh, that's okay," Kat says. "Our boyfriends are picking us up over at the Ville. See you there though."

He mumbles a line about missing our chance, then he slouches away. He knows he's been had. Kat is good. She's showing me how to be a townie and I'm teaching her how to steal.

At night, we slip into the basement laundry room, sit on the washing machines and drink Thunderbird from paper cups, keeping our eyes peeled for rats, spiders and peeping Toms that often turn out to be Willy. But once it looked like Mr. Winger.

"I think I need a few shots of this before class tomorrow," I say. "Biology. Puke class. Dead frogs everywhere. I can't eat for days."

"Wait till you get to the piglets."

"What?"

"And sometimes kittens."

"No. Never. What?"

"Why do we study the insides of frogs anyway?" Kat says. "It's disgusting. What are we going to be, frog doctors?"

"There's a frog doctor?"

"I suppose," she says. "Somewhere in the universe."

That's when we hear a knock on the basement window and see a man's face pressed against the glass and we both scream loud enough to scare him and the rats away.

"I'm going to get that gawker asshole," Kat says,and grabs the hammer but when we get to the top of the stairs we see it's Willy with a stocking pulled over his face.

The next morning in biology class, the formaldehyde stinks like pig knuckle juice and my stomach heaves. Mr. Boyle, hands out a diagram of a frog on its back with dotted lines that show where to cut but I can't. I don't want to see the insides of a frog. Frogs belong in water or under rocks. I see the frogs lined up next to the stainless-steel probes and slicers. I place my thumb on my frog's crown and cast a spell—but the frog stays cold and dead. If only there were tiny squares of white cloth or paper to cover the bare, belly-up body; its legs bent at the joints ready to leap down the hall searching for a way out, swimming through the pipes back to the shore, back to sand and water.

I study the chart, the naming of parts, memorize so I can pass the biology exam without cutting: Per-it-on-um, Liver, Heart, Gallbladder, Spleen. I memorize the page top to bottom:

Peritoneum: A spider web like membrane that covers many of the organs, you may have to carefully pick it off to get a clear view.

Lungs: Locate the lungs by looking underneath and behind the heart and liver. They are two spongy organs.

Gall Bladder: Lift the lobes of the liver, there will be a small green sac under the liver. This is the gallbladder, which stores bile.

I tell Mr. Boyle the class makes me puke but he says I'll get over it. I feel sick all the time and stop eating, every time I try I see the insides of the frog that other kids in the lab slice open. I tell Mr. Boyle I will pass the exam if only he will let me take it and not cut up the frog. He says no, no exceptions.

On the scale in the girl's room the needle jumps to 94. After a while, I don't even feel hungry. I like feeling empty and watching my ribs pop out from my skin. I stop going to biology class, then math, English and history, geography and gym.

186

Newsreel

GRANDMA AND ME WALK to the movie show. We pass the park, and the green grass waves, the school flag snaps in the wind, the white church in the colored section rings a bell and we whiff tomato sauce floating from an open window.

"How about some lunch?" Grandma says. She's been selling her pies at the football games so she has some money.

"Sure," I say.

"Let's go to the ravioli place," she says. She's wearing her black coat with the glass buttons and sparkles on her ears.

"I'm hungry and I don't feel like frying nothing today."

Her pocketbook swings as we walk and the rhinestones on her ears shine rainbows in the sun. I hope no one sees me.

"I packed some hard boiled eggs and jellybeans for the picture show," she says.

At the ravioli place we sit at a booth and Grandma gabs to the waitress about how she grew up in town over on Eastern Avenue where her father was a barber and a jeweler at the same time and how she used to play the organ at the cinema and was the first person to sing on the radio.

"It's nice to live in town, don't you think?" she asks the waitress but the waitress walks away.

"I'm getting a job at the thee-ate-err," she says. "I bet I can take orders for pie there."

I forgot how it is to be with Grandma when she's happy and smelling of talcum powder. Since Zuzu, all she does is pray, cry, pray, cry, wash clothes, pray, fry pork chops, cry, scream opera then cry, pray, fry. But she says you can't forget to laugh no matter what happens and a picture show is a magic potion.

Our ravioli comes and Grandma says, the Italians sure know how to cook and the sun breaks across our table and lights our blue plates.

"Even if they are guineas," she whispers. Then she laughs and ravioli steam swirls around her face and fogs her glasses and rhinestone

187

earrings and I wonder if I will remember this day, eating ravioli with Grandma with the sun on the blue plates.

At the movie show is a glass booth where you give an old lady your money. When you walk into the lobby the chandeliers shine from the ceiling and in the mirrors on the walls so you see yourself walk in all different directions at the same time. Everything smells of popcorn. By the velvet curtain is a long glass candy case like Snow White's coffin in front of the popcorn maker. Grandma says in the old times people wore evening gowns to the cinema and she sat up on stage and played the organ when a lady got tied to the train tracks or when someone was running from a bank robbery or murder.

Grandma sits in the aisle seat. Always, before the movie starts, they show Popeye if you're lucky and scratchy newsreels if you're not. Today there is a newsreel so I take a stroll out to the candy counter but you can't steal, all the candy locked in the coffin. I take my time and study the posters of actors dressed in green and gold, kissing or shooting rifles and posters of war planes flying in a row.

When I get back to my seat Grandma is digging her hands inside her pocket book. A newsreel is on, soldiers waving flags, then another rolls on, a reel with black lines and cracks and an airplane taxiing to the sky. My eyes fix on the plane as it lands and out pops a woman. Her blonde hair is short and her goggles are pushed up on her head and she wears a leather hat with earflaps. I get a spooky feeling like you meet someone on the street and you know you met them before but you haven't. My arms tingle when I see her high boots but the reel cracks and the screen goes blank and ja-voo creeps up my legs and the back of my neck and there's wild in my heart.

"That's the girl in brown who walks alone," I say, and look behind me to see if someone else said the words. But it's a matinee and no one is there. I'm not sure where I've seen the girl before only that I have.

"Grandma who was that in the reel? Who was the girl in the plane?"

"How should I know?" she says. "I was peeling my eggs."

My leg and arm hairs stand and prickle my skin like straight pins.

Knife tells me it's someone from the dream world and there are a lot of them between the movie projector and the cinema screen, slipping in and out. I twirl the airplane charm on my wrist. Knife tells me to think of fairies and how only some people see them.

When I get back home, me and Willy find the airport on a map in the drugstore. It's a mile and a half down 29 then over to Prince and down to Airport Road. We skip along the shoulder of the highway, trucks whizz past, honk horns at us and wave. It's a clear blue day and up the way we spot a red plane lift and fly over our heads trailing a stream of white smoke. The engine roars and Willy covers his ears till the sound melts into the clouds.

We sit on the grass across from the runway and watch the planes taxi and lift and the wind blows our hair sideways. When the wings rise my heart goes with them and I feel it deep in my stomach like when you are in the plane and you get a flutter that means you are airborne. While some are taking off others land, glide down and the wheels spin over the black top. We watch the pilots jump out and later drive the planes into the hanger, putting them away like toys.

Knife thinks maybe we could live in the hanger with the planes and play pilot when no one is there, study the dials. Willy says he knows how to fly and Knife says: Woah!

Stealing Lockwood

WHEN I GET TO KAT'S HOUSE she is in the bathroom staring in the mirror and drawing on her eyes, gliding black eyeliner across her lids, making little black half-smiles in the corners.

I go, "Kat, have you ever shoplifted?"

"Some gumdrops and peanut butter cups when I was a kid," she says.

"That's it?"

"As far as I remember."

"I think you'd remember," I say.

She's brushing on gold eyeshadow that glitters on her lids.

"Well," I say. "I'm a thief and I dig it."

I tell her it's from the fox gene because foxes are chicken snatchers and she goes:

"Fox gene?"

I explain about Waco my pet fox as she draws a brownish line around her lips so it looks like she has two sets.

"How come the light is off?" I say. "Don't you want it on?"

"No," she says. "Don't!"

"Okay," I say.

"I can only put makeup on in the natural light."

We drag ourselves to school up Davenport and spot colored girls with beehive hair and tight skirts and wish we were colored and could be in a singing group. Some girls give us slit eye, some pretend we are invisible, but a few say "Hi." They're probably the ones who go to the white painted church on the corner.

The trouble is, we get to school but we don't go in. I can smell biology class from the street and Kat whiffs the chalk of equations on the blackboard so we march past Lockwood High straight to the park.

Pretty Park has trees drowning in the brook and we throw down our books and shoot stones at them in the water. Some of the trees, the hickory and the birch, bend toward the water so far over I can see the twisted roots.

"My father is dead," Kat says. Her hair is a sand color and

190

sometimes she rolls it with Snow Crop orange juice cans, today it's pin straight and her bangs a wedge across her forehead.

"So is mine," I say. "What happened to yours?"

"He was a model. He hung himself." she says. "Last year."

"Oh," I say. "Is that why you live at the apartments?"

"Yeah. We had to sell our house and my mother got a job at the asshole bank."

"Same here," I say. "My mom punches holes in cards."

"Why?"

"Something like Morse code. My father got a job building stages for rock bands," I say.

"You said he was dead."

"He is," I tell her.

After the park, we zip down side streets to avoid the cops, patrol cars and slip behind trees if we hear one on our way to Kat's apartment to case out the liquor.

"What's this?" I say, snatching a bottle form the liquor safe.

"Cognac," she says, "It's French."

Kat reaches for two glasses from the cabinet.

"You drink cognac from a snifter," she says, and hands me a glass that is wide at the top and skinny on the bottom. "My father drank cognac."

It's not bad after a few sips and we empty what's left in the bottle then make grilled cheese and rummage through Kat's closet for something to wear downtown.

At night we hunt the streets tracking down a happening. Boys pass in shiny cars, radio tunes slicing through the air and boys hoot from rolled down windows. Kat says maybe someone will take us to a party so we can get drunk. We watch ourselves in all the storefront windows. I'm dressed in Willy's jeans and my brown cowboy boots, a white shirt and brown vest. I stole the boots from a store called Bootery. I just strolled in, tried them on and when the cashier turned around I walked out the door.

"I have a secret," I tell Kat.

Kat is staring at herself in the glass and doesn't turn her head so I talk to her in the glass.

"What?" she says, to my reflection.

"I stole everything I'm wearing. Even my jeans from my brother."

We swim like fish with the shiny blue and yellow cars down Main Street that pass us in the window glass.

"How? You stole everything?"

In the reflection she looks taller because her hair is teased so high tonight.

"I've been doing it for years," I say.

She stares me down.

"Years?" she says.

"Want me to show you?" I say, and the next day we walk along the highway to a big store called Mindy's.

I work on my shoplifting every day. If I wear a skirt into Mindy's I can roll on at least two more underneath. The coat racks are high and stuffed—no peep holes. I pick out three skirts all the same but in different colors a red, a gray and black

"Watch this," I tell Kat, and roll up a skirt under the one I'm wearing.

I pull them up one by one under skirt number one.

Her eyes pop and she hugs her jacket and yanks on the ends of her hair.

"I'm checking out," Kat says, and walks away.

I put on a leather jacket, rip off the tag, drop it into the garbage then wait for a customer to walk into the store and that is when I slip out, feel the hot white rush inside.

We walk to our apartment. I unload my loot: four skirts, three shirts, a leather jacket. Mother Blind is at work and Willy is in his room building an alien detector set with a slew of antennas he picked at the garbage house.

"Wow," Kat says, eyeing my stuff. "But I don't know," She twists her fingers around her wrist. "I can't have the law on my ass," she says. "The cops are all assholes."

On my dresser is a ceramic bowl, blue, busting with charms: the silver fox with the gold eye, the gold horse, a pink poodle with a clear eye, a sparkly black dog with a red eye, a white cat with a green eye, all the stuff I stole that never looks as good when you get it home except for the silver airplane. It's heavier than the other charms and a brighter silver. There is a heap of rainbow colored sweaters, a pile of 45's I robbed from the record store: The Everly Brothers, Chuck Berry, Little Eva.

I lock the door and we sit on my bed and listen to: "No Particular Place to Go." We blow smoke toward the ceiling and watch it snake in the sunlight.

"Everything is weird," Kat says. "Why are we here? How is it we have mouths and eyes? Why were we born to die?"

"Creepy," I say. "Why do we have toes?"

"I know it's evolution," Kat says. "But it's still queer when you think about it."

"Let's get back to shoplifting," I say. "I'll write down the rules."

Kat looks at herself in the mirror and glides on flesh colored lipstick.

"That color makes you disappear."

"It brings my eyes out," she says.

Her eyes are sunk deep into her sockets as though she is always looking at me from far away.

"At night, I go over my shoplifting lists for the next day," I tell her. "See."

I open the pink diary.

Tuesday
brown leather jacket with zipper pockets
leather pants
new pocket book
map of Florida

"Why a map of Florida?" she says.

"I'm running away," I say.

"How? How would we get there?"

"Hitch hike," I say.

"I don't know," she says. "Truck drivers are such assholes."

Kat twists her bubble gum ring around.

"These are the things I'm gonna to do when I get there." I show her the page in my diary.

get tan
learn to like coconut
learn to surf (steal surfboard)

steal a bikini (black)
get a job at a hotdog stand (no stealing)
make friends with a pilot (lots of them there)
find out how old you have to be to take flying lessons
look for dolphins

Kat rolls her hair in her finger. "I want to learn to tell fortunes," she says. "You know, on the boardwalk."

"In Florida you don't have to go to school or dissect frogs," I say.

"Really?"

"What are we going to do about tomorrow?"

"I wish I'd get sick or break my leg," Kat says.

"Maybe we can make ourselves sick."

"I know. What if we catch pneumonia?"

"How?"

"At the hospital?"

"You mean go there? But how would that work? You'd have to kiss them."

"I know," I say. "Shower. Wet hair. Put on a bikini. Run around in the cold. Grandma said you can catch your death that way,"

"Let's go to New York instead," Kat says.

Kat says I'm weird but so is she. I never knew anyone to roll their hair with orange juice cans before and make it look good and she never knew anyone that could steal half the town.

I turn up the volume on the record player and we dance the hitch hike.

Freddie

WE WALK DOWN BRIDGE STREET and the maple trees along the sidewalks drop red leaves that catch in our hair, me on the house side, Freddie on the street side, my books tucked under his left arm as his right hand brushes back the leaves. I know Freddie from English class. Well, from the few times I went to English class. He's tall with reddish hair, kind of a good looker though his head seems too small for his body. His eyes are black and small but fierce. He wants to carry my books and walk me home so I let him because he is the first boy who ever asked. Not that I can't carry my own books. I don't like him. I mean, like a boyfriend. Not that I ever had one. Neither has Kat. We're working on it though.

Keep your blades sharp, Knife says.

When we get to our porch stoop Mother Blind is sweeping purple and yellow leaves across the brick lined cement and there is apple pie in the air from Mrs. Winger's kitchen window.

"My Mother," I say.

He reaches out his hand to her.

"It's a pleasure to meet you Mrs. King," he says, and his voice sounds like an actor on a stage, different than when he told me he was hit on the head with a golf club.

"This is Freddie from English class," I say.

"Well, what a gentlemen to carry your books," she says with a smile.

Freddie is dressed in a suit and tie, his thick hair is slicked back behind his ears. He's not shy in class and likes to talk about Animal Farm and Hamlet more than anyone except Mr. Cooper our teacher. I like English class. If I could just go to English class I'd go to school everyday. Kat says maybe we can start our own English class with library books, an actual house filled with books they let you borrow, then read them and talk about things like plot and theme and why didn't Hamlet just kill the king right off?

I let Freddie carry my books home a few more times because I didn't go to school more than a few more times. But one hot day I see him on Main Street. It's summer and Kat has gone to Boston to visit her Grandmother for a week but she'll be home tomorrow.

"Hey, my friend has an in ground pool," Freddie says. "Want to go night swimming? We can walk there. It's across the highway."

I think about this--going alone with a boy without Kat there and how it would feel to wear my bathing suit in front of him. Willy is the only boy who's seen me in a bathing suit but he doesn't count and neither does Grandpa.

"Why at night?"

"It's more fun and my friend's parents are leaving this afternoon on a trip."

"Who is your friend?"

"Jimmy. Jimmy Smith from the football team."

"But he's a senior."

"So."

I know who he is. The best looking boy in school. He could be in a movie. It's as if he's been eating moonlight, born in moonlight, baptized with liquid gold, everything about him glows, especially his eyes. I've noticed lately I am a sucker for eyes like his.

"Will Jimmy be there?"

"Yeah," he says, and stares at me with his small head and eyes that make me think of a weasel. His hair isn't slicked today. It's wild now and red stubbles cover his chin.

"Can we wait till my friend Kat comes back tomorrow?"

"It's going to rain tomorrow and Jimmy's parents will be back so we won't be able to drink. I have a six pack."

"I guess," I say.

"I'll stop by your house at 7:30 and we'll walk there together."

"Will any other girls be there?"

"I invited Sandy Moore and her sister," he says.

"Okay," I say.

"Don't forget your bathing suit," he says. "It's a great pool. Has a changing house."

Freddie shows up at exactly 7:30 dressed in long shorts and white tee shirt.

"I dropped off the six pack before," he says.

We walk not speaking, Freddie with his transistor playing "You

Don't Own Me," as we cross the highway and climb the hill of white houses.

It is a fancy house, big with a red front door and black shutters on all the windows. The pool is lit all around and the water is clear and blue.

"You can change first," he says, and points to a wood shed.

I'm thinking how much I wish Kat was here but Knife says not to worry because if anything weird happens I know how to scare people. I hook the door shut. The room smells of wood, chlorine and rubber from the collapsed floaters on the floor. I change into my red bathing suit. I felt too weird about wearing my bikini without Kat. I take a deep breath, make sure my bathing suit covers all the right places and step down onto the stone patio.

"Where's Jimmy and the other girls?" I say, and notice a bright orange scarf flung over a black chair. "Is Jimmy in the house?"

"He went to pick the girls up," he says, and hands me a beer. I chug it down not because I like beer but because I feel lonesome and naked without Kat.

Freddie is already in the pool drinking a beer. His legs are white and hairy. I get in and the water is cool, silky, the sun melting orange over the hill, the clouds over me like raggedy wool blankets, pink and rose colored and there is a sweet smell in the air from the garden. I rub my finger over the smooth tiles of painted waves that line the cement.

Freddie swims to the middle of the pool, his head above water his body white beneath. He is staring at me and something in his face has turned dark. Something familiar somehow.

"When will the others be here?" I say, but he doesn't answer. He just stares, his face getting darker.

"I'm not feeling good," I say. "I'm going to change and go home."

"But the party hasn't even started."

I pull myself up out of the water and grab my towel from a chair and walk into the changing house making sure to hook it shut. I roll down my suit and step out of it when I hear a pop at the door, the latch swinging open and Freddie is standing there looking at me. His face has changed into a mask of another person. He steps toward me, the orange scarf in his hand.

"If you touch me I'll kill you," I say, and I mean it. It comes from a deep place where Knife was born.

He stands frozen for a few seconds then turns and leaves dripping water, dragging the orange scarf across the floor.

I jump into my clothes, leave my bathing suit behind, run across the highway ducking cars. I make it home thinking how I can't wait to tell Kat.

Well done, Knife says. The Perfumo boys practice paid off.

Wha?

THE JESSE JAMES RUNS ON A SLOW TRAIN SCHEDULE, old, rickety, like the wooden station that leans to the tracks, the roof a torn hat, the bench rusting under the big clock, a clock that forgot how to tell time. The Jesse James gets you to Manhattan though, if it doesn't jump the tracks or lose its wheels. It's about the only thing that happens in Lockwood besides the suicides. It's usually the Billy the Kid train, a lot faster. Billy the Kid gets the goners, the ones who stand on the tracks and wait. Across the street from the station is the Harding funeral parlor where Kat says there is a one-eyed undertaker, Charles Wesley Harding who handles the suicides.

"A bloody mess," she says.

"Why would someone do that?" I say.

"It's quick I guess," Kat says.

Kat knows the New Jersey track from the New York track, which pee smelling stairs to use, how to make the Newark connection, where to hop the underground cars to get places and once you get there, how to walk fast and pretend to know where you are going at the same time.

"You have to stay chill," she says, standing under the lamplight with silver bracelets and platinum hair.

You wear black in the city, she tells me. I rob two pair of black stretch pants and black turtle neck sweaters. I'm so fast they never know I was there. Kat thinks we need spiked heels. We find two pair at the garbage house, one silver and one still sort of gold, most of the glitter rubbed off but a smudge of sparkle sprinkled at the toes.

"Use the black pencil like this," Kat says, staring into the mirror. "You want to look like part of the tribe. The beatniks. Draw on your war paint. This color is Blue Coal."

She is doing an eye makeup demonstration for me, dabbing white around her eyes then lining her lids with black, smudging the lower lids raccoon style.

"Keep your lips pale. I use this pancake makeup. We need to look older."

199

"But it makes you look dead."

"That's the point," she says.

With a foam pad she smears her lips with Nude so they disappear.

Kat's been to New York with her brother Nick who's eighteen and wears ribbed turtlenecks, blue jeans and a Navy pea coat. He took Kat to a place named *Cafe Wha?* She says it's where the gone people go, gone from everywhere they used to live, singing about war and Siamese cats, poets too.

"Beat poets."

"I read Frost," I say. "In school. "The woods are snowy, dark and deep." That's the only part I remember."

"Well, not pretty poetry. Mostly, a lot of college kids who write crazy poems about supernatural darkness, for instance."

"You mean like Poe?"

"You and bloody Poe," she says. "Sort of, but not really. My brother hangs with them. They smoke weed. Pop orange sunshine.

I don't know what that is and I never heard anyone say "Bloody Poe" before, but Kat's father was from England where everything is bloody.

"There's a lot of assholes too," she says and slicks her bangs down. "It's a happening. If you're lucky a stranger walks on stage and blows your mind. You know, like Alice down the rabbit hole. Where am I?".

"What's orange sunshine?"

"I haven't done that," she says. "But Nick says it feels like you are in a cartoon," she says, smoothing out her hair. "Not sure about the heels now," she says. "I think flats. Do you have a hammer?"

I bang on Willy's door but it takes him forever to hear me because he is blasting a 45 of "Bread & Butter." He finally opens the door a crack and says: "Bop?" His hands are black with grease and it's smudged beneath his eyes and across his nose and the air smells of diesel fuel, flint and Gypsy Rose wine.

"I need a hammer," I say.

"Yoyo," he answers, and squeezes a hammer through the crack so I don't see what's going on inside.

Kat knocks the spikes off the heels and they pop and leave a circle of glue. We try them on and they look weird around the pointed toes but Kat says they'll do but we need berets and sunglasses. I tell her

I can rob the sunglasses from the Wald's Drugs but I doubt there is one beret in all of Lockwood but she says that's okay because there are armies of them in Manhattan.

"Have you been to the village?" Kat says.

"No," I say, pretending to know what she means. "I went one time with my Grandmother. On a bus to the eyeglass store and a place with sandwiches in glass closets."

"Oh, no. That's midtown. Greenwich Village is different. It's a scene."

I don't ask her what that means because I'll find out soon enough.

We settle on black framed sunglasses with mirrored lenses. I pop them in my pocket as Kat asks the woman at the counter if she carries My Sin perfume. We meet outside and head to the train station. Kat has dyed her hair platinum and wears it straight as spaghetti.

"Tickets," the man in the little wood station says, and we each give him ten dollars but he said it's eleven dollars for the roundtrip fare.

"But we only have ten each," Kat says.

'Trails of troubles," he says, and hands us our tickets anyway. "Next time you give me twelve," he says.

"Up the castle steps," Kat says, and I follow her to a scary cement hole in the ground that smells of pee and we climb the stairs to the open light, the steel tracks, hug our wool coats against the icy wind that stings with ice pick teeth.

We hop on the Jessie James and it rocks along braking at all the towns along the way: New Brunswick, Metuchen, Plainfield, Westfield, Cranford, Nether wood, Newark. People get on and get off. An old woman in a pea green coat and hat drags a little boy by the hand and they sit in front of us, the boy standing on the seat facing us with a snotty nose and chapped cheeks. He looks somewhere around three years old, about the age Zuzu would be now and a picture pops up in my head of Zuzu with her root beer eyes and dandelion hair and my heart cracks so I look away out the window at the low metal buildings and heaps of stone.

At the Newark station I follow Kat like a ghost. I could end up on the wrong train to a place I've never been or even a different state and that scares me but Knife asks me if I'm going to spend the rest of my life scared like Grandma saying: *Lord help me.*

At Penn Station New York we move with the crowd up the stained cement steps to the elevator that I am afraid of at first then we walk out into the cold sunlight, the barking cars and coast down Broadway. We barely need to walk there's so many people crossing like one body, freezing in the bone cold, blue-finger cold, ice cube toes cold. I see people disappear a little at a time into the ground, fog coming from their mouths, steam snaking up from iron and climbing the tall buildings to the sky. We float past signs for peep shows, an xxx movie house, a strip club and Kat points them out and tells me it's where old dirty men go to see naked women and yank on their boners. I never knew about these things in the country. But, maybe I did

We step over bottles and bodies in the gutters, crumbled newspapers, old men on benches, a black horse with a silver carriage, diamonds in windows, people with tin cups, the smell of pizza, bread, peanuts and pee taking turns in the air. I didn't see any of this the time with Grandma, it's like the boardwalk at the lake, only this boardwalk is a sidewalk with way more people and every kind of dog, every color of baby in carriages spin wheels through the slush.

"Don't lose me," Kat says, her cheeks red, her platinum hair smacking her face, her eyes stone cold blue. "You'd never find your way home."

I remember all the times Willy and me were lost in the woods before we discovered the pond but we always found our way back.

"Don't be so sure of that," I say.

I trail Kat down the stairs to cars like silver bullets where people hang onto shower curtain bars like monkeys and we zip along below the city streets to the stop at MacDougal, trip the stairs to the street and enter Wonderland: the smell of cinnamon and skunk in the wind, mopey people dressed in black smoking cigarettes pinched in leather gloves, a midget woman with an orange cat on her shoulder, a store front filled with skeletons hung from cord.

"What's that skunk smell?"

"This is Greenwich Village," Kat says. "There's weed everywhere."

"Where?"

"Not that kind, silly. Weed. Grass. Makes you high."

The streets are curvy, narrow and made of stones that shine with melted snow and flecks of diamonds when the sun shines.

"This way," Kat says, and I track her to the lit sign that says: Café Wha? on the corner.

Inside it's dark and smoky, a cigarette and coffee bean smell, candle wax and rows of black leather booths, girls with straight hair, bangs and black eyeliner. One with gold hair wears a red beret. We never did get our berets. There are candles at the booths and a stage with a mic and a wooden stool and a girl with a red guitar.

Holy, Knife says.

"Try not to look so, you know, spooked," Kat whispers.

I study the floor, disconnected shapes of marble laid out like a crazy quilt.

We order coffee and Kat opens her pocketbook under the table and shows me two tiny bottles of Baileys Cream.

"This is what I meant by a happening," Kat says. "Far out, right?"

"Yea," I say. "I wish we came here all those days we skipped class."

"True," Kat says, and knocks on her pack of Newport's. "But you need money here."

After the waitress walks away Kat opens the bottle slides it up the elastic cuff of her coat and in a flash she pours a shot in our coffee and we watch the steam curl as the girl with brown hair and a black guitar sings about glory.

I feel stupid but I have to ask Kat anyway.

"Have you, you know, smoked weed?"

"With my brother a few times."

On stage the glory girl steps down and a girl with long blonde hair sits on the stool and tunes a red guitar and then she starts to strum her fingers across the strings, her hair in waves over her shoulders and the black sleeves of her sweater. She hums then sings out with a voice like honey a song about a bowl of oranges.

"Is it like drinking?"

"No. It's a mind trip. Each time is a different color."

"I want to try it," I say, hoping it's not like the cough syrup. "Does it make you sick?"

"No. It's not like that. If there's any around," Kat says.

I never heard anyone sing about a bowl of oranges before and it's like waking up, like I've been sleeping. It's like discovering the pond with the bicycle. A surprise.

"I don't ever want to go home," I say.

"Joie de vivre. It digs right?" Kat says.

"Nothing like this in Lockwood," I say. "Nothing."

I don't know what Kat's French words mean but I feel them like the stars that time in Mr. Zagoria's class trip to the planetarium, skipping diamonds, not caring where you end up in the black sky. In the light from a high window the smoke is colored blue and I watch as it twists through the dark and blurs the ceiling beams.

I notice a guy with curly hair and nice eyes that look green under the light. He wears a black cap and carries a guitar and there is something about him that makes me gawk.

"Who is that guy, Kat?"

Kat scopes out the room.

"The one wearing the cap," I say.

"I never saw him before. Only been here a few times. With Nick," she says.

The girl on stage finishes the song and sings another about robbery and there's a few cheers but not many people yet and she steps down from the stage and her hair catches light and candles flicker as she glitters by.

The guy in the black cap steps up to the stage with a contraption around his neck that holds a harmonica and he lugs a big guitar. He's skinny and plays with the mic sliding it up and down till it locks into place then he bangs out some chords, blows into his harmonica, fiddles with his cap, clears his throat, taps the mic that makes a loud fizz sound.

"I'm gonna play a tune written by Woody Guthrie," he says. "It's called Airline to Heaven."

Kat and me are frozen to the leather though neither one of us know who the hell Woody Guthrie is.

"There's an airline plane
Flies to Heaven every day
Past them pearly gates
If you want to ride this train
Have your ticket in your hand
Before it's too late."

204

His voice sounds like sand mixed with glue and when he sings it's like a highway with cars made of words that travel fast going in their own direction down a road not on a map. I feel for my airplane charm to make sure it's still there and he looks my way and nods and I freeze with his stare for a minute before he sings on.

> "If the world looks wrong
> And your money's spent and gone
> And your friend has turned away
> You can get away to Heaven
> On this aero-plane …"

My head is loose, Knife says.

His voice isn't that good really but you pay attention.

Kat and me share a look.

'Bloody good,' she says.

When the guy with the black cap finishes his songs there's more people than before and they whistle at him and some just sit like they don't know whether to clap or boo and Kat and me never want to hop the Jesse James back to Lockwood.

"Let's go outside," Kat cat says. "If someone hands you a joint, inhale like a cigarette but deeper and hold the smoke in your lungs as long as you can. Not everyone gets off the first time."

We lean against the building and light our cigarettes waiting for something to happen then before we go back inside two Poe guys and the kid with the cap walk out the door and light up. The smoke is strong, skunk mixed with cattail weed. On fire.

"A hit?" the guy in a gray pea coat," says.

"Sure," Kat says, and he nabs her the joint, a fat cigarette, the kind I saw Daddy Dead roll one time with leaves of Virginia tobacco.

I zoom in and watch so when my turn comes I won't look like an asshole. We lean in a circle toward one another, close to the building, the air chill, icy, mixed with frost from our breath and the smoke from the skunk. The joint passes to me and I suck it in and jam my lungs but end up hacking like a dog. It comes my way the second time. I don't suck in as much. Keep it in my lungs till I am ready to burst and the smoke drifts out blue. A woman bundled in black, wheels a baby carriage, the baby buried in a cloud of blankets, the carriage bumps over the stones and I stare and wonder who invented it, the carriage. Who thought it up? A carriage with a *hood*. But then I remember the stagecoach and cowboy movies.

"Where you shacking up?" the Poe guys asks the guy with the cap.

"Home is where I Find Myself," the guy with the cap answers.

WOAH, Knife says.
"The sidewalk is shaking," I say.
"It's the subway," Kat says.

The guy in the black cap is standing next to me, his pant leg touches mine and I stare at the side of his face, half smile, eyes that say he knows something I don't. Then the three of them walk back

under the sign that blinks: Cafe Wha? Café Wha? Cafe

What?

"Feel Anything?" Kat asks.

"Noooooo," I say.
We lean against the cool stone and light another cigarette and I

see a full FuckinG Moon like it's the first time, my feet on the crystal sidewalk, head in the stars. Moon. MOON. MOON MOON MOON. MOON. Hooked to a star? Or,

FLOATing? HOW? It's huge and yellow tonight and the brownish spots are clear--two at the top like raggedy windows and

one on the bottom open. A SKULL with babies leaping out, chains of babies like dolls snipped from black paper holding hands. But then I see it is a projection from a toy store window, dolls or small skeletons.

GRoovy. Knife says.

You could throw a L-A-A-A-A-s-o around it, George.
"Remember that in the movie?" I say out loud.
Does the rain FALL? Knife says.

We've watched it a M-i-l-l-i-o-n times on

MILLION$$$$$$$$$$$MOV-

IE, eight o'clock weeknights channel 5.

A MOMENT in Time, Knife says.

I wish Willy could see how much BiGGER the CITY moon
is and how King Kong's shadow sits on the Empire State Building.

U N D E R t o n e s, Knife says.
"What???"
The shadows.
"Do you have the matches?" Kat says, and I see there are cars splash-
ing snow onto the sidewalk, neon blinking in the wet street and I
pull the matches from my pocket and study the flame at the end of
Kat's white cigarette.

"How are we here? On earth I mean, turning, and not F A L L I N G
?"

"G r a v i t y," Kat says, and the word stretches out and floats
in the air to the other side of MacDougal and back again.
"How L   O   N   G have we been out here?" I say. "It seems

like hOURS."

"Look," Kat says, "The moon is the same color as COrnbread. I guess I'm hungry. Have you ever really, really tasted corn-

bread? With BUTTer?" Kat says.

I smell Grandma's oven, her cornbread made of yellow kernels, or,

TEETH, depending. Teeth left behind on the Cob.
"I want cornbread SOOOOOOOOOOOOOOOOO

OOOOOoooooooooooooooo fucking bad," I say. "How does it

F E E L?" Kat says.

"W h a t?" I say.
"Let's go back in," she says, and I follow her inside where the cups and spoons are

C L A N G I N G. Someone has taken our booth but we grab another.

"Two EXp--r--e--s--s--o--s," Kat says.

The guy with the cap gets back on stage and blows into his

H A R M O N I CA and the notes play like I've never really heard music awake before.

"Where R R R we?"
"Café Wha?" Kat says.
I notice colors reflect in my coffee and realize the guy in the cap is floating in my cup, and he strums his guitar there on the black surface and blows his harmonica and sings at the same time and his words roll

out of his mouth hard like different colored Stones.

In the R a i n, Knife says.

"I think I like this," I say.

A guy with dark rimmed glasses and a beard is on the stage and he is reading words sewn together and some of his words go off like little word explosions in my head. Words I never heard strung together before: *hydrogen jukebox, naked-starving-hysterical, supernatural darkness, steam heat and opium.*

Holy, Knife says.

And the words stay behind in my head staring little fires.

"That's Allen Ginsberg," I hear a girl behind us say.

"Wow," Kat says.

"I'm Starving," I say. It sounds so silly because I'm not *really.* If I were all my ribs would be poking out and I'd be nakedstravinghysterical and almost Dead.

"You're Stoned, Kat says.

"What Time is it?" Kat says, and we see it is time to go. We've run out of money.

Jessie James rocks us home with a rhythm and beat like music and it nearly puts us to sleep but then a hard stop at the Lockwood station and the engine reels us forward and we stumble down steps,

that smell of rubber, that lead to the Biack Path lined with lamps, clear bowls of yellow alongside a clock with black hands that point an arrow toward the green glow of: 2:49.

"We're stuck inside of Lockwood with the I high school blues again," Kat says.

Juju

WE'VE BEEN CUTTING CLASSES for a month and now we're in a black sink hole of hell and in trouble. Lockwood High has papers on us and Knife thinks this could be another juju headed our way, a cat 5.

We make it back to the Village a few more times, huddle in the cafe spilling spoons of liquor in black coffee. We try to look dead and beat with leopard eyes and coats, thigh high black skirts and "Kick'em dead" boots, all of it stolen. On the city streets we see people in rags crying in boxes under neon and stars, some without teeth, a guy with no arms preaching on 52nd Street, we stare into store windows on 5th Avenue, mannequins with lemon-suck faces wearing animals, we hear poets read about steam heat and opium, building harpsichords under the Brooklyn Bridge in the dark, we go to Washington Square park where there is holy water we and huddle beneath the arch, we shiver through snow and ice but nothing matters except all we want is to be out of Lockwood High School. I memorize the details, the thirteen stars.

A moment in space, Knife says.

But first we have to go to court and to make it worse we have to go with our mothers.

The courthouse is made of melted white marbles and it smells like an aquarium inside. The judge says we have to go on a thing called "probation" and report to an officer guy in the building on Bridge Street and if we miss anymore school we are being sent away to some kind of school on a farm, or a crazy house, or Barbizon, or a cave on a mountaintop, or a place like in the movie *Suddenly Last Summer* where they were going to take the memory part of Elizabeth Taylor's brain out due to cannibalism on a beach where newborn turtles get eaten. We just don't know. And we don't really believe that any of those places exist.

"Habitual truancy is an act of juvenile delinquency," the judge says. "Do you understand that the Lockwood superintendent of the board of education has brought truancy charges against you?"

He has cloudy hair and a mustache in the shape of a hedge and big ears like on the gargoyle on the Grant Building and I can see wires of hair inside his nose. He looks at my mother then Kat's.

"Do you understand these girls can't miss school again," he says.

"I do, your honor," my mother says.

"Yes," Kat's mom says.

"Why haven't you made sure they were in school?"

"I work. I'm a key punch operator at IBM, your honor. I didn't realize."

Kat's mom says the same thing. She's a teller at the First Union Bank.

Then he turns to me and Kat and I know what Kat is thinking.

"I sentence each of you to one year of probation," he says. "Failure to meet the obligations set out by your probation officer will result in further charges and detention," he tells us.

He signs papers and we go to an office where a young guy tells us probation means we'll be supervised and need to follow rules like go to school and don't break laws. Our jail sentence has been suspended.

"You have been continuously defiant of school rules," the probation guy says, as he taps his pencil on his desk. "You are habitually truant. This is a court order. It has the weight of the law. Do you understand?"

Kat and me look at one another and I know she is thinking: this guy is an asshole. But we don't really understand any of it and don't want to.

Now we have to meet with him once a week but not together, alone. I don't like this.

For a while we force ourselves through the big red doors of Lockwood High but we are both behind in all the classes and can't figure out what is going on and the reading assignments are piled up and so are the exams we have to make up. Still, we go and sit in the back of our classrooms like we both had lobotomies, all the missing information. I slide down in my seat and keep my head down and after a few weeks we take a day off and write sick slips that say we have a contagious virus and sign our mother's names and when the truant officer comes to the door we don't answer it.

We're only thirteen, well Kat is fourteen but I figure they won't do anything to us because we're not really breaking any laws that they *know* about.

"It's a free country," I say.

"We have to go to school," Kat says. "It's the bloody law. One thing I don't want is those assholes on my back."

"No way. How can they make you go to school? I already know how to read and write and add and subtract and multiply. Everybody's going to stare at us. I'm not going to dissect any frogs or baby pigs. Not. If we can quit at sixteen, why not quit before?"

"I know but my mother says I have to. There are laws in New Jersey like it or not."

So we walk up Davenport and I say hello to the colored girl who is so pretty with her beehive but she just gives us the look.

"Why does she hate us?" I say.

"Because we're white and we owned slaves."

"I never owned slaves. That was my father's family," I say.

We are becoming our other selves with each step. Our honor selves. Good students who earn A's. The selves that finish assignments and ace exams. One of the holy. We're going to help one another study and cram. We'll dress in skirts and puffy sweaters like the honor girls and we're going to take glee club and learn to twirl. Kat says, maybe she should be in the marching band and play the tuba. But when we get to the big red double doors and smell rubber, lead and disinfectant and we want to run.

"I don't want to be here," I say.

Kat looks at me and takes a deep breath.

"I *have* to go to asshole class," she says.

We walk down the corridor and our heels click hollow against the waxed tiles.

In science lab Mr. Boyle tells me I have a lot of work to make up. They've already moved onto fetal pigs and I'm still on the frog.

I stare down at the chart and pick up the scissors. I try not to look at the small grayish bodies of the baby pigs. My stomach is queasy but I force it down and read the chart in front of me but I can't stop thinking frog soup.

1. Place the specimen in the dissecting pan ventral side up.

212

2. Use scissors to lift the abdominal muscles away from the body cavity. Cut along the midline of the body from the pelvic to the pectoral girdle.
3. Make transverse (horizontal) cuts near the legs.
4. Lift the flaps of the body wall and pin back.

David Solomon sits next to me with his baby pig and his scalpel and the room buzzes with voices and the sound of metal hitting metal and lids being unscrewed from jars and the air filled with death and vinegar.

I snip open the fat belly and the smell goes up my nose and I gag when I peel back the skin and see orange and yellow spaghetti and run for the door, make it to the girl's room and puke a corn muffin into the toilet and the corn kernels float to the top like yellow teeth.

Sally Sands is posed at the mirror with her blonde ponytail, doing her lipstick.

"Hey in there," she says. "Are you pregnant? Everybody says you are. Is that why you haven't been in school?"

"What are you talking about?" I say, slamming the gray door.

"Everyone's talking about you," she says. "You and your friend. They're saying you're both pregnant by Johnny Smits."

"You're lucky I don't kill you," I say and I am a lion with a thousand teeth.

I make it to the side door and run all the way home.

The next day I tell Kat: "There's a rumor we're both pregnant."
"What?"
"I can't do it. Let's go to the park."
"But we have to report to asshole probation," she says.
"I'm scared of him," I say.
"He's just a stupid asshole probation officer," she says.

We met with him once, first Kat then me but I couldn't talk to him, only nod my head and twist my charm bracelet, hold on to the silver airplane. He is young and cute with brown hair and eyes and he makes me nervous, ashamed for skipping all those days. He asks questions. "How are things at home? Am I doing my homework? Who am I hanging out with? What about my father? Did

213

I make up all the work I missed at school? Do I date any boys? Do I have regular periods?" After he asks me that I know I can never go back and I fly home down Davenport Street.

I unlock the door to my room, yank out my travel book and flip straight to Paris. I can't say the names of the streets except for a few, De Belleville and Saint Martin. At night the Eiffel Tower is lit with a million stars.

Don't forget the Yiddish bakeries, Knife says, and I flip to the page with the yellow store front, a gold bunch of wheat painted against a shining black surface and I concentrate hard until I am there in my head making my way around the twisty Paris streets.

In the morning, the rabbis will hand me free samples, lemon cookies, chocolate cake. There is a photo of two rabbis at the bottom of the page with white beards, wearing black hats. They bake pastries inside huge black ovens. I think about what would happen if my whole family was there. Everyone except Daddy Dead: Grandma flipping pies under the Eiffel Tower and Mother Blind dancing at the Moulin Rouge, or she can be taking bows in a Shakespeare play with a red velvet curtain. Willy could build mechanical sculptures that write messages on pieces of paper, then throw them in the air at every corner, all the people running after the notes, looking for answers to their questions. There won't be probation officers or school laws or papers served in Paris and Grandpa can work at an angel factory and apply his years at Mack Truck making sure the wings curve at just the right angle, me and Kat clicking down the winding cobblestone in black boots, spotting all the assholes.

But New York is a lot closer.

We hop the Jessie James. At Café Wha? we hear the guy in the cap sing: "So long New York. Howdy, East Orange."

"Hey, that's in New Jersey," Kat says.

"Why would anybody sing about it?" I say.

Inkblot

MOTHER BLIND LEANS TOWARD THE KITCHEN WINDOW and a circle of sun lights the red in her hair. On the stove a pot of water bubbles with egg noodles and she stirs the steam, her eyes faraway, steam snaking to the ceiling. When the noodles are done she'll melt in butter and salt from the pale green shaker, ridges all around, a silver lid filled with tiny holes and dented from Grandma banging it on the soup pot.

Last week the school called IBM and Mother Blind had to meet with Mr. Carpenter the principal with his suit and bow tie and swivel chair. He tells her I'm in a fix for cutting so many classes again and I am headed into traffic on the wrong side of the road and Lockwood High is ready to press charges, serve papers, run me over with a school bus, a lawn mower, a train with boxcars. He says he's arranged an evaluation and that means inkblots and word puzzles, lobotomy. "When I say a word, you say the first word that comes to mind," the woman tells me.

"Slope."

Slip.

"Green."

Frog.

"Bird."

Fly away.

Next, she shows me cards with inkblots, cannibals, men on motorcycles, cauldrons of fire and a sky full of babies. That was last week and yesterday she called my mother and probably told her I'm on track to become a serial killer.

Mother Bind opens the freezer and a cold cloud of air puffs across the room. "I want to tell you a story," she says, and drops ice cubes into the glass.

"There's some things you need to understand. The counselor said you are very angry."

"Me? Angry? I saw a dead man on a motorcycle and cannibals. What's wrong with that?"

215

She pours coffee over the ice and the cubes crack inside the glass.

I'm cutting a stack of cards, trying to shuffle and cut the way Daddy Dead taught me a long time ago shuffle, shuffle, cut, cut, smack on the table, gin rummy.

"I want you to know your father wasn't always an idiot," she says.

Is the circus coming? Knife says.

"I don't care about him no more," I say

"Any more," she says and sighs, and her shoulders slump.

She tells me the story about Daddy Dead being adopted when he was ten and his real daddy a drunk that his mother divorced to marry the tall man with the egg farm and the pig out back. Before long the tall man adopts my father and for a while the other father, the drunk one, left them alone in the white farmhouse with the round oak table and the yard with the chickens and eggs and the pig and the duck, my father happy with his new adopted self and new name.

I pull at the threads unraveling from my blouse then go back to cut my cards and Mother Blind rings her spoon on the side of the pot and outside the one o'clock siren blows from the football field.

My mother stirs the wooden spoon and stares at the boiling water, not looking at me, but into the pot as if it's telling her the story like alphabet soup. "Your father had a colored nanny," she says. "He loved her and was punished for loving her, clinging to her legs when she left."

"One day," she says. "Something terrible happened."

"An apocalypse?" I say. I learned about it from Rosemary Ryan who is Catholic.

She tells me that the Richmond high school, where my father was a senior, the other father, the real one, shows up in his police uniform and waits until my father is out of his classes. He says to Daddy Dead, who wasn't Daddy Dead yet: "I'm your real Daddy."

Then the real daddy walks away in his uniform with the badge flashing and goes home and shoots himself in the heart.

"His name was Virginius Parker McGowan," she says, and how that is my real last name and not King but King is my real legal name, but not really, not blood and I think about legal and names and how Aunt Oink got the name King legal but not us because there's no holy matrimony and it's not legal and stamped by the government and signed on the line.

216

I square the cards off and stack them on the table, pull each thread of my gauzy white blouse until it is free and hold it up to the light, watch it disappear.

Outside the wind is crazy and I watch Mr. Winger's lawn chair somersault down the sidewalk then tumble across the street toward the highway.

Mother Blind says, that my South grandmother had a switch, same one she used on Daddy Dead and she swatted me with it but I grabbed it out of her hand then I laid down with it in the crib and went to sleep. There's more grandparents that are great and came from Donegal, Ireland and Scotland. She says my great grandfather joined the civil war rebels and died and then the great grandmother ran the coal and ice business and they called her the Ice Queen of Richmond and that is where my crazy comes from.

I imagine a woman with white hair and a long black dress with an ice crown on her head and she is gliding on a frozen river, twirling around then skating away, her blades silver and sharp enough to kill people.

"How come I didn't know this before?"

"You knew about Ireland," she says. "And Scotland. But I wanted to keep The South in the South."

"Tell me everything."

Mother Blind turns on the facet, and the water knocks somewhere in the pipes then rushes out and the sun catches on the collar and pocket of her dress and she tells me the story of how she met Daddy Dead in New York City on an autumn day, the trees washed red and yellow. He was in the Army, handsome with black hair and blue eyes. He was smart and played a Gibson guitar and sang "Your Cheatin' Heart" and she sang "Crazy" by the fire. He was a pilot with a Piper Cub and a photographer with a twin reflex camera. They set up house in the blue bungalow with the willow tree out back and yellow pies on the windowsill.

"Can we move to New York?" I say.

"Of course not!" she says. "You're not listening to me! I am trying to tell you a story."

"Alright," I say, and cut the cards in half.

"The blue bungalow. Do you remember it?"

217

A moment in time, Knife says.

I remember Daddy Dead lift me on his shoulders, the green backyard, I'm wearing my white sundress, red around the edges, bow at the back. He rubs my back and smells of apples, cinnamon, he is a movie star. Every night I wait by the door holding my papers for him to sign. When he picks me up I rest my head on his shoulder, he calls me baby girl, no, not really.

Tell the truth, Knife says.

He calls me *nigger baby*.

"We were happy for a while," Mother Blind says. "Very happy. You remember that?"

"I remember a lamb on my crib that glowed in the dark," I say. "And the blue tree at Christmas. I remember the colored doll in the gold box."

Supernatural, Knife says.

"That was your father's idea," she says. "It was a joke. He's a tease."

I shoot her my mean eye.

"He isn't all bad but if you bait the hook, well the fish will bite and that's what happened." She tosses yellow noodles in a blue bowl and sprinkles on the snowy cheese.

I fan my cards on the table. Jokers and spades.

In bed I wonder if Toro misses me. I hope not because I want him to be happy but I miss him, his head on the pillow just like mine. I dream of different ways to get him back and hide him in my room. Willy and me are taking a bus back to the Texaco. There we can cut through the field that runs into Cherokee Road toward the dead end. We'll pack our flashlights and bring peanut butter sandwiches and a bone I stole for Toro. We think maybe the kid will let us stay at his house, help him watch for trappers and the probation officer won't ever find me.

Knife thinks maybe that way the juju won't get us because she's tracking it and it's locking down, getting closer.

Toro

MOTHER BLIND SAYS WILLY HAS TO GO to Virginia and live with Daddy Dead on the farm with the pig and the round oak table but Willy doesn't want to and I don't ever want to go back to school so we hop the Route 22 bus on our way to the House of Toast Diner. This time we'll make it to Florida. When we get there I'm going to send Kat and postcard and her brother is going to drive her wherever we end up. Knife says the juju is a cat 6 and its eye is heading this way.

I tell Willy about Café Wha? and Greenwich Village and the girl with blonde hair and the guy with the black cap singing a song about a train but he's not really interested until I tell him about the guy who said hydrogen jukebox, then his eyes light up.

We drop coins into the slot and the bus driver asks no questions.

"We're getting out at the House of Toast," I say, and he nods.

He hands us blue tickets and we sit in the back on a long green seat. Out the window, trucks whizz by and tails of black smoke blows out of the dusters.

I've got five dollars saved in the pocket of my jeans and when the bus screeches at our stop we climb down and head straight to The House of Toast.

The waitress asks us what we want to order and Willy says: "*Basghetti.*"

"He means spaghetti," I tell her, but they're all out so we order grilled cheese.

He opens his grilled cheese and sticks some French fries and the pickle slice in the middle then closes it back up.

"*Welp,*" he says, and shrugs his shoulders.

The waitresses wear blue uniforms and white aprons, fishnets on their heads, one with teased up hair and red lips gives Willy a wink.

We cut through the field on toward the dead end on Cherokee. It looks different than before. Not as long. At our old house we can't believe what we see—there is another house on top of it piggyback style. It's big with an upstairs and no qua-qua out back. Where we lived looks so small. How did we fit? But the cherry trees still line the backyard and the dogwood tree out back and there's a patch of dirt where King Car once sat.

"Bugger," Willy says.

It's as if we are ghosts and the house can't see us anymore.

Our swing is gone and over where the dingy-barrow was is a big garage with a basketball hoop, black top, two shiny bicycles.

A head of dark hair flashes out the front door, a tall kid bouncing a basketball. He stares at us.

"Lookin' for something?" he says. "This is a dead end."

"We used to live here," I say.

He jumps up and tosses the ball into the hoop.

"Oh yeah?" he says, and dribbles the ball. "Well, we live here now."

We skip the path to the field, the kid staring till we get to the trees where he can't spy us. We crack branches, beat the ground the way we used to like time travel and we search for the stone hills we built. At the pond we look for signs of King Car, find the rusted fender bobbing near the dirt bank.

Willy picks it up, rips it back into the pond.

"Do you think we'll find the kid?" I say.

"*Bemay*," Willy says.

We poke sticks in the water, feel for King Car but don't hit until Willy shimmies a tree, splits off a limb, punches it deep into the black water and Willy gets a hit and the pond boils rings and bubbles. We find some of our old stone Alamos, sticks with our names carved in, a pile of ashes. I rake a hill of leaves and a plastic teacup rolls out, pink with a blue handle.

Holy, Knife says.

"Let's go find the Stovekin place," I say.

Willy kneels in the dirt, burrows a hole where he buried armies, the spot marked with a red metal flag snapped off our mailbox. He digs out soldiers caked with mud gripping rifles and aiming smack at the sky. Willy lines them up across the clay.

"Which direction should we take?" I say

He leads and we hike toward the hills ahead, past the trees to the north. We walk miles, rest, eat apples, have a smoke.

"It has to be somewhere," I say. "He said there is a sign outside."

Over hills and knots of scrub pine. We climb over a creek with clear flashing water and we spot a herd of deer but still no Stovekin Estate and it's getting dark. I spot a broken sign at the end of a narrow path of rock. It says in green painted letters: *ekin state*, the post cracked down the center.

"This is it, Willy."

We follow the footpath and our sticks gnaw tracks in the wet clay till we discover a white house with green shutters at the end of a lane by a line of the brown heads of bush clover. Their seeds spin in the air. We stop and stare. The house is crippled, leaning to the right, the front porch crumpled. Dark and broken windows, the frames peeling green paint.

"Nobody lives here," I say. "We'll never find Toro."

But Willy crawls over the broken porch and jams open the door.

In between the torn wood I see a paper that reads:

This Property Is Condemned.

"Willy don't." I holler. "It's condemned."

There is another paper stuck to the window that says:

New Jersey State Property No Trespassing

Between the porch floorboards Indian pipe grows and the woody heads brush my knees with their rough shells.

It's ghosty here, a corner where a witch might live, still I trail Willy, stumble over warped floorboard and dive into black space. It's hard to see but then I spot a stack of empty soup cans, bags of garbage, an empty Coke bottle. Willy jumps the stairs, me behind him casing out the mostly empty rooms. I follow Willy up the second set of stairs and the steps creak and groan as we go. At the top is a door, shut, a blue light shining through the crack.

"Is anyone here?" I holler. "Hello?"

I hear a yap and I know it is Toro.

"Ro," Willy yells.

"Hey. Can we come in?"

Willy bangs on the door, it opens and the kid stands there, his yellow hair lit, his eyes flashing.

"I've been waiting for you," he says. "Double trouble."

He still wears black boots with silver buckles but the leather is scuffed and the heels ragged.

"How did you know we were coming?" I say.

221

"Your dog," he says.

I spot Toro in the corner switching his tail, his ears perked.

"*Toro.*"

He chases his tail and the boy opens the door all the way and I run to him and he whines but doesn't look at me, he stares at the wall. With the light I see his eyes aren't black anymore, they're dark blue and filmy. I kiss his head, rub his ears and he barks and licks my fingers. I rub his pink belly.

"How come his eyes look funny?"

"He's blind," the kid says. "Been blind a year now. Otherwise he's healthy and a good watch dog at that. What are you hoodlums up too?"

"We're running away, hitching cross country," I say.

"*Florry-da,*" Willy says.

"Florida," I say, but it sounds empty like something old, the teacup in the dirt.

"Oh really?" he says, and clicks his tongue. He knocks a cig out of a pack of Camels and strikes a match. "Well, I hear you're taking a different kind of trip and you're going to be away for a good long time."

"Huh? What kind of trip?"

"One that don't take you too far," he says.

"What's that supposed to mean?"

He blows smoke from his nose, leans against the wall, his boots crossed. On the floor is a can of tomato soup with a spoon in it.

"I thought you'd be a pilot by now," he says, and snickers.

"I'm learning," I say. "I have a flight manual and we go to the airport and watch the planes take off and land."

"You can't just read manuals. You have to put in flight time."

"I already know," I say.

Willy rummages his sack, snaps out a Salem and we both light up. I plop on the floor and Toro jumps on my lap.

There's stacks of books around the room, some covered in leather and others in cloth, fat hardcover books thick with words and photographs, a few say *Poetry,* a stack of paper and a typewriter. I spot a huge aluminum pipe about seven feet long and there are blankets and pillows inside, a book with the pages flipped with lines of typed words. The kid sees me stare.

"That's my dream tunnel," he says. "You need one of those for your trip. You can dream anything you want in there. Go any place on earth when you read. I've been all around the world."

"Can we stay here?" I say.

"Stay here? You're already trespassing. No. You can't stay. If you try I have my walkie talkie right there and you know who has the other one," he says, and crushes his cigarette on the floor.

"Can't have no underage kids living here. I'm eighteen."

Willy kicks at his sack and looks at the floor. The boy's hair is longer now, down to his shoulders and he pushes it back behind his ears and crosses his skinny legs.

"Will you still take care of Toro?" I say.

"He's mine now," he says. "You know the rules of the Stovekin Estate."

It's dead on dark out and cold and we have to track back to the bus stop and hope we find it before morning. I kiss Toro's head, smell his fur so I can remember it later on.

Willy and me hook on our packs, Willy flicks his flashlight off and on spotlighting the boy's dream tunnel.

"I guess I'll be seein' ya sometime then," the kid says. "When you come back from your trip."

We slip down the trail.

"He don't know nothing," I say.

I can't keep the tears away but Willy pretends he doesn't see.

We dig our way back over the hills and fields of tickseed and water willow, back to the dead end where the windows are lit in our King Car house and we spy straight through to the hallway, all our tribes papered over with flowers.

Baby No

IT'S COLD AND RAINY and there's mud everywhere, so much mud in the football field you could ride a sled in it, it's on our coats, shoes, the sidewalks, the grass and Aunt Oink is in trouble again.

"A curse," Grandma says. "You make room for the devil..."

Aunt Oink is pregnant again, not sure if the father is the guy from Spain with eight kids or the one-night stand at Ralph's Ranch House the night when the Impalas played and she was dancing the Fish and the Mashed Potatoes.

Mother Blind rolls her eyes, fat pink rollers in her hair, a mud mask on her face, bubbling chicken cacciatore on the stove, onion clouds over the stove and she says there is a way out of the *situation*—a colored doctor in Edison by the name of Dr. Sash, an office next to the Exxon oil drums off Route 22. Mother Blind said she had *one*, whatever it is. Everything hush-hush. A pitcher of beer sits on the kitchen table, corn cobs bobbing in a pot of salted water, Grandma smacking an avocado into shape.

"I don't know," Aunt Oink says. "Against the law. Esther said to down a bottle of Tanqueray and soak in a hot tub of Epsom salts."

"Tie a string around a lock of your hair." Grandma says. "Then set it on fire and say a prayer."

"Three months gone," Aunt Oink says. "How will I finish nursing school?"

She started nursing school and already learned how to stick a needle in a vein and draw blood.

"Besides, how will I pay for it?" she says.

"Grandpa can take out another loan from the Credit Union," Grandma says.

"Pay for what?" I ask. I'm sitting on the sofa tearing into a Mars Bar and breathing onions.

"Oh just women stuff," Mother Blind says, and lights the tip of her Salem.

Willy's bombarded in his room clicking dials, twisting spools of wire around a television antenna.

"There's a shot." Mother Bind says. "It works sometimes."

"Can't use no coat hanger," Grandma says. "Elsie Hager died of it."

"Died of what?" I say.

Baby-no, Knife says.

I heard something on the news, a woman who died from a knitting needle.

"I'll make you the appointment," Mother Blind says, the smoke of her cigarette snaking up from her French twist. "The sooner the better."

"How'd you become the authority?" Aunt Oink says.

"Well, if that's how you feel you're on your own. Make your own appointment." Mother Blind says, but Aunt Oink don't answer.

On Thursday night I drive with Aunt Oink to Dr. Shay's office. We pass oil drums, white and huge, lined up across a bare field like spaceships glowing with the light of the moon, a greenish tint and it seems we're on another planet, not in New Jersey anymore. I wait in the doctor's office flipping Woman's Day magazines while Aunt Oink gets her baby gone shot.

But a week later we go back because the shot was a blank.

"Will you come with me?" Aunt Oink says. "I'll buy you some wine if you do."

So, we ramble back down route 22 past the green and blue neon bar signs, the billboards advertising Marlboros and correspondence courses, past the rows of spaceships, and on the radio a song called "Take Good Care of My Baby" and we look at each other then Aunt Oink shuts the radio off and stares down the highway, all the wheels spinning in her brain.

Dr. Sasy pops from the door. He's tall and very black, handsome and speaks with a soft accented voice. I flip the magazines and after about a half an hour and I hear Aunt Oink cry out: *It burns* and I wonder if Dr. Sash is lighting matches inside her belly burning baby no to ash. Another half hour and Aunt Oink stumbles through the door, her face pale, her eyes puffy and red.

In the car she pukes three times on the side of the highway. I am never having sex even it's the best thing in the world. Aunt Oink says she's okay to drive now and we peel down 22, drop the spaceships behind us and speed toward Orchard Street.

She asks me to spend the night then she skids off to the liquor store and I watch as she wobbles in the door then stumbles out with a bottle Gypsy Rose.

She makes me a bed on the velvet sofa and pours two glasses of wine. Half way through her wine she doubles over with cramps and tells me her insides are crammed with gauze stuffing like a turkey.

Wha? Knife says.

A candle on the coffee table flickers and I track the time as long drips of wax slide down in puddles on the glass and the flame makes shaky shadows across the red walls. Even the bathroom is painted red now.

"I'm in labor." Aunt Oink hollers.

Boil water, Knife ways.

I freeze. I thought the baby was gone already.

Her cramps come faster and sharper all through the night and she is folded on the floor.

"Should I call an ambulance?" I say.

Never. Knife says.

Aunt Oink shakes her head and says she might get arrested and how I can't tell no one about this *ever*.

At 5:10, the sky is lighting gray and she stops moaning and tells me the pain is over and she has to pull out the stuffing.

"Why did he do that?" I say.

"How should I know," Aunt Oink says. "They don't teach abortion in nursing school."

She shuffles into the bathroom.

"Zoe, come here," she hollers.

I don't want to see but she kicks open the door, bloody gauze is on the floor, so much I can't believe it could all fit inside.

She pokes the bent end of a hanger over the toilet stabbing the bloody water.

"Look," she says.

In the bowl there is a baby bobbing in the water, pink and tiny with arms held in and legs bent at the knees, tucked up to its belly as if it trying to hang on. She jabs at it with the hanger making sure it is dead I guess. The head is bigger than other parts but no eyes. I can't breathe and everything stands still and I feel sick when she puts her hand on the handle and flushes the baby away.

"Remember this," she says. "This is what happens when you fool around."

I'm thinking I couldn't forget it no matter how hard I try.

"I'm getting dressed for school now," she says, and reaches for her uniform. "Thanks for staying."

"How can you go to school?"

"The pain is gone now," she says. "I can't miss class. I don't want to. Besides, I need something else to think about.

Outside the sun is coming up over the purple hills turning them red and orange.

Gypsy Rose Lee

WILLY IS ON THE FLOOR IN HIS ROOM with his hair sprayed green and a pencil in his mouth. I step over empty cans, monkey grease, chop suey noodles, the crunchy kind, empty potato chip bags, beer bottles, loose nuts and screws rolling in all directions.

"*Wabbershuck?*" he says, his round eyes lit.

I reach into my jeans pocket and pull out some coins.

"All I have is thirty cents," I say.

He charges entry to his room because he serves alcohol.

"*Sic Em,*" he says, and holds out his palm.

The room reeks of grease and oil. A tune blasts from Willy's red transistor, guitars racing down an interstate, zigzagging in and out and over, crashing through the speakers. Willy jumps up and slides across the slippery floor, his blue socks surfboards.

He spins an old turntable with his finger and sinks down next to me, radio parts spread around transmitters, a receiver, a silver antenna, copper wire, a pair of horn shaped speakers, red knobs, dials with numbers and arrows, the base of a blender. On the wall is one of his new formulas:

$$468/f in \text{MHz}$$
$$\leftarrow\leftarrow\leftarrow \ \rightarrow\rightarrow\rightarrow$$
$$710 \text{KHz} = \text{½ wavelength} = 659 ft$$

He's grown tall, scrawny and his green hair waves below his ears.

"What are you building now?"

He's wearing a plaid flannel shirt and Grandpa's old silk tie.

"*Rad-o-machine,*" he says. "Mars. *Buzz-ware.*"

He's connecting copper wire to the motor of the blender. On the window sill is a can of lighter fluid, an empty green bottle of Gypsy Rose with Lee scribbled under Gypsy Rose, and a Playboy centerfold that is taped to the glass window pane, a redhead not wearing anything except red lipstick hanging alongside a can of motor oil.

"Doof-wolfers to Mars?" I say.

That is Willy's word for speakers.

Lately, even I have a hard time understanding him. In school he is a genius at math and science but the teachers gave up on his language skills so they let him do math and science projects in the lab and they are helping him write his very own dictionary.

"*Roof-totters and shimmy-gigs,*" he says, and points to a heap of reels and strung out tape.

He swivels a penknife, jacks open the blade, aims and stabs the nude redhead.

Glitter is in the basement with the washers and dryers. His girlfriend. He tells me he she plays a black guitar and writes and sings songs in Willy language. The last one she wrote was called *Doorshock* and he listens for it on his transistor. I don't think Glitter is real.

He tells me she wears black boots that come up to her thighs.

Groovy, Knife says.

There is a bar set up in his closet, our old wooden coasters turned upside down, a bottle of Seagram's, ginger ale and Thunderbird. He mixes himself a cocktail and stirs it with a broken piece of antenna. It's easy to buy liquor in town, you just ask one of the bums outside Jimmy's and pay them with a swig.

"Where's mine?"

He hands me a glass and I take a chug and we light our Salem and blow smoke through our noses and Willy spins O's through the haze.

I ask Willy if he thinks the Stovekin boy is taking good care of Toro and he tells me he is because he can see him through an old television picture tube in his closet and we don't have to worry. Ziggy is in the tv tube keeping watch over things. In his crazy head part of him is still six years old.

He taps copper levers in code so the martians will know we are here on Orchard Street in Lockwood, New Jersey in our crummy apartment house with the peeping Tom's, steel wash lines and garbage houses. If he gets the code right the Martians will be at his window and we'll get to ride the green neon saucer. There are wires that travel from his bed out the window hooked up to antennas that tap out code to wake him in the night when the Martians buzz him.

"I'm in a lot of trouble," I tell him. "I might be going away but not to Mars."

"Heavy," he says, and offers me another cocktail.

"It must be like boarding school where the rich girls go to study which fork to use."

Willy clicks on the Frappe button and the room fills with rotten egg smell before the blender motor catches fire.

"Kat and me went to Greenwich Village," I say.

"*Yup*," he says.

"I know I told you but I didn't tell you everything. I smoked weed."

His eyes drill me to the floor, then he moves on to his wires and antennas.

"Kat says there are all kinds of happenings there. During the day they have acts, comedians, strippers, and magicians."

This gets his attention.

"*Dang!*"

"We'll take the train one day," I say, but he's already on to squirting different patterns of lighter fluid across the floor and he says: *Raggy* out of nowhere and her name hangs in the cigarette smog and there's a quiet blue chill in the air but I don't ask him any questions.

Jelly Jam

MOTHER BLIND GOT A PROMOTION and that means more money but not much. She practices walking in her heels with a Shakespeare book on her head and afterward she reads the book and memorizes the lines so she can repeat them at work and wow everyone. She's decked out in a pink sweater with the rhinestone buttons and patent leather heels, ready for a night of rock n' roll and fast dancing at Jasper's.

One of her boyfriends is a guy with blond hair and muscles and he don't like me and Willy. He says we are rude to him just because Willy tied his shoes together in a hundred knots and I never say hello, and pretend not to see him. We don't like strangers sleeping over and Mother Blind kissing them. But when she has a boyfriend over she forgets about me getting home before midnight.

Kat tells her mother she's staying over at my apartment and I tell mine I'm staying over Kat's. At night we go to a diner called Mary Lou's Jelly Jam and order grilled cheese, fries, lemon pie for dessert, put quarters in the record box and out comes the Duke of Earl. They mostly have old songs from a couple years ago. When we spend all our quarters we slip out the door as the waitress flips through the swing doors to the kitchen. I wear my tight leather pants and jacket and Kat her black capris and white shirt.

"I'm hungry," Kat says, and we walk up Maple toward the highway where Mary Lou's flashes pink and blue neon. From a block away you can see the aluminum siding and it mirrors the speeding cars that look as if they are racing straight through the diner walls. It's shaped like a bullet, like a subway car. Inside, we pick our favorite booth by the window next to the door so we can make a fast getaway.

"I'll have a grilled cheese with tomato and fries," I say. "And a lemonade."

"Me too," Kat says, and the wrinkled waitress with teased hair writes it down on her pink pad. There's a little hat on her head that looks like a boat pinned to a wave.

We hear the swoosh of the door and turn our heads and in comes five James Deans. They pick a booth across from ours and sit, their knees bumping under the table their legs are so long. They're old enough to drive a Chevy Imperial, blue with a white roof. I notice the lookers. Only one is good looking though they are all pretending to be. I never kissed a boy and don't think I much want to yet but probably soon.

They order hamburgers and fries and cherry Cokes all around then the best looker calls across the aisle at us.

"Aren't you girls a little young to be out this time of night"" he says. "How old are you?"

I light my Salem and blow the smoke at his face and say: "Aren't you boys a little young to be out at night?"

"A wise ass," he says. "Come on, you can't be more than fourteen more likely thirteen."

"It's not polite to ask a girl her age?" I say.

I'm feeling the zombie cocktails Kat and me drank before.

"I like those pants you're wearing," he says. "Did you paint them on?"

They get a good laugh out of this and I give him the killer look Knife taught me and don't blink. Kat has her head down in her lemonade.

Slay, Knife says.

"A guy could get the wrong idea about you in those pants," he says. "Where'd you get them at the jail bait store?"

I suck the bottom of my glass and it makes a loud slurp.

"I'm bored," Kat says. "Let's get outta here. This is deadsville, man."

"Hold on!" the boy says. "We're going to a party at midnight. Time enough to finish our grub and take you girls with us. Keg shindig and you can drink all the beer you want."

"What brand of beer?" Kat says. "I only drink Miller."

"Well we must of knew you were coming then. How about it? You aren't scared are you?"

"I don't know," the boy with the butch hair says. "How'll we all fit?"

"They can sit on our laps," the cute one says.

Kat and me check each other and we're both thinking, go.

"You sure you got Miller?" Kat says. "If you say you do and you

232

don't you're an asshole," she says.

Kat and me wait till the waitress pops in the swing door and make a getaway.

We pile in the car and I sit on the cute boy's lap, Kat on the other end of the seat with buzz boy. Kat never kissed a guy either but this might be the night we both get it over with.

Down the highway there are neon lights from the bars and the strip joints and the guy at the wheel is speeding, windows rolled down, the radio blasting "Only the Lonely" and we're headed for a shindig. But the car turns off Route 22 and cuts a side road and I'm not sure where we are. The car brakes and I spot the blacktop of a huge parking lot.

"Where's the party?" I say.

Outside it is coal black except for one thin line of blue neon along the edge of a sign across the highway. Trailer trucks hum past and shake the ground.

"Right here in the car," the driver, says.

Kat and me stare at one another the thoughts passing from me to her and back around thinking these guys are murderers but we can't let on or act scared.

"Oh yeah? The beer is in the car?" I say.

Silence. I hear Knife in my head say: *Hightail.*

"Let me out," I say.

I dive for the door but it's locked and the kid blocks me with his shoulder.

"I knew you'd be assholes!" Kat says.

The driver taps his nails on the dashboard and someone lights a cigarette and the car's jammed with the windows rolled up.

"I'm thinking those leather pants look pretty inviting."

"Ummm Hmmmm. Tight," another guy says.

"And look at this, stretchy black pants."

I see him rub Kat's bare knee and she smacks his hand.

The boy I'm sitting on pulls me close to kiss me so I smack him across his cheek.

"Damn!" he says. "A spitfire. I could have a good time with you."

"Jimmy," the driver says. "Let's go find some real women," he keys the ignition and takes off down the road.

"Hey!" the kid says. "We were just getting started."

He puts his hand on my thigh and moves it up all the way and I squeeze my legs together as tight as I can till he pulls his hand out.

"I'll kill you," I say.

They drop us off at the diner and tell us we're lucky and we run all the way up Maple and over to Bridge.

"What do you think the assholes were planning to do?" Kat says.

"Kill us," I say.

"Rape is more likely," she says. "That's when a guy screws you without your permission, just in case you didn't know."

"I knew that I say."

"Tomorrow is probation," Kat says.

Morning comes and I don't go and Kat does. She's don't want the law on her ass.

I wear my leather pants and the jacket with the zippers. If I go to probation the cute boy will ask me if I went to school and I'll have to lie or say yes. The probation guy said we are in double trouble and might be sent somewhere like over the rainbow.

The Sheriff

FROM MY BEDROOM I SEE A MAN march up the path, but not just any man. He's dressed in a khaki uniform with a star on the pocket and a hat on his head like the guy on television, Andy Griffith. Only this sheriff has papers in his hand that I imagine, by the way his boots point, are signed and stamped and I wait for him to pass number 124, our number, but he turns, climbs the steps of our porch stoop and the bell rings and splits my ears three times and I run and hide in my closet.

Mother Blind answers the door and I hear the rumble of the man's voice through the walls. He might be related to the boy at the pond. Maybe I should tell the sheriff I'm a friend of the boy. I know about Flipper and her bike in the pond. I know the boy set the fire. I know he's a trespasser.

Don't serve the papers and we won't tell, Knife says.

But he is already gone.

"You're going to court." Mother Blind yells down the hallway. Her voice is both hard and soft around the edges and I know she is mad and sad at the same time.

Though I want to lock myself in my room for the rest of my life, but she sits with her face in her hands, a cigarette pinched in her fingers and tears down her cheeks telling me I am charged with juvenile delinquency and failure to report to probation.

"I'm sorry," I say, and I am. Sorry to make her more trouble than she already has.

The probation officer told us last week, when we finally had the nerve to show up that we're going to be sentenced. But that's for criminals who rob banks and shoot people. They don't know about the stealing so they can't put me in prison for that.

"Can't we get a lawyer?"

"No lawyers for juveniles," Mother Blind says. "The state is in charge of you now. Nothing to defend, they decide and that is that. You'll just have to take your sugar and lump it."

Fishtails, Knife says.

The phones rings and I know who it is. It's Kat telling me the sheriff served papers on her mother too.

"I bet they just give us more probation," I tell Kat. "This time we'll have to go and not miss any appointments."

"I don't like this," Kat says. "Judges are all assholes."

"Nothing bad will happen," I tell her. "We're just kids. You have to do crimes to get sent away."

That afternoon Willy lit a cigarette at the horse farm and his pant leg caught on fire so he hopped on his bike and rode home till the wind ate the flames but his pants leg made a chimney and the skin on his left leg is melted. Mother Bind says she can't take no more. She drives him to the hospital in Grandpa's car and I stare at the state papers. The stamp says New Jersey. Willy has to get pigskin on his leg and Knife's forehead dents.

Runaway

It's the Friday before the Monday when we have to go to court that Kat and me run away. We take Duke's, the back road that leads out of town and it's a dark and curvy road and when a car comes we duck down in the weeds till it passes then track the road to wherever it leads. There's no moon or stars tonight and it's chilly. We shiver, pull our sweaters tight under the empty sky with one pack of cigarettes and a bottle of codeine cough syrup to get us high. We finally figured out you can't drink half the bottle at once.

There are farms along the way. White barns that glow and fields spread purple out to the hills, meadows where deer leap without a sound. We walk to a clearing, sit on the ground, light a cigarette and pass it back and forth, down a chug of cough syrup. It tastes so bad I almost puke but keep it down and then my body warms up and nothing seems so bad. We watch deer point their heads our way then stand stone still as lawn ornaments until they decide we're okay and go back to munch on the grass. In the dark we see the white of their tails aimed at the black sky.

"Where are we going?" Kat says.

"We'll just follow the road until morning and see where we end up," I tell her.

We talk about periods and I tell her the truth. I tell her I knew about it from school, still, I was eleven and afraid to tell Mother Blind because she don't talk about those things and how I thought Kotex was something you pad your brassiere with. How the first day I got my period was the same day at the awful church camp, bawling the whole time because I was homesick for our little apartment. I didn't want to tell anyone about the blood. I was ashamed so I kept wadding toilet paper in my underwear so the blood wouldn't soak my shorts and that didn't always work out so well. We weave along the road in the dark, the light just beginning over the hill where the sky is gray.

There is a steep hill, so steep it hurts to climb it but when we get to the top the sun burns the edge of a field and farms spread out in front of us, red barns and silos, square fields with rows of green, black and white cows in a line crossing the road to the river, everything in order.

"Wow, I want to live here," I say. "Maybe we can hide out in a barn for a while."

The air smells of hay, clover, cow dung and the only sounds are the blue jays in the trees.

"Yeah," Kat says, "We'd be better off in the city with all the other homeless people."

That is our way out though. You can get lost in the city. They'd never find us. Just some money to get by till we get jobs.

"What do we do now? I'm hungry," Kat says.

"I've got two dollars," I say. "Look, there's a gas station along the highway. Maybe we can rob the cash register. Let's walk there. Probably be a vending machine."

"I'm tired," she says.

"Think of it this way," I say. "You are in prison and about to be hung or electrocuted and you have to walk to your death. Think about that for a minute, how bad that would be. Now compare that to this moment right now. See? This is nothing."

Nothing but a juju, Knife says.

"Stop it," I say.

"Stop what?" Kat says.

When we get to the gas station a man with white hair and silver framed glasses says we can stay for the rest of the day, hang in the garage. He gives us free Cokes, Hostess cupcakes and we sit on a tool bench and gobble them down. Everything smells of gasoline, motor oil and we watch as a Chevy lifts high in the air over our heads and the man works his wrenches. We feel pretty good. We're on our way, really going somewhere. We'll send ourselves over the open roads, fields and gas stations along the highway. We'll make it to Pennsylvania where there won't be papers on us.

The man asks us where we live and what we are doing out of school and we tell him our school is on vacation week.

He ties a red bandana around his head and looks at me with his blue eyes.

"Vacation, huh?" he says. Then he walks away into the store part of the gas station.

We're feeling pretty okay until the police car pulls up and tells us to get in.

The Law Won

I'M ONLY THIRTEEN, NUMB AND SLEEPWALKING passing through the walls of our apartment. Can't wear my jeans to court, so I wear a stupid green dress. Knife says it's not my style but only temporary. I brush on eyeshadow, coat my lids blue so I'll look grown up for the judge, Mother Blind in a black suit, hair in a twist, pearls at her ears and neck. Daddy Dead is supposed be in court but I'm glad he won't be. Mother Blind chain-smokes, paces the kitchen and I keep redoing my eyes, the shadow, black mascara, pale lips, thinking nothing bad can happen if I look good.

Prepare for orbit, Knife says.

"It's time to go," Mother Blind says, and snaps the gold clip of her pocketbook shut. "You shouldn't be wearing makeup. Too late to change. Let's go."

The courthouse is white, and shaped wedding cake style, all the white layers stacking up. On the top is a gold lady tipping a scale, she flashes in the sun and burns my eyes. Inside it's made of stone, smooth, cool when I run my fingers over it. We climb the stairs to the dome painted blue as the sky with gold that's bright around the edges. Kathy and her mother lag behind us on the winding staircase. We climb to the top layer, look down. How would it be to jump, the railing? It only comes up to my thighs. If I dive off they can't send me anywhere except to a morgue and for a second, I think I can do it—jump.

The door is marked: Juvenile Court.

Kat stares at the floor. Everything smells different here like the grave stones that night we drank Thunderbird at the cemetery.

Big wooden chairs are the first thing you see in the courtroom, then a giant desk and an American flag in the corner and we wait for the door to open and the judge to fly through the door in his black robes. Everything about the room is heavy, important, at attention. There is a high ceiling, a painting of an eagle gawking down. Every sound, shoes against tile, the screech of chairs, a hum from the hall, gets trapped on the ceiling then bounces down in echoes. There is a man who stands stiff, and dressed in a dark blue suit, red tie, the collar of his white shirt ringed brown at his neck. He looks straight ahead but I can tell he is spying us with his side glance.

Kat is in a black pencil skirt and red turtleneck, her blonde hair waves over her shoulders. She twists her gold ring, a red birthstone, around her finger and I know she thinks the man in the red tie is an asshole.

Papers and old leather books line the shelves and smell of dust and history like in class, tiny flecks in the air. On the desk it says: The Honorable Judge Leahy.

The door opens with a swoosh of air. It's the probation officer in a dark suit. He sits in the chair to the side of the judge's desk and stares hangdog at the floor. When the judge stomps in, his black robes swish, the thick door bangs, Kathy jumps in her seat and her birthstone dings against the tiles then spins across the floor and the man with the dirty collar bends over and picks it up.

The judge is big, bald, with wire rim glasses and I study his face to see if he is nice but I can tell he's not. He's made of stone like the walls. The chair makes a loud groan when the man in the suit slides the judge's chair out from the desk. The judge wears a fat gold watch on his wrist, a gold ring on his finger. Papers are on the desk and he shuffles them, stopping to read then he looks up at me with his judge eyes, his glasses sliding down, hairs in his nose.

"State your name," he says.

"Zoe King," I say.

My voice comes back around at me.

"And you?"

"Kathy Blue Atwood," she says, in her flat "You're an asshole" voice.

"Do you understand the nature of the charges?" he asks, but we don't know what to say and don't answer at first.

"Answer the question," he says.

"Yes," I say, lying.

"Yes," Kat says, pretending.

"I will read them to you: You are charged with violation of probation and truancy. Code 679 of the New Jersey Board of Education. What is the reason you did not attend school or report to probation after you were told of the repercussions of your failure to do so?"

241

He looks at me then Kat with his eyebrows up and his glasses sliding down from his hairy ears to his nose.

I think the right answer might get us off.

Kat's legs are crossed and she is swinging her left.

"The weather was so nice," I say. "We just wanted to go to the park. We weren't doing anything bad and I was scared of probation. It would be better if the probation officer was a girl. I didn't want to cut open the frogs or pigs in biology class. It made me sick. I couldn't do it."

Mother Blind clears her throat.

Someone coughs.

The leg of a chair scrapes.

The judge stares through me with his gray speckled eyes and the room is silent till he turns to Kat and asks her the same question but she doesn't answer, she just swings her leg. Then he asks my mother and Kat's mother how come they can't control us.

"I'm alone. Her father lives in Virginia and I have to work full time," my mother says.

"My daughter was never in trouble until *her*," Kat's mother tells him and points her finger at me.

The judge taps his pen on the desk and looks at me then Kat.

"You are incorrigible," he says, looking at me, and the word bounces back from the ceiling and back again I wish I knew what it meant.

Kat's mom cries and blows her nose and I wonder if the judge will say: "Order in the court." But he doesn't, he reads from a paper held close to his eyeglasses and I notice the paper doesn't bend.

I look at my hands, the lines crossing over a triangle, my fingers numb and cold but my palms sweaty.

"Your honor," the clerk says, and hands him another stiff paper then walks away. The soles of his shoes tap against the floor like typewriter keys.

The judge clears his throat and scratches his head.

I turn my bracelet around on my wrist. Only the silver plane is left and I hold onto it and run my finger over the tiny wings.

"Your honor," my mother says. "May I please address the court."

He looks up from his mustache, his bushy eyebrows raised.

"You may," he says.

"Your honor, my daughter is not a bad girl. She has problems and I am alone and have to work and her father lives in Richmond. Please, be lenient and I promise to send her to live with her father in Virginia where she will be more closely supervised and will no longer be an issue here in New Jersey."

I lose my breath for a second. I can't believe what she said and I'm not sure now what is worse, getting sent away to a girl's school or getting sent away to my father.

"The court has made its decision," he says. "You may be seated."

Kat's mother stands.

"Your honor," she says. "I'd also like to address the court."

The judge sighs and says," "You may." But I can tell he's in a hurry to get this over with.

"My daughter was always in school, she was studious and obeyed rules until she met this one," she says, and points her finger at me again. "Her father died two years ago. I too have to work. Please, consider."

"You may be seated," he says.

I want to shrink into my hand and run down all the paths on my palm.

The judge leans forward and stares at me then Kat. He clears his throat again and I flip the plane on my wrist back and forth. Then he speaks.

"I hereby sentence you for an indefinite term to The New Jersey Training School for Girls," he says, and the words lock shut. I hear my mother gasp. There's an animal sound and the floor collapses under my chair and I fall into a pit of nothing familiar or real all the pieces of me coming apart.

Training?

The man with the red tie and dirty neck says:" This way."

Kat's mother cries, "God help us."

My mother sobs, hugs me before the man leads us down a long hallway then through a passageway to another building next to the jail.

"Where are we going?" I ask, but he doesn't answer.

Kat is dead quiet, tears running tracks through pancake makeup.

"It won't be so bad," I hear myself other self say. "It'll be like boarding school." I start to feel happy. "You know, rich girls going to study manners, Kat, an adventure."

Jet-down, Knife tells me. Now.

But I can't. It's a training school, I tell her. It must be nice.

Models get trained.

The man brings us to a smelly office. He carries the papers from the courtroom, signed and stamped, New Jersey.

"Wait here," he says, as if we could go anywhere and points to a bench.

I look for ways to escape but he locks the door and there's not one window in the room.

"This is bad," Kat says. "This is a fucking asshole bad."

I'm so sure the school will be a boarding school I start to get excited and picture myself learning French, how to properly fold a napkin, which spoon to use for soup, tea and dessert, walk with a book on my head. When I get out in a month or so, I'll walk and talk same as the girls in honors classes, majorettes, the ones who live in the white mansions on the purple hill.

The man unlocks the door and tells us they are getting the papers together and waiting for a car.

"Where are we going?"

"Trenton," he says.

"That's for crazy people," I say, but he snaps the door shut.

Kat stares at the floor in a trance, all the pancake streaked with white lines of bare skin and I wonder if I am a witch and the reason we are here and I know the answer.

"I can't believe I miss my asshole Mom," Kat says. "And I thought I hated her yesterday."

"It's my fault," I say. "Your Mom said you were good until you met me."

She looks at me with her far away eyes.

"You didn't make me do anything," she says. "I was bored before you came along."

"I hope we are in the same room at the school," I tell her, then the man comes back with keys and this time there is an old lady in a brown wool coat and she stares at us as if we're two mangy stray cats she wants to scat from her yard.

The man steps in front and the brown coat walks behind us through a passageway that leads to a scary garage. It's as if we aren't human anymore. We're green aliens with eyes like insects or frogs, piglets about to be dissected.

Rain beats on the metal roof of the garage and the sky is so dark it could be nighttime though it is only two in the afternoon. Thunder breaks from the purple hills like in a movie before Elizabeth Taylor has a lobotomy or a cigarette. Nothing seems true. Real. A gray car waits, an ugly car that says State of New Jersey Department of Corrections across the door.

Kat and me sit in the back seat and stare out the windows at the wet highway, the trees drooping with rain, the fields dark, the streetlights cartoon green, yellow, red against the dark blue of the sky. We pass farms and fruit stands, rain runs off tin ridges and onto sacks of potatoes, crates of onion, apples and pears. We listen to the conversation in the front seat about rheumatism and cataracts and hearts. The thunderstorm beats a rhythm on the roof and I wonder if the car might split in half from the lightning and we can escape, run down the highway to the barn with the horses and cows. On the right, a river rushes by, the muddy water over the bank and onto the highway and we drive through a highway stream. The tires spin mud onto the windows, little smacks of brown. I tell myself it won't be so bad but Kat is not convinced. It seems as if the car's not moving at all. Like being stoned but not good.

"What do you know about where we are going?" I ask the woman. "We're scared."

"Well, I guess that's the point." she says. "What did you do?"

"Skip school," I say.

"Surely you did more than that."

"And not report to probation."

She turns and looks at us with her baggy eyes.

"I don't know that much about it," she says. "Only that the population is colored and a lot of those from Newark."

Kat honks her nose in a Kleenex and I wonder if the colored girls speak French and know which fork to use or if they are going to kill us.

Part Three

French Lessons

THE FIRST THINGS I NOTICE: wet grass, a lot of it, and some of it fenced with metal barbed wire. But there was a white mansion with columns on the porch, just how I imagined a boarding school would be. Over the door I see the house has a name: Fielder. The car stops outside the black door and we walk through in a trance like twin Frankensteins.

Inside are desks and two colored women tapping on keyboards. They look at us, bored, then back to their Remington's. One woman is handed my papers and the other woman Kat's. The driver man and the old lady sign on a line and skit out the door. They don't even look back at us or say goodbye.

A big woman with short arms wearing a saggy purple dress and thick eyeglasses says to take a seat, her eyes big, magnified behind the lens. Another woman, wears a headscarf puffed with green petals and she steps from a slanted doorway, the sheer petals flapping as she walks. She tells Kat to take a seat at the warped desk, the stacks of papers and heaped knitting books tipping toward the floor and I look up at a sign that says: Tomorrow is the First Day of the Rest of Your Life. After the rain, the sun is out and splatters shadows across the floor and the walls, hand shadows, long fingers and thumbs.

The woman gives me a clear plastic bag that says: *New Jersey* across the front in black letters and over the top is a yellow sticker that says: Zoe King.

"This is for your possessions," she says. "You'll get them back when you are released."

"When will that be?" I ask, but she just gives me a cold coffee stare and picks up the black telephone. I see Kat across the room with her head in her hands and her hair stuck to one ear from leaning against the car window. She's looking pissed off enough to die from it and I know what she is thinking.

"Zoe King ready for orientation. Five minutes," the woman says, into the black receiver.

"Step this way," she tells me. I look back at Kat slumped in her red turtleneck, most of her pancake gone except for her forehead and chin.

The woman fills in the blanks on the paper.

"Follow the Intake arrows." she says. "Through the metal door."

"But can't we wait for my friend?" I say. "We came here together."

"Oh no," she says. "You won't be seeing her till you are twenty-one and by then you won't want to, take it from me."

"We need to be together. We don't know anyone else."

"This way," she says, and pushes me through the heavy door.

"What do you mean twenty-one?"

"If you want to get along here you'll learn not to ask so many questions. Where do you think you are, boarding school?"

She follows me down a narrow hallway without windows only long tubes of light that shade the walls green and the air stinks of rubbing alcohol that gets stronger as we go. Our shoes echo and bounce wall to wall, until we come to a thick steel door and the woman rams a red buzzer with her brown thumb. On the other side of the door is a white skinned, white haired woman with a nametag pinned on her shoulder that says: Mrs. Bates. I watch the red nailed hand of the colored woman slip Bates my papers stamped and sealed, papers that say I'm the property of New Jersey and Bates holds them with her clubby fingers.

"This way," Bates says.

A moldy bathroom is on the left, white tiled, huge, smelly, with open stalls, rows of toilets, sinks, a shower room, chrome heads lined up, a path of matching silver drains. In between the floor tiles, streaks of brown and rust, maps of creeping water. The room smells like one big toilet.

"Strip," Bates says. "Put your bracelet into the bag."

"What?"

I touch the silver airplane and rub its wings with my finger and try to wish myself back to our garden apartment, it seems so pretty now, then I can go to school and have my room back.

"I need my bracelet," I say.

"That's not allowed," she says.

"Take off your clothes."

I notice the gaps where tiles are missing, bare spots, globs of glue in clumps, hair ripped from a scalp, spaces to fall through, Mrs. Bates checkered dress, my head so light and dizzy I tumble into the white squares of cotton.

"Why?" and the word ping pongs wall to wall.

"Do what I say and don't ask questions. Strip and off with the bracelet."

I wonder how she can be so mad at me when I just met her.

I take off my shoes, my dress, and my socks till I'm wearing only my black bra and black Friday underpants and the woman stares me up and down.

"I said strip!" she says.

"Everything?"

She nods. "And the bracelet," she says. Now.

My face is hot but I'm cold, shivery, my teeth chatter.

Knife says to coast but I can't.

"This is an order," Bates says, and shakes the keys in her hand. "No jewelry."

I unclasp my bracelet and it falls to the floor.

This is an order, Knife says. Orbit.

A silver drain in the tile catches my eye. I slip down a hole, miles of iron pipe to the core and Atlas has let go, only dark space, the stars are gone.

"Why do I have to undress in front of you?"

"You're a ward of the state now. If you don't obey there are guards and a padded cell."

"There's been a mistake," I say. "I don't belong here."

"They all say that," she says.

The floor is cold, slick with water. I drop my underwear, black puddles on the floor.

"Turn around," the woman orders.

I hide inside and Knife sharpens her blade.

"Put your arms out at your sides."

A white sink is filled with green drips.

"You need to delouse your hair."

She hands me a plastic bottle with a skull and bones label, turns a crusty knob and a showerhead sputters and shrieks before the water breaks from the spout.

"I don't have lice."

"It's *mandatory* get in."

I stand under the rush of cold water then hot and pour the goo on my hair. It smells like Shelltox. Termites eating wood. King Car waiting. I cover my face, melt into water and salt. Pipes rumble from deep behind the shower wall and I rub the goop into my scalp and it stings, drips in my eyes, burns my nose. I rinse and rinse.

Bates throws me a towel and locks me in with her eyes. Rat eyes. I dry off, wrap the towel around my naked self, feeling my arms and legs drop off, my neck loose and I rise through the shower steam to the ceiling and look down.

Good, Knife says.

"Brush," Bates says, and hands me a toothbrush and paste.

"Over there," she points to a greenish bowl. The trouble is that I have to drag my body as if I weighed three-hundred pounds. I lean against cold porcelain. In the mirror I am drowned, my hair matted, dripping, my eyes red, stung, swollen. Alien.

Bates shoves me a bag of clothes: brand new Fruit of the Loom underwear, thick white cotton with a stamp that says "New Jersey." An ugly green uniform with snaps up the front, black and white shoes, bulky white socks, all too large or I am too small and the shoes so heavy my legs won't stay on.

"Down the hall," Bates orders.

She is at my back. Her keys jangle.

We stop at a wall of iron bars that reach to the ceiling, bars painted pink and the gate slides open, grind and clang, an empty sound, the scrape of concrete and iron, pink paint flaking, showing rust and iron teeth, slots where the locks fit together. I step through the gate. I am not really here. I ride the ceiling like a trapped fly.

A hallway, dark, rows of doors cut with barred windows, Bates keys a door at the end.

"Get in," she says, and I zombie through.

"How long do I have to stay in here?"

"That depends," she says. "Quarantine is two weeks but that is if you adapt."

"What's quarantine?"

"You could be diseased," Bates says.

I am little, then big—the rabbit hole, my body tiny but my heart too large, my head hits the ceiling then I shrink to the size of Knife and we square dance for a minute, like in school, pick a partner, spin around and around, *dosey-dough*.

The room is empty except for a metal bed and a dirty striped mattress.

"What will I do in here?"

"Well you can start by thinking about what got you here," she says. Her face is wrinkled, white elephant skin, her eyes dead, her words hammer.

"Please don't make me stay here. There's been a mistake. I want to go home."

I look down and see the baggy green uniform and the clunky black and white shoe under the green hem and blood goes out of me.

"I need to talk to the judge. Please."

"Pay attention. If you persist to conduct yourself in this way, I have a cell for you in the basement. You won't disturb other inmates there." Bates says, Her words banging together.

I peek past the bars in the door and see another window across the hall and a big black head with full frizzy hair and black eyes staring at me. She looks scared too.

A woman who is not Bates hands me scratchy brown paper towels to blow my snotty nose.

Dust is in the air, clouds, dots like water or bits of broken glass or rainbows glide around the room. In the cold white sun, I notice the wall scratched with words and symbols.

"How long do I have to stay?"

"The state can detain you till you're twenty-one," the new woman says, and it sounds as if she is very far away on another planet.

"I'm only thirteen."

"There's a girl here is nine," she says. "Had one a few years back was eight."

A window with bars looks out over a field of weeds blown flat from the wind and rain. Further on, where the sky turns dark blue, a line of black branches shakes twig fingers, and I remember what the Ouija board said, the picture of the woman with her hands and hair flying in the air.

253

"Now, if you don't settle down, see this?" she says, and holds out a long silver skeleton key. "We have a strait jacket and a padded cell."

She steps into the hallway and the key turns in the door and clicks the lock.

There is a bare mattress, maps of pee stains across it, brown patterns, the charts on a bad moon and I say a kind of prayer that this isn't true, I'm not really here. The mattress reeks. On the wall names and dates scratched into the iron, Mary, Joan, Maureen 5/5/1959, a heart and a dagger.

"They'll bring you a tray at five o'clock," Someone somewhere says.

I imagine Willy tapping his secret codes and wonder if he can reach me, invent a formula to dematerialize me and shadow me out of here.

The black face fills the window square again, moving back and forth, one eye then the other, one at a time, framed by the square barred hole in the cell door across the hall.

"There's a pot in the corner," a voice says, and the words echo.

Beside the bed and pee mattress, there is only a pot and a magazine, Good Housekeeping.

I pace from the door to the window, window to the door and back and when I look up at the cut out in the door, across the hall, two dark eyes stare back in a face round and sad.

"Who are you?" I say.

She doesn't answer just gawks at me with dim eyes.

"Judith" she whispers.

"What are you here for?"

"We ain't 'lowed to talk."

"Okay," I say.

"Fightin'," she whispers. "I hurt somebody."

"I do that too," I say. "I beat up a girl in sixth grade," I tell her. But of course it's a lie.

Her eyes are black and she stares so steady and deep, so still and blank, it seems she's blind.

"My friend Kat is here too but I don't know where."

"You won't be 'lowed," she says. "They keeps you apart."

I sink deeper. Listen for keys down the hall and if I hear them she tells me to stop talking. Her hair is a black hedge, square and thick.

We shift inside our squares. She disappears. Comes back. I wait for her. Tomorrow, she says, I'll get something called an internal. It gives me a chill.

"What's that?"

"You don't know?"

"No."

"It's when that mean doc sticks her nasty finger up your pussy to see if you got a gonorrhea or a baby."

"Oh that," I say. Mother Blind don't talk about that stuff. I'm not even sure what my girl body parts are called, except for boobs and triangle.

I tell her I've never gone all the way with a boy so I can't have a disease that sounds like an animal and for sure I'm not knocked up."

"Girl, everybody here has fucked."

"Yeah, I did that," I tell her.

Keys jangle in the hall; Judith's face disappears.

I fall apart on the bed. Disintegrate—the snail that time when I poured salt on it and it disappeared. Soon I'll wake up at home. Willy tapping his wires. Mother Blind in the kitchen with a pot of boiling egg noodles and butter.

I flip the pages of Good Housekeeping and the photographs make me sad. How lucky the women are in the ads, free to wax a floor or polish a window, make a Duncan Hines cake or a tuna casserole. On page 59 is a photo of a white cottage with blue shutters, a yellow fence, roses and I remember Shari's house, Shari from my school bus, Shari with the pink cheeks and rabbit hair sweater. I open the cherry red door and step inside. The wood floors shine, the windows too and they look over a garden and everything smells of oranges. Shari's mother bastes a chicken. She's dressed in white heels and a yellow party dress. She asks me if I'd like a Manhattan and we sit at the table and clink glasses, cross our legs, light our Salem's. I ask if she wants to do Paris and she says she'll pack her Samsonite and be ready in a jiffy. Music plays from a kitchen radio, "Moon River," and Shari's mom asks me if I want to Walz. I say, *sure* but then there is a clang and I look up from Good Housekeeping and see a dark arm slide a gray tray in the slot in the door: cold meatloaf, oily string beans, a brick of striped ice cream wrapped in a white paper envelope, the food sectioned off in pie wedges.

I eat only the ice cream and slide the tray back under the door.

"You don't want your grub?" Judith whispers.

Her eyes steady, her teeth bright white. It feels as if we are in a zoo.

"I can't eat it," I whisper.

"Can you slide it over to my slot?"

I shove the tray hard and it rams into Judith's door. Judith hooks her empty tray under her door and sends it back to mine.

"Do you have any magazines in there?" I say.

"Vogue," she says.

We trade and I study photographs of boney, flat chested girls with fake eyelashes and zombie eyes, girls decked out in silver, black cut out dresses, tight pants and sharp boots.

I notice the sky is black and a bare bulb flips on from the ceiling. I read all the names and dates on the wall, a row of seven lines: ~~1111111~~ then another ~~1111111~~ and another, ~~1111111~~ day after day, week after week and someone has carved in:

Bitch of Jesus Christ.

Judith says they call it the spelling wall and all the cells have one.

"How do they do it?"

"Bobby pins," she says. "Pull the rubber off."

I bury my face in the gray pillow. Chicken feathers and the hairs of the girls who came before. I'll write a letter to President Kennedy, tell him about the eight-year-old and to Judge Leahy, tell him I don't normally wear blue eye shadow. I think if I wet the bed here it won't matter but I don't pee the bed anymore. Figures.

Orbit, Knife tells me. Open the book of dreams.

So, I dream about the way the pond changes every day, sometimes muddy, sometimes clear, silver and gold, black and orange, the eye of the sun and the moon, the rain and the clouds, the stars falling down. I think about how I can't live in a world where people cut the feet off of pigs, eat lambs and baby cows, send dogs and monkeys to outer space, order children to prison but Knife says: NO. That's the wrong direction.

I must be making a lot of noise because the keys turn in the door and a tall cocoa-colored woman in a French poodle skirt shakes me by the shoulders saying: *hush, hush.*

She hands me a set of white sheets and a gray blanket and says I must stop. I am disturbing the others. I ask her where Kat is but she won't say. There is a place for girls who can't calm down, she tells me.

"If you don't settle down they will send you to the home for the feeble-minded."

She says if you get sent there the girls scream all day and in a faraway time one girl had her brains beat out with a bedpost. Says they don't call it a home for the feeble-minded anymore but that is what it is just the same. I ask her what feeble minded means but she just looks at me.

"I just want to go home," I tell her. "Can you get me out of here?"

"Sure, you and two hundred and thirty other delinquent girls," she says. "And when they do get out most of them get sent back."

I tell her how the boys in my school beat people. Rob cars. Cash registers. They don't get sent away and that is why I didn't think Kat and me would.

"You're very naive," she says. "It's the system, she tells me. The system is harder on girls. Boys are expected to misbehave. Girls are not. Girls are supposed to be ladies and keep their legs crossed and their lips red at all times.

I tell her it can't be possible that they can keep me here until I'm twenty-one. I say I'll run away then. She tells me about Dora, her name scratched in the wall under the window. Dora who ran away twenty-six times. Stayed in this very cell each time she was caught but she never got further than the edge of the woods. The last time she ran they found her body frozen in the canal, her eyes wide open, hands up as if trying to break through the window of ice.

I ask her if I can write to the president and the judge and she says she will bring me a pencil and paper in the morning but judges orders are final and the president is too busy to read a letter. I tell her I need to get home because I want to be a pilot and she says: *sure honey*.

The door locks behind her.

"Wait," I say. "Can I please use the bathroom?"

Judith laughs.

"The pot is in the corner," she says

I have to pee in a pot. It's part of the training. The system. I'm to see a Dr. Singer for an exam early in the morning. I tell her I'm a virgin from the country. Not a city girl. I only went there a few times.

"Goodnight," she says, and locks the door. I can tell she is kind and I don't want her to leave.

I pull my knees to my chest, my arms around my body on the pee mattress, Knife in my head telling me to orbit the moon lights the ghost names in the dark.

When I pee in the pot it makes a terrible loud speaker trickle that I am sure everyone across New Jersey can hear.

Turbulence

THE ONLY TIME THE PAIN GOES AWAY is when I sleep. Waking up is a different story. Orbit, Knife says, and I find a way out. I close my eyes, shut this nightmare down and let the clouds of subway smoke take me away. We walk down the stone streets of New York, my eyes ringed in black, Kat's hair a polished platinum, her lips pale with pancake, her eyes lined with Blue Coal Maybelline.

We go to Cafe Wha? Redo the Before, like reading backwards, carried with the crowd across Broadway, disappear into the subway station, the silver bullet cars that land at MacDougal. On the corner are three guys huddled together. They pass us a joint. I go the place where everything is covered with the gold from the moon. I remember the moon that night. We sit in the black leather booth. Candles turn shadows. The guy in the cap sings strings of words. An *areo-plane*. A bluish mist rises and I'm flying high. Stoned. I stay with that dream for a long time then flip the page and go to the yellow plane and the girl with her goggles dripping wax from the moon.

"Hop in," she says, and I stare into the gold of her eyes.

She sets her goggles back on her head and says:

"The stars seem near enough to touch. The reason I fly."

Stars large and small explode around us. I hold onto the steering to keep my head from knocking against the roof.

"Turbulence," she shouts. "A storm. We have to fight. Stay the course."

She tells me there are four layers below the earth and four layers above. We pass through time and space. The danger is getting trapped in a layer, she says.

"I'm flying blind so hang on. Easy to get lost. The fog. I have to land this baby," she says.

In the light from the stars her gold skin looks blue.

She angles the plane closer to the ocean, so close I can see the waves break, then a sea of green that is Ireland and we fly low and drift over the purple mountains and jagged cliffs.

Judith

I OPEN MY EYES. WHERE AM I? The spelling wall, words coming at me and someone in the hallway rattles a tray under the door: a tiny box of corn flakes and carton of milk, a hardboiled egg and a white paper cup of apple juice. If they give you a glass, fork you might kill yourself. It seems that the sun shouldn't shine here but it does right on the spelling wall.

Dead Bitches

A few spaces below it says:

Dream Baby

Judith moans from across the hall and I peek through the bars and she is staring out of the hole and straight at me with her sad eyes.

"If you don't want your grub slide it over," she says.

I take the egg and the apple juice, check the hall then slide the tray across to the slat in her door and quick she pulls it in then shoves her tray back to me.

"What's going to happen today?"

"It's like I told you. You get the exam," she grumbles from the square.

"How do you know what's going to happen?"

"Been here before," she says.

She tells me about a fire set by girls with rags and kerosene and how there are bones buried under cottages from the girls who didn't make it, how they put you on a table with metal stirrups like a horse so they can put a tool inside you, a tool made of cold steel clamps that jack you up like a truck.

"I never had sex."

"Well, I'm just tellin' you the rules. They go by rules here and nothin' you say is gonna do any good."

"Don't I have a say over my own body?"

I think to myself that the doctor can't touch my body even if I'm in prison my body is still my body my hand still my hand. This is the holy matrimony of me.

"Not no more," she says, and her face comes back and fills the

260

window with one eye.

We hear the keys ring from down the hall and go back to our stinky mattresses and I think how colored or white don't make no difference in here.

"King and Jones," a voice says, and the keys turn in the door.

A tall brown woman with blonde hair trails us into the big ugly bathroom. She tells us to shower. After about two minutes she says time is up and hands us white towels and underwear. I don't look at Judith but from the side of my eye I can't help but see her naked body, black and big as a mountain wearing a white towel.

We dress back into our New Jersey underwear and uniform.

"To the left," the woman points. "Follow the signs that say INFIRMARY."

Nothing looks real and my head is helium drifting to Mars.

I find myself on a long white bench in a green uniform, Judith next to me as we wait for Doc Singer. I think of the frogs in biology class and how the scissors split them down the middle to open the flaps of skin, doors to the inside parts.

"What is the doctor like?" I whisper.

"An old hatchet with eyes and white hair."

Judith sits with her elbows resting on her knees and her chin in her hands, fed up, bored. She's done this before.

It's a white room that smells of bleach and rubbing alcohol, the windows, glass, ice cubes, fat foggy cubes that don't open or close, look out or in. Everything here is Poe.

Judith shifts on the white bench, leans against the painted brick wall, her hands at the back of her head, ankle over ankle, hair frizzed out on one side and flat on the other. She says she needs grease. Her hair. I think of Crisco, Willy rubbing it into the track of our roller coaster. Willy working his wrenches and screws, his nails set to hammer, his fingers tan from the sun, crunched on his knees tuning his radio. Before.

Keys. Keys everywhere: skeleton keys, keys made of bone, locks, keyholes cold and grinding. A giant belly comes through the door and the girl attached to it sits at the end of the bench away from the green that marks us as *quarantined*. She is pretty and has thick black braids that hang down over her watermelon bump. I think of the baby inside and the baby Aunt Oink flushed down the toilet. I think of Zuzu.

A nurse, short and round and wearing a white hat, a paper sailboat on her head, walks toward me.

"Doctor Singer will see you now," she says, and she is staring at me.

I follow her into a room with bottles, tubes, cotton, sheets of white paper, giant napkins, metal things that shine in the light. White and chrome everywhere. Out walks Doc Singer and she is exactly as Judith said: Dr. Hatchet with her sharp beak, pointy chin, a white pile of hair. A spotlight shines on a table with green vinyl and metal horse things.

"You need to take off your clothes," the nurse says, and hands me a paper napkin.

"Again? I don't need an exam," I say. "I've never had sex with anyone so I can't be pregnant or have a disease." I am so sure this will save me.

I tell her it's my religion and I have to wait till I'm married and this is my body and I don't want to be touched and what about rights? What about the Constitution? I need a lawyer. Get me out of here. This is a mistake.

"You need to get undressed," the nurse says. "There, behind the screen."

The doctor arranges instruments on a steel table.

"No. I won't."

"It's the rule," the nurse explains. "Every girl that comes into this institution has to have a physical examination including a test for gonorrhea. Venereal disease and pregnancy."

"I don't have those things."

"Get undressed," the doctor says, from across the room. "If you don't I'll have to call in the guards and they'll do it for you. You are under the jurisdiction of the state of New Jersey now. You are a juvenile. A delinquent juvenile."

I walk behind the screen and my hands shake. My mother standing in the doorway of the bathroom ordering me to undress. I peel off my clothes and put on the paper napkin.

"Come on now," the doctor says. "I don't have time for nonsense."

262

She makes me get up on the table. The vinyl, where the napkin ends is sticky like that time with Wilma. Put my bare feet in the chrome. Cold.

"Spread your legs," she says, but I can't and I don't know what she means. I open them a little but that's not what she wants. My knees knock together.

I call out to Knife in my head and her eyes spin into mine and she tells me not to let on I'm afraid.

"*I said open your legs*," the doctor says, and pushes my knees apart and tells me to relax but my legs won't and my knees clamp her hands together so the nurse comes and says I have to let my legs go limp and dead and when I do I squeeze my eyes shut against the world and the Poe pendulum story blows through me. Knife tells me to begin planning our trip to Paris but all I can think of are the silver trays lined on the steel counter, the small green bodies belly up, the legs spread, the dotted diagram, the broken line that shows you where to snip the scissors, the drawing I memorized, the naming of organs, the inside parts: Peritoneum. Lungs. Female. Heart.

Play dead, Knife says.

"You're no virgin," Dr. Hatchet says.

It's a lie: *starving, hysterical, naked* a voice says.

"Next," the doctor says, and the nurse helps me back to the screen. I hear papery sounds and low voices in the walls and I think I hear someone say: *hydrogen jukebox*.

I Like Your Wife

KNIFE SAYS I CAN LEAVE MY BODY, slip out through the window in my head so I go back to the Before to stop dying. I press my eyelids down with my fingers and colors start to pop.

Cut to Paris, Knife says.

I count the street lamps, count the angels, the horses, count everything everywhere, count the cracks between sidewalks the bells in churches, one hundred, one hundred and one, one hundred and two, count the monsters on the roof of the church, count the number of teeth the horses have on the merry-go-round, count the loaves of bread at the Jewish bakery, count the times a rabbi prays.

Turn the page. I am walking in the sun with Grandma. We are going to the ravioli restaurant, Grandma in her rhinestone earrings, the ravioli like pockets on a rag doll, zig zagged around the edges hiding the cheese inside, steam rising from the sauce, the red and white checkered curtains, Grandma talking to the waitress, Grandma peeling eggs while the newsreel rolled the girl in brown who walks alone. Turn the page.

I run and run through the fields. The tall weeds wave against my calves. I run so fast I am nearly flying. Run. Run. Run. Run to the pond. Sail over the dark water. Run.

"Zoe," I hear someone say and I open my eyes, and see I'm not at the ravioli place with Grandma or the cinema. I'm in a cell. I don't remember being led back here from INFIRMARY but I am, staring at the names scratched into the iron walls.

"Zoe."

I walk to the door and look out at the dark eye.

"You okay?" Judith says.

"No. But don't tell nobody."

"Got it," she says. "Lock you in a looney bin you ain't gettin' out ever."

Keys down the hall and we slip back to our beds. Someone slams a tray through: meatloaf that looks like dog food, stewed tomatoes and peas and the same brick of ice-cream you get once every day. I take the ice cream and shove my tray over to Judith.

After lights out I go back to Cafe Wha? and fall asleep hearing that guy in the black cap sing about a hard rain and the poet that time, the guy who the girl at the next both said was Allen Ginsberg reading the words: *supernatural darkness* and now I know what it means.

In the morning I ask for a paper and pencil to write to President Kennedy:

~~Dear President Kennedy,~~
~~I like your wife.~~
~~Sincerely, Zoe King~~
I tear up more than a few and have to ask for more paper.

Dear President Kennedy,

You may have heard of Trenton New Jersey. There is a place here called The New Jersey State Home for Girls. (also known as Training School for Girls) I am here because I didn't go to school for a long time due to great weather and frogs.

In biology class they make you cut up frogs. It makes me very sick. I memorize all the parts of the frog: the liver, the heart, the lungs, the eggs and know where they fit but I can't cut the frog the way Mr. Boyle said. I don't think this should be a reason to be sent to reform school.

You don't have rights here. I don't think this is part of The United States. I saw The Statue of Liberty once and I read The Constitution in history class. How come in this place you don't have rights for your body? Ask your wife about this.

I did also skip school due to sunny weather. I am thirteen years old and kids like to be in the park (like Caroline and John John) when the weather is warm because you are only a kid once so why do I have to spend it in school were I don't want to be. I already know my tables and division and how to read and write. (I am writing right now and I love to read but they don't have many books here)

I know there are laws and I promise to obey them every day if you can call Judge Leahy (very mean) and get me out of here where I don't belong. I want to be a pilot when I grow up and you have to go to a different kind of school for that. They can keep me here until I'm twenty-one. By then I'll be too old to be a pilot.

You probably don't know this but they put you in a room made of iron with bars on the door and the window. There is a wall of bars in the hall that locks and unlocks and slides open and closed and these bars are painted pink because it is a girls' reformatory, I guess.

I really like you and your wife and if I could vote I would vote for you to be president for the rest of my life.

Please write back,

Zoe King

p.s. I did steal a couple times but I didn't get caught

I fold my letter and slide it into the envelope.

President J.F.K.

White House

Judge Leahy

EVERY MORNING WHEN I OPEN MY EYES I still don't know where I am. I count the days by the number of trays and so far I've counted twenty-one. In one week I will go somewhere else. Houses called cottages where we'll be assigned according to our crimes. Cottages with names: Murphy, Voorhees, Wilson, Fielder, Edge to honor all the rotten governors of New Jersey.

Judith says it is better in the cottages but you are still locked into rooms and have to bang on your door to use the bathroom. But she says you can come out of your cell to go to school and work in the laundry or kitchen mopping the floors. Kat and me and one other girl are the only white girls out of 234 colored girls, she said. I think of my father and how he'd call all the girls *niggers* here including me.

I ask Mrs. Webber for more paper and an envelope to write the judge.

Dear Honorable Judge Leahy,
A week ago you sent me and my friend Kat away to a terrible place. You've probably have never been here. If you had you wouldn't have sent us here.

I only wore blue eyeshadow to court because I wanted to look pretty and grown up so you wouldn't send me away. (guess that was a bad idea). When I told you the reason I didn't go to school (the sunny weather and the frogs) I forgot to say that my mother needs me at home. I wash the floors and keep things neat and clean and do the laundry and cook spaghetti and sauce for my brother. My mother has to punch cards full time at the IBM factory. So, that is why I was too tired to go to school and dissect the frog.

My brother, Willy, fixes and builds things but he speaks another language that no one but me understands. If you don't send me home, he will have no one to talk to and he might not be able to invent his earth to Mars radio.

I know I played hooky but I never smoked a cigarette or drank alcohol like some other kids I know. Besides, I want to be a pilot when I grow up and I need to study. The only books they have here are lady magazines and some textbooks from 1919 and they don't let you have storybooks because they might give "one ideas."

Mrs. Webber says they can keep me here until I am 21. That is not right. This is the United States of America and we have rights under the laws. I thought I had a right to a lawyer. How come not?

Another thing is, there are boys I know, Skippy Weeks for instance, who did more than skip school. They got in fights and hurt Randy McNeil so bad he had to stay in the hospital for weeks. Also, they busted the windows out of the boy's room and wrote bad words with magic markers all over the mirrors and walls and robbed a gas station. They steal cars. And they skipped school too. How come they didn't get sent away and we did? They are fifteen. Maybe you didn't know about them?

Please let me come home now. I've already been here 9 days.

Sincerely,

Zoe King

Mrs. Webber makes me give her the pencil back because I might kill myself.

I ask Judith what they train you to do at the school. She says if you are sixteen they train you to be a hairdresser and not burn scalps or cause explosions. They give you hair rollers and dye, a hairdryer and a curling iron, permanent lotion and pink curlers with teeth.

If you are not sixteen, they teach you to make hospital corners on sheets and how to give a bed bath to a dummy. You take your own temperature and pulse, listen your heart to make sure you are alive. They give you bandages, gauze and tape to wind around the dummy's head. They teach you hygiene, how to tweeze eyebrows, wash feet and clip toenails on sick people, how to prevent bedsores and make cancer bandages, stuff you never wanted to know like how to fry eggs, bleach toilets, wash clothes, properly apply lipstick, iron shirts, all the things they don't teach in boarding schools. But for poor girls and the feeble minded these are valuable things to know. You aren't smart enough to finish school and could never get into college but you'll still have to get a job.

Deadbeat, Knife says.

I ask Judith what the other girls are like. She says some are nice and if they like you they will ask you to be part of their *family* a wife or a daughter or husband or brother, a grandmother or grandfather, cousin or aunt. They will give you a new name and make sure you have talcum powder and lipstick, candy from the training school store. They'll make sure you don't get beat up. They give you their dessert at dinner or extra mashed potatoes if you want. They'll write you letters called *kites* which means they are folded into teeny triangles that fit into the palm of your hand to be slipped beneath tables. If you get caught with one you get locked in your room for a week or something worse if you are caught more than once—bread and water. I thought that was just in movies.

Rotten

At night, I lay on the smelly mattress of maps, the *supernatural darkness* pressing down, a pillow over my face and I think when I wake up I'll be home in my own bed and everything will go back as it was only this time I will go to school. I'll be good. I'll be free. I never knew what it meant before.

The doctor said I am not a virgin but I know this is *not* true.

Who cares? Knife says.

Virgin means you never let a boy put his Henry in your triangle. Judith says if you don't bleed at the exam than that means you fell on your bike or slammed down on a tree branch there and then you bleed but your just a kid and don't pay it no mind because you bleed all the time.

I think a lot about what a rotten person I am.

1. I call people names
2. I don't help my mother
3. I only think about myself
4. My mother sleeps on the sofa and I get my own room because I was so mad about leaving our King Car house and what about the law? Half of the house is ours, right? But I forgot something else about the law of matrimoney--you have to be married.
5. I'm a thief and I like it.
6. I drink but Grandma says it's okay before you go to bed.
7. I don't appreciate.
8. I don't believe in the God of the Bible sort but I would never kill a lamb or any animal but probably would kill a person.

When I get out I'll probably still want to smoke and drink and I'll still call Aunt Oink, Aunt Oink but just to Knife like always. I'll try and help Mother Blind but I'll probably forget. I'll still think about myself and I won't believe the Bible. But I will go to school because Mrs. Webber said that pilots have to finish high school. I think it is true. Also, I won't steal. Okay, I'll try not to. I don't think you can be a pilot if you get arrested.

I don't ever want to come back here. Judith said when you leave here, if you look back you will come back. She looked back and now she IS back.

This is the bottom of the Loch Ness Lagoon, Knife says, dark and slimy with the angry dead children who didn't get to grow up. It seems I won't grow up either. If they keep me here until I'm twenty-one, every day will be the same color, black and I'll be the same as I am today just older, madder, meaner, each day a dark hole, falling and falling and falling.

Out the window past the gates is a field, I see sunflowers with wind-snapped necks.

Cut, Knife says.

"I can't stand being alive anymore," I tell her.

Coast, she says. Then launch into orbit mode.

I close my eyes. Willy and me slide the muddy trail to the pond, the weeds shoot seeds into the warm air, we catch them on our tongues, our bare toes caked with mud, sun on our faces, the fox in my heart, free. I miss everything free. Free to use the bathroom without asking, without the ring of keys.

Judith said the wall in our cells are iron because the girls in isolation from Before times tore down the plaster walls with their fingernails. All just to see the person in the cell on the other side. Weeks locked up alone, nothing to do but tear down the walls. Judith knows the history of this dungeon. New Jersey re-plastered the walls but the girls licked them down again. So, New Jersey put up iron walls but the girls still left their marks.

I stare at the iron because there is nothing else. What happened to J.C. 1952? What about Carrie who loved Johnny or Gloria who loved Gwen?

This is Judith's second time here but two of her sisters were here before her. She tells me things in between trays when the hall is empty. There was a cage in the attic for girls who didn't stick to rules. One rule was to always wear lipstick.

"What? Why?" I say.

"Don't want no dikes," she says. "You knows, girl on girl. Don't

271

want no girls looking like dikes when the big wigs from Trenton shoe up.'"

Judith says tales get passed down year to year like hand-me-down rags so no one forgets the girls from the Before who had it a thousand times worse than we do now. Staring at the iron, the cement floor and pee mattress it's hard to believe but I *do* because Judith is a mountain. Judith is not a sissy girl who'd deal out gossip. She knows things from her sisters, her mother, even her grandmother who all did time here in the Way Back.

Judith says in the beginning of reformatory time it was all white girls, hell raisers they called them, mostly from around Trenton. Her grandmother was the first colored girl sent here because she was in the car, pregnant, when her boyfriend robbed a bank. Before her Grandma moved up from Alabama, Newark was a nice place where people wore ironed clothes and dined in white tablecloth restaurants. When the jobs left, the paint stirrers and mad hatters, closed and white people moved out, coloreds from the south moved in, like Judith's Grandma.

"Pregnant with my Mama," she whispers, from her window, her dark face in sections, slivers, sliced by the bars, one black eye staring at my one green eye, shifting right to left to show the other eye. "She the only colored here, she says. "White girls' tough as hell. Auntie Gloria took in my Mama. Raised her most."

After her Grandma, the colored girls came more and more till vanilla turned chocolate until today only 3 white girls and I'm one of them. Judith says the white girls didn't catch any breaks either, they were beat, locked in cages, called imbeciles, morons and feeble minded. Back then if a guard decided you were feeble minded, well things happened, that's all it took to get you sent to Blackwell's Island or some other looney bin.

"Had it shit badder than us," she says. "A fire. Roof burned off Murphy. Six girls locked in the jailhouse. One snitch blamed the other five. Beat confessions out of 'em."

She tells me the big wig at the school at the time, a Mrs. Harris, charged the girls in court for arson in the first degree but that wasn't the end of it. They threw the girls in the county jail in Trenton but that was against the law for girls aged 11,12, 13,14.

"Trenton papers told it," Judith tells me in between mashed

potatoes and squares of ice cream. "Arms waving from the bars out to the city street. Screams. They got attention. The papers licked up the story. Should 'a burned the place down."

Keys in the hall and so we move from the door and wait for the plastic tray to slide through the slot.

There are no good books here so I wait for Judith's stories whenever the hall goes quiet. I've already reread Good Housekeeping, Woman's Day, and Vogue, the most interesting, many times. I have seven more days in the iron cell, that is if I don't turn imbecile and get sent to the asylum but Knife tells me to orbit and before I know the Now will be the Before but when I think of being here for 8 more years I'd rather be an imbecile.

I ask Mother Blind for books. The superintendent of New Jersey has to *okay* the books first so my mother sent me one called: *The Nun's Story* and that's okay. Only, I can't have my own books in isolation because I am only supposed to think about what got me here and when I think about it I know why I am here, I'm here because I'm me. I don't follow rules. How did the weegee board know I'd end up here? Knife says it is because of layers, the board can read the different layers of our lives. I won't ask it anymore questions.

Grandma sent me a white bible with gold edged pages and a gold ribbon to mark off your page. But first they checked it for weapons and secret messages from Grandma. Grandma was happy I asked for it. I'm going to *saved* and not go to *purgatory* or *limbo* now that I am baptized.

I think about Grandma and the day we ate ravioli in town and then went to the movies, Grandma's jelly beans and hard boiled eggs rolling down the aisles. I was free then but I didn't understand it yet. I miss Grandma most.

I miss Mother Blind too.

Find a moment in time, Knife says.

And I go back like flipping pages backwards to the moment with Willy and me by the warm oven our arms hugging Mother Blind in a circle of sunlight because she was so sad and crying, drowning, her life gone wrong, down the drain and she didn't deserve that. She knew Shakespeare for instance. I go back to the Before when I was the only kid and she read me *Little Black Sambo* every night because it was

273

my favorite one, the only one I knew where tigers could turn into butter. Sambo's parents were named *Mumbo Jumbo* and *Mumbo* and his mother made him new clothes but he had to take them all off when he got to the woods because the tigers would eat him otherwise. They fight about who got the best of *Sambo's* clothes, biting each other's tails racing around a tree so fast they melted. When Daddy Dead called me *nigger baby*, because I made Mother Blind read it every night, she read it to me anyway. In my head I am small and tucked in the twin bed in and the light from the lamp shining down on the pictures of tigers.

I try to read the Bible but it don't make sense everybody getting killed and walking on water. I like Jesus but the rest is like a movie that never ends. I can't believe any of it is real because men wrote it and they lie about everything. How come there isn't a girl Jesus? I flip through the pages and find a page that reads: "This too shall pass."

Knife's been saying that for years.

Judith believes the Bbible so I don't tell her how I feel about it because it's her second time here and she don't know if she has a home to go to when she gets back to Newark. I don't want to make her start not believing, not that I could.

I ask Judith if her grandmother knew the story of the white girls who tore down the walls. I want to hear that story again and again.

"Call them *weeds*, the girls," she says.

Judith tells me the *weeds* tore down seven connected cells in Murphy in only a few hours. When they asked them why they said they had nothing else to do and they were lonely.

"Wow, that's impossible," I say, but Judith stares straight through me not smiling and I know she knows things I don't and that a lot of things you don't think are possible, are. Look at me for instance.

Judith says to look behind the radiator and the window sills for a bobby pin. You can usually find one, she says, from the girl before you. I find one between the radiator pipes the rubber already skinned. I scrape the wall with the sharp end over and over carving three lines for the letter Z but it's invisible.

All the Colored Babies of the World

ON THE BLACKEST DAYS, Knife says you can stretch a memory like bubble gum like getting stoned. Time slows down. I go back to Greenwich Village and drift inside a cloud of blue smoke that lifts me up and over the Cafe Wha? away from the Here. I see the universe inside a speck of sidewalk glass, the moon hung golden over the city lights, the sky black, the three windows shaped like maps, brown stains clear enough to see the windows are open and I fly in and out and around.

By the time I leave the dream of New York, I am ready to I stretch further back to Willy and me jumping our horses silver and gold, their manes wild with wind. We duel, die again and again, *kilt*, on the dirt hill, the bicycle buried deep in the water, dripping mud and hairy weeds as we lug it to the bank. Go back to King Car when the engine fired and flattened a path to the pond, the motor swallowing gulp after gulp until the gas tank choked and King Car died at the edge of the water. It seems a fairytale, now, Here.

Tomorrow I leave quarantine after two weeks of iron walls and go to Murphy cottage. I hear Kat is going to Voorhees for *honor girls*, the Honorable Judge Leahy thinks I am the troublemaker and I guess he's right about that. Honor cottage means you get more privileges. For instance, you can walk to and from the laundry house without a guard, leave the lights on till 10:30 instead of 10.

Mrs. Bates hands me some clothes that belonged to another girl the same size 5 as me: a cotton skirt with flowers on it and a white blouse, silly looking, a joke but I don't care so much because I can feel the sun on my face again. Still, I miss my cowboy boots and jeans. Knife says it's just temporary, like everything.

"This way," Mrs. Bates says, and Judith and me walk single file to Murphy happy we'll be together and to be out of our cells. From across the field I see Kat in a red jumper with her hair tied up in a ponytail. I put my hand up to wave but Mrs. Bates says: "No communication of any sort is allowed with Kat." She looks much smaller than before somehow.

The cottages are brick and I look over at the infirmary, Doctor Hatchet with her cold clamps and wiry white hair wedged between legs searching disease and babies.

Edge is the cottage where the pregnant girls stay. Next to the infirmary. Judith says you only see the pregnant girls at sundown, their egg shaped bellies black cut outs against the moon.

"Why?"

"Like the lipstick rule," she says. "Don't want to advertise what goes on behind the doors so they only allowed out at night, the pregnant ones, and walk circles around the grounds wondering what's gonna happen to all the colored babies of the world. For us, this *is* the world, at least for now. A world in a world like a snow globe filled with doll heads. Different shades of brown faces looking up searching for their mothers from the glass, the snow falling down. Judith knows things because she's been one of the girls in Edge but we don't talk about that much. I only know she was there.

One week after they are born the babies are gone. If no one in the family wants the baby, then they put it up for sale though they call it adoption and the baby mamas never know where their babies end up. It's as if the babies are dead like Zuzu, gone babies, like Aunt Oink's Baby No.

"Hundreds of babies been born at Edge," Judith tells me. She says you can hear the mothers cry at night, from an open door or window. The pregnant girls don't runaway. Where would they go? And if they did runaway New Jersey would pretend that they were never there. More money for them. The pregnant girls cost a lot. Some of them are as young as me. There is a rumor around from the Way Back that Doc Hatchet smothers the babies they can't find a homes for and buries them under the sunflowers. That is why they are big as dinner plates but always get their necks broken by the wind. No one cares because they are colored babies. People with money to buy them are white, most of them, and they only want blonde babies. Judith says there is a tombstone hidden in the field outside Murphy that says: BABIES.

Inside Murphy the colored girls sit at rickety tables and knit or shuffle cards and they turn their heads and stare at me all the way up the hall. Everything smells Lysol and there is a sign on the wall that says:

This Friday: The Debbie Reynolds Festival Begins!

The Murphy girls crowd around me as if I am a star they want to touch. They check me out up and down, want to know where I came from, why I'm here, if I have a baby, a boyfriend, they almost pet me like a kitten or a dog. I ask Knife what to do and she says to play it cool, they weren't expecting a white girl from Lockwood.

"You're pretty," someone says.

"No I'm not," I say, and they laugh at me.

"You have a nice figure," Miss Vivian, the house mother says.

"I like your hair," a small girl says.

But not everyone thinks I'm special because I am the only white girl in the cottage of thirty colored girls, a tall girl with a half-moon upper lip that shows her white teeth stands with crossed arms scoping me out with her bad eye.

Miss Vivian shows me to my room, same size as the other cell but with more light, no iron walls, a window in the door with thin wired glass in a crisscross pattern but no bars. The outside window has curvy bars, rust colored and flaky.

Miss Vivien says I can send home for my very own bedspread, twin, and curtains that measure 36 inches and one stuffed animal no bigger than a kitten. She is tall and young and her skin is deep tan. She looks at me and says: "My, my you have long hair! You'll need a trim. The superintendent doesn't like long hair."

I wrap my fingers around my hair and tuck it inside my shirt and Miss Vivien locks the door to my new cell.

I look around, a dresser and a bed. Out the window I spot something small and black in the field running in the wind through the tall weeds, in and out and jumping in the air and I see ears and a tail and can't believe that it is Toro. The boy must know where I am. Toro racing, flying toward the window, closer, bigger until I see it's not Toro at all but a black plastic bag twisting in the wind.

I sink down on the bed and stare at the plaster walls counting the cracks until dinner. My new cell is better than the one in isolation but only because there aren't iron walls and there is a window where I can see trees.

At dinner we sit at a round table and eat mashed potatoes, and platters of potato pancakes, applesauce and high stacks of white bread. There is some kind of stringy meat and I give mine to Judith.

"Where you from?" a girl with stick out teeth asks me.

"New Jersey," I say.

"I said where you from?" she says, and her top lip curls. "East Jesus?"

"Lockwood," I say.

"You're a farm girl?"

"Lockwood's not country," I tell her, but she looks away at a light skinned girl with green eyes and shifts her hands under the tablecloth.

"My name is Gwendolyn," the small girl tells me. "But everyone calls me Gwen."

Forks clink on dinner plates and everything smells like boiled potatoes and disinfectant. It's not really a cottage, it's a building like a doctor's office or a small hospital with rows of locked doors down a long hallway of cells called rooms.

"Mr. High-Pockets out there with his burr-head," a big boned girl says. On her head a tight red rag tied at the back in a knot.

Outside the window stands a tall brown man with tight kinky hair and he's trimming some bushes and cutting the grass. There are guards that drive around the reformatory making sure there's no runners.

"Those ditties always peeking in the windows," Cora says. "They be out there spyin' in the windows cuffin' their meat."

The tall one, the one they nicknamed Mr. High-pockets, is a looker with a face like the guy who sings the banana boat song, smooth and buttery skin and a head that seems carved out of cherry wood with a sharp blade.

Gwen tells me she is ten years old. She has thin nappy hair down to her shoulders, big eyes and a long nose with a bump on it. She is so skinny you can almost see through her.

"My name is Zoe," I say. "I'm thirteen."

"I already know that," she says. "Everybody knows the new girls. Why you here?"

"Skipping school. How about you?"

"Arson," she says.

"Who's on duty tonight?" someone asks.

"Blizzard," Margo says.

"Who's that?" I ask Gwen.

"Bates," she says.

Dinner is pretty much always the same: potatoes, string beans, meatloaf, squares of striped ice cream, chimneys of white bread, stacks of butter squares, fish sticks, bowls of soggy noodles, stew of unknown ingredients.

Pig livers, cow tongues and fish eyes, Knife says.

Everyone eats as if it's their last meal because it is until morning.

I learn the routine.

5:30 am: Morning wake up siren. Wait in line for shower. Try not to look if someone is naked. Brush teeth.

7 am: Get in line for breakfast. Sit down next to Gwen. Eat Farina and white toast.

8 am: Go to laundry detail and wash tangles of bras and underpants.

12 pm: Lunch. Potato pancakes or potato soup. Towers of gummy white bread.

1 pm: Go to school. Don't learn anything because you already know what they teach: multiplication tables that you learned in third grade. Practice hospital corners on sheets. Give CPR to dummies. Get straight A's on all tests because they are stupid. The teacher tries to teach math and English and History but hardly anyone pays attention. I do though and get A's on everything which comes as a revelation, as Judith likes to say, *Jesus walking on the water.*

4 pm: Tea time, not really. Lock up in cell from four o'clock to five o'clock.

5 pm: Dinner Bell: Sit next to Gwen or Judith. Eat potatoes and corn, applesauce and don't look at the nasty meat.

7 pm: Twiddle thumbs or count floor tiles or the stitches on a knitting needle.

9 pm: Bedtime. Wait in line for wash up. Go to the bathroom because later you will have to pound on your door and hope someone comes.

10 pm: Lights out. Get in bed and listen to girls sing if Blizzard

Bates isn't on duty, Mrs. Voorhees doesn't care, she likes it. Read or say a million prayers that you will wake up on a beach in Florida.

11pm: Strange noises in the night. Gone babies. Things scrape against windows and doors; howls from the woods. A fox?

On Saturday night we play Fish. There's a storm, a tree cracked in half and the rain beat so hard shingles flew off the roof and Gwen cried. I hugged her to calm her down but Mrs. Bates said:

"That's not tolerated! No touching! She'll get over it."

Everyone here agrees on only one thing: We hate Bates.

Tonight at dinner, I give my chicken to Judith. Cora got sent to Edge because she got pregnant by immaculate conception or Mr. High-Pockets though no one knows for sure but her stomach got too big to ignore. I'm gaining weight too, now I have to wear size 8 but Knife says not to worry. There's always Jack La Lanne.

Afterwards, we sit in a room with wood tables and chairs where girls cut cards and knit pink and blue booties. I ask why and some say for the gone babies and others say for the mirror in their boyfriend's Chevy. They smile at me and I smile back. I am white and there's nothing I can do about that. Judith tells me they think I am cute and want to be my boyfriend. I am something called a white hammer but Judith says it's not a bad thing at all, it means sexy. Everything here is weird. I don't get the boyfriend thing, Judith says I will.

The metal chairs are set up row after row in the gym and the girls from the other cottages shuffle in single file and I see Kathy in a cherry colored sweater. She spots me and winks then turns away and Mrs. Stiles makes sure we sit far apart. I spot the other white girl, tall and pretty with beehive hair that they'd never allow in our cottage, Murphy.

When the movie rolls, they turn down the lights and even the guards watch just to get away from this hell for a while and see some color. Some girls to my left and in front of me do things with their hands, palms on chairs, slipping things to the palm in the next chair. I wonder what the notes say.

We watch a movie called *Tammy*. It's about a silly white girl who wears blouses that look like the tablecloths and pigtails in her hair. People like her because she is a cheerleader who lives next door and sings, *Tammy's in Love*. She looks about seventeen and already knows how to tap dance in the rain. No one like her is ever going to live next door to anyone here at the reformatory.

Tammy looks at herself in the water, she sings to the moon, and the stars, Tammy in her bobby socks and ponytail, Tammy with her tiny face and turned up nose. Tammy's in love with Tad and lives in a white farmhouse with ruffles at the windows, like Shari from my school bus back then. Debbie Reynolds and the colored girls of Newark who pass love notes palm to palm in the dark and carve initials into their thighs. Next Friday they're showing *Singing in the Rain*.

On the way back to our cottages Judith points to the field where the moon seems to have landed and I see the outlines of the Edge girls walking two by two, and I wonder about all the colored babies of the world.

Nurse Poe

I'VE BEEN HERE FOR THREE MONTHS and still no word from Judge Leahy or the president. Mother Blind and Grandma come to visit and we sit in the gym with the guard at the door. Mother Blind picked up Grandma after work and she wears a wool suit and heels and Grandma hides her house dress under her black overcoat. She eyes the guard and clutches the collar of her coat.

"Zoe," she says, "I don't like this place. I want you home. It's not right." She pulls out a rag and honks her nose.

"Did you talk to the judge?" I ask, Mother Blind.

"Zoe, the judge won't talk to me. What's done is done. There's no going back. Just behave."

"But they can keep me till I'm twenty-one!"

"They won't. They can, but I spoke to a lawyer at work and he said it's rare. Typical stay is fourteen to fifteen months. Unless you get into trouble."

Grandma clicks her tongue and unwraps a Ludden's cough drop.

"That's a year away!" I say.

Panic.

"Lord, help us," Grandma says, her hair gray at the part.

"Good news," Mother Blind says. "Your Aunt Allie finishes her medical training in a few months. She's been through so much."

Nurse Poe, Knife says.

"Figures, I'm in reform school and she's in nursing school."

"Have you been drinking vinegar again?" Mother Blind says. "You should be happy for her."

I lean back on my chair and the metal legs scrape against the linoleum. The gym reeks of rubber.

"Do you like the Bible I sent you?" Grandma says, and reaches into her purse, the guard eyeing her. She rummages through small jars, Kleenex, Spearmint, a bag of jelly beans, lipstick and a book of green stamps and plucks out a white tube that says: Vick's in bright blue letters and jabs it up the right nostril then the left each time making a little snort noise from her throat.

"It's pretty Grandma," I say. "Thanks."

"The twenty-third psalm will get you through," she says.

The guard walks over, in his brown pants and shirt, "NJTSG" over his pocket.

He looks at his wrist watch and says: "Ten minutes."

"What?" Grandma says. "It took us an hour to get here. Can't you make it last longer?"

"Sorry ma'am," he says. "I don't make the rules."

He walks back to the door; his boots echo against the walls.

"What about Willy?" I say.

Mother Blind tells me Willy is in Virginia with Daddy Dead till he gets over his beer drinking and fire setting and she don't know how long because Daddy Dead has emphysema and it's getting worse.

"He won't quit smoking. He hasn't been able to work the last few weeks," she says.

Grandma tells me she got a job at the cinema selling tickets and candy and taking orders for pie on the side. She made friends with the cinema owner a big woman with white hair and a Cadillac.

"The time will pass quickly," Mother Blind, says as they leave but I don't bother to tell her it won't.

"Don't forget your pray-dens," Grandma smiles, her red lipstick smudged at the corners. She kisses me on the cheek and leaves a red heart there.

"I wish I had some whiskey sugar water," I tell her, and the guard gives me the eye.

One day I get a surprise visitor, Daddy Dead. Not a good surprise. "Look at all the trouble you caused," he tells me. "You know I have to pay a lot of money to New Jersey because you are here?"

He has a coughing fit and I hear the loud wheeze in his lungs.

"Every month I have to cut New Jersey a check just so you can live with a bunch of niggers from Newark," he says, and lights a Camel.

"Why didn't Willy come with you," I ask.

"He can't be no place with a locked door like this. "You know how he is. Has your Aunt Allie been here?" he says, and has another hacking attack and stubs his cigarette in the ashtray.

"You mean my aunt-stepmother? No. She's in nursing school."

"Is she seeing anyone?"

The guard looks at his watch and lifts five fingers in the air at Daddy Dead.

I tell him I wouldn't know if Aunt Oink is dating. He tells me he still loves her and can't get over what happened with Zuzu and the divorce. He says how Aunt Oink is the love of his life.

Kill, Knife says.

I'm glad when the guard unlocks the door and he leaves with his hack and his wheeze and his broken heart.

Beauty Lessons

IF YOU ARE SIXTEEN and have the money to buy cigarettes you are allowed four a day at set times, nine o'clock, one o'clock, six o'clock and eight. Mrs. Bates keeps the matches and her eye on Gwen.

The smokers sit on painted blue chairs crammed in the corner by a pile of magazines: Seventeen, Family Circle and Woman's Day, the pages worn and rippled.

Bertha, a tall hunky girl with boobs as big as Aunt Oink's, paces the room singing "Prisoner of Love," a song by James Brown. I never knew about him till now but almost every girl here is in love with him and when I see a photo of him and hear his voice I'm not colored enough yet to think he's cute or even has a good voice. He's scary to me. I can't help it.

Some nights, if Mrs. Bates isn't on duty the girls sing down the hallway after lights out. Judith sings "Amazing Grace" in her deep voice, almost like Grandma's when she sings opera but Judith's voice is deep as a well and coated with honey, not scary like Grandma's. Afterwards, Margo tries to outdo Judith with "Locomotion" but she never can.

This month I have kitchen duty: bubble Farina, burn stacks of white bread and fry about two hundred sunny side eggs. Margo wants her eggs blindfolded so I flip them over. For lunch I boil rice for jambalaya, chop tomatoes and cry over onions.

My kitchen duty doesn't go so well the day I use salt instead of sugar in the cake recipe. They reassign me to scrub the bathrooms but I mix ammonia with bleach and they have to evacuate the building. Mrs. Bates says it's a miracle it didn't explode and burn the place down. I wish. Now I am assigned to laundry duty.

I could train to be a beautician in the beauty study program like Margo, Linda, and Denise but then I'd probably ruin someone's hair but I'm not old enough. They spend the whole day at the beauty parlor because they already quit high school so they don't have to take moron classes.

I stuff the laundry bags till they're fat and heavy and try not to think about whose underwear I touch, collect the wash from outside the pale green doors and fill the straw baskets, carry the baskets on the wooden cart to the laundry house, sort the white, separate the colors, if you mix a red shirt with a white you could end up with pink, (did that) don't use too much soap or suds bubble out of the lid and cover the floor, (did that) fill the driers and Margo's clothes touch Gwen's, Gwen's feel up Linda's, Linda's rub on Cora's, Cora's sleeves tangle in the strap of Margie's bra, all of us tumbling--iron the collars and the hems, lift the lid of the ironing machine and press it onto the table cloth, try not to get a steam burn, if lint gets up your nose blow it, check the names on the collars and waistbands, the socks and the underpants, the bras and the night gowns, fold and fold and fold and don't forget to smile and always wear your lipstick.

I wheel the cart over to the beauty school, pick up the ether smelling towels that burn my nose. Margo tells me not to forget the "doo rags" in the closet. They're what some of the girls use to make their hair flat like a man's. Margo was sent here for selling her body to men so now she wants to be one. At the beauty school, they teach girls to try and be pretty. While I am collecting laundry I listen to their stories.

Linda is telling Rose a story as she rolls Rose's black hair with prickly rollers. The story is about Linda's grandmother Sophie and her neighbor Beatrice and how Beatrice caught fire on Chestnut Street when she lit a cigarette and the fake peony on her felt hat caught flame. She was wearing the dress she borrowed from Linda's grandmother Sophie and when Grandma Sophie saw neighbor Beatrice on fire, she thought for a minute she was seeing herself on fire in the dress she bought for fifteen cents from the gooseberry man who steals wash off neighbor's clothes lines.

Linda clicks the pink rollers tight on Rose's scalp and I remember the night Grandma told me to leave the Toni Perm rollers in all night. Rose is big and tall with creamy tan skin and black eyes and some girls, Cora and Rose for instance, call her Big Mama.

She sits in the chair and files her nails, her long brown legs crossed as Linda snaps away with the pink teeth.

Sophie, I'm sorry about the dress, Beatrice said. *If I die will you put a pitcher of water on my grave? Then she collapsed on the ground.*

"What happened to her?" Rose asks.

"She died." Linda says, and smacks a clean towel around Rose's neck.

I stuff the wash slowly, hoping to hear more stories but Linda stops to put lotion on Rose's hair, squeezing from a plastic bottle across each roller. At the next beauty station Denise tries to calm Gwen's crazy puff of hair with grease from a jar.

I drag the heavy laundry bags past Margo who's soaking brushes and combs.

"Wait," Linda says. "Here, take this towel."

She flips me the rag and presses my palm. I feel the point of the triangle, the edges stiff and thick. I know it's a kite and I can get in trouble. I turn toward the door and bend down to tie my shoelace and stick the kite in my sock.

"Hold on," Margo says. "Did you know these old lady beauticians' are coming here to do makeovers? They're from Pink Poodle Salon in Princeton. Little blue-haired ladies." Her lip curls and there is a half-smile across her lips.

"No," I say.

"Well Blizzard said you're one of the models." Margo gives me an odd smile. All her smiles are odd. "She didn't tell you?" she says, and purses her lips into a tight bud.

"No," I say, "And no one is *touching* my hair."

"We'll see," Margo says, and makes a scissor motion with her free hand through the air.

After lights out, I take the kite from my sock and open the folds and read by the little light I can catch from the outdoor lamp.

> Dear Z,
> Honey and me think you are sweet
> and pretty and we'd like you to join
> our family and be our daughter.
> Love, Your Mom, (I hope)
> L J

I figure LJ is code for Linda. I'm not sure who her husband Honey is but I'm guessing it's Alex. As it turns out, when you are a member of a family they carve your code name into their thighs with raw bobby pins. Not allowed but a lot of girls do it. The only other white girl at the school other than Kat and me, Laura, has been here for three years so far, carved her leg till it exploded and she spent a month in the infirmary with Dr. Hatchet but when she got an infection she got to go a real hospital. But of course they sent her back since she didn't die. Laura had a mixed baby last year but they snapped it up one week later.

Vulture beaks, Knife says.

I hide the kite inside my sock.

On Tuesday, an hour before lockdown, we are in the rec room. Gwen is shy and thin next to me with brown eyes and light brown skin. She set her neighbor's house on fire and someone died. I never ask her about it and if I did she'd run away. There's only certain things you can talk about with her. No one wants to cry till they get home. Margo tries to tame Gwen's hair with irons and grease but it's stubborn. Gwen sits by me at meals and on movie night.

Gwen tells me my hair is the silky kind and she touches it with long fingers and asks if she can brush it. Mrs. Voorhees is on duty tonight so it's okay. Gwen separates my hair in three bands then braids them together. She says never to let them cut my hair and I tell her no one is ever chopping it again after Daddy Dead and Aunt Oink put the bowl on my head and clipped around the rim. Gwen tells me Mrs. Bates thinks my hair is too long. She heard her tell Mrs. Voorhees. I don't like the sound of this. You don't have the right to *not* have your hair cut? What country is this anyway?

On beauty makeover day, the ladies from Pink Poodle step out of a pink Cadillac toting pink boxes and suitcases. They look us over in the gym and write names on a clipboard. Mrs. Bates calls my name. I tell her I don't want a makeover and to let someone else have it. She tells me I will do what I'm *told*. That is why I am here. If you get a write-up the parole board adds a month, or more, to your sentence. I want to get home while I'm still a teenager. I miss Willy and Grandma. Hell, I miss everybody even Aunt Oink. I think I can't stand it here one more day so I go to the damned beauty school on makeover day.

"Hello, I'm Mrs. Fern," the lady says. "Sit down."

I sit in the chair and she spins it around till it is the right height.

"I don't like hairstyles," I say. "And I don't want my hair short."

"It only needs a trim," she says, and promises not to cut more than one inch. Her arms clink gold bracelets in my face. She tells me to relax.

Margo sneers at me in the mirror with her snake poison. Linda is curling Vicky's straight hair. She looks at me and throws a secret kiss when Mrs. Fern turns her back.

"Don't worry, we'll make you pretty," Mrs. Fern says.

Linda pats a hand over her heart, then points to me.

Another lady in a mint cardigan unloads a cardboard box of pink nail polish and remover stacking them on the shelf, all the ladies of Princeton here to rescue us from our hair and grubby nails.

"You know that story about neighbor Beatrice you were telling me?" Rose asks. "Where did your grandmother find a dress for fifteen cents?" Today Rose is having her hair styled and her makeup done.

I squeeze my eyes shut and think about Beatrice who died from a flaming peony and wonder how a dress can cost fifteen cents. The plastic goes around my neck and over my chest and smells like the swimming pool Grandpa bought me and Willy. I lean my head back over the sink and Mrs. Fern massages my scalp with suds that smell lemony. Her hands knead my scalp and she showers my head with warm water, then rubs coconut in and rinses again, pats my hair dry with a soft towel and I start to relax a little. I keep my eyes closed and listen to Linda.

"Grandma Sophie said the investigators told her the artificial peony Beatrice sewed to the felt hat was flammable.

"Huh?"

"Yeah. As it is, Beatrice already had a hard life after her daughter's nightgown caught fire. She was at the ham joint picking up some grub when it happened. The poor girl was walking past the kitchen stove and poof!"

"Lordy," Rose says.

"That's terrible," Mrs. Fern says.

"I knew a boy set the woods on fire once," I say.

"One of the girls here is an arsonist, I heard," Mrs. Fern says.

Mrs. Fern leads me back to the chair and I feel a chill up the back of my neck and the comb on my back. I relax a little, but then I hear a click and a touch of cold steel at my ear and the sound of scissors going snip, snip. When I open my eyes, I see Mrs. Fern has butchered one side of my head.

"You said you wouldn't." I holler.

Then a crash, glass bottles breaking and an ether smell burns my eyes.

"Oh my god." Mrs. Fern screams. "Good grief."

"A broom, please."

"Towels, someone yells.

Margo pinches her nose.

I look in the mirror—something moving in the corner, red and blue—Gwen in a blue sweater holding a large bottle of nail polish remover and a small red box. I jump out of the chair right before Gwen strikes the match and the flames zip across the floor toward the bottles of permanent solution and there is a rush to the exit before a *pop, pop, pop* of little explosions then a loud hiss of flame.

After the fire trucks grind down the lane, we look back at the beauty building still smoking but standing just the same. The firemen were able to put the fire out so not everything was burned and before the night is over the cleaners come in and work overnight to put things back in order by morning.

Gwen is locked in isolation and I lose my privilege to walk outside without a guard because they think I told Gwen to start the fire even though I didn't. But I still have to be in the fashion show with my hair short and stupid and I want to die.

Hair

THIS IS BAD. SHORT. Up to my ears and now poor Gwen is padlocked in isolation. The old ladies from the Pink Poodle ran out the door crying and jumped in their cars not even taking all their pink suitcases. Linda had to finish my hair but there wasn't much she could do because the left side was already chopped up to my ear and Mrs. Bates told Linda no hip hairdos and that she had to put my hair in a flip.

Oh god, I hear Knife say.

I had to walk up and down the gym to model the awful hairdo. I didn't look at anyone, not even Judith, only the floor. I can't look in the mirror it's so bad. I could try and style it with grease I guess. After I wash the hair style out Judith gives me a do rag to tie around my head.

Today at lunch, Cora passed me my second kite and I don't know what to do about the first so I tell Linda okay, I will be her daughter. It's what they do here. Families they call it, like Judith told me back in quarantine. The second kite is from Mary Corpreau, the light skinned girl with pretty green eyes. She wants to be my man. Nothing makes sense here.

I never wrote a kite but it feels dangerous and fun so I ask for some more paper to write the judge. This is what I wrote:

> Dear L J,
> Thanks for wanting to be my mother.
> I would like that because you are always nice.
> Your daughter,
> Z

Gwen showed me how to fold the kite but it takes me ten times to get it right but finally I have a tiny yellow triangle that I tuck into my sock. Sometimes they do random checks of your pockets and socks. At dinner I whisper Linda in Rose's ear and she passes it down to Linda.

I wonder what I am supposed to do as her daughter? Gwen told me it's just about writing the kites and making plans for going home and living together on the outside but I saw Judith and Cora doing stuff under the table with one hand while pretending to read the Bible with the other.

I write Mary back that she can be my boyfriend because she is pretty.

Holy, Knife says.

Colored

SOMEWHERE BETWEEN GETTING HERE and six months later I turned colored. I don't feel white anymore. I'm colored all the time and I know when I get out of here I'm never going to be white again. The only thing that's not colored about me is my skin and hair. I like everything colored: The Temptations, Smokey Robinson, Motown all the way but I still don't like James Brown, yet. Linda says I will and how I can come visit her in Newark, and maybe we can go to his concert.

Linda's mother bakes sweet potato bread with butter and honey, and when she goes to church on Sunday to sing, her mother wears a yellow dress and a hat with red flowers then she comes home and cooks chicken or ribs and they eat in the sunny dining room at the walnut table with her aunties and her brothers and sisters and Mr. Johnson from down the street who is very old and lonely. Afterwards, they play piano and sing and sometimes the minister comes over but he's colored and doesn't preach outside the church. I tell her I can't eat the chicken and ribs but I like cornbread and apple pancakes. Linda said she didn't know how good she had it at home but she fell in love with a guy and was in the car when he robbed a liquor store and shot a man and she didn't rat out her boyfriend to the cops. She says I can come to her house on Sundays once we get out. We'll meet at the train station in Newark.

"You okay doing that?"

"Yeah. I took the train lots of times," I tell her, picturing Kat's platinum hair wave in strands across her face as the air from the subway blew us up the steps to MacDougal.

She says I will still be her family even then, my other mother.

Linda showed me her thigh with a Z carved in, the scab still there. The Z is for me. There are other initials in her thigh and those are healed over, the scabs gone and she slips me a new bobby pin.

After lights out I start to carve the top of my thigh. It doesn't hurt so bad and I keep going until I see the blood. Linda says to let it scab over then pull the scab off and carve some more. I make a letter

M. M for Mary. Mary Corpreau, my boyfriend. She has creamy brown skin and lime colored eyes, the prettiest girl I've ever seen. She winks from across the table and sends me kites that say she loves me and signs with X's and O's. Sometimes, we brush hands standing in line or outside the mess hall and once she touched my hair when Mrs. Voorhees turned around, then kissed me quick on the lips.

I write her kites that tell her I like having her as a boyfriend and when she touched my hair and my hand it felt good and made my heart pound. I tell her I love her eyes.

I sign with red lipstick kisses. I never had a boyfriend and now I have a boyfriend that is a girl. Everything is different here.

Sometimes I think about going home but not all the time anymore. After a year passes they tell me I am coming up for parole and I don't really care because I'm not sure I want to leave Linda and Gwen and Mary. When Gwen came out of isolation she wouldn't speak for three weeks. She is a tender bean.

What will I do when I have to go back to Lockwood High with all the whites separated from the coloreds. I don't want to be with them. I'm not one of them anymore. Will I always like girls? If I like boys, I know they won't be white boys. What about that? What will Grandma and Grandpa say? Mother Blind? They still say *nigger*, well, not Mother Blind. They still want a place for white people and another place for coloreds.

I look in the mirror in the bathroom. We aren't allowed mirrors in our rooms because, you know, we might see ourselves. I see I am still white after all this time. My skin hasn't colored brown like the others and my hair is still straight but long again. I turn over my palms and they are the same shade as the rest of my hand. I think when I get home I will get a dark tan, perm my hair buy a doo rag. I think when I get home I'll start a singing group with two colored girls and we'll snap our fingers and work on our dance routines, practice our moves in the mirror, pack blades in our beehives just in case.

What about pilot? Knife says.

I keep forgetting. In here, sometimes you forget about the world before this one.

"I'm sure you'll be there to remind me," I tell her.

At lunch I see Honey pass Cora a kite under the table. Linda looks at her over, checking out her tapioca pudding and Honey pets Cora's knee then her thigh all the way up. I think this isn't right. Honey is married to Linda with three children a son and two daughters: me, Lulu and Fran and Cora is Linda's sister.

I don't say right away though. I wait till I see Honey rub Cora's ass outside the wash house.

"I saw Honey and Cora touch under the table," I tell Linda. "Cora is your sister who used to be your daughter, right?"

"Don't you dig no dirt, girl. I forbid you to do that. Cora is your Aunt."

"But she used to be my sister," I say.

"Well, things change," she says, and twists her hair into a knot.

"But don't you care that Honey is feeling her up?"

"You must be wrong about that," she says. "Honey and me are in love and jump the broom married."

"Well, I'd be mad," I say, but Linda's knitting needles are stabbing the pink yarn in and out and around and she don't look up at me.

When I see Honey at the wash house I say:

"I know about you."

"Don't need you collaring no jive," she says, and gives me her dead cat eye. "Stay outta my ass and I'll stay outta yours. It's deadsville, man, you hear?"

Judith and Jen have five children, two daughters and three sons': Macy, Lacy, Tracy, Sorrow and Morrow.

Judith says everyone needs a family. Especially in here. Nothing else really matters until you get out. And if you leave your family behind well that usually means you'll come back because your family on the outside is not your family any more.

Parade

WHAT I HAVE BEEN DOING THESE DAYS: I was a sailor in Mrs. Voorhees Harvest Home parade on the "Red Sails in the Sunset" float. Don't ask what that means because I don't know except it is a song, a stupid song. Mrs. Voorhees sewed me a sailor outfit and bought a sailor hat at the Five & Dime and I'm on the back of a truck holding a white flag, the sail part and the truck, the boat, sailing a circle, the girls on the lawn eating hotdogs and fries on the shaggy grass.

The other floats: Gwen as Betsy Ross in a blue gown with a white napkin pinned around her neck, Cora as Molly Pitcher, a tall girl from Wilson dressed as Abraham Lincoln with a beard and a black top hat and a girl from Taylor wearing a white wig dressed like George Washington. Nothing in this place makes any sense and after a while you give up on sense if you had any in the first place.

There was a dance too and I saw Kat there and I could tell she thought it was an asshole thing to do and it was. It was Mrs. Voorhees idea, a dance in the gym with the boys from Jamesburg, nobody dancing, gawking back and forth. Kat is different now, in love with Chancy Grey, a tough girl with silky skin and hair. Kat ignores me and doesn't look back when I stare across the gym.

It is a dumb dance with boys on one side and girls on the other feeling like morons. There are three white boys to match up with us three white girls but I only notice the colored boys and not even sure I like them. Nobody moves until Mrs. Voorhees pairs people up and makes them dance to stupid "Red Sails in the Sunset" again. Margo said Mrs. Voorhees is trying to be white and that is why she died her hair blonde and always acts as if everything is right with the world.

296

Normal

TODAY I TURNED FOURTEEN and Mrs. Voorhees gives me a tube of lipstick and I a card that says: Life is a Bowl of Cherries. Happy Birthday!

Judith made me a pair of mint green baby booties and Alex a string bracelet, Linda a necklace made from pink yarn, Margo her black eye stare. She doesn't like me being friends with Judith and Judith doesn't like me being so close to Gwen because Gwen used to be her girl. Everybody jealous. Rose and Carol are getting a divorce over Rose letting Sammy stick her hand up her skirt while she spooned her Farina.

The way you get a divorce here is you get a kite saying: I want a divorce. Then, Joanne tries to keep it from happening. She tries to patch things up talking about commitment and love everlasting and holy. But after three or four tries if that doesn't work she sends you a kite that says: Divorce Is Final, sign below and then you are free to marry another girl.

It's crazy but after a while the crazy seems normal just like every other place in the world.

Some days I lose my temper. I get in trouble when I slam the cabinet door in the kitchen. Kitchen duty is better than laundry but I don't get along with Mrs. Dash the cook, a white woman with long arms and short hair. Mrs. Dash doesn't like me because I'm white. She only likes the colored girls. She told Laura all the girls in the reformatory have "done it" with boys, there is no one here who hasn't and she looks my way and I slam the cabinet door and the glass breaks. I wish I did it with one of those diner boys that night so I could be like all the other girls who did it. Mrs. Dash writes me up and I get locked in my room for a week and get a demotion. I get mad when people say things that aren't true. Not every girl is the same. I know where I come from. The country. The woods. East Jesus as Margo would say.

Virgin Mary

IT'S CHRISTMAS AND WE HAVE A SKINNY TREE in the corner with colored paper chains on it and no lights or glass ornaments. We aren't allowed gifts from home because some girls wouldn't get any so we open donated gifts, tubes of lipstick, socks, Bibles, chewing gum, Mars Bars, plastic jewelry, composition books, colored pencils.

Margo wears a furry brown sweater with stripes and plops down next to Gwen and cases out her loot sniffing for something she might want for herself.

"I can use this," she says, and takes a pack of gum, a candy bar and a set of colored pencils."

"You tell Mrs. Bates, I'll smash everything in your room," she says, and her lip curls over her buck teeth, her mouth a skinny line.

"Goddamn bitch!" Judith says. "I'll kill her. That cunt thinks she own everything and everybody."

Margo turns her head and stares at Judith with her yellow eyes.

One night, after the movie, *Gidget*, Judith and Margo get into a fight over Alex. Margo hit Alex in the thigh where her fresh carving of L J was and Alex's leg busted open and bled all over. Judith told Mrs. Bates and then when everyone else was watching the movie *Tammy's in Love*, for the second time, Margo snuck out without Mrs. Webber catching her. She went into Judith's room and smashed her figure of Virgin Mary from the dresser, the head snapped off, the hands left praying in the corner, all the pieces on the floor.

When Judith got back from the movie she was mad.

"Who broke my Virgin Mary?"

"Maybe it just fell," Alex says, her green-yellow eyes cut down the center with a black slit.

"It don't just fall," Judith says. "It was cuffed."

"What's going on?" Mrs. Bates hollers.

"Somebody smashed Virgin Mary."

Judith kneels on the floor and picks at the pieces, tears running down her slow eye.

"Judith, no one was here hon. It was an accident. A draft maybe." Mrs. Voorhees says.

Mrs. Voorhees don't want to know. More work for her writing up the papers.

"Maybe a ghost," Alex says.

"We'll never know," Mrs. Voorhees says, playing her keys. "Time for lock up girls. Get ready to wash up. You have ten minutes."

Outside it is raining hard, silver needles beat the sidewalks muddy and the sky is dark a brownish red the color of Grandpa's cigar. Grandma visits and tells me that since Grandpa don't work anymore after his stroke, he lays on the bed all day smoking cigars and nipping whiskey. She put up a little Christmas tree with colored lights and silver cookie cutters hung from string. Grandma says our tree, the one Mother Blind decorated is the prettiest with pretend snow on the branches, blue lights and silver stars and that next year she hopes I am out of this place on Christmas day and I can hang my stick people on the tree because she saved them, the ones I made when I was nine or ten, set in her red and gold Luzianne coffee tin.

At dinner Margo says:

"I'll have some a that meat tit," Judith.

"Like hell you will," Judith says, and pulls her plate closer.

"How about you hay-eater?"

"Go ahead and take it," I tell her. "I don't eat it anyway."

Margo sucks on the meat, grease dripping down her chin.

"How come you a hay-eater?" Cora says.

I think about the pig's knuckles but don't say.

"I like animals," I say.

"Oh ain't that sweet. I could go for some wag myself. Cow wag, Dagwood. Know what that is?" Margo says.

"Don't want to," I say.

"It's a good thick cow tongue sandwich," she says, with her snarl. "Just cuz you can afford to be picky. You learn to like what you can afford to eat."

I throw down my fork. Even the potatoes make me feel sick.

"We're poor too," I say.

299

"You ain't po, you white. Even if you is po you still white. You don't know nothin' about po."

"But I know about poor," I say. "I can't help it if I'm white, I don't even want to be. I want to be colored like the rest of you."

"Oh really? You don't know nothin' bout being a nigger," she says. "If you did you wouldn't want to be one."

"Hey," Margo says to Cora. "I'm feeling your draft way over here. Got a problem?"

Cora stares back but don't say anything. Nobody likes Margo. I bet her own mother don't even like her.

"Is it true your father went to the burner?" Margo says. "I heard they fired him for raping that white can of goods."

"Don't be digging dirt on her," Linda says. "She's not feeling well. She got the cramps."

"All you need is some choke dog for that. Fix you right up. Wish I could get a bottle of that in here. That would cheer up the place." Linda says.

Cora rolls her eyes.

"No. What I need is to get my black New Jersey self outta here so I don't have to listen to no more from you," Cora says.

"Don't argue," Alex says. "We're all stuck in here. Ain't nothing we can do about it."

"Stuck in deadville with no bucket to escape in," Margo says. "Just so the white girl knows, since she wants to be a *nigger*, a bucket is a car fresh out the chop shop. An old car put together with thief parts like Frankenstein."

"I had a car like that once," I say. "King Car."

"Girl you ain't got no license, you jiving me."

"No," I say. "It was a junk in our backyard."

"Well now ain't that honey," Margo says.

Judith gives Margo her steady eye and dips her bread in the meat gravy, chews it hard keeping her slow eye on Margo.

Alex says she's worried about Celine's baby. Celine was only in Murphy for a couple weeks. She's tall, thin with toffee skin and big doe eyes so pretty she could be a princess but she's pregnant by her brother. Just the same, she don't want to give her baby away. She don't want a gone baby. Gwen says the gone babies come back on full moon nights and float down the walkway of Edge like paper dolls, thin and looking for their mamas in all the windows.

"Celine say if try to take her baby she'll run with it," Gwen says.

Judith says they're babies owned by the state. The state can kill the babies. The state can kill us.

I almost believe her.

Mrs. Voorhees wants us to sing Christmas carols after dinner but nobody feels like it with all the rain pounding the roof and no lights on the tree. Nobody here sings Christmas carols anyway, nobody except Gwen and she stands in the rec room and sings "Silent Night" in a high voice, her big eyes rolling, staring at the dusty ceiling fan as if she's seeing something there the rest of us don't see.

"Thank you, Gwen," Mrs. Voorhees says. "Nice to see one of you has some holiday spirit."

Margo scowls from the corner chewing on Gwen's Mars Bar, Judith knitting a pair of pink baby booties for her gone baby, tiny pink and white booties with ties pulled threw the ankles and looped in bows and the two connected with string to hang on a mirror or a door knob as a reminder.

Alex says they should make them for real babies and maybe they'll end up with the ones who are gone at the orphanage. Maybe the babies will somehow know where the booties came from so a part of its Mama will be there. Linda says she's learning how to make a bonnet and Joanne says she's knitting a mint green sweater when she figures it out but she don't have more yarn and no money to buy any at the reformatory store.

"I'll have my Mama bring you some," Alex says, braiding her potholder on the square green frame.

After lights out, I hear noises from Margo's room next to mine. It sounds like a dog scratching dirt, scraping and I hear a sound, pebbles falling onto the floor. When the night watch walks the hall the pebbles stop and when she is gone Margo digs some more, pebbles rolling on the floor, and I wonder if she is digging a hole in the floor and scooping out a secret tunnel like in the prison movies.

In the morning there are rings around Margo's yellow eyes and I notice her fingernails are nearly gone.

"What are you doing in there?" I whisper. "You kept me awake last night."

Her eyes have green speckles and they stare back at me like glass rocks.

"I'm bored aren't you?" she said.

"Yeah."

"If you mention this to anyone," she snarls. "You'll end up with the other buried bones, understand?"

"Yeah," I tell her. "I don't care what you do."

"Only a few girls know. You're next cell over so I knew you'd find out but I don't see you as a snitch. But it comes with a price."

"Okay," I say. "But what are you doing?"

But Margo stomps away, her large shoulders all muscle beneath her striped sweater, her hair a bright red mop from all the experiments at the beauty school.

The History of Aviation

"You have a package," Mrs. Bates says. She gives me her scowl and throws the package at me and it lands heavy in my lap.

> To: Zoe King
> Trenton State Home for Girls
> Trenton, NJ

The package is big and square with no return address and I see where it's been inspected by the asshole specking for secret codes, guns and knives and cupcakes filled with keys and rat poison.

I unwrap it in my room, slowly, so I keep guessing for a time. It's a thick and heavy book with a brown leather cover and when I turn it over the title is:

The History of Aviation.

What? This is fat city, as Margo would say. But who sent it?

I leaf through the pages. There are photographs of people wearing flight suits and jumping off barns and mountains and all kinds of contraptions that didn't work and killed people. There is the story of The Wright Brothers, Charles Lindbergh and then on page 365 a woman waving from the hatch of her plane and she has bobbed yellow hair and wears a brown leather cap with earflaps and goggles on her head and she is smiling, showing her white teeth. I stare and bumps crawl up my arms and down the back of my neck when I read the name: Amelia. Amelia Earhart. Disappeared. On the Island. Lost contact. Headline News. Foggy weather blamed.

Knife says you can't know everything about the world. You can't know how the weegee board knows the future or how the moon hangs in the sky or why the sun doesn't burn out like other fires, and what about the stars? You can't know for sure how the stars shine and make patterns in big and little dipper shapes. Only what books tell you but what do they know?

In the morning I sass the cook in the kitchen and get sent to lock down so I can read the book and study the photographs the rest of the day and into the night.

I read everything in the book and the parts about Amelia I read over and over especially this one part because it gives me chicken flesh and prickly pin hairs.

Amelia flew through clear skies for about three hours. Then the altimeter failed so she couldn't read how high or low she was flying. Flames shot from the exhaust and a raging electrical storm bossed her around violently for about an hour. Ice was now coating the wings adding weight so she flew lower to warmer air until she could see the waves break beneath her. When low fog rolled in she had to fly higher. She was flying blind with a leaky gas tank. At dawn she spotted the Irish coast and looked for a place to land and followed a railroad but instead of an airport she found miles of green farm pasture and she brought her plane down in a long sloping meadow frightening sheep, cows and horses and landing in front of the farmer's stone cottage. The farmer said at first he wasn't sure if she was a man or a woman.

"Have you flown far?" he asked.

"From America," she said. "My name's Amelia."

I read this so many times I have it memorized. I was in the other layer on the other level and she was there and I was there and Knife was there and I know she is the only one who understands.

I slam the book shut and hide under the blankets and hug it, afraid to open it again but I can't wait to. I wonder if the gone babies are out tonight? Anything is possible. Maybe the president sent me the book, the judge. Nah, not him. Maybe the boy in the woods. Yeah.

A Hole in the Wall

AT NIGHT I HEAR MARGO CRACK THE PLASTER, piece by piece, knocking through the wall. Then later in the night I hear a groan, some kind of crack and a loud thump on the floor then silence for a long time until the night watch makes her rounds and all falls silent.

At breakfast Margo asks me to pass her the sugar bowl and slips a kite into my palm and I slip it into my sock making sure Mrs. Voorhees isn't looking.

Alex looks especially upset today, hunched over her Farina bowl and eyeballing Margo, then back to the bowl not looking at the rest of us.

Judith is quiet and dark today too, still fired up about her Virgin Mary, her steady black eyes on Margo as she breaks the yolk of her egg, all the yellow oozing out.

> The Kite says:
>   The Plan:
>   We're busting a riot and breaking outta here.
>   You're either in or your out. If you're out and rat
>   on us we'll kill you.

In the rec room that night I think about Margo's plan and whether or not she'd kill me. I think she would. I ask Judith what happened to the girls who ran away the last time she was here.

"Depends," she says. "Somebody paying for your ass they add time. Nobody paying for your ass they don't. Just lock up. Why?"

"Just wondering," I say.

"I hear somebody planning a break out," she whispers. "Margo, I bet."

"I wouldn't know," I say, but her dark eyes know I am lying.

"They always come up caught, sick, drugged out, pregnant or dead," she says.

After lights out and final check, I hear plaster crumble to the floor and can't believe they didn't get caught by now since it happens

305

every night. Maybe they know about it and don't care since they'll get caught anyway. Or, maybe they're busy smoking and eating all the leftover cake in the kitchen after the new girl's birthday. There's always leftovers of cake since they give us slices skinny as paper.

Night after night the sound of falling plaster. Then I don't hear it so much till one night Margo starts scraping my wall down near the floor on the side where my bed is. I press my ear to the wall and listen to the pebbles drop and the grind of something metal.

I'm scared because Daddy Dead is paying so I'll get more time and I don't want that.

I flip through my diary in the moonlight past about twenty pages that say:

     I can't wait to get out of here

But, truth is, it don't seem so bad in here anymore. I'm not really sure if I want to go home some days but other days I dream about running wild through the woods and feeling the air and all the creatures there waiting for me to come back. Back to the pond. I'll live there, build a little house and the Stovekin boy won't kick me out this time.

Then the next day I think maybe I should get in enough trouble to stay here till I'm sixteen so then I can quit school and go to beauty school instead. Judith says they only keep girls till they are twenty-one if they killed someone. But in the back of my brain Knife is there reminding me that I want to be a pilot and live in Greenwich Village with the beats and the poets with long beards howling words. I never knew I liked words so much until that night with Kat, stoned and listening to that poet guy, Allen Ginsberg and his *supernatural darkness, hydrogen jukebox, boxcar, boxcar, boxcar*. His words woke me up, high.

On Friday night I hear a chunk of my wall fall out and I crawl under the bed and see Margo's hand chip away with a nail file she stole from the beauty school. She sticks her hand all the way through and she gives me five.

"I'll have this busted out by tomorrow," she whispers. "Alex is here."

Margo's hand goes away and in comes Alex's, small chicken boned hand. She gives me five too and her is hand warm against my own.

Keys playing down the hallway. We are silent in the dark, Alex holding onto my hand.

"Everyone in bed in there?" the new guard hollers. I quick jump back in bed and pull the covers up and everything goes quiet till I hear the key turn in my door and the light flick on. I spot a piece of plaster on the floor but it's rolled under the dresser.

"Everything okay in here," she says.

She's young and tall and light brown. It says Miss Cooper on her nametag.

"Yes," I say, rubbing my eyes.

"I thought I heard something," she says, and looks around the room.

"I was sleeping," I say. "I didn't hear anything in my sleep."

She stands there for a few more seconds looking around but she doesn't see the chunk of wall hidden by the leg of my dresser.

"Okay," she says, and locks the door again.

I hear her unlock Margo's door and figure they've had enough time to make things look normal. I see the light flicker on the wall opposite Margo's.

There's a pause. Then I hear Margo say "What is it Miss Cooper?"

"Just checking," Miss Cooper says. "Heard something, must be the wind."

Once I hear the key lock Margo's door shut I can start breathing again.

Pillowcase

It's Sunday night when Margo chips the hole big enough for me to climb through, my heart crazy as I squeeze in the tiny space wondering what would happen if I got stuck.

Alex sits on the bed in the moonlight, her eyes shining dark.

What about the plaster? Someone will see it broken on the floor."

I pick up a piece and put it in my pocket.

"You have laundry duty right," Margo says.

"Yeah."

"Okay. You sweep the plaster in your pillowcase. When you get to the laundry there is a garbage bin at the back of the room by the water heater. Dump it in there and cover it with whatever else is in there."

We sit in a circle of light on the floor and talk about busting the outside wall but this will be harder to hide though there are bushes outside.

We play jacks on the floor until we hear the keys and quick crawl back and sneak into our beds.

All day I wait for the night. When the moon is out we scan out the window for the gone babies that ghost around Edge. Alex says she saw one floating with a blanket but I didn't see nothing and neither did Margo. Still, we watch.

One night I saw something strange but not out the window. After I crawled back in my room tired and ready to sleep a warm cloud of air blew in my room from somewhere. I felt the heat hang over my bare feet and I got spooked so I squeezed back through to Margo's room but she was in bed and so was Alex and they were under the blankets, Alex upside down and the blankets were rolling like crazy.

That's when I hear boots down the hall, Blizzard Bates, and I quick slip back into my room.

I hear the key turn and the light flicker from Margo's room.

"What's going on in here," Bates says, and Margo starts to cry.

"What is it?" Bates says.

"I was having a nightmare," Margo says. "A bad one."

"Well, go back to sleep," Blizzard says. "And stop moaning, you'll wake the others."

"But how…" Margo starts to say, but her door locks and the light caught on the wall across the hallway goes dark and we listen as Blizzard's boot steps fade down linoleum floor.

That was scarier than the gone ghost and I wonder what Margo and Alex were doing in bed together and how Alex made it back to her room so fast but whatever they were doing, I'm not telling anyone.

My Dad

JUDITH IS MAD AT ME because now I am friends with Margo but I have to be friends with Margo. Judith says Margo used to be her husband but left her for Judith's sister who used to be her child. Just like real families in here.

So this is how it goes with me:

Linda is my mom, Honey is my dad, Mary is my boyfriend, Viola is my sister, Cora is my brother. Kites are flying everywhere all day and hardly anybody caught. I think all the women guards are only interested in the keys and look the other way if they see anybody passing a kite.

Linda has my whole name carved into her leg now. Right next to my name is Viola and on her shoulder is Honey. The M on my thigh for Mary is healed up now but I don't carve any others. Not since the only other white girl in here besides Kat and me nearly lost her leg when it got infected.

Mary and me kissed again. She is so pretty and sweet and always winks at me and blows kisses. What I don't understand is what would we do if we were alone? I saw Honey stick her finger up Linda's dress underneath the table in the rec room so maybe that is what you do. Linda made a howl sound but then Blizzard walks in the room and Linda says she stubbed her toe.

I guess everybody is crazy everywhere. Only place sane and quiet is in the sky.

Parole

WE GOT CAUGHT. While we were in the mess hall eating runny eggs Blizzard Bates had our rooms searched. Margo got two weeks isolation and so did Alex but I only got one week and my parole is still on. Weird. I thought I'd get another month. I kind of hoped I'd get another month. Lock up wasn't so bad because they didn't take my book so I studied how to land this time since I already know how to take off.

At the parole board I had to sit in front of four people who sat at a long table, me in a straight back chair in front of them.

"Have you learned your lesson?"

"Yes."

"Parole means you need to follow the rules of the parole board."

"Yes"

"The rules meaning you must attend school or if you decide to quit school at age sixteen you must work."

"Yes."

"You are to have no contact with Katherine Blue Atwood.

"Yes."

"You'll have to come to my office once a month," a thick faced woman with man cut hair says. She wears clunky wedged Army boots. She speaks with a loud and rough voice, deep and scary.

"You'll have to take a bus to Elizabeth and arrive on time."

"Yes."

"If you are caught drinking, partying or having contact with Miss Atwood or breaking the rules of your parole in any way you will be returned to this facility. Do you understand? You are still a ward of the state of New Jersey."

"Yes."

"Why were you sent here?" a man asks. I recognize him as the psychologist I asked to see. I tried to tell him that sometimes I wanted to die either by sticking my head in an oven or drowning in a toilet bowl. He stared out the window the entire time. I never went back.

Then they spoke in low tones to one another.

"Parole granted," Army boots says. "Keep in mind it can be revoked at any time."

"Yes."

It's all about the landing when I get home.

Normal landing can be made with the power on or off, with or without flaps. The kind of landing you make depends on different things: surface wind, turbulence, size of landing patch and the air temperature. Clear the engine with the throttle so the cylinders don't load with fuel. Hold your glide at 70 to 80 mph and enter at an angle of 45 degrees. Hold your glide with the flaps up. Check air traffic. Break your glide with back pressure on the wheel at 10 or 12 feet above the surface. Hold the nose high and touch down on the two main wheels. Don't ride the brakes. I imagine parole is a lot like landing in a country you haven't visited in a long time. Freedom to be good. Freedom to be bad. But the freedom I want most I know I'll only find in the sky.

Glitter

NOW THAT MY PAROLE'S BEEN STAMPED and signed, I get to go home for one day until the release date July 15 when I leave for good, maybe. Kat went home last month. Judith tells me not to forget: Don't look back.

Mother Blind drives an old green Chevy up the drive in the rain and the pavement glints blue beneath the black tires. I see Grandma and Aunt Oink, Grandma with her big earrings and Aunt Oink in a white uniform. It feels strange getting in the car. Everything is different. Yet the same. My first time out of this place in a year and four months. It doesn't seem quite real like stepping out of one of those glass bowls filled with tiny green plants and slate colored stones. Something like an aquarium. The willows by the entrance drip green leaves.

Grandma says to hurry up because we've got to be back by 7 o'clock and still have to drive an hour just to get home her red rhinestones shine even in the rain.

"I can't wait till you're out of this dump," she says.

"How can you stand being in there with all those *niggers*," Aunt Oink says. She is wearing her white uniform. On the pocket it says: Allie King.

"You don't call Johnny Mathis that," I say.

"Oh he's half white," she says. Her black hair is in a twist and she is wearing her red lipstick. A smoke cloud from her cigarette hangs in the air floating tiny sparks of lint.

"They're my friends," I tell her. "And I don't call them that. It's a bad word. It's a South word."

"Hmm," she says, and her smoke twists through the air.

Pig ears, rat tails and snakeheads, snort, snort Knife whispers.

"Do you want to go get ice cream?" Mother Blind says.

"Sure," I say, and feel as if I am sailing, too fast.

"How come you're wearing your nurse uniform?"

We slip down the hill, fog blowing up from the wet asphalt, I grip the door handle.

"Going to work at three."

"Can you slow down?" I say. "You're driving so fast."

"I'm only going forty," Mother Blind says. I take a deep breath.

"Do you like it? Being a nurse."

I roll down the window to breathe the free air.

"It depends on what floor they put you on," Aunt Oink says. "But there's a lot of cute doctors."

"Do you see dead people?"

"Oh yeah," she says. "I have to put them in the body bags. They're heavy."

"Isn't it scary?"

"Not after the first few," she says. "Just a body like an old overcoat you try to give away."

"There's something I need to tell you," Mother Blind says.

"What? It's not Willy is it?"

The rain beats down on the roof and makes green puddles on the road ahead.

"No. Your father."

"What about him?"

The windshield wipers aren't working right and everything is blurry.

"Allie, could you light me a cigarette."

"Dope stinking," Grandma says.

"He's in jail and he's not getting out for a very long time."

"For What?"

"Rape."

"What?"

"He raped a teenage girl," Aunt Oink says, and her pocketbook snaps shut.

"I don't understand."

"He had sex with a young girl against her will," Mother Blind says. "In her college dorm. An eighteen year-old. He'd been following her. Drunk. He climbed through the bathroom window. She was in the shower. They found a photograph of her in his wallet. Dark haired. Big boobs."

"Sound familiar?" Aunt Oink says.

"Why?"

314

But no one answers, only the sound of wheels as they slap the wet and hilly road. I wonder if he'll have to pay for himself to be in prison. Did he hold a pillow over her face? I know she wished him dead over and over. But I don't ask how he did it or if a college dorm is like Murphy without the locked rooms. But the lock would have saved her. Will she be able to fall in love like the brides and housewives in *Woman's Day*? What will happen to her? Will she finish college or have to get a lobotomy like in the movie with Elizabeth Taylor? Will she ever want to be touched again? The line of trees along the road melt watery and bleed into the ditch and I watch in the rearview mirror the rain hit the road we leave behind.

"What about Willy?" I say.

"He's back home waiting. For you," Mother Blind says, and it seems as if it takes hours to get to the garden apartments.

I'm not sure how I feel. Nothing seems real anymore. Maybe the sky.

I order a coffee ice cream cone and Grandma orders butter pecan.

"I love ice cream so much I could swim in it," she says, and I think how she never got to see the world except for her little patch and even that wasn't so good. I wish we made it to Florida that time. At least she'd get to see some state other than New Jersey. Maybe I can fly her there someday before it's too late. I'll show her the secret parts of New York City.

When we get to the apartment it's like walking through a tunnel and nothing looks as before., everything smaller and further away. I look around my room at the white furniture and the unlocked door. I think of the day we went to court and how I was so sure we wouldn't be sent away. So sure if we were it would be a boarding school. How I could be such an imbecile? I didn't know about the iron world then. Everybody is so damned white out here.

I knock on Willy's door.

"*Doorshock*," he says.

I open the door and he looks up with his round eyes, his hair streaked blue and down to his shoulders. My mind skips back to the pond and Willy with his cape and his fox crown, a filmstrip, images connected together in frames: Knife in her leather outfit flying to Paris, the roller coaster, the bike, King Car, Willy always under the hood spinning sparks and plugs, Toro jumping through weeds, the boy with gold hair. It seems it never happened now.

"Helmet," he says, and points to on the robot parts spread out on the floor. I help him put all the different parts into separate categories dropping them onto paper plates and into cups.

"*Wabbershuck?*"

"I don't have money and I can't drink," I tell him.

"Why?"

"Okay," I say, "I still have six hours. But just a short one and I don't have any money."

He pours Gypsy Rose into a jam jar.

"Woah," I say. "I have to go back."

"*Formeration?*"

"Yeah," I say. "Formeration, but I'll be out soon. What are you making?"

"Roof-totters and shimmy-gigs," he says, and points to a tin box that beeps and has knobs and antennas and speakers.

"Are you sad Daddy went to jail?" But he doesn't answer. He is busy turning knobs and adjusting his antennas. I don't need to ask him to explain. I feel woozy from the Gypsy Rose but Mother Blind boils angel hair and her special cherry pepper tomato sauce and the dizzy goes away. It tastes like the best food in the entire world and I eat way too much.

After, Willy calls me back to his room.

"Glitter," he says, and opens his closet. She pops out with her beehive sparkling, her hair blue-black and her skin ghost white. She's wearing a very short blue skirt and white boots.

"What say?" she says.

"Hi. You must be Glitter."

"What's happening?" she says.

On the way back to the reformatory we don't talk about Daddy Dead or the girl. All the lights are on in Murphy and I wave to the car and walk up the path with the guard.

Back to formeration, Knife says.

316

Grease

It's July fourth and soon I will be home.

I'm in Fielder Cottage now where the doors are unlocked and all the girls who are going home stay. Judith is one of them and she is across the hall from me. The rooms are big here with regular furniture and big windows without bars and your own bathroom. We can keep our doors open during the day but aren't allowed in one another's rooms.

At night there is a living room with a television and girls playing cards and Monopoly but I stay in my room feeling quiet but I think I'm happy about going home. Mrs. Webber comes in my room and wants to know what is wrong with me and how come I'm not socializing with the others and I tell her I am studying my aviation history but she doesn't like that and says I need to join the others.

I tell her okay and she leaves.

"I'll see you downstairs then," she says.

There is an upstairs and downstairs here, a big stairway outside my room. I can see into Judith's room, her dresser where everything is lined up neat: lipstick, combs, deodorant, soap, talc, lotion, hair grease. I wonder how the hair grease feels and how it would look on my hair. I check down the stairway and see Judith at the table shuffling cards with Rose. I tip toe into her room and open the grease, stick in my finger in and scoop up a small glob, go back to my room but before I can rub it in my hair I hear footsteps. It's Judith and she stomps into her room and walks straight to the jar of grease.

"Who touched my grease!" she says. "Was it you?"

"No! What would I do with it?"

"You were the only one up here."

I pretend to dry my hands on a towel in my bathroom.

"Mrs. Webber!" Judith calls down the stairs. "Someone was in my room! Someone was in my grease."

Judith is angry. I don't know how she can tell anyone touched it. I hardly took any.

"Zoe was it you?" Mrs. Webber asks.

"No, what would I do with it?" I say.

"Judith are you sure?"

"Yeah, I'm sure. I'm real sure," she says

"Let me see the jar," Mrs. Webber says, and Judith unscrews the lid. "Now how can you tell? It's full."

"I can tell," Judith says. She is staring at me with her sharp black eyes.

"Come on, now. You're just tense about going home. Shut your door and come on back downstairs. You too Zoe. You've been keeping to yourself a little too much. You have to get over that. You're going back out into the world, girl."

Don't Look Back

THE JUDGE NEVER DID ANSWER MY LETTER and neither did the president.

Mother Blind and Grandma are coming to pick me up, I'm to meet them at the gate with the guard. I can wear what I want so I ask my mother to send:

> my black jeans
> cowboy boots
> leather jacket
> white shirt
> black eyeliner
> hairspray

I think about going back to Lockwood and how I'm colored now but no one can see. I think about Mary and wonder if we'll meet up on the outside the way we plan. If Daddy Dead knew he'd be mad as hell but he called me a *nigger* before anyway. I'm not going to let white people tell me I can't have colored friends. Will I always like girls? I kissed Mary on the lips those times but I still haven't kissed a boy so I can't say but I figure a kiss is a kiss and it don't much matter if it's a boy or a girl, colored or white.

Mrs. Webber hands me my bag, my bracelet with only one charm. But the important one. I slip it on, trace my finger around the smooth edges of the wings that flicker light from the late day sun and I notice this, unlike the others now lost, the silver coated ones, this charm has weight, pure silver.

My boobs got bigger since I've been here and there's nothing can be done but I'm going to get skinny now that I won't have to eat bread and potatoes all day long and I'll be able to do things like ride a bike and run the football field. I think maybe once I start running I might not be able to stop.

Mother Blind sent me the clothes, the hairspray, the black eyeliner, the back jeans I asked for but I'm ten pounds heavier now and the pants are pretty tight so I rip them up, the threads as so worn, until they fit and there is a hole on my right leg and one on my left knee. The M shows where I carved it into my thigh. I don't have to hide it anymore. I make two rips on the side of the waistband because it's too small now and pull on my boots, button my shirt and slip on my leather jacket and put the piece of the wall in my pocket..

I hang my head over and spray underneath my hair so when I stand up it looks like I'm in the open hatch airplane with the wind blowing and no helmet on. I line my eyes with the black pencil till I look like a cat.

My aviation book is under my arm, , Amelia is on page 359, the chip of plaster in my pocket, my silver airplane on my wrist.

Don't look back, Knife says.

The clouds are purple, blue and spread out like feathers over a moon hung thin as paper.

Julia Van Middlesworth earned a BA and MFA from Fairleigh Dickinson University. She's the recipient of the New Jersey Council on the Arts fellowship, the winner of the Fish Anthology short story prize, the Sean O'Faolain short story prize and has been published in *The Literary Review, Southword, The Horizon Review, Fish Anthology, Sean O'Faolain Anthology, Long Story Short, Broadside, Hibiscus, Bottomfish* and *The Plains Poetry Journal*. Julia is a founding member of The Sourland Mountain Workshop and editor of *The Sourland Mountain Review*. Julia lives in Somerville, NJ, with her husband Lawrence, rescue cat Barnabus Collins and rescue dog Horatio.

Thank you to everyone along the way who helped me with *Daddy Dead*. The FDU MFA program, Walter Cummins for all his work and insight, his elegant prose, improving the entire novel with one word: consequence. Mentors: Tom Kennedy, Rene Steinke, Ellen Akins. Much appreciation to Brian Bradford for his brilliance and steadfast encouragement, Cory Johnston for his honesty and keen eye and for telling me to "be even weirder." Special thanks to my brother William Atkinson for inspiring "Willy" in the novel (I made a lot up, okay?). Sourland Workshop: Helen Branch, Vicki Brand, Jin Cordaro, Lauren Gusastella, Elizabeth Jaeger, Stephen Kahofer, Kitta MacPherson, Jessica Brokaw Shearer, and Regina Toth. Without our group this novel would still be a short story. Special thanks to my three children for never discouraging me. Most of all thank you to my husband of twenty-five years Lawrence Jay Kroehling for his love and support.